THE BLOOD SAGAS

BOOK 1
BLOOD & LOYALTY

Avery Brown

DEDICATION

The Blood Sagas is a story of great people and great ideas. A time of ambitions, egos, wants, desires, and all that comes with that, including magic and madness.

It's a story of men and women with different beliefs and opposing faiths, forging a nation, a concept, a rule—either by given vision or perceived destiny. Whether motivated by revenge, greed, fear, love, lust, or hate, connected by humanity as we are, cooperation as a people of one voice eludes us because we are entangled in our arrogance and hubris. Thus, words of peace and equality for all are enforced by the gun and acts of attrition, violence, and anarchy in the pursuit of happiness and even an aristocracy that sees itself above it all. This is where this story begins, and where it ends can only be told by the women and men who live it.

Enter the great plains, where good and evil become grey depending on the day, where power shifts like the wind, and we humans are willing to kill to keep it, even the aristocrats. This is a story of deals made behind closed doors by people who would rule the world and handshakes given in deserts by comrades that could change it. This is a story of blood spilled and loyalties upheld.

This is a story dedicated to my brother, friend, comrade, and most importantly, my pal…

Garland Tyree AKA S.I., NTG. RIP.

THE BLOOD SAGAS

BOOK 1
BLOOD & LOYALTY

Introduction

Welcome to Keystone, a modern-day metropolis in the great plains and entry point for most everything imported from foreign lands. Keystone is also the only landmass connected to all the great plains states—save Noble Haven, a sovereign state of aristocrats governed only by themselves. Although people of influence and power can be found in Keystone from all over the plains, none dictate how Keystone is run, save the Mayor.

Hence, Keystone is a bustling city where fortunes can be won and lost. Everything is here, from the finest restaurants, hotels, casinos, and theaters to the grandest of fashions. This is the bright vibe of Keystone, but there is also a dark side—the seedy side with wild saloons, brothels, back-alley gambling, and poker houses, not to mention the best weed and smack dens around. All of this keeps money and people flowing in droves through Keystone's streets.

Yet, above all that is Keystone's neutrality and indifference to the laws that govern most other places among the plains, making it a very appealing haven of sorts. And as a result, the best and worst of people descend ceaselessly into Keystone, seeking to indulge in all manners of taboo.

Therefore, it is nothing to see a wanted man politely chatting with an aristocrat from Noble Haven or even a Benta soldier in the stands cheering with a tamer from the Republic because they bet on the same horse. Ultimately, this is a place where any debauchery can be realized without judgment. If you can pay the tab, then you can surely have. Money truly makes this world go 'round. Yet, be ever wary and aware. For just as sure as Keystone is a place where dreams can come true, there are many who realized their worst nightmares here.

Chapter One

NoLove sat at the window, watching the streets below his hotel room on the second floor. He was fresh out of Fort Prison after doing a dime stretch and already back in Keystone. Things had changed since he was last here—not by much, but just enough to notice if you knew how to look.

Things will be different this time, NoLove thought to himself.

He had a purpose now, an actual cause he felt was worth going to the limit for. He was no longer just a hired gun. He was now a catalyst for change, a harbinger of an approaching movement. He was given a vision in prison, and he accepted it. He now had a destiny to manifest that he was willing to die and kill for if necessary. As the sun started to set on Keystone, it cast a purple haze over the city that reflected off the ocean it bordered. The deeper the sun sank, the livelier the city became on this summer evening.

Horse-drawn carriages were steered up and down the exciting dusky streets. Men crowded in saloons, and the smell of weed wafted subtly through the air. A bevy of beautiful Lucys selling pussy on a corner caught NoLove's eye. As one smiled up at him, he reminded himself now wasn't the time for that. He was here to perform, and perform he would. For now, he would just watch. Watch and await the moment. NoLove knew he could be patient; doing time had taught him that. Working out had made his mind as strong as his body—his brown skin vibrant with the penal glow.

"Goon, is everything ready?" NoLove asked, still peering out the window.

Goon was in deep concentration as he prepped the guns spread out on the table before him.

After a moment, without looking up, he responded, "Yeah. I'm just finishing the trigger on this Flesh-Eater. All you gotta do is tap the trigger, and you'll turn a man into a sprinkler. As far as skat guns go, it's heavy-duty. Three shots at once, much better than a double barrel. I'm right good with it, so I'll be toting this, bruh."

NoLove nodded his head in understanding. "What about the pistols?"

"Check," said Goon. "It's six pistols, all six-shooters, and I got 'em all loaded up with bone crackers. Big calibers...all man stoppers!"

Goon's excitement was palpable, but NoLove simply nodded.

"I can't speak for TwoFace, though. Nobody touches his guns but him," added Goon.

"Don't worry none 'bout the kid. I'll vouch for him. He'll show out when it's time to get the guns off. I done seen him perform 'nough times. The kid's got rattler in his blood."

"Then I guess we're good," Goon said, still transfixed on the weapons.

"Matter' fact, where *are* TwoFace and Swindle?" asked NoLove, peering over his shoulder, briefly turning his attention away from the bustling streets below.

"I reckons they're still in the back flippin' that Lucy."

"Time for her to go. Tell 'em toss her a coin and get her gone," ordered NoLove.

"Gotcha," Goon answered as he rose from the table.

A short, stocky barrel of a man, his skin as black as a starless night, Goon was every bit of what his name implied.

"Aye Face! Swindle! Lose the Lucy and get out here!" Goon shouted through the door of the room, followed by two loud thumps before turning abruptly to get back to the table where he began loading the Flesh-Eater, a three-barrel shotgun that fired three rounds of buckshot in unison, vaporizing skin and bone.

This crew's young, but they've got heart and are loyal, which is enough for me, NoLove reminded himself.

TwoFace emerged first. A tall, lanky kid, standing at six-two exactly. His smooth copper skin and thousand-yard stare helped him fit in well in Keystone. Two gleaming black Colt magnums hung from his holster in a cross clutch. He was barely twenty-five and rumored to have already killed as many men, most notably by quick draw. He could be hot-tempered and reckless, but NoLove knew he had a good enough reason to recruit the young regulator, albeit he had to agree to bring his cousin Swindle on, as well. But for what TwoFace brought to the table, it was a deal NoLove was willing to make. Swindle was young but eager, and as NoLove saw it, he would either do or die—with what was to come.

"Where's Swindle?" asked NoLove.

"He's still in there sayin' his goodbyes, I reckons," answered TwoFace as he pulled back a chair and sat down at the table with Goon.

"Sayin' goodbye to a Lucy?" Goon laughed with NoLove joining in, followed by TwoFace.

"I believe it was his first time," said TwoFace in his cousin's defense.

"How is it you guys nowadays learn to kill before you learn to fuck?" NoLove asked no one in particular, turning away from the window to join his men at the table.

"Shit, some of us learn the guns before the girls," answered TwoFace, tapping his fingertips on the guns Goon had displayed out on the table.

"You got that right," Goon added, stroking the Flesh-Eater. The sinister smile on his face revealed an empty space where a tooth should be.

Just then, the back door opened again, and Swindle, a slightly shorter, darker, and heavier version of TwoFace, emerged from the room holding hands with a brown-skinned Lucy with enough ass and tits for every man in the room. And a face that'll raise any man's eyebrow.

She smiled at them all as Swindle walked her to the door. After reaching the door, she blew NoLove, Goon, and TwoFace a kiss over Swindle's shoulder as he hugged her. Then she kissed him on the cheek and was gone.

Swindle closed the door behind her and turned around to three pairs of eyes and grins. At that moment, he felt every bit like the youngest guy in the room.

"How was she?" Goon teased.

"Hey, bruh, she's not that kind of girl!" Swindle immediately responded.

The room erupted in laughter, but NoLove was the first to ask what everybody was already thinking.

"Really? How you figure that?"

"Because she told me she loved me, and she proved it," said Swindle.

"How'd she prove it?" Goon asked, now bent over with laughter in his chair.

"Because she told me so. She let me cum in her mouth, too, while TwoFace was fucking her, and she only charged me half price."

The laughter broke loose again.

NoLove stood up and walked to Swindle, placing a hand on his shoulder. "Lil bruh, I got two questions. Do you know what a Lucy is, and do you know what a trick is?" NoLove pressed, but before Swindle could answer, someone began knocking on the door.

Knock, knock, knock.

The knocks came again, urgently and impatiently this time.

Finally, the moment has arrived, thought NoLove.

They opened the door, and into the room slithered a Stoneman—the so-called walking law dogs of Keystone. He was a greasy pig of a man, and it nauseated the gunmen to deal with him. NoLove would have killed him on the spot, but he needed information.

The fat Stoneman entered the room and removed his badge as if that extricated him from being a man of the law. He sat down at the table cluttered with guns and began to spill as NoLove and his crew listened intently.

"Okay, it's going down tonight," the man started. "All the

players are present. They're meeting in the backroom of the Blaze. It's fifty pounds of pure smack and just as much kush. At fifty-five grand a pound on the smack, ten grand a pound on the kush, and the buy money there, too, it's a big lick. And the take for me and my men is one-fourth of the haul, as we agreed."

The man paused, looking at NoLove for confirmation.

NoLove nodded in agreement to the deal, thinking in the back of his mind that he would give the Stoneman a lot more than what he had bargained for. The Stoneman nodded, too, and continued.

"I got two of my guys doing security, and they already know to take a walk as soon as you show up."

"What about our escape route after the job?" NoLove cut in.

"I've got you six fresh horses at the meeting spot—fed, watered, and ready to run. So, soon as we divvy up, we part ways, and you guys make a beeline for the Barren Plains. And it's gotta be tonight because, as I hear it, the Republic will be here tomorrow to collect their muscle money."

NoLove and his crew nodded in unison. All of them had run-ins with the Republic before, and even though Keystone was neutral to what went on out on the plains, the Republic was known for bending the rules when it came to getting their man. NoLove, the crew leader, had just gotten out, but TwoFace and Goon were definitely on the wanted list.

"Don't worry. Soon as we do the deed and give you yours, we're gone," NoLove assured the man.

The Stoneman got up, emphasizing with his hands, and said, "Just remember, no murders. Robberies in Keystone happen all the time, but when people get killed, FatPockets wants answers. He probably won't trip as much about a murder as he would for not gettin' his cut of whatever caused it. Fact being, money will likely be the root of any killing 'round here."

The Stoneman looked at the men confidently, sure that he'd gotten his point across. Then he walked to the door, turning a final time to address them as he reached for the knob.

"And no cuffing, fellas. Any jewelry or personal valuables you take, I get to cherry-pick. Got it?"

NoLove was the only one to respond. "Got it."

I can't wait to kill this man, NoLove thought as he rubbed his hands together in anticipation, knowing red blood would cover his brown skin soon.

TwoFace was the first to voice what they were all thinking as soon as the Stoneman left.

"I can't wait to kill these pigs."

"You and me both, brother," added Goon as they all began getting ready, strapping on their guns.

No more words were necessary. The moment was approaching, and they would readily embrace it.

*****

StreetLife entered the Blaze Saloon, pushing through the swing doors. With people from all over the plains in town, it was packed and very lively, teeming with music, loud laughter, good smoke, and cheer. The Blaze had a certain air of elegance that couldn't be denied—even the Lucys were classy.

StreetLife had to admit to himself that this was one of Keystone's favorite spots for pleasure, but he was not here for pleasure this time. He was here for business and big business at that. He was trying to cop three pounds of pure smack, the high-grade shit that you sniff and couldn't feel your face for about an hour. He also wanted to get a few pounds of weed. He'd heard it was kush, a strain hard to get, and from what his plug had told him, this load came from El Chablo.

As StreetLife observed all the other high rollers perched at the poker tables or dice shoots, he knew he wasn't the only person in town trying to score. He had already decided that whatever he got his hands on, he would push it back up north through the Republic and Noble Haven, where it would be worth two to three times as much. Although it wouldn't be easy moving smack through the Republic where it was outlawed, the risk was surely justified by the reward.

StreetLife was a Rollack, just as the two-gun tattoo on his right hand pegged him for, and the only life he knew was sex, money, and murder. The big gun tucked in his wing-clutch guaranteed that he would never go back to The Fort nor face The Worm. When and if it ever came down to it, whether Republic soldiers, tamers, or any other oppressors coming for him, it would be guns up, and he'd let God decide the sentence. The years he served in The Fort were more than enough for him to know he'd greet the grave before another cage. But perhaps after he handled his business, he would ball a bit, grab a Lucy or two, take in a show, or take it to the tables with the rest of the shark eaters. Pete's luck, the last time StreetLife was here, he blew damn near a hundred bands.

Nah, just get the work and hightail it; that's the plan. Then again, plans do change, he thought as a scantily clad waitress approached him to take his order. She was all body and cherry-faced—just his type.

"What'll you be having, sexy?" she asked, staring into Streets' eyes and leaning in close to make sure he could hear her over the noise around them.

"I'll have you in a bottle," he responded, speaking coolly into her ear.

They both laughed as she placed her hand on his chest and responded, "That can be arranged."

"I'm sure it can, ma, but business before pleasure. In the meantime, how 'bout you bring me a bottle of Whiskey 25 and a cigar? I'll be over there."

Streets pointed to an empty table against the wall, away from the crowds. There he would have a perfect view of the entrance and the stage. It was also the ideal spot for a person who didn't want to be noticed.

StreetLife stood over six feet tall and was well built from years of working out while serving time in The Fort. His complexion was what some referred to as high yellow. Under normal circumstances, he'd be hard to miss, but he could blend in, in a city like Keystone. Putting his eagle eye on the crowd, he noticed people from all over the plains present. He even spotted two Republic soldiers, their black uniforms announcing to all who they were and who they fought for.

As the waitress hurried off, an announcer called a singer to the stage by the name of Mary J., and by the way the crowd reacted, StreetLife was sure she was going to be a powerhouse.

She came to the stage, appreciative of the standing ovation. A brown-skinned woman, she was beautiful to look at and put together like a stallion. A scar under her left eye indicated the hardships she had overcome, but once she started singing a ballad about real love, the force of her voice left no doubt that she was anything but phenomenal.

StreetLife sat down just as the waitress made her way to him.

She placed the bottle down on the table along with a cigar she pulled seductively from between her perky breasts.

"Here you go, sweetie," she said with a wink.

"Much obliged," StreetLife countered as he handed her several bills.

At a quick glance, it was clear to the server that he was paying for more than whiskey. When she saw the denominations of the bills, her eyes lit up with motivation for what she would do to earn them. Grabbing the cigar, she put the tip of it between her lips, puckered seductively, and then slowly spun it around, moistening the end. She then pulled out a wood-base cutter and skillfully clipped the tip before placing the award-winning cigar to StreetLife's lips. Striking a match on the table, she held the flame to it as she leaned in to whisper into his ear.

"And I swallow," she added with another wink.

"Well, I reckons to have a mouthful for ya," said StreetLife with a wink of his own.

"I guess it's a date then," said the waitress as she folded the bills, tucked them into her bra, and sashayed off.

At that moment, StreetLife noticed four men entering the Blaze, and the look on their faces was all business. Three looked a bit young, early to mid-twenties, and they were all packing iron. But the one in front looked familiar. When he realized why, he had a feeling things were about to go sideways.

It was NoLove. He and StreetLife had served time in The Fort together, but the look on his face told StreetLife it was not a pleasant time to approach him to reminisce.

One of the four men posted at the door while the other three proceeded to walk through the crowd, straight toward a hall on the right side of the stage. They were focused and moved with a menacing purpose.

StreetLife calmly pulled his gun, cocked it, brought it under the table, and waited. Blood was about to hit the floor if NoLove's street game was anything like his jail game. StreetLife would make sure it wasn't his blood.

He grabbed the whiskey, took a long swig, and listened as Mary J. brought the house down.

Chapter Two

The four men were on a mission. They were given a vision and had the conviction to see it through. Destiny was about to be manifested. Words between them weren't necessary. Instead, they moved as one cohesive unit. Immediately upon entering the Blaze, Swindle had taken a seat by the entrance. Mary J. had the place in such an uproar that their approach went unnoticed. The other three men sliced through the crowd straight toward the back as they had been instructed—making no eye contact and moving virtually undetected by all except for one man, who had his gun cocked under the table while burning a cigar.

***

As soon as the two Stonemen guarding the meeting room door saw the three men approaching, they nodded and got lost. The hallway was dimly lit as lights aimed at the stage cast a glare down the hallway. NoLove and TwoFace entered the room as

Goon closed the door behind them. He put his back to the door, pulled out the Flesh-Eater, and began watching the hall as Mary J. continued to blow.

When NoLove and TwoFace stepped into the room, the discussion taking place inside abruptly stopped. Several men seated at a table seemed to take up most of the room, and a servant moved about, seeing to the men's needs. It was evident to all that NoLove and TwoFace were not welcome. The air was thick with smoke, and the odor of strong booze and men of all persuasions were present.

Suddenly, a man sitting at the far side of the table with mounds of drugs stacked in front of him spoke out.

"Are you two lost? Because this here is a private affair."

"Nah, I reckons from all that I see, we are right where we need to be," said NoLove as he pulled back an empty chair from the table and sat down, while TwoFace stood directly behind him, his face blank and disposition stoic.

"By the looks of ya, I'd say this meeting is above your pay grade," said another man seated at the table whose face was decorated with a long, intimidating scar.

NoLove chuckled at the comment. He then placed his palms on the table, looking at every man seated around the table before addressing the one who had just spoken to him.

"You hear that, TwoFace? Scarface here says this meeting is above our pay grade."

The mere mention of TwoFace brought a whole new level of tension and awareness to the room since it was a name widely associated with murder.

NoLove savored the shock that came across their faces now that they knew it was no longer a game.

"I see you're starting to get it. Now, we can do this the easy way or the hard way, which is to say…" NoLove paused, then looked at the scar-faced man before finishing. "…the Mob way."

"Look, bruh, you're either here to spend money or waste time, and by the looks of it, you ain't got much money, and your time is up," said the man.

"You're right. I'm not here to spend money, and we've wasted enough time talking. I'd say it's time to cut butter. Listen up, because I'm only gonna say this once. I'm here to deliver a moment," NoLove stated.

"And what moment is that?" asked a skinny white man who looked like he indulged in every drug on the table.

"A moment of revelation. Allow me to introduce myself. My name is NoLove, and by the look on most of your faces, I trust you know of my brother TwoFace. We represent Goodfellas. From this point on, spread the word: if you're eating, you either cut us in or you cut it out. And by the look of this table, I see a lot of eating that we are not involved in."

TwoFace sucked on his teeth, letting a hand drop to the handle of one of his guns.

"And you still ain't involved. So, what you think, because you push off in here like the big bad wolf with some colorful names we're supposed to shake in our boots and cough up muscle money? Bruh, you got me fucked up. My name is Leggs Shyne, and I'll die about mines," said the man with the scar as he let his hand also drop to his gun—a move mimicked by several other men at the table as the room fell deadly silent.

Your scar makes sense to me now, Mr. Scarface, but it doesn't matter much. I'm going to kill you all, NoLove thought mischievously.

"You're right, Leggs. You will die about yours because I'm gonna kill ya to take it. TwoFace!" NoLove shouted, and the next few seconds were a blur of movement and gunshots.

Blam! Blam! Blam! Blam! Blam! Blam! Blam! Blam! Blam! Blam!

A total of ten shots were fired, and ten men lay dead at the end of it with holes in their heads.

TwoFace again sucked his teeth, now aiming his smoking guns at Leggs seated at the other end of the table, the only one left alive along with the waiter.

"You're pretty goddamn fast," said Leggs, acknowledging.

"I keep hearing that," TwoFace responded. "Care for a shot at the title?"

"Nah, bruh. I know when I'm outgunned."

Just then, Goon busted into the room, Flesh-Eater at the ready. The room looked as if it had been repainted. Sprays of red blood and brain matter were everywhere.

"Mob shit," Goon whispered as he looked around the room, taking in the scene. "TwoFace?" he questioned, knowing this had to be his work.

"Reloaded and ready," TwoFace answered, his twin guns still aimed.

"Goon, what we look like out there?" NoLove asked, rising from his seat and drawing his gun as he approached Leggs.

"We're all good out there, bro. The crowd is gone on Mary J. Shit's so loud out there that the shots were drowned out," Goon answered.

"Good. Grab the smack and the weed," ordered NoLove, his gun still locked on Leggs. "Waiter, stop shaking and bag up that money before your brains find their way to the wall or floor."

The waiter, who had been trying his best to be invisible, jumped up and immediately began doing as told, shoving stacks of bills into satchels on the table.

"You know this ain't gonna end here, right?" said Leggs as NoLove took his gun and tossed it aside.

"Perhaps not, but you are. You know, Leggs, I was locked up with a few Shynes in The Fort, and bullshit aside, they were some of the hardest. But now, we're out on these streets, and I reckons in killing you, I'll put that hardness to the test," NoLove told him.

"Well, it is what it is," countered Leggs, looking up at NoLove. "I hope you don't expect me to beg for my life 'cause that ain't 'bouta happen," he spat.

"Of course not. You Shynes are made of sterner stuff, and I know the fact that you got a scar on your face means something with you Shynes."

"Yeah, it means Dempaku will welcome me in death and that your head will end up on a stick before my grave."

"Is that right? Well then, I'm up to the challenge, bruh. Trust me, I'm up to the challenge. Wherever, however, whenever. Win, lose, or draw. But when my time comes, you will still be dead."

"Got it all bagged," Goon said, throwing the sacks over his shoulder.

NoLove nodded. "Bartender…fix this man a drink and make it stiff. It'll be his last."

Determined to remain on the living side of all the death around him, the waiter again followed directions despite the fear raging through his body. He fixed the condemned man a drink, his hands shaking as he passed it to him.

"Much obliged," said Leggs as he took hold of the drink and swallowed it in one gulp. He then turned all of his attention back to NoLove. "You think you 'bouta challenge the world? You think you got a plan that big, and it starts with a robbery?"

"Nah, bruh, we got a plan that big that starts with us and ends with the Mob. You know the slogan: We came, we saw, we murdered shit," he concluded and leveled the gun at Leggs' abdomen.

Blam!

The shot punched right through Leggs' stomach, blowing his back out.

"You son of a bitch! You shot me in the gut!" Leggs shouted, clutching his stomach.

"Yeah, that means you got 'bout an hour or two of life left. Enjoy it."

"Bitch, I can't wait till my bros cut your fucking head off!"

"You won't be alive to see it," NoLove shot back as he snatched up the two sacks of money and headed for the door, followed by Goon.

"What about him?" asked TwoFace, aiming a gun at the waiter.

NoLove and Goon both turned to face the man as he stood at the side of the table shaking.

NoLove tilted his head to the side as he pondered the question and finally said, "When you tell the story, make sure you tell it right. It was the Mob, bitch!"

He then turned to the door and stepped out, followed closely by his men.

***

StreetLife looked up to see NoLove walking back into the

crowd, his two men close on his heels, lugging stuffed satchels they hadn't been carrying before.

The way they're clutching their hammers and quick steppin', something happened in the back somewhere, StreetLife figured.

The crowd was wild with revelry; many people were locked arm in arm, singing and dancing along with Mary J. as the bandits pushed through the crowd toward the door with no stutter in their step.

A moment later, a frightened waiter came running out of the back hallway and headed straight for the stage. He pushed Mary J. aside as he began to holler and scream into the microphone.

"They killed them! They killed them all! There's blood everywhere!" he shrieked while pointing in the direction from which he had come.

He almost knocked Mary J. to the ground, instantly silencing the crowd with the spectacle he was making on stage.

"What's wrong with you? Who are you talking about?" asked Mary J., trying to soothe the man.

"Bitch, get the fuck off me," he shouted, shaking his arm free of her grip. "I'm talkin' 'bout them muthafuckas right there! The Mob!" he barked, pointing right at NoLove, Goon, and TwoFace, who had been inconspicuously making their way through the festive crowd up till then.

Time froze as everybody locked in on the trio knifing their way to the exit. StreetLife tensed up, ready to fire as soon as he could figure out who to fire at. In an instant, a Republic soldier jumped up from his table, aiming a gun at NoLove.

"Stop movin'!"

A second later, a gun fired, and the soldier's head exploded, splattering blood all over NoLove. Immediately after that,

TwoFace stepped past NoLove and fired another bullet into the face of the soldier who was sitting at the table with the now headless one.

"Mob shit!" TwoFace barked, and all hell broke loose inside the Blaze.

Taking in the scene, the bartender reached under the bar and pulled out a fifty-shot Tapper, ready to get involved.

Boom!

Swindle had risen up and blew the back of the bartender's head off with one of his Colts before he could even take aim. Swindle then turned on the crowd and started firing.

Boom! Boom!

"Let's go!" he shouted.

NoLove, TwoFace, and Goon also began firing into the crowd as they backed out of the saloon, shouting "Mob shit!" after each shot until they got to the doors and vanished into the night.

*****

The three Stonemen were eagerly waiting at the edge of town in greedy anticipation of their reward regardless of the shots they heard, knowing their scheming helped bring about the chaos in the Blaze.

As NoLove and his men stepped into the alley carrying their take, the Stonemen pulled the horses into view. They were all too thirsty to collect their cut. Goon walked straight past them to the horses, grabbed the reins, and immediately started loading the saddlebags with the bricks of smack and weed while Swindle stood watch at the entrance of the alleyway to be sure no one had followed them.

The Stoneman who set up the heist spoke warningly. "I thought I told you no shooting," he stammered. "Now, let's see what you got." He faced NoLove and TwoFace.

"You did tell us no shooting, but what made you think we'd listen to you?" NoLove responded coolly.

In an instant, TwoFace drew his guns, pointing each at the head of the Stoneman who covered the door at the Blaze.

"Listen here, Lawdog!" NoLove barked. "We the Mob, and we don't pay. Nor do we obey. What's ours is ours, and what's yours is ours. So, take that with you to the resurrection."

Blam! Blam!

The two shots vibrated in the alleyway as the two Stonemen's brains were blown out of their skulls, and their bodies fell lifelessly to the ground.

"You backstabbin', double-crossin' sons a bitches!" exclaimed the final Stoneman, backing up as NoLove stepped forward.

"You really didn't see this comin', did ya?" NoLove asked.

The Stoneman backed up until he felt the fat barrel of a Flesh-Eater against the back of his skull, freezing him in place as NoLove, TwoFace, and Swindle walked past him and started to saddle up.

"Aye, Goon," said NoLove as he stepped in the stirrups and hopped on the horse.

"Yeah, bruh?"

"Everybody's made their bones t'night. I reckons it's yo' turn," said NoLove as everyone else watched.

It was barely a second later when Goon let off the Flesh-Eater.

Bloom!

The thunderous sound ripped through the night, blowing the Stoneman's head clean off and startling the horses.

"Never doubted you," NoLove chuckled wickedly as all three men tipped their hats to Goon.

"Mob shit," Goon said and jumped onto his horse.

"Mob shit!" they responded in unison.

"Let's ride!" NoLove shouted, slapping leather to his horses' flanks.

Heading hastily for the Barren Plains, the men felt elated, accomplished, and ready for more. They had represented their name and delivered a memorable moment—one of many to come.

***

The Blaze was in a state of frenzy as bodies lay sprawled out everywhere. Some looked like monsters from a child's nightmare with half of their faces missing or the tops of their heads gone. StreetLife watched it all play out as NoLove and his gang made their getaway, even firing raw in the crowd to do so. However, that didn't worry StreetLife as much as knowing the work he came to buy had surely just left with NoLove.

Another thing that stressed him was two Republic soldiers were among the dead, tamers at that—the so-called elite—and that would bring Republic heat. That was heat he couldn't afford, but curiosity forced StreetLife through the crowd—the bodies on the floor and the moans of agony from those hit by the shots now crying out for help.

He walked down the hall that NoLove and the waiter had emerged from. Seeing a door to a room wide open, he knew it must've gone down in there, and once he stepped inside, what he feared was confirmed.

Several bodies—all still seated—had a hole in their head or

face, and the backs of their skulls were blown out. It was indeed a grotesque scene, he understood better the waiter's panic as he rushed to the stage. But what really blew StreetLife away was seeing his connect now among the dead and knowing NoLove jammed on him right under his nose.

He heard a shuffling noise and quickly pulled his gun, cocking and aiming it in the direction of the sound.

"Relax, bruh, I'm already on my way," said Leggs.

StreetLife realized the shuffling sound was coming from a man as he tried to stand up in his blood-slicked boots, his gun on the floor next to him.

"What happened here?" StreetLife asked, still keeping his gun trained on the man.

"Dig, bruh, I'm Shyne, so even in dyin', ain't no snitchin'. But look around you. What's understood doesn't need to be explained!"

Leggs coughed, blood dripping from his mouth as he spoke. Holding both hands over his stomach, he made a futile attempt to keep his insides from falling out onto the floor. Yet, the blood continued to cascade through his fingers. Leggs' breath had become labored, and he could feel his life ebbing away.

"Guns to suns," StreetLife said as he got close to Leggs, still not re-holstering his gun but knowing the scar on his face marked this man as a Shyne, confirming what he just said.

"Suns to guns," responded Leggs, invoking the greetings between Shynes and Rollacks.

StreetLife was now standing over Leggs, looking down at the wound. Leggs removed his hands so StreetLife could see it.

"Damn," StreetLife grumbled as he shook his head hopelessly.

First, he studied the strawberry-sized hole in Leggs' stomach, then bent over to see the apple-sized hole in his back. He looked back at Leggs, his eyes saying what Leggs already knew.

"Yeah, they got me good. Ain't no need in you bein' cotton about it. I can smell my own insides! Of course, the bastard hit me in the gut just to bleed me out, but I guess I fared better than the rest of these muthafuckas. At least I still got my head. Look, you know what that means?"

Leggs tilted his head to the side so StreetLife could see the scar on his face. StreetLife nodded to let him know he did. He also knew he'd been in this room too long and needed to breeze before the law arrived. It was too much killing to go unanswered for.

"Look, bruh, I need you to take me to Shynetown. Take me back to my hurks so they'll get blood back for me. Tell Alkada I put him to the oath on a man called NoLove, and see to it that my son, A1, gets my guns, earns his scar, and that a head is put before my grave, real proper like." Leggs paused, looking up at StreetLife. "Put it on Pete that you'll see to this," Leggs insisted.

StreetLife looked at the man—now closer to death than being alive—and nodded, assuring him that he would.

"Nah, bruh," Leggs piped up. "You got to put words to it. Now, come on. I can already feel Dempaku pulling at my soul."

"That's on Pete, bruh. Now, let's go! This place is 'bout to be swarmed over wit' heat."

Leggs nodded and held out his arm for StreetLife to help him up. StreetLife grabbed Leggs' gun, then swung Legg's arm over his shoulder and pulled him to his feet. Again, he heard Leggs say, "Suns to guns."

Those would be the last words he ever uttered.

Chapter Three

Keystone was in a state of chaos, gripped by the horrors that took place the night before, and the sunrise brought with it all manner of rumor and speculation. At the heart of whatever was being said, the facts were that at least eighteen bodies lay dead throughout Keystone, and two of them were Republic soldiers. Telegraphs were sent, and the word spread like wildfire.

Sergeant Grimble was over all the Stonemen of Keystone, and after hearing the news of what happened, he raced to the Blaze, totally unprepared for the carnage that awaited him. He was a man of average height and frame with pale skin, long hair, and a beard. He thought himself to be a ladies' man. But once he arrived at the Blaze, he did not swagger around the crime scene like the grizzly he had fashioned himself to be. His beet-red face betrayed the unease he felt around all this death. Instead of representing the attack dog leader of the Stonemen he usually portrayed, he acted more like a dog being forced to smell his own shit.

He began to feel queasy at the sight of the headless bartender, and when he looked down at the shattered skull of the Republic soldier, his brains sloshed on the floor like mush, he nearly lost his shit. The other soldier's body was still seated in his chair—his head leaning back and mouth wide open like he was yawning at the ceiling. He also had a hole in his head with his brains on the floor behind him, looking like a pile of bloody dog shit. Vomit rose in Sergeant Grimble's mouth, but he caught it and swallowed it back down, not wanting to look weak in front of his men.

"Come back here, Sarge," called one of his Stonemen from a hallway that led to the back.

The sergeant started walking that way, stepping over two more bodies.

"They were killed when the culprits fired into the crowd while making their escape," the Stoneman reported as he led the sergeant to the backroom.

This is bad, Grimble thought to himself as he brushed away the heavy perspiration forming on his brow. The two dead republic soldiers were issue enough, but when Sergeant Grimble stepped into the back room, he was shocked with disbelief at what he saw before him.

This is just too crazy. His mouth became watery as he felt the vomit rising again. He worried he wouldn't keep it down this time. Suddenly, the room began to spin, and Sergeant Grimble felt himself falling backward as he passed out.

"Sarge! Sarge! Wake up, Sarge!" shouted one of his men as he tried to shake him awake.

Grimble was on his back when he regained consciousness. He gazed up at the ceiling, his face contorting in disgust at the stench of death that permeated the room. When he lifted his head slightly, he noticed his chest was covered in what he had eaten for breakfast. The man continued shaking him in panic.

"Get your goddamn hands off me. I'm fine," Sergeant Grimble grumbled, smacking the man's hand away as he got back to his feet to look around the room, trying to make sense of the senselessness before him. "Ten dead bodies, all shot in the head. What kind of mad dog kills like this?"

Grimble shook his head in disbelief, wiping regurgitated bits of food off his face and shirt.

"Okay, what happened here?" Grimble shouted to the room full of Stonemen and dead men.

A close look told him that his Stonemen also had a problem wrapping their heads around the scene—most of them looking as sick as Grimble felt. A few moments went by in silence.

"Don't everybody speak at once," Grimble pressed.

"It looks like there was a shootout," offered one of his men.

"Shut the fuck up, clown!" barked Grimble. "How the fuck was it a shootout when, as I look around, not one of these dead men even drew their pistol." He pointed his finger at the holstered guns strapped to the dead men as he sauntered around the table.

The men lowered their heads in silence.

"So, they all either waited to be shot systematically—which I sure as hell wouldn't do with iron on my hip—or the rabid dog who did this had to be fast as fuck. Given the evidence, I'd be inclined to think it was the latter," Grimble stated as he approached an empty chair with blood on it. He studied the chair and the blood on the ground around it. "It also looks like somebody was dragged off. Do we have a witness?"

"There was a waiter who says he saw it all, but he's still in too much shock to talk," a Stoneman responded.

"In too much shock to talk? What the fuck? Well, let him know he'll be shot straight if he doesn't. Now, get him the fuck in front of me!" Grimble shouted, stepping forward and slapping a smaller Stoneman on the back of the neck to drive his point home.

"You. Take off your shirt," Grimble ordered one of his men.

Sergeant Grimble took off his vomit-drenched shirt as he waited for the other Stoneman to give up his.

Okay, I'm getting my swagger back, he thought, relieved his nausea had dissipated.

The next voice they heard was one they all knew all too well. The voice reminded all of them of an angry father calling out to his child to take leather to his ass. It was the voice of Fat Pockets, and Sergeant Grimble was the child being called.

"Sergeant Mutha-Fuckin' Grimble!" roared Fat Pockets as he stepped into the room.

He was a short, robust man—barely five feet tall but well over 280 pounds of balls and bluster—and white as the driven snow. He had a patch of hair that he combed over to the right to make it look like more than he had. Always slick mouthing and dressed to impress, he ran Keystone with an iron fist.

"What the fuck happened here?!"

Sergeant Grimble quickly walked back toward the entrance of the room.

"Mayor Fat Pockets, sir, everything is under control," Grimble muttered, not sounding a bit convincing.

"Bitch, what the fuck you mean everything is under control? Control where? You call all these dead bodies control, Grimble? I'll slap a year outta you if you tell me this is under control again. This is anything *but* under control. In fact, it's totally *outta* control. This is death—black and nasty," Fat Pockets fussed, waving his hands around. "This is bad for business, bad for Keystone, and bad for me! A bunch of dead bodies I don't have to explain to nobody, but you tell me how the fuck do I explain two dead Republic tamers who have had their heads turned into stew, and we don't even know who, what, or why yet. I swear to you, Grimble… If I find out your monkey-ass was in hot pursuit of prostitutes and tricking on Lucys while people were being killed in my city, I'm telling you right now, boss to bitch, I will have you raped and murdered just as sure as my name is Fat Pockets, you fucking clown. Now, tell me something right now that will keep you alive!"

"There is a witness. A waiter," said Grimble, the words barely stumbling from his mouth.

"Then what the fuck am I talking to you for?" Fat Pockets barked at the visibly shaken sergeant.

Then a messenger hit the doorway, yelling.

"Fat Pockets! Fat Pockets!" the messenger hollered, pointing back out into the hall while trying to catch his breath.

"What, boy?"

"Fat Pockets, the military is here. They're waiting for you at your office," he announced.

The messenger then peered into the room. His eyes widened at the sight of all the carnage, and he promptly fainted. Shaking his head, Fat Pockets stepped over him and left the room with Sergeant Grimble in tow.

***

The morning had only just begun, and already the sun was beating down on the people of Keystone. Fall was approaching, yet summer refused to let go. Nonetheless, the Republic was here to pick up their seasonal money and supplies. Fat Pockets could have sent a delivery transport to the Republic, but the Republic had to flex their muscle, and as usual, they showed up in full force to do it. It was just his dumb luck that two Republic soldiers had been killed the previous night, and somebody would have to answer for that.

Fat Pockets approached Council Hall feeling apprehensive. A pig of a man, Fat Pockets had built his reputation and stature by bullying, intimidating, and manipulating those under his authority, but that would not work with the Republic. Not at all. Marshall Stryfe and his brood were the real monsters of menace.

His feeling of dread deepened as he climbed the stairs of Council Hall, now fully aware of the faction of soldiers scattered all around him. Fat Pockets pushed through the Council Hall doors only to find several more grim-faced soldiers lining the halls that led to his office, all standing rigidly in their black uniforms with their hands on their guns as if waiting for the order to gun him down.

"Fat Pockets, Captain Hammer is in your office," said his secretary as he passed her desk, but Fat Pockets ignored her and the soldiers that eyed him with hatred for the death of their comrades as he and Sergeant Grimble proceeded to his office.

Fat Pockets and Sergeant Grimble stepped into the Stone Room and found Captain Hammer sitting at Fat Pockets' desk staring out the window. The closing of the office door brought forth a crisp, stern voice.

"Fat Pockets, I presume," said Captain Hammer as he spun around in Fat Pockets' chair.

Fat Pockets was very familiar with the name Captain

Hammer but had never met him until now.

Captain Hammer was a man of grit—a barrel-chested man of average height, with a mane of silver hair that spoke more to his experience than his age. He had an eye patch that covered a barren hole where his eye once was—an eye taken from him at the hands of a Shyne during the Death Sagas, where he'd slaughtered hundreds.

"Please have a seat, Fat Pockets," said Captain Hammer, gesturing towards the empty seat on the other side of the desk.

Fat Pockets proceeded to sit down, feeling like a guest in his own office. He introduced Sergeant Grimble, who sat beside him, but Captain Hammer aggressively cut him off.

"It doesn't matter who he is!" Captain Hammer yelled as he pointed his finger at Sergeant Grimble. "Nor did I invite him to sit!"

Sergeant Grimble looked at him dumbfounded.

"In fact, get up and stand back there in the corner and admire me from a distance," Hammer ordered.

As taken aback as Sergeant Grimble was, he was not a fool. One look at the expression on Fat Pockets' face told Grimble that Captain Hammer was not a man to be trifled with. Then as if in cue to Grimble's thoughts, Captain Hammer flicked his finger for Sergeant Grimble to do as instructed. Grimble immediately got up and went to the corner of the office, where he stood as if he were a child being disciplined—hands at his sides and looking at Captain Hammer, who now returned his single eye glare to the mayor.

"Just so we are clear, Mr. Pockets, I don't care what goes on in Keystone. Honestly, I believe you are living the life here and will continue to as long as your tributes continue," said Hammer with a sinister grin. "But what I am concerned about is how did not one, but two Republic soldiers…" Hammer held up two fingers. "…get killed in Keystone? Two Republic soldiers?" he reiterated. "Now, for that, you have warranted my undivided attention. So, tell me, Fat Pockets. I'm sure you're familiar with a telegraph, are you not?"

"Yes," Fat Pockets responded meekly.

"Okay, good," said Hammer. "The device you see before you is called a Limelight, and it works under the same premise as a telegraph, except it allows you to send and receive spoken words for about five minutes before fading."

Fat Pockets looked at the device on his desk, wondering how he had failed to notice it before. *How is it possible to communicate with a person so far away through this little black box the size of a man's head?* he wondered in amazement, his eyes glued to the contraption.

Captain Hammer yanked him out of his trance with a snap of his fingers.

"Focus, Fat Pockets, and prepare yourself. Marshall Stryfe would like to speak to you."

After being shown how the device worked, the mayor put the funnel-shaped object to his ear and positioned the other part over his mouth. Both were attached to a length of black cord that led back into the device and another one that traveled out the window to the telegraph lines.

After a few moments of Hammer fiddling with the knobs, the commanding voice of Marshall Stryfe came through, sounding like controlled thunder being directed right into Fat Pockets' ear.

"Fat Pockets?" the voice asked.

"Yes, sir," answered Fat Pockets, rising to his feet.

40

"This is Commander Stryfe. Would you please enlighten me as to the events that have taken place in Keystone?"

"Well, at this point, I really don't know, sir," Fat Pockets answered.

And the thunder lost control.

"You don't know!" blasted Marshall Stryfe. "What do you mean?! You have a massacre in your city, and you don't know?! Is this your final answer to the commander of the Civilized Republic? I don't know, Fat Pockets. Perhaps I should uproot you from your little cubbyhole, have you brought back here to Independence, and have General Lynch put you to the testing of truth to see what you really *don't know*. You'd be surprised at the secrets one could be made to reveal during a testing. Fat Pockets, you run Keystone only because I allow it. You are allowed your plush life because you are paying for it. So, have no illusions, Fat Pockets. In the grand scheme of things, you are my pet, my paying pet, not even worthy of being my puppet. Your revenue, economics, and docks are greatly appreciated, just as I'm sure you appreciate the air I allow you to breathe. But if you can't control what I allow you to control, you will be replaced right after I have you erased. Do you understand me, Fat Pockets?"

"Yes, sir."

"Also, Fat Pockets, you are aware that under my rule, prostitution and poison pushing are crimes that can be taken beyond incarceration at The Fort and punishable by death, if I so choose. And I've been given to know that both practices take place in Keystone with impunity. And if this is so, let me now ask, are you aware of my new implementation of the death penalty?"

"No, sir," Fat Pockets answered as Captain Hammer and

Sergeant Grimble watched him.

"Delightful. Let me tell you about it. No, better yet, let me enlighten you on it. I call it 'The Worm.' And it is as creative as the Limelight we are speaking on. The Worm is actually a jungle slug of some type that drops down from the trees onto its victims while they sleep, or so I've been told, and I import them right through your docks, I might add. But I digress. The Worm is implanted into the brain by way of the ear canal. It then eats away at the brain matter, replicating itself as it eats, without the need of a mate. It's truly unique in that aspect. Within ten minutes, there will be two or three eating the brain, and let me tell you, from watching this, it truly drives a man mad. The longer a man endures, the more worms he will incur until he is begging to be killed. At which point, a gun loaded with a single bullet is slid into the room with him. He can either kill himself or be driven crazy. Trust me, it is truly fascinating to watch. So, tell me, Fat Pockets, would you like to fascinate me?"

"No, sir."

"Then I suggest you satisfy me," Marshall Stryfe said before the line went dead.

Captain Hammer looked at Fat Pockets, winked his one eye, then dismissed the mayor from his office with a wave of his hand as he spun the chair back around and continued to look out of the window.

***

Mayor Fat Pockets left Council Hall, walking in a daze.

"What are we gonna do?" Grimble asked desperately.

He felt Fat Pockets' gaze piercing through him and turned to face him.

"We gotta talk to that waiter," said Fat Pockets, still slightly shaken up—Marshall Stryfe's words still playing in his mind: *Fascinate me or satisfy me.*

***

After ending the connection, Marshall Stryfe turned to his assistant.

"Mr. Happy."

"Yes, sir, Marshall Stryfe," Mr. Happy answered as he rose from his seat before Stryfe.

"Send for Sheldon Drake. I have need of his skill set."

Chapter Four

Shyne sayings: *Keep your gold and silver; we deal in blood and lead. Cross us, and your blood be owed. Our lead is yours to keep. I'll kill and die for any pal of mine, but I'll take your head if you kill a Shyne.*

***

It was midday as StreetLife finally entered the city limits of Shynetown. The sun was up high, and his horses needed water. He was thankful they'd brought him this far; he could smell the ocean not too far off in the distance. It had taken him just over three days to get here, towing the body of Leggs by wagon. But he gave the man his word and intended to keep it.

As he entered the town, he read the sign that revealed all it stood for: *Visitors, you are now entering Shynetown, so beware as Shyne law is the only law here!*

The sign had been there way before StreetLife was born, and

he was sure it would be there long after he was gone.

The last time he was here was for the burial of S.I. of the Billies, killed by oppressors not even a year out of The Fort.

StreetLife had taken up with the Shynes and the Billies in the skirmish until they got blood back for S.I.'s murder; Alkada took it upon himself to sever the head of the man who killed S.I.—an act that StreetLife partook in and that made him a wanted man. But as StreetLife saw it, he would die a wanted man, for he decided long ago he would hold court in the streets before going back to The Fort where he and Alkada first met.

Those were some wild times, but if this body he now carried into Shynetown were any indication of things to come, there would be even wilder times ahead. And StreetLife knew he would be right in the thick of it, along with Alkada and anyone else who rode with him—that was if Alkada was obliged to honor Leggs putting him to the oath. Knowing Alkada as he did, StreetLife was sure he would. These Shynes were extremely loyal to each other in this life and the next, as they were known to say.

There were pikes with heads erected on them in damn near every yard he passed, standing as a testament to that loyalty. They were sticking out of the ground like some grotesque tree, an ungodly tribute planted in front of the headstone of the man or woman who demanded it.

Shynetown was a bustling city, and pretty much anyone was allowed here as long as they followed the laws. And the laws that were not allowed to be broken revolved around stealing and hard drugs. Get caught doing either, and you'd suffer the consequences, which was more than StreetLife cared to ponder.

He passed numerous merchants plying their goods, but he had no time for that. He weaved his way through the streets, getting closer to his destination. He pulled off into the more secluded areas of Shynetown, passing several houses until he got to the road that led to Alkada's home. Getting close, he saw he was being approached by two men, both clutching their guns. StreetLife respected it, knowing he was a little too deep in Shynetown unannounced and unexpected.

"What's your business, partner?" one of the men asked StreetLife, his gun already half pulled and cocked.

"Whoa, bruh," said StreetLife, bringing his wagon to a stop.

He looked at the two men, noticing they were younger than he thought and probably kids the last time he was here. Neither had a scar on their face yet, but he could see the eagerness in their eyes to kill.

"I'm here to see Alkada. He and I go way back. I'm an old friend."

"Oh, yeah? Well, how do you know Alkada wants to see you?" said the other young boy, pulling his gun completely out and cocking it.

"Look, scraps, my name is StreetLife. Now, Alkada's house is only a stone's throw from here. So, I suggest one of you run along and get Alkada before you do something that's going to end up with somebody dead, and I reckons if it's me, it won't be me alone," StreetLife warned, dropping the reins of the horses, ready to draw iron.

The two looked at each other and then back at StreetLife, ready to start something wild.

"Streets, is that you?" called Alkada from two houses up, leaning on his fence, breaking the moment of tension between the three of them.

"Yoo, what's betta, bro?" StreetLife responded, grabbing up

the reins of his horses and urging them forward.

"Drummer Boy, you and Shotta, holster them irons and step aside. That's a Rollack and my friend ya blockin'," Alkada yelled out.

"Say no more, Big Bro. Shyne Love!" Drummer Boy called back as he and Shotta stepped aside, allowing StreetLife to pass.

StreetLife again looked at the two scraps and nodded, knowing Shyne culture would live on in them. He pulled his wagon to the front of Alkada's house, and a grand house it was: two floors, big and spacious, more pristine than he remembered. There was a big lawn with four tombstones and a pike with a head mounted on each.

"Well, well, well. So, it really is you. It's been a while," Alkada shouted, stepping outside his fence to meet his old friend. "You ain't afraid to come to Shynetown?" Alkada laughed.

"I'm Rollack, bro. You know ain't no fear in me now or never!"

"I know that's right, bro. Suns to guns…"

"Guns to suns," StreetLife responded.

The two men locked hands in greeting and then embraced each other as comrades and pals.

Bullshit aside, StreetLife had to admit Alkada looked to be doing well for himself. He looked healthy, still solid at about six-feet, two-fifty, with his trademark bald head and two long scars on the side of his face. StreetLife could see that Alkada still had fire in his eyes and movement.

He has to be pushin' fifty at least, and the only sign of aging is the salt and pepper beard. He has been keeping himself up well, StreetLife thought.

"Wussup, bro? You gotta pardon the welcoming committee.

We don't get many light-skin bros this way, and you never know when Marshall Stryfe or his attack dog, Captain Hammer, might try and send a move at me. I know he's still sour about that eye I took from him," Alkada said.

"It's all good, bro. Can't blame the scraps. Remember, we were scraps once."

"Yeah, I guess you're right. So, wussup? Split the middle. I know you must've come here for a reason."

At that very moment, a young girl of about twelve appeared in the doorway of Alkada's house.

"Daddy, who's that?" she called out, pointing at StreetLife.

"Never who dat," StreetLife said, smiling and digging in his pocket for two gold coins as the young girl approached them.

"And what might your name be, little missus?" StreetLife asked as he tossed the two gold coins to her.

She extended her hand mid-air and caught both the coins in one fluid motion, quickly burying the coins in her pocket without breaking her stride. Her gaze never left StreetLife's face as she stood in front of him.

"I'm Nefertiti," said the girl, pointing a finger to her chest. "And this is my father, Alkada." She pointed directly at her daddy. "But I still don't know who *you* are…and around here, that could get *you* killed," she finished matter-of-factly, now pointing at him.

Her eyes held the same fire as Alkada's. Alkada could only shake his head at his daughter's audacity before interjecting himself.

"Well, Nefertiti, this is my good friend StreetLife," said Alkada, planting a hand on his shoulder. "He and I go back quite a ways in the good ol' days."

"Umm-hmm. Well, where's his scars then, like yours?" asked Nefertiti.

Recollection flooded back to StreetLife. According to the Shynes, killing a man for killing one of yours was simply revenge and expected. But placing a head on a pike was a mark of Shyne love, loyalty, honor, and respect. Whether it was for family, a comrade, or a pal, it would earn them a scar—a Shyne medal of sorts.

"Well, little lady, StreetLife reps a different banner, that of Pistol-Pete Rip. Ain't that right, StreetLife?"

"Till my casket drops!"

"Whatever, Daddy," Nefertiti cut in. Then turned to StreetLife and said, "Well, Street! Life!" She deliberately punctuated each part of his name. "You know my daddy ain't 'bout that life no more. Four heads in our yard are more than enough, and I got a brother or sister on the way, so he ain't goin' nowhere. So, you might as well climb right back up on that wagon and take your problems to the next town."

"Nefertiti!" Alkada barked, cutting off her verbal barrage."You will respect your elders. Now get your ass in the house and tell your mother we have a guest for dinner before I take a switch to you!"

Alkada reached for her, but she quickly sidestepped him, immediately turning to run for the house, shouting all the way.

"Ma! Ma! Daddy got one of his old gun friends in the yard, and he looks like trouble!" Nefertiti hollered as she stepped back into the house, slamming the door behind her.

StreetLife was bent over with laughter. Even Alkada joined in for a moment.

"Say, bro, she is most definitely your daughter."

"Yeah, she is that. She has all of my fire and her mother's defiance and mouth. Not to mention she's touched by Dempaku's insight like you wouldn't believe. So, the fact that she doesn't want me to go anywhere means you must need me to go somewhere," Alkada said, now looking at StreetLife in earnest, waiting for the truth.

"You got a good life goin' here, bro. Big house. Wife and kid. Land. And respect the world over. I hate to even be here for the reason I am here, but I gave a man my word."

"Bro, good, bad, or ugly—split the middle. What's up?"

"I just left Keystone," answered StreetLife, looking at Alkada.

"Is that right?" Alkada said as he rubbed his beard, grinning at StreetLife. "Well, you know word travels faster than horses, and I heard it got kinda dicey up that way—heavy killin' and all. I even heard two Republic tamers were killed, and a big score was taken. Whoever did it sounds like my kinda guys. You mixed up in all that?"

"Not exactly, but before you start rootin' for the villains, you need to know that the guys who did do it put your Shyne bro, Leggs, in the box I'm luggin'," StreetLife said, nodding his head toward the back of the wagon.

All good humor and cheer were gone at that moment, replaced with the hate and evil StreetLife remembered Alkada possessed from their time in The Fort.

Just then, Yemi appeared in the doorway with Nefertiti at her side, arms crossed, tapping her foot in vexation. Alkada's wife was shooting daggers at StreetLife with her eyes as she called out to him.

"Streets, what's up, stranger? It's been a long time. You stayin' for dinner?"

"No, he's not!" Nefertiti answered.

"Get in the house," Yemi snapped at Nefertiti.

Grudgingly, Nefertiti backed up as Yemi turned back to StreetLife.

"Don't mind her. She's just acting like her father. You know you are more than welcome here."

"Much obliged, Yemi. I reckons I will stay for dinner."

"Good. You know, between feeding Alkada and this one in me…" she said, rubbing her stomach, "…we have to keep plenty food on deck."

"I know that's right. It takes a lot to feed this bear right here. I'm surprised there are any chickens left in Shynetown," StreetLife said, clamping down on Alkada's shoulder with his hand.

"Well, I'll leave y'all to it. Dinner will be ready by sunset," she said before stepping back into the house, followed by Nefertiti, but not before Nefertiti quickly looked at StreetLife and stuck up her middle finger.

***

Alkada stood stoically at the edge of the wagon while listening to StreetLife pour him up about the events that had taken place in Keystone. When he was done, Alkada nodded and placed his hands on the box containing Leggs' body, speaking the only words that needed to be said.

"Shyne loyalty, Leggs. May Dempaku receive you."

"So what are we doing?" StreetLife asked after a moment.

"The only thing I can do. When my father was killed in the Death Sagas, and after Axx returned to exile, Leggs took me under his wing. He taught me what my father wasn't able to. Although Axx taught me how to kill, Leggs taught me why. I gotta get the head of the man who killed him and bring it back to his family. He did no less for me when my father died, but I don't expect you to be part of this. You kept your word well enough, and I'm grateful you brought his body back."

"Come on, bro, don't try me. I'm a Blazer, and we don't back down. We get down, dig? So now what? I'm at your side just as I know you would be at mine. Besides, from what I saw, you're gonna need some real shooters with you on this."

"Do you know any?" Alkada asked laughingly. "Just kiddin', bro. I know you're with me. I expected no less. Go ahead inside and make yourself at home. Tell Yemi I'll be back by dinner. I gotta take Leggs' body back to his family and get his son ready. He's a scrap, but he's ready and eager to pick up the gun. My father dying gave me the hatred to be the Shyne I am, along with Axx giving me the joy of killing. Perhaps Leggs' dyin' will push his son just the same. Either way, this will make or break him," said Alkada as he grabbed the reins and climbed up into the wagon. "And you say it was NoLove who was in The Fort with us?"

"Copy. He's the only one I recognized for sure. The other three were kinda young, but they handled the metal well enough. Reminded me of us in our younger days, gunnin' shit down. But one was toting two guns in front on a cross clutch. He's the one who killed the Republic soldiers. Now that bastard was *fast*. I'm talkin' quick like. The tamer had flat got the drop on them. The next thing I know, his skull exploded. Brains hit the floor like hot wings. Then, before the other tamer could even flinch, the back of his head was on the floor. So, they're for real. Ain't no stutter-stepping."

Alkada nodded.

"That sounds like TwoFace. I heard the name a lot lately coming outta the Barren Plains. Slim, mid-twenties, wears two colts on a cross clutch. They say he killed the James brothers up in Black Creek a while back. So, I reckons we're gonna need HardBody," Alkada said, looking off into the distance.

"No, bro. I *know* we're gonna need HardBody," Streets countered.

"Anyway, go ahead and get cleaned up. I'll be back in a bit," Alkada said, slapping the reins on the horses' backs as he headed off.

***

Alkada approached Leggs' manor, a grand house built on land passed down for at least two generations. Apple and peach trees lined both sides of the house's carriageway; it was clear Leggs had lived in style. His ancestors were among the founders of Shynetown.

Although smack was forbidden in Shynetown for use, sale, or purchase, Leggs was always one to think outside the box, and whereas most people dealt in smack going hand to hand, Leggs had no time for that. He made his money by getting the smack where he needed it to go. "The money is in the smuggling," he always used to say.

Aside from weed, he was sure to keep that smuggling out of Shynetown, even though he spread love in Shynetown with the money he made. "Ain't nothin' wrong with pushin' poison as long as you don't poison your own," was another one of Leggs' sayings—one of many. But among the most significant was the one he had told Alkada so long ago: "A man kills your father; he deserves to die dirty and without mercy." This saying played through Alkada's head as he severed the head of the man who killed his father while Leggs and Axx stood at his side, encouraging him. And it was this saying that Alkada would tell Leggs' son. A saying he would one day, in turn, pass down. As long as action enforced the sayings, Shyne culture would never be watered down.

There were already several pikes in the yard; all had heads on top. Alkada looked to see Leggs' twin daughters among them, obviously preparing to add to them. Leggs' daughters were a few years older than Nefertiti. He dreaded the thought of someone one day bringing his body to his wife and daughter in the event he was killed in the field—like he was now doing with Leggs. But Dempaku willing, it would never come to that, and if it did, so be it. All he could do was embrace and respect death the same way he did life.

"Where's Lafern?" Alkada called out to the twins as he brought the wagon to a stop and started climbing down.

"She's 'round the back of the house, takin' ax to wood for our father's pike," said the first twin.

"You can leave the body where it lays. Our brothers will be along to tend to it," finished the other twin.

Alkada nodded as he started to walk toward the back of the house, relieved that they already knew and he did not have to look them in the eyes and tell them their father was dead.

Like him, the twins and their mother practiced the Dempaku belief, as did most of the women in Shynetown, to a greater or lesser degree. And due to those practices, they could sense and feel things that others couldn't. Thus, Alkada was sure they knew the moment Leggs had returned to the essence.

Alkada walked along the soft grass of their massive estate, and the closer he got toward the back of the house, the louder he could hear the steady chopping of wood.

Thnk, thnk, thnk was all that could be heard as he made his way to the rear. He stepped into the backyard only to be confronted by Lafern's back as she swung an ax up over her shoulder and then down into a small tree she'd fallen.

Lafern was an elder among the sisterhood and emanated great spiritual power. Although not as strong as Petra, her blessings from Dempaku were noticeable enough.

"Is that you, Alkada?" she asked while continuing to chop, not even turning around to face him.

"Yes, Lafern. I've come to—"

"No need for your words, Alkada," she said, cutting him off. "We both already know what has happened, and we both already know what is expected. My son will have his father's guns, knife, and sack, and you will have my son. This pike and my husband will be in the ground by sundown, and my children and I will be awaiting your return with a head to put on it. And should my son die upholding his duty to his father, I expect you, Mighty Alkada, to bring back two heads instead of one. This is Shynetown, Alkada, and what is understood does not need to be explained."

Alkada remained quiet, letting silence fill the air between them.

Moments later, she said, "Shyne love, Alkada," then proceeded to chop more wood.

"Shyne loyalty, Lafern," Alkada responded.

Lafern stopped chopping wood, again letting silence fill the moment between them. Then, turning to face him, she coldly and sternly she spoke.

"Alkada, when there is a head on a pike for the death of my husband, then it's Shyne loyalty, not before. Good day, Alkada."

With that, she turned back and let the ax swing.

Chapter Five

Alkada took his time returning home, getting his mind right for what was to come and for what he would tell his wife and daughter. His wife would understand, but his daughter would not. Regardless, they would have to respect his decision.

The setting sun brought a cool breeze through Shynetown. News of Leggs' death spread like wildfire since he was well-loved and highly respected among Shynes.

The residents in the neighboring houses saluted and nodded at Alkada as he passed several houses to head back to his own. The salutations were not merely greetings; they were moreso acknowledgements of what was expected of him. The nods were assurance that he would successfully complete the task he had accepted since all knew Alkada had been put to the oath.

Leggs was dead, and many would mourn, but there would be no funeral until there was a head present to proceed. Leggs would just lay in the ground until then, but the rules were clear. Every Shyne deserved a funeral, and Leggs would have one. Alkada would see to it.

He pulled in front of his house, stopping a second to think about what his life had become and all he had accomplished. Although not as big as Leggs', his house was bigger than most. He had a suitable amount of land and a good bit of coins saved up from his days riding wild, not to mention he was the youngest sitting member on the council. There were heads in his yard, a testament to his loyalty to the Shyne way of life, but most importantly, Alkada thought about his prized possessions: his beautiful wife and daughter. His wife was loyal to him above and beyond all others who had his back. Even when Alkada put foolishness before her, she remained beside him. She had even given him a beautiful daughter, whom he loved beyond words. Alkada thought about how, even now, his wife carried another child for him—another addition to their family and securement of the bloodline.

Alkada inhaled deeply. *I am Shyne*, he thought to himself as he hitched the horses to the fence and entered his yard. Walking toward the porch, he was immediately struck by the aromas of his favorite foods, a sign of his wife's acceptance of him leaving. As soon as he opened the door, he caught sight of his pregnant wife sitting in the living room while talking to StreetLife about the old days. His daughter was standing over her shoulder, brooding, her eyes locked on StreetLife. She hated that this man was here to take her father away. She immediately ran to Alkada and embraced him when he came into the room.

"Hey, Nefertiti. Something smells good in here," he said, hugging her back in an attempt to keep the mood jovial, but his daughter ignored him.

"'Bout time you got back. It's time to eat, and this one inside me is tired of waiting," Yemi said, rubbing her belly and then balancing her hands on her sides as she straddled to get to her feet.

They all followed suit and headed for the dining room. Only briefly did Yemi and Alkada make eye contact—a passing glance, but the message was clear: they needed to talk in-depth. All this from a silent language they had developed over their twenty-five-year relationship.

"Yeah, bro, it smells too good in here not to be eating," StreetLife beamed.

"I know that's right! Let me clean up, and I'll be right with you," Alkada offered as he headed upstairs to wash off.

After Alkada returned, they settled in the dining room at the table set like a buffet. Barbeque chicken, lamb, spiced potatoes, fried cabbage and catfish, fresh biscuits, cornbread, and yams covered the tabletop—all of which Alkada intended to taste.

They all sat down and gave thanks before taking their first bite. Alkada sat across from his wife, and Nefertiti sat across from StreetLife. The only sound heard was the forks and knives hitting against the plates.

"This catfish and yams are the truth, Yemi," StreetLife said, forcing the words out as he chewed profusely.

"Thanks, Streets, but I can't take the credit for Nefertiti's work," Yemi admitted proudly.

StreetLife nodded as he turned to Nefertiti to praise her, but before he could utter a word, Nefertiti asked, "May I be excused?" her eyes shooting daggers at him.

"Go ahead, Nef," said her mother, already knowing the worry her daughter must have been feeling.

Nefertiti immediately got up and walked to the stairs leading to her room, only turning one final time to stare more hate at

StreetLife. She stomped up a few steps before stopping to shout, "Answer the door!" to the three adults sitting at the table, then continued on her way.

Yemi reached over to StreetLife and apologized for Nefertiti's behavior.

"You know the Shyne way of life is hardest on the children. To me, you are a friend and comrade of my husband who has come to call him back to the gun in a debt of loyalty, but to her, you are a thief who has come to steal him away." Yemi paused before adding, "And in you doing so, you take away a daughter's greatest love."

Streets nodded his understanding, knowing Alkada's daughter and wife didn't welcome his arrival.

Alkada broke up the solemnity of the moment. "What does she mean, answer the door? There's nobody at the door."

No sooner had the words left his mouth, there was knocking at the door. Yemi gave Alkada a knowing glance of their daughter's budding abilities as he rose from the table to answer the door, wondering who would be calling at this hour. The sunset meant the easing of the day and family time in most Shyne homes.

"It's Petra!" Nefertiti shouted before slamming the door to her room.

Alkada shook his head, again amazed by his daughter's heightened awareness. And sure enough, as he opened the door, there stood Petra before him. *Dempaku,* was all Alkada could think, acknowledging his daughter's connection to their higher power—a connection Alkada, Yemi, and Nefertiti all shared.

Petra smiled at Alkada; she radiated an aura of power. She was a petite woman, about five-five in height. Her complexion was reminiscent of honey and cream, and her short hair truly accentuated her sharp facial features, bringing to mind a cunning fox. Yet, her most amazing feature was her captivating eyes—one was coal-black and the other the clearest blue. The power of her gaze was said to beguile and bend most to her directing, especially men. Those who were weak often avoided eye contact with her for fear of being pulled into her gaze. And at over fifty years of age, it was said that she was still untouched. Most whispered *that* was the source of her power—a power that placed her at the head of the Sistahood and center of Dempaku's order.

"Shyne love," she greeted Alkada, stepping inside his home, draped in a cloak of red and gold, pulling her hood down to reveal her face.

"Shyne love," Alkada responded, holding out his arm to the hall while closing the door behind her.

Petra made her way to the dining room.

"Safu, Sista," she said upon seeing Yemi sitting at the table.

"Sista, Safu," Yemi responded, careful not to title her in front of StreetLife, who didn't practice the faith and thus didn't know their structure.

Petra then stepped over to the stairs, placing her hand on the railing and peering up towards Nefertiti's room. "Safu, young Sista," she called out.

"Sista, Safu," Nefertiti responded as she cracked her door open and immediately closed it again.

Next, Petra turned her attention to StreetLife, her stare strong and penetrating, feeling him, testing her instincts on him. This lasted for several seconds as Alkada and Yemi both awaited the outcome.

Petra nodded to herself and smiled before saying, "Greetings, friend. You are true."

"Well, much obliged," StreetLife answered, knowing something mystical had just taken place.

Petra looked back at Yemi. "Sista, I've come to speak with Alkada, mind you?"

"No, Sista, not at all. Would you like to join us for dinner?"

"I'm good, Sista. How's the baby?" Petra added, coming close and bending down to place her hands on Yemi's belly.

"Well, Sista, and eager to get here."

"I'm sure, and all feels in order," she said before standing upright. "Alkada, to me," she said, walking back towards the front door.

Stepping outside, they began to walk to the front gate of Alkada's house.

Petra went right to the heart of her visit.

"So, Alkada, what do you intend to do?"

"Take to the road at sunrise. I've been put to the oath. I gotta do for Leggs what he and Axx once did for me."

The mere mention of Axx brought up ire in Petra, but she didn't show it. Instead, she pushed on.

"So you accept?" Petra asked, cutting her eyes at the four pike-mounted heads that already stood in Alkada's yard.

"What choice do I have? I must accept. Besides, Leggs was an elder, and at times, he filled the void my father could not. I wouldn't be showing Shyne honor if I allowed the men who slaughtered him to live. Petra, I'm Shyne, and Shyne life is one of absolution. It is part of that calling, and I know what I would expect of my bros had *I* been the one in the box instead of Leggs. And why do you question what I've done for years? What vision have you seen for what is to come?"

"I have seen many," she answered, looking into Alkada's eyes with her motley pair. "But know this, Alkada. You must be absolute in this and without a doubt, for the men you hunt are animals and care not whose blood they spill. And you must be the same. I know that you know the sweetness of Mugasa's wine, a necessary evil you've been known to play with. But no matter, for Dempaku has already claimed your soul. So, don't be concerned about deliverance or redemption in the bloodletting to come should you fall. But you must be a wolf and wanton in your slaughter. The theater of terror is forming all across the land, so you must kill without hesitation or question. Let Dempaku sort the souls of all who rise against you. Leggs' death is only the start. Many more will fall, and few will rise in what I sense is to involve us all."

"What is your vision, Petra?"

"Too many to say. Too many possibilities. But I will give you the gift and the curse of one vision that I am certain of. It is right what you do. It is loyalty that drives you, but if you fail or fall — only by death– you die loyal to your oath, and Dempaku will welcome your soul. That is the gift. However, the curse is, should you fail, your daughter will not. So strong is the psyche of Dempaku in her, and her love and loyalty to you so relentless. You dying will born a hate in her so powerful none will stand before her that will be matched with a madness unseen before. So many possibilities, Alkada. Much surrounds her. Fire and ice meet in her soul. She will need you just as the child that your wife now carries will need you. Life and death are the natural way of things, but if you die before your time, the ramifications of that will be greater than you could imagine. I dare say no more than this, Alkada. Go back inside, and on this night, you will take your wife. Do not love or caress her tonight. You will begin the taint of hatred on this night for what you are needed to do. Leave by sunrise. The wind will be with you, and I will be in the wind."

Petra then stepped closer to Alkada and put two fingers to the right side of his temple as she whispered into his left ear.

Alkada heard the words before but was too helpless to repeat them.

Petra stepped back from him and said, "One final thing, Alkada. Should you seek the aid of Mugasa, as I told you, you are covered. But know that you *will* be used." She paused and handed him a pouch full of an unfamiliar powder. "Take it. You will know when to use it *if* you need to use it. Shyne love, Alkada," she said before pulling up her hood and walking away.

"Shyne love, Petra," he responded as he turned to walk back to his house, at once remembering a question he needed to ask her. However, as he turned back around to call her, she was gone as if she had blended into the wind now blowing around him.

***

Alkada stepped back into his home to find StreetLife still eating at the dining room table. He looked up at Alkada, his face asking the question his mouth didn't.

"We ride at dawn," Alkada said. "You'll find linens and whatever else you need in the closet next to the guestroom."

StreetLife nodded in agreement and went back to his meal while Alkada climbed the stairs, heading to his bedroom. Once he reached the top, he looked across the hall to Nefertiti's room, only to find her standing in the doorway staring at him, her eyes projecting a fury Alkada could literally feel. She was vexed he would be leaving but knew it was his duty to go. They exchanged a glance that only a father and child could until Alkada turned away, walking a few steps to his bedroom, opening and closing the door behind him gently as his daughter watched.

Yemi stood at the window, her nightgown blowing against her naked body as she gazed into the distance. She was all woman, all beauty, and black as the night she was looking out into.

"Are you leaving?" she asked, her back to him.

"You know I am."

"Why must it be you? There are other Shynes," she pressed.

"Because he put me to the oath," he countered.

"And you so blindly obey!" she hissed, refusing to face him even though she felt him coming closer.

"That answer should be as clear as the scars on my face or the scars on your face. It's for loyalty that I go, just as it was for loyalty that you've gone. A loyalty you will respect as I had to respect."

"You have a family now, Alkada. A wife who needs you. A daughter who loves you and one on the way who deserves to know you. Tell me, Alkada, what am I to tell our unborn child if you don't return?"

"You will tell the child his father was a Shyne."

"*Hmpf*...who said it would be a boy? So entrenched are you that you are eager to have a boy and bring another life into this world. Yet, you are just as eager to run off into the Plains and take life from this world. A true hypocrite you are, Alkada."

She knew her words would anger him, but it was this exact ire that she wanted to bring out in him.

"I am no hypocrite," he said, now standing at her back. "I am Shyne, as are you...and killing is part of that. Not *all* of it, but, if you must know, a part that I enjoy."

"Just as Axx and HardBody…and both of them are probably consumed by the maddening," Yemi spat.

"Funny, you of all people would say that when both their blood flows in your veins. Now, stop suffocating me with wordplay. I'm leaving at sunrise, so am I going to spend this night loving you or raping you?" he stated.

Finished with the issue, he reached out to caress her arm.

"What the fuck ever. Get the fuck off me!" she said, snatching her arm away.

Alkada immediately regripped her arm, turning her around to face him, conscious of her pregnant belly between them yet uncaring in his efforts as he placed his lips to her ear.

"Hustle or muscle, Yemi, when I ride out into the Plains, I will do so with the scent of you on me."

Again, she pulled away from his grip, stepping toward the door as Alkada reached out, clasping her arm and pulling her back. She turned into the pull and lashed out with her free hand, violently striking Alkada in the eye. Alkada felt the blow, accompanied by a flash of silver in his mind that ignited his rage, his anger, his evil.

The blackness in his soul bubbled to the surface, and he backhanded her across the face while maintaining his grip on her arm. He pulled her aggressively to the bed, tossing her before him. Then he ripped off her nightgown, tearing away the remaining shreds as he bent her over and began to take her from behind, despite her fighting and resistance. Not moved by Yemi's tears, he pushed deep inside of her, holding her at the hips and pulling her to him as she tried to get away to no avail. He plunged deeper and deeper into her with each thrust.

Yemi could feel him filling her insides. She felt his rage, force, and power. Most of all, she felt his evil—the thing she wanted to feel most, the evil he needed to embrace, the evil that would bring the killing out. So, she surrendered all of herself in every way. What she did not give, he took, and he took deeply and without mercy throughout. She struggled, cried, and felt pain, but none of that mattered because she had created the monster he was, and it was this creation that would bring back the man she loved.

***

Alkada rose with the dawn. His clothes had already been laid out for travel, so he stepped into the bathroom to wash out his mouth and clean his face. His wife lay on the bed, rubbing her belly like she was assuaging the baby to come.

They locked eyes for the briefest of moments, speaking their silent language.

Her eyes said, *Come back.*

His responded, *I'll do my best.*

Aside from that, no other words would be spoken. *What is understood doesn't need to be explained,* Alkada thought as he finished dressing and left the room.

He expected to see his daughter standing in the doorway of her room, but she wasn't. However, after walking down the steps, he found Nefertiti sitting at the dining table. Before her on the table were his guns—two big revolvers, one he assembled himself and one he pried from the hands of his dead father—along with his belt, straps, knife, ammo, and a sack. All were cleaned, loaded, and ready.

No words could describe the feeling between them at that moment. It was more than a father's love and more than a daughter's love; it was a formed bond of raw emotion, impressed upon them by Dempaku. Alkada was sure of this, remembering what Petra had told him.

Nefertiti rose from the table and went to him, hugging her father at the waist. She held back words but not tears. He was again proud of her for respecting the Shyne way, knowing there were no words to be said.

Alkada bent down and kissed her on the forehead. Immediately after which, she turned and disappeared up the steps.

Alkada stepped to the table to strap up. He holstered one gun on his left hip and tied the other to his right leg strap before sheathing his knife at his back, embracing and mentally connecting with his metals. Next, he grabbed his sack and cinched it to his belt, then grabbed the three rolls of food set out for him. He headed for the door, snatching his brim as he stepped out of the house.

StreetLife and A1 were at the edge of the fence, readying the horses. A1 was Leggs' oldest son. At nearly eighteen, he was all too eager to be Shyne. Although Alkada was barely fourteen when he became Shyne, he hoped A1 was ready. He'd been given to know that the Passing was a ritual A1 had already been through, so now it was time for the final steps into Shynehood.

Well, he'll know the measure of his metal soon enough, thought Alkada as he walked to them, closing the fence behind him.

"Top of the morning," he greeted them, tossing over the food rolls.

"Top of the top," they both replied.

Alkada then looked directly at A1, who stood barely five-feet tall, and placed a hand on his shoulder.

"Rise and Shyne," Alkada spoke, invoking a Shyne greeting.

"I Shyne, you Shyne," A1 responded, trying to sound and appear grimmer than the situation called for.

It occurred to Alkada that losing a father makes you hard the way losing a mother softens you up.

"You ready for killing, scrap?" Alkada asked.

"I reckons so," A1 answered.

"Good, because we are about to do plenty of it. A man who kills your father deserves to die dirty and without mercy. So, we're 'bout to get our hands filthy and have no cares about it. Taking heads is a nasty business," Alkada said, pointing at the heads in his yard. "And by the end of this, I'm s'posing our sacks will be full, and your pa will have his funeral."

"*Raaaaah*!"

A loud shriek ripped through the air as if giving an order for attention. They all looked up to see a giant black eagle with red splotches descending on them from the morning sky. It spread its massive wings as it landed on the head that stood before S.I.'s grave. Again, it shrieked in defiance as if telling the rising sun to go back down. It then looked directly at Alkada, and the message was clear: *Do you intend to leave me?*

"Skully, why would I send for you when I knew you would come?" Alkada asked, holding out his forearm for the large raptor.

The bird shrieked again as if mocking him but obeyed, flapping its wings and coming to its master. Alkada brought the eagle to eye level, establishing their connection and awareness of each other's minds, solidifying their link. He told the bird two simple words: "Seek HardBody." Then he projected the image of HardBody into Skully's mind.

The bird nodded and leaped back in the air with a final earsplitting shriek that caused the horses to jump skittishly as Skully flapped his massive wings with enough force to bring up a twister of dust from the ground. StreetLife and A1 marveled at the whole spectacle. Alkada was a man with many talents.

"Hold on, brothers," Alkada said, turning to StreetLife and A1.

Going back into his yard to the four heads erected there, Alkada spat on the head that stood before S.I.'s tombstone. He then kneeled, placing his hand on the grass above S.I.'s grave, and spoke a few words that only they would know. Next, he grabbed a handful of the grass, stood up, walked back to the horses, and rubbed a dab of grass on the crown of each horse. Once he finished, he reached for the reins of his horse and jumped up onto the saddle, ready to ride.

Yemi appeared in the doorway just as they were about to push.

"StreetLife," she called, sure not to utter a word to Alkada. Yet, all three men looked at her.

"StreetLife, you brought the news that took him away. So, you be sure to bring him back, or you bring me the head of whoever takes him away," she ended, saying no more, for there was no more to be said as they turned their horses.

StreetLife nodded and threw up the gun salute. He then looked up to see Nefertiti in the window, pointing at him with one hand and her pocket with the other.

At first, StreetLife was confused, but then understanding reached him as he dug into his pockets to find the two gold coins he had given her and a small note. He opened the paper and began to read:

KEEP YOUR GOLD. BRING MY DADDY BACK, OR ONE DAY YOUR HEAD WILL BE IN OUR YARD!"

— NEF

StreetLife looked back up at the window, only to find an empty window staring back at him, but he knew she was watching and would be waiting.

Alkada asked if everyone was ready, and his question was answered with a pair of nods. He then pulled the reins on his horse, snapping them to life, and they rode off, heading northwest—riding for loyalty and all that came with it.

Chapter Six

NoLove and his gang were posted up on a hill overlooking the valley below them. The clouds forming in the sky were dark and heavy. A storm was coming. Strong winds and the stronger smell of approaching rain guaranteed it.

They were now in Reach Providence, civilized Republic land—not a place to be caught after what they had done in Keystone. Yet, NoLove felt they were close enough to the border of the Barren Plains if they had to make a quick escape. It had been nearly a week since they pulled off the rip in Keystone, and rumors were swirling all over the Plains and Republic about the massacre they had left there.

In the week since then, they heard it was everything from a deal gone bad, to corrupt tamers on the take, to El Chablo sending a hit squad to deliver a message. NoLove laughed at that one since it *was* a message of sorts, but it wasn't from El Chablo—it was from the Mob, and it was loud and clear. *You cut us in, or you cut it out*, NoLove thought to himself with pride.

But if what they had just done in Keystone earned the Mob

honorable mentions, then what they were about to do would really make them something to talk about. Things were moving. The world was spinning. Change was coming, and the Mob was a part of it. Still, the sooner they hit this lick and were back across the border, the better. Killing two tamers in Keystone was nothing, but running into a battalion of Republic soldiers this deep in Republic territory and things would get lively.

NoLove took out his longeye and looked down into the valley at the train tracks they had been watching for the past two hours. The tracks ran like a snake's tail right past them, entering a mountain tunnel to Republic City, Noble Haven, and Keystone. The train would be loaded with freshly minted money and gold for circulation down from Independence, the heart of the Republic—at least that was the word from Foot two days ago when he and NoLove met. Foot also let him know that, aside from all the gossip, four men were being sought for the killings in Keystone. They called themselves the Mob, and they were last seen headed west into the Barren Plains; the waiter had gotten it right. To play it safe, NoLove added four more guys to the crew to mask their movements for the time being.

Thunder rumbled in the distance. The ambush would have to be before the train entered the tunnel to Republic City, and with the hills concealing their move on each side, they could remain undercover and have all the time they needed.

Peering through the longeye again, he finally saw what he had been looking for: telltale puffs of smoke rose in the air before quickly dissipating into the wind, announcing the train's rapid approach. Although they couldn't yet see it, it would be coming around the bend right into the bottleneck entrance of the mountain tunnel.

NoLove gave the signal to Goon directly across from him on the opposite side of the hill. They both carted a herd of cattle right up to the hill's edge, and it was time to put them to use.

Goon gave the sign to his men at the back of the herd, and they immediately began to fire shots in the air, causing the cattle to stampede down the hill. NoLove's group did the same, and then they all watched as the cattle cascaded down the slope until they covered the tracks and blocked the entrance to the tunnel. The train would be forced to stop.

NoLove and his men were on both sides of the tracks, keeping the animals bunched together as the train cleared the bend. It was half a mile away and immediately started to slow down when it turned into the gulch and the cattle came into view.

The engines suddenly began to power down—steel, steam, and forward momentum all beginning to slow as the train came to a halt. The speeding mammoth of metal came to rest just shy a hundred feet from them, like a lumbering giant who had suddenly decided to take a nap.

The gang then snapped their horses to life and converged on the lead car. NoLove pushed his horse to the side of the car, and with guns drawn, he called out to the conductor.

"Come on out! Hands high!" he barked.

The conductor peered out from the door to see several barrels aimed directly at him and instantly shot his hands in the air as he began stepping down. He was a short, frail, white man, followed by a hulking, black cabin boy, who also raised his shaky hands in the air as he stepped off the train. They were equally confused, looking at each other as if whatever was happening was the other one's fault.

NoLove and Goon unsaddled, guns still held at the ready, and stepped to the two frightened men, backing them up against the train.

"Okay, who's in charge of this train?" asked NoLove, waving his gun between the two.

An ear-splitting voice answered from the second car behind as an older man yelled while charging at them. He was all balls and bluster, a true Republican straight out of Independence.

"What's the meaning of this? Why has this train stopped? Who are you men? And get these cattle out of our way *now*!"

This old bastard has no idea, NoLove thought as the man continued to rage.

The conductor and the cabin boy looked at the man with pointing eyes, nonverbally answering NoLove's question of who was in charge.

As the man came within arm's reach, Goon slapped him into the cabin boy.

"Shut the fuck up!" Goon shouted.

The man became indignant as he fell to the ground, smacking away the cabin boy's attempts to help him up.

"I'll have you men know this train is under the personal protection of the Civilized Republic, and I will personally see to it that you are all sent to The Fort for interfering with our course, perhaps even The Worm," the man raged as he stood to his feet, still holding his now bruised face.

The gang began to laugh as they gathered around the three men.

"I'll see how much you laugh when you're put to The Worm," the man offered, attempting to remain defiant.

NoLove approached the man. "Is that how you feel? Well, let me tell you what's going on. I know this train is loaded with money and gold, and we're here to impose Mob tax."

"I have no idea what you're talking about," he retorted.

"Okay, have it your way. I see you're not gonna be satisfied until I make you a believer."

"A believer of what?"

"Of the Mob, bitch!" NoLove barked, backing away from the man while nodding as he internally decided what course of action to take.

"Okay, pretty boy, tell me, you ever see what a Flesh-Eater can do to a man at close range?" NoLove asked as Goon stepped forward, grinning at the man's confusion. "Aye, Goon, why don't you show 'em what it can do."

NoLove stepped aside. Goon raised the Flesh-Eater to face the conductor and pulled the trigger.

Kra-Boom!

The blast echoed off the hills, causing the cattle to bristle up, some even running into the tunnel.

From the chest up, the conductor was gone. His head, face, and neck were blown onto the train side, plastered there like some grotesque painting momentarily come to life and now dying as clumps of shredded flesh began falling to the ground along with the body.

Upon seeing this horror, the cabin boy immediately jumped on the man, shouting, "Give 'em the key! Give 'em the muhfuckin' key!"

He reached for the neck of the man, who had slid to the ground in shock. The cabin boy, now on his knees, turned to NoLove.

"Please, sah… Please don't eat me, sah," the man pleaded. "This crack got a key around his neck to the cargo hold in the last car. On everything I love, he got the key to what ya want."

"What's your name, bruh?" asked NoLove.

TwoFace bent down to snatch the key from the man's neck as he sat there in a stupor of disbelief and passed the key to NoLove.

"Peppy, sah," answered the cabin boy.

"Okay, Peppy, here's your chance at survival." NoLove tossed him the key. "You open the cargo hold for me, and you won't end up like that guy." NoLove nodded towards what used to be the conductor. He then turned his attention back to the man on the ground. "Aye, Pretty Boy. I bet you never thought your day would go like this. You said you'd have us all sent to The Fort. Well, look here…I just got out of The Fort. I'm never goin' back, and that's on the Mob! My life is just beginning anew. However, it's the end of the road for yours. When you get to hell, be sure to tell 'em NoLove sent you."

NoLove raised his gun to the man's face.

"No, no…" he protested, waving his hands in front of his face. *Blam! Blam! Blam! Blam!*

The bullets blew the man's head and brains into the train's wheels. NoLove then turned to his gang and casually reloaded his weapon.

"Okay, you three," NoLove said to the new guys, "pull the horses up along the side of that last car and get the hitch ready. TwoFace, Goon, Swindle, new guy, come with me. It's time to do the devil's work. Let's go, Peppy," NoLove ordered.

They all walked to the entrance of the second car and stepped up into the train. NoLove was in the lead as he pushed the cabin boy ahead of him and down the train aisle. True to his word, NoLove entered the car like he was the devil himself and the men behind him the devil's helpers.

A couple jumped up in the aisle and asked, "Who are you?"

"The end," No Love responded bluntly as he pointed his gun at the man while his wife stood behind him.

Blam!

NoLove fired, blowing his brains on the woman's face. She turned to run but lost the back of her head as NoLove fired again, a bone-cracker slug punching through the base of her skull, causing her head to leap forward as her body tumbled clumsily to the train floor.

TwoFace was next to release, firing point-blank range into the faces of several passengers sitting in their seats. Complete pandemonium broke loose as Swindle and Goon joined in, killing whoever they looked at as they made their way up the aisle. Lost in their bloodlust, they ignored the cries and pleas of mercy shouted at them. They were the Mob, and this was Mob shit. They blew through the car, stopping at the end, and reloaded their weapons as they prepared to enter the third car.

Leading the way, Peppy was too scared to turn around for fear of falling victim to the carnage he heard happening behind him. They stepped out of the car and entered the third to perform an encore. Just as NoLove set foot in the car, a woman wearing a neck full of emeralds as green as her eyes jumped in front of him.

Looking at NoLove, she said, "Take my life, and you get nothing. Take me with you, and I promise you I'm worth my weight in gold."

Not one to falter, NoLove made the split decision in a split second. He lashed out, smacking her with the gun, then turned her around and pushed her down the aisle behind Peppy to the last car.

To NoLove's right, a man stood up in protest only to have the top of his head explode as a large caliber bullet tore through it. Behind that was more of the same—men, women, and children slaughtered in their seats. No one was innocent, and none would be spared.

They entered the final car, where numerous crates and boxes greeted them. One crate in particular—a large, metallic chest secured with locks and cornered with clamped latches—caught their eye. This had to be it.

"Okay, Peppy, show me the money," said NoLove, holding the woman by the arm, his gun in his free hand.

The cabin boy immediately went to work, unlatching and releasing the large locks that held the chest in place. Once it was free, Peppy undid the bolt that opened the lid, revealing the trunk inside. On seeing this, they all stepped forward and crowded around as Peppy stuck the key into the keyhole and turned it, popping open the top. Inside were two neat piles—money on one side and bars of gold on the other. They all smiled at this glorious sight, even Peppy, as if he had just presented them with a gift and sought their approval.

"Okay, close it up," NoLove ordered.

The side door to the car slid open just as a streak of lightning snaked through the dark skies above. The three new guys were there with the horses and a wagon, ready to work, although they looked a little nervous.

"It's time to move! Storm's about to be on top of us," one of them yelled.

NoLove nodded and looked at Peppy. No words needed to be said. You would have thought Peppy was down with the Mob the way he was working to unload the crate and get it hitched up to be carried off. Once the cargo was locked in place, they all started to re-saddle to make their escape as NoLove looked on. Swindle, already on his horse, urged it forward to where NoLove was standing, checking to ensure the take was secure on the wagon.

"Who's the dame?" Swindle asked.

NoLove looked back at the pale-skinned woman, then back to Swindle.

"I don't know yet, but I think she'll come in handy," NoLove answered.

Just then, they heard a baby crying back in the third car. TwoFace, already saddled up, looked at the new guy who had been with them in the cars.

"Aye, I guess the new guy missed one," TwoFace stated.

"Goon!" NoLove barked.

"I got it," Goon said, hopping off his horse and running back into the car in search of the crying.

The Flesh-Eater roared a few moments later, and the crying stopped forever.

"New Guy, you okay? You look a little sick. You sure you got the stomach for this?" asked NoLove as Goon stepped down from the car to rejoin them.

The new guy had a look of disgust and contempt on his face as he looked at the Mob.

"Why?" he started. "You killed them all. Why'd you do that? They didn't pose a threat. They weren't even armed."

NoLove looked the man dead in his eyes and answered deadpan, "Why not? We're the bad guys, remember?" With a hand on his gun, he approached the man as he sat on his horse. "You best get your mind right, bruh. There is no grey to this. It's straight black and white. We are the bad guys, and those cars full of dead people are the good guys. So, I reckons you pick well the side you claim. Besides, if you kill one man, kill a hundred. It's all the same, even if they catch you. They can only hang you once."

The thunder rumbled overhead, followed by the first drops of rain.

"Let's ride!" NoLove shouted.

After walking back to his horse, he grabbed the woman by the arm and ushered her up into the saddle before hopping on behind her. The horses began to pull the wagon with the loot uphill as his men fell in line behind it.

"Well, Peppy, I guess this is where you and I part ways," NoLove said, holstering his gun. He then dug into his pocket, pulled out a roll of bills, and tossed it to Peppy. "I reckons you never make no mention of ever being on this train. It'll be mighty hard to explain all this killin' and you still livin' but not havin' had a hand in it. So, I suppose you grab a horse and get lost."

"Yes, suh," responded Peppy, stuffing the money into his pocket, thankful he wouldn't be killed.

The rain was coming down harder now. NoLove pulled his horse to start up the hill but paused and looked back one last time.

"Aye, Peppy," he shouted through the rain.

"Yes, suh," he answered timidly as fear overcame him and his thoughts raced.

"If you ever *do* decide to tell it, be sure you get it right. Let 'em know it was The Mob."

With that, NoLove kicked his horse and headed up the hill to catch up with the others as they headed south into the Barren Plains. They had come to the crossroad and crossed the line well beyond the point of no return. It was either destiny or death from this point forward, and the future was sure to be filled with both.

Chapter Seven

Mayor Fat Pockets was seated at his desk in total distress. Although the military had left well over a week ago, the effect of their visit could still be felt. No sooner than they were gone, another horrendous event occurred—a train slaying. Over forty men, women, and children had been killed. There were no survivors, and it was very messy. On top of that, it was on Republic lands.

Whoever the bandits are, they're not afraid to up the fire, Fat Pockets thought, finding the location of the tragedy particularly disturbing. *Two massacres in two weeks. These guys are for real, and they want to make their presence felt.*

Marshall Stryfe wanted answers, and if none were forthcoming soon, heads would roll. The pressure was on, and Fat Pockets had to produce. Thank God for the waiter who was able to put a face and name to the ones responsible for the killings at the Blaze and offer why the massacre occurred. That would buy him a little time, but it wouldn't negate the fact that over fifteen bodies had been dropped in Keystone, and the count would've been higher had Fat Pockets not been able to keep the dead Stoneman found in an alley a secret.

Nonetheless, a massacre here, and now one in Reach Providence, had to have been done by the same people. But what was the purpose for such ruthlessness? He knew it was for money and drugs in Keystone, and money was often a good enough reason to kill. But why the killings in Reach Providence?

Everybody kills to some degree, he reminded himself. *Shit, Shynes won't just kill you. Fucking with them, you might also find your head on a stick, depending on the reason. If Baron Black got a hold of you, you might find your asshole stuffed with baby rattlers and then have your poison-ravaged body left in the desert to kill off the buzzards that fed on you.*

Yeah, there were some very notable ways of killing folk, but he couldn't wrap his head around the recent indifferent killings. The witness said they called themselves "The Mob"— a sweet piece of information Fat Pockets had been glad to deliver to Marshall Stryfe. And he was sure by now any man with a connection to them had a price on his head.

These fools done defied the Republic and all it stands for. The Republic will not just turn a blind eye to it as they did in the Death Sagas, Fat Pockets thought confidently.

Marshall Stryfe would see to it that somebody paid. *Marshall Stryfe.* Just the thought of him caused anger and fear to stir in Fat Pockets' heart and mind. Finally, he had to admit to himself that ever since Marshall Stryfe seized control of the Republic, he proved to be a man unburdened by norms. He did what he wanted, when he wanted, and to whomever he wanted. Fat Pockets knew he had nowhere to run, nowhere to hide from Marshall Stryfe's reach.

He had been called a pet—a "paying pet," to be precise—and was even threatened with The Worm. Fat Pockets didn't like to be threatened, especially by somebody who had the capabilities to carry them out. He preferred to be on the sending end of the threat since the receiving side was for suckers.

Marshall Stryfe had his foot on the collective neck of Keystone, and Fat Pockets knew he had to be smart, especially dealing with a man born of the devil himself. However, Marshall Stryfe had exposed a vital flaw: he needed Keystone, or at least the contributions and resources Fat Pockets generated for him off Keystone.

But what if I started sending those contributions elsewhere and provided resources and the use of his docks to those that would be more appreciative? he wondered, pondering the future and his fate in it.

Fat Pockets leaned back in his chair, mentally probing the possibilities of such a bold and reckless endeavor. Red Rock wouldn't do. Whether Shyne, Billy, or Blazer, they were a society far too tribal and attached to their beliefs of ritualistic and spiritual loyalties. More times than not, incurring the fury of any one of the factions almost always brought forth the ire of all three. And to Fat Pockets' way of thinking, that would be like playing spades against two brothers and a cousin, which he knew would be a bird move.

El Chablo wouldn't work either because he generated more money than nearly all the Plains combined. As far as the drug trade went, he was Big Boss, and he didn't care who had to die to make sure he and his crew kept eating. As they say, Fat Pocket was "'bout the money," but he felt smack money was a little too dirty for him. And the Vasas couldn't be trusted; Fat Pockets knew that was a bed he could never get out of once he laid down. If the Diablo ain't kill ya, his daughter Elvira surely would. Fat Pockets shook off a shiver, thinking about what he had heard about her.

But what about Baron Black? He also defied the Republic like the rest and had outrightly battled back their encroachment for years, calling for everybody to do the same. "Unity is power," he was known for saying. He perpetuated talk for democracy, and the more Fat Pockets thought about it, the more it made sense to him. A lot more sense than the dictatorship of Marshall Stryfe and his vision of authoritarian rule.

One thing was for sure—to get from under the Republic, Fat Pockets would need help. Better yet, he would need protection, and he knew where to find it. Getting up from his desk, he walked to the door and peered out down the hall to see Sergeant Grimble talking to his secretary like he didn't have a care in the world.

"What the fuck?" started Fat Pockets, stepping out into the hallway and approaching the desk, all boss and bully. "Are my motherfucking eyes playing tricks on me? Tell me this is an illusion."

He stood directly in front of Sergeant Grimble and his secretary.

"Sergeant Bitch Grimble, what the fuck are you doing? If memory serves me right, not too long ago, a man made you stand in a corner, and like a bitch, there you stood. Now, here it is, I find you in this mud duck's face trying to mack, yackety-yakkin' like two bitches. Like we ain't just have a *Little Shop of Horrors* here in these streets, with more bodies than one man could count. Now, get the fuck out this hoe's face, and beat your feet and find me a messenger for the long run before I have your stupid ass raped and smacked!"

"Yes, sir, Mayor Fat Pockets," responded Grimble, grabbing his hat off the desk and leaving immediately.

Not finished with his rant, Fat Pockets turned to the secretary.

"Bitch, what the fuck you smirking 'bout? I remember you were a Lucy suckin' dick for soups and jellybeans on the shady side of Keystone when I found you. But now, you sittin' behind that desk actin' like the belle of the fuckin' ball. Bitch, skip your ass down the block and get me some fried chicken from that Busy Bee spot, and try not to trip on a cock along the way. And it best be hot when you get it back, or that's my word I'm gonna stick you on a corner with a 'for sale' sign 'round your neck. Now, kick rocks!"

"Yes, sir," she said, rising from her desk.

"Yes, who, bitch?"

"Yes, sir, Mayor Fat Pockets," she answered.

"That's right. Get it right, 'cause I'll put hands on a bitch and still make her trick. If I ain't a boss, then a boss is a bitch."

He walked toward the doors of Council Hall, standing on the steps as his secretary ran past him.

"And make sure you get hot sauce," added Fat Pockets, looking down on the streets of Keystone, feeling back on top and in control. *But for how long?* he wondered.

***

Mr. Happy knocked on the door to Marshall Stryfe's office and stepped inside.

"Marshall Stryfe, Mr. Drake has arrived to see you, sir,"

reported Mr. Happy.

"Ahh, yes. Send him in," said Marshall Stryfe, getting to his feet.

"Yes, sir," Mr. Happy answered.

"Oh, and Mr. Happy," called Stryfe.

"Sir?"

"Please, next time, wait until I tell you to enter before stepping into my office. We are the Civilized Republic; thus, decorum must start with us. Next time, you will be disciplined," said Stryfe, waving him off.

Mr. Happy nodded as he exited the office. A few moments passed, and then another knock on his door.

"Enter," said Stryfe coolly.

In strode Mr. Happy, followed by Mr. Drake. Stryfe stepped from behind his desk to meet him. Mr. Drake was a slender man of average height, but his talents in the art of espionage were renowned.

Mr. Drake was impressed by what he saw when he stepped into the office—treaties on the wall and the paintings of forefathers. Just the sheer majesty of Stryfe's ambition and his accolades up to this point served as a testament to what Stryfe hoped to accomplish as leader of the Civilized Republic.

Marshall Stryfe was a tall, stern man with a full head of salt and pepper hair. His steely grey eyes gave away nothing but sought everything. They had met many years ago, only in passing, before Marshall Stryfe became who he was now.

"Marshall Stryfe," said Mr. Drake, extending his hand.

"Mr. Drake," answered Stryfe as the two men clasped hands.

"Please, have a seat," said Stryfe, gesturing to the seat before his desk. "Can I offer you a drink?" he asked while making his way behind his desk to sit down.

"Yes, after we've handled the reason for which you contacted me," answered Drake.

"Business before pleasure; the markings of an astute businessman. I like that," Stryfe admitted.

Mr. Drake nodded.

Stryfe looked up to Mr. Happy, who was standing behind Mr. Drake. "You may leave us."

Once Mr. Happy was gone, Marshall Stryfe faced Drake, ready to deal with the matter at hand.

"How are you?" Stryfe started.

"I'm well; I'm alive. I'm here upon your request."

"Yes, and I greatly appreciate you coming despite the short notice. I trust your getting here was uneventful coming down from Noble Haven."

"Yes. Aside from the nasty rumors about the massacres in Keystone and Reach Providence, the trip was fine."

"Well, those were no rumors. A nasty lot that is being sought as we speak are responsible—no doubt bandits out of the Barren Plains, which brings me to the heart of this meeting. Mr. Drake, I would like to unify the Barren Plains under the banner of the Civilized Republic and stop the banditry and lawlessness that goes on there. But, as you well know, certain obstacles stand in my way, and I require a man of your skills to remove them."

Mr. Drake leaned back in his chair, finally realizing what this meeting was about.

"Marshall Stryfe, unify the Plains? Well, wasn't that the whole aim and failure of the Death Sagas? Albeit it was before my time, many of the players who partook in that affair are still alive and kicking. And please call me Sheldon; all my friends and employers do. And as I'm sure you are about to be both, let's be frank, for there is no need to mince our words. You do, in fact, mean El Chablo, Baron Black, and Diablo Vasa?"

"Of sorts," answered Stryfe, who wasn't liking Drake's smugness but respected his perception on the matter and his resolve to handle it nonetheless. Thus, he proceeded on in full disclosure.

"El Chablo only cares about money—the money he and his cabal make off the poison he peddles. Granted, he's a big fish, but it's my pond. And as a result, we've captured him twice."

"And twice he escaped," Drake interjected.

"Trust that there will not be a third time," Stryfe promised.

Drake only nodded.

"As for Diablo Vasa, he only cares about power—power over his people within his borders. Both men are quite simple in their ambitions, and, therefore, can be easily outthought. But Baron Black is an altogether different viper. See, like me, he wants the land, but for all the wrong reasons. He wants the land for the people's sake. However, the people don't know what's best for them. They are little more than sheep or cattle to be herded. And *I* will be that shepherd, not him. His way of unification is by way of democracy, allowing the lawless to thrive, and I can't have that. My way of unification is with the eradication of this riff-raff—the desolate, savage, and uncivilized. And more precisely, the death of Baron Black. So, tell me, Sheldon, are you interested in my proposition?"

"Well, that depends on what I stand to gain because what you're asking is no easy fuck of a Lucy, even if at all possible. Thus, the risk I am to take must be justified by a grand reward I stand to gain," countered Drake.

"Okay, then, Sheldon Drake, let's not trifle. I offer you Keystone to run as you will. The imports, exports, gambling, and all other under-the-table dealings that go on there, which I hear are very lucrative and have made Fat Pockets quite wealthy. You will answer to no one but me, and even in that, it will only be in regards to an annual contribution to the Republic of your intake of revenue."

"And what about Fat Pockets?" Drake asked.

"What about him? Trust me, Sheldon, you handle Baron Black, and I assure you when you reach Keystone, Fat Pockets will be hogtied and on a platter with an apple in his dead mouth," Stryfe responded coldly.

The offer was more than Drake could've dreamed of. The possibilities of what he could do as a ruler of Keystone were endless. Control of the docks alone would make him a force to be reckoned with, and he'd bide his time, first getting from under the rule of the Imperium across the water and then from Marshall Stryfe. Then he'd be the man behind the desk instead of in front of it.

Marshall Stryfe looked at the man before him and could almost read his mind, seeing his facial expressions as what he could have and do bloomed in his mind. Stryfe could see the deceit making its way from the back of his thoughts to the front of his face. And while Sheldon Drake was still going through his decision process, Stryfe had already decided that although initially he would've honored his word and given Drake control of Keystone, it would be so much better to have Drake kill Baron Black. Then, in turn, he would have Drake and Fat Pockets killed and then assimilate both the Barren Plains and Keystone into the Republic.

Both men now studied each other—gauging, thinking, plotting. The silence lasted nearly a minute before Drake spoke.

"Marshall Stryfe, you dangle a carrot that no donkey could refuse. So, if what you ask can be done, I expect you will make good on your end when the time comes," Drake stated.

"Then we agree?" asked Stryfe.

"Agreed we are," responded Drake.

"Then let us toast to our venture of civilization," offered Stryfe as he stood up, followed by Drake.

"Do you have brandy by chance?" asked Drake.

"Yes, of course. The devil's cut," laughed Marshall Stryfe, reaching his hand out for one final handshake, solidifying their deal.

All men have their price—whether for honor, loyalty, riches, or women, thought Stryfe. *They can all be bought, and if not, killed and replaced by someone who will say yes when they said no.*

Chapter Eight

Several days had passed since Alkada and his band set out. Hot days and cold nights on the open plains. They rode west out of Shynetown and, after two days of riding, headed north. It was a given that the men they hunted had not come south out of Keystone since that would've brought them smack dab into Red Rock and north into Republic Lands, which would've been a death sentence. So, west out of Keystone made the only possible sense, and under this pretense, they headed north in hopes of picking up their trail.

They had just entered the Canyons of the Benta Territories, lands ruled by El Chablo, the lord and master of the drug trade, and he didn't take kindly to trespassing. Thus, Alkada knew they had to pass through these lands as quickly and quietly as possible, but that wasn't in the cards for them. Alkada sensed they were being watched. At first, the feeling was light—the curious gaze of a mere scout. Yet, as the day wore on, that curious gaze turned to stalking.

It was midday, and the sun was bearing down on them. The canyon walls prevented the sunlight from getting to them, but the heat was oppressive and draining. As they pushed on, the feeling of being watched could no longer be denied, especially since the watchers stopped being so subtle about their watching. Alkada could notice how the shadows moved with them through the canyon, only stopping when Alkada looked right at them.

StreetLife brought his horse up alongside Alkada to confer, but before he could utter a word, Alkada asked the obvious.

"How long?"

"'Bout the last two miles," StreetLife answered.

"How many?" Alkada said as he readied himself for combat.

"I'd reckons fifteen to twenty," StreetLife responded, doing the same as they approached an opening in the canyon.

A1 looked on, baffled, not understanding. However, as soon as they cleared the canyon walls, a semicircle of Benta soldiers armed with rifles and machetes greeted them. They were short and stocky men, their skin the same color as the beige and red canyon walls, but as Alkada looked more closely, he realized these were not the elite soldiers of El Chablo. They were more like a ragtag group of rejects that fell victim to the very drugs they smuggled.

"Greetings," said the one who appeared to be the leader.

"Greetings, friend," responded StreetLife as they brought their horses to a stop.

"Yes, friends we are," started the man. "Well, friends, it seems the three of you have traveled through our lands while we silently protected you, and here it is, you near the border, and you have yet to make a contribution for that protection," said the man, grinning wolfishly as he gripped his rifle.

StreetLife began to reach into his pocket when the de facto leader interrupted him.

"Ah, my friends, I'm sorry, but surely the contribution we require cannot be found in your pocket."

All the troops clutched their weapons more sturdily. At this, Alkada stilled himself and prepared to take life.

"Well, what are you asking for?" StreetLife asked.

"How 'bout we start with your horses and weapons," the man responded. Then his gaze fell to A1. "And the young boy," he added, looking at A1 in a lustfully and weirdly as his fellow soldiers chuckled.

What kinda soldiers are these guys? Alkada thought.

"Raaaaaah."

Just then, the air was ripped in half by Skully's arrival, his shriek echoing off the canyon walls as he floated down and landed on Alkada's shoulder, flapping his massive black wings like the regal creature he was.

At this, the Benta leader said, "We'll be taking your bird, too. He'll taste good with some sage and salt over a spit."

More sneers and snickers from the soldiers followed his words.

"Or how about this?" said a newcomer, whose sudden appearance cut the sneers and snickers short. "My bros and I go about our business, and you Bentas go on living."

HardBody nudged his horse in from behind the soldiers to post up with Alkada.

"Shyne love, Alkada. What's up, Streets? It's been a while. Who's the scrap?" HardBody asked, pointing at A1 with his chin.

When no immediate answer came, HardBody turned to see the gun-clutching, now menacing-looking Benta soldiers. "You guys still here? I can dig it. I reckons we might as well get to the last stop on this train," he said, turning back to face Alkada, shaking his head.

The Bentas remained fixed in their positions.

"Bentas. I *hate* these guys," HardBody said as he drew his guns with lightning speed and began firing at the closest Benta to him. Alkada and Streetlife followed suit.

Boom! Boom! Blam! Blam! Blam! Boom! Boom!

The next few seconds were a blur of hand movements and muzzle flashes. These were professional gunslingers; killing was their true calling. As the shots rang out, eyes and teeth were blown from heads, along with fleshy skull chunks. Spirits could be felt floating away as bodies crashed lifeless to the ground. The only Benta soldier left standing when the smoke cleared was the leader.

HardBody started chuckling as he reloaded and holstered his guns. Alkada and StreetLife did the same.

"Okay, I bet my offer to go on 'bout your business sounds real good now, doesn't it?" HardBody asked the remaining soldier.

"Yes, yes, my friend," responded the soldier standing among his dead men.

"Too late!" snapped HardBody. "Now unstrap that rifle and drop it to the ground."

The soldier did as told.

Directing his gaze at A1, HardBody said, "Hey, scrap, I guess you forgot you had a gun on your hip. And I reckons if you be Shyne or Rollack, it doesn't much matter. But you for sure can't be vegan. So, this one is for you." He gestured towards the lone soldier before them.

A1 reached for his gun but was stopped by Alkada.

"The time to do it that way just passed you by. You got a knife on your hip. It's time to let your nuts hang and ride or die, scrap."

A1 nodded, passed his guns to StreetLife, and hopped down from his horse. Then, with knife in hand, he approached the soldier.

The Benta knew he was about to die no matter what, but at least he would kill one of them before he did. He was five-ten, two hundred pounds, and his adversary was only a kid. HardBody threw the Benta a knife. He bent down to pick it up, then looked at A1 as he began to wave the blade back and forth as if slicing the air.

Grinning, he said, "Little man, you should've used your gun when you had the chance. Now, you will die with me."

A1 ignored him as he got close.

"Remember, A1, he called you a 'young boy,' which means they meant to fuck you!" StreetLife screamed out.

As the realization of what StreetLife said dawned on A1, he stopped walking. Consumed with anger, he choked up on the handle of his knife, holding the tip-up. As he got within a few feet of the Benta, the soldier immediately lunged at A1, his knife in his right hand held out like a spear before him. A1 sidestepped to the left and tried to counter but was kicked back, falling to the ground. He rolled into a tuck and then rose to one knee, holding his stomach in anticipation of the rush. And rush him the Benta did, thinking the child was injured. He raised his knife high and came down murderously. At the last second, A1 sprung up, ducked beneath the soldier's striking arm, and stabbed the soldier in his midsection, pulling the knife across his belly. A1 then reversed his grip and brought the knife back full-thrust to the back of the soldier's neck, pulling it out of his throat.

The Benta immediately reached up for his neck, dropping the knife to cover the gaping gash as he fell to his knees and then forward flat on his face—dying as he did so.

"Shyne shit!" HardBody barked from his horse, so caught up in the moment that he reshot the already dead soldiers scattered about.

Skully ruffled his feathers and shrieked, taking back to the air, while Alkada handed the reins of his horse to HardBody and nodded as he approached A1. StreetLife nodded his respect, as well, and tossed A1's guns back to him. Alkada placed his hand on A1's shoulder as they stood over the dead soldier.

"It's nothing personal, son," Alkada said, reaching down to pick up HardBody's knife. "I just had to be sure you could show your fangs when the time came." He then crouched down and stuck two fingers into the dead man's neck, slicking his fingers with blood and standing back up to smear the blood down A1's face. "Let that dry," he said.

HardBody kicked his horse forward, handing Alkada back the reins to his horse, and reclaimed his knife.

After saddling up, Alkada looked back at A1 and told him, "Look here, scrap, go ahead and cut his head off and put it on his chest. That will let anybody who picks up our trail know that there are Shynes at the end of it."

Alkada then pulled his horse along; HardBody and StreetLife followed. As HardBody passed A1, he stopped his horse.

"Congratulations, kid. You passed the test. Be sure you let that blood dry on your face and fall away on its own."

"What was the test?" A1 asked, amazed at all the scars on HardBody's face.

"It's called the Hardening," he answered.

"So am I a Shyne now?"

"Hell nah. Fuck nah, you ain't no Shyne now. You got a long way to go. But at least you're on your way. You see my face, kid?" HardBody pulled his hat back to reveal at least twenty scars. "I've taken a head for every scar you see, and I still got a lot more to get, dig? So, you best be knowin' this is only the beginning. And we got a long way to go. Got it?"

A1 nodded, excited to be in the presence of HardBody. There was nobody in all of Shyne history to carry more scars than him; HardBody was a household name on the plains.

"Well, that's good, kid, because the killings we'll be doing are for Shyne love, loyalty, honor, and respect."

HardBody cut his eyes to Alkada, who was talking with StreetLife. He then leaned down close to A1 and whispered, "Say, kid, there's a saying for men that kill like us, and I reckons you might as well get to fixing your mind around it now and make it part of your reasoning whenever you pull the trigger. It goes: *You kill one man, kill a hundred. It's all the same. Besides, they can only hang you once.* You understand that?"

A1 nodded, grinning at the profound saying that had just been handed down to him. Once again, HardBody glanced at Alkada and back to the kid.

"So, tell me, kid, do you want to be a servant in heaven or a star in hell?"

"A star in hell," A1 shot back instantly, already familiar with that saying and its meaning.

"Come on, kid, get to cutting that head off so we can ride out!" shouted Alkada.

"Relax, big bro!" HardBody stressed, kicking his horse forward. "I was just fixing the kid up with the killer instinct."

"I know that's right!" Alkada responded as he locked hands with HardBody in greeting. "The only problem with that is if you took the kid under your wing, he'd probably end up consumed by the maddening."

Alkada laughed. He was happy to see the man who was raised like his little brother. The bond between them was solid as stone.

HardBody was as black as night with a soul to match, slim built with a face that was a montage of scars.

HardBody then shook hands with StreetLife and greeted him. "Suns to guns, bro."

"Guns to suns," StreetLife responded as the three men turned back to A1, who was busy cutting the soldier's head off without any hesitation.

The sight brought back memories to Alkada and HardBody when they went through their first trials to become Shyne.

After A1 finished his business, they prepared to head north, with Skully flying overhead.

***

They rode hard until sundown, making up for the lost time. Nearing a mountain range, they found an enclave alongside a river and made camp there. After tending to their horses, they raised a fire and gathered to pow-wow. Skully remained in the air, a quiet sentry watching for any danger as the men spoke around the flames.

StreetLife recounted what had happened in Keystone for HardBody and A1. Alkada could see that StreetLife's telling of Leggs' last words stirred up emotions in A1 and sought to end it.

"Choke up on the soft shit, kid. Ain't no room for it here. Your father's dead, and tears won't bring him back, but they will get you killed. The men we're gunning for don't give a fuck 'bout killin'. They'll kill a man just the same as killin' a bug. Now, I know you're in pain, but there's power in pain. So, I reckons you pull the power out of the pain you're feelin'," Alkada said, studying A1's face through the fire.

A1 nodded, getting a hold of the emotion rising in him.

HardBody then told them what he had heard about a train massacre in Reach Providence, and they all agreed it had to be NoLove on both accounts. So, they would continue north until they picked up the trail.

"So, that's Leggs' kid?" HardBody asked Alkada.

"Yeah. His name is A1," Alkada answered.

"Say, A1, you think you ready to be scarred?" HardBody said, now looking at A1.

"Already," A1 responded.

"Damn, HardBody, it seems you've earned a few more scars since the last time I saw you at S.I.'s funeral, and what the hell were you doing this far out?" StreetLife inquired.

The mention of S.I. brought an ire feeling to Alkada—ire and hatred for the law dogs of oppression who killed him, but S.I.'s death didn't go unanswered. Just as sure as S.I. was laid in the ground in Alkada's yard, so was the head of the man who killed him—one of the reasons Alkada was now a wanted man by the Republic.

"Yeah, I picked up a few more scars for the Billy bro. S.I. was one of the realest, so I ain't mind spillin' blood for him. Besides that, me and Ammo runnin' a bet for who will get to fifty scars first," HardBody answered with a hardy chuckle.

"So, I guess you were out here tryin' to ante up," StreetLife added.

"Nah, Streets. I was out here lookin' for answers to my past, you might say."

StreetLife nodded, a bit confused by HardBody's answer. Alkada wasn't, though. He knew HardBody was out here looking for Axx. And secretly, Alkada hoped he would never find him.

"Well, I'm sure you'll be able to catch a scar or two on this one. It's sure to be a smoker."

"I hope you're right, Streets," said HardBody as he stood up to stretch his tall, lean body.

Even though night had set upon them, one could still clearly see the scars covering his face regardless of his dark skin.

"It's funny that it's come to this," HardBody continued. "NoLove was a solid dude in The Fort. I reckons he's gotta know we'll be comin' for him. And me and the kid, TwoFace, crossed paths in the Barren Straights—had a facin' at high noon. But before we could get to it, tamers hit the town on a raid, so I had to skin out. As I hear it, there is still a 'kill on sight' decree for any Shynes caught on Republic lands."

"Or anyplace outside of Red Rock for that matter when it comes to the Republic," Alkada cut in. "I'm sure Captain Hammer is still holdin' salts for that eye I took."

"And his brothers you killed," StreetLife added.

"Yeah, well, the Hammer brothers should have thought about all that when they killed my father and S.I.," Alkada said as he, too, stood up to stretch.

"*Our* father," HardBody interjected, to which Alkada nodded, remembering how his father had raised them both.

"Either or… TwoFace is 'bout as fast as they come, and I'm glad to know I'll get another chance at him. He'll either be another scar for me or the death of me," Alkada expressed.

A1 sat amazed at hearing all the information being passed before him.

"However it plays out, stutter-steppin' will get you killed. So, keep ya hammers on cock. Now, go on and get some rest. I got first watch, and we ride at sunrise," Alkada said.

As his men laid down to rest, Alkada sat in the lotus position for a spell of meditation, but first, he reached out to Skully with connection and awareness, seeing through his eyes as he flew above them. Certain there was no danger, Alkada severed the link and returned his focus to his meditation and his bond to Dempaku, offering prayer to his higher power and readying his mind for what was to come.

***

They broke camp at dawn, continuing to head north toward the Sanchie Lands of Diablo Vasa, a man Alkada had also respected as a father figure and who also fought in the Death Sagas. Riding halfway through the day, they stopped in a small town for supplies and to see if there was any new news from up north. The scene was quite rural and sparse when they pulled into town, but still, they would be able to get what they needed.

Alkada stepped into a small supply store while StreetLife and HardBody stood outside with A1, who watered the horses.

Watching the going-ons of the town, StreetLife noticed a young boy being jumped by four other young boys while tied to a post in the ground. One of them had a stick. The kid looked to be only a year or two older than A1, and although tied at the waist, he seemed to be holding his own against his attackers. But it was only a matter of time before he would be overwhelmed.

"What's goin' on there?" StreetLife asked HardBody, knowing he frequented these parts.

"It's a game…or more like a rite of passage into manhood called Beating the Dog. Each boy takes a turn attacking the boy who's tied up for one-on-one combat. If the boy who is tied up starts to get the best of his attacker, he gets hit by whoever's holding the stick, and then it's his turn to fight as he passes the stick to the kid beside him. It goes on until each boy beats the one tied up one-on-one or until they decide collectively to beat him to death. And whoever strikes the killing blow is considered a man, which by the look of things, won't be much longer," HardBody explained.

StreetLife looked on, digesting what he'd just been told. Then he exploded.

"Oh, hell no! Fuck no!" StreetLife barked as he started walking toward them.

HardBody followed right behind, smiling and clutching his guns.

StreetLife stepped directly into the middle of the fray and yelled, "Untie him!" to the boy who was holding the stick.

"Not untie till he die!" a boy spat back at StreetLife.

StreetLife instantly drew his revolver and slapped the boy on the side of his face, firing it simultaneously.

Boww!

The shot shattered the boy's eardrum as he fell to the ground in a heap of dust and dirt, holding his bleeding ear and screaming out in pain. All the other boys jumped back, and StreetLife fired another shot, popping the rope that held the boy in place.

Now freed, the boy immediately went on the offense. He

lunged forward, grabbed the stick, and swung it at one of his tormentor's heads, dropping him cold. He then spun around on another, swinging across his face, knocking him onto his back. The final boy turned to run, only taking one step before being elbowed and knocked to the ground unconscious by StreetLife.

The freed boy then shot to the ground and began choking the boy who StreetLife had gun slapped, slinging him up and down, slamming him into the ground as he strangled the life out of him while StreetLife and HardBody looked on.

A village elder, who had been watching from his fruit stand, grabbed his rifle and marched toward the fiasco. He raised his rifle and began to take aim when he felt a barrel pressing at the back of his skull.

"You pull your trigger, and I pull mine," A1 said, holding his gun steady, ready to make good on his threat.

The old man immediately dropped his rifle and raised his hands.

"Whoa, whoa," said Alkada, taking in the scene as he stepped out into the street. "What's goin' on?"

As StreetLife filled him in on the turn of events, Alkada's face showed the same disdain that StreetLife felt over the situation.

"What was his crime to be treated so?" Alkada asked the elder, who stood stiff as a statue with A1's gun still cocked and pressed against his head.

"He got caught stealing bread," answered the elder.

"And for *that*, he must lose his life?" responded Alkada, dumbfounded. He signaled for A1 to remove his gun from the man's head.

The elder lowered his hands and then brought a hand to his face, pulling it along his jaw, indicating the scars on Alkada's face.

"Who am I to say what makes sense in Shynetown?" the elder replied.

Alkada nodded his understanding. This was not his land. Nor was it his place to question their laws.

However, StreetLife did not share this sentiment as he reached into his pocket.

"Fuck all that!" StreetLife barked as he flipped a gold coin worth twenty times the bread's value to the elder.

The elder bit down on the coin, then shoved it into his pocket as he shooed the beaten boys away. Then he picked up his rifle and went back to his fruit stand. Several gawking villagers quickly dispersed after noticing Hardbody's scarred face. They knew what the Shynes were about, and they did not want to meddle.

HardBody noticed the fear and seized the moment.

"Okay, problem solved! Everybody go back to living and breathing!" he shouted, caressing his guns while looking around as the villagers bowed and looked away to avoid eye contact. Then, he turned to Alkada. "Sanchies—I hate these guys."

"Alright, StreetLife, you saved a life today! You got blessin's comin'," Alkada said. "Now what? Is he comin' with us? Are we pickin' up strays now?" He looked at the boy as he untied the rope from his waist.

"I don't know," StreetLife started, also looking at the kid. "I just couldn't let him die like that," StreetLife continued, now facing the kid in earnest. "So, kid, you comin' with us. Can you handle a gun and ride a horse? We don't hold hands here, bruh. Either you ride, or you *will* die," StreetLife told him.

Looking up at StreetLife, the kid replied, "You saved my life, so I'm with you until I repay the debt. And I know many things. Like the men you hunt are not far from here. They are in a place called Shameless, and death surrounds them as it surrounds you."

StreetLife looked at Alkada for some sort of confirmation. Alkada pushed his senses onto the boy and nodded subtlety to StreetLife, indicating he sensed Dempaku's energy on the kid. Even Skully shrieked above in agreement, also feeling what Alkada did.

"You got a name, kid?" StreetLife asked.

"Yes. I am called London."

Chapter Nine

NoLove and his gang crested in a heavily wooded area off the roadside that overlooked the town of Shameless. They decided to wait for sundown before entering. This way, they would attract little attention since Shameless was a midway town and attracted numerous travelers headed in all directions.

After the train heist, they rode for two straight days south out of Reach Providence, only stopping to feed and water their horses. Now that they were back across the border in the Barren Plains, they could breathe a little easier. So, they made camp and waited. It was still early enough in the day for a cool breeze to blow through the trees before the high noon heat kicked in.

Now is the perfect time to make plans, NoLove thought to himself.

NoLove had to be back across the border to meet Foot in Republic City in a few days to execute the next phase of events. All in all, he had to admit that things were going well. The feeling of change was real, and they were the harbingers of it. NoLove smiled, looking down at Shameless.

Taking the woman had been done in the heat of the moment, but now, given time to think on it, NoLove wondered what purpose she would serve beyond sex. Perhaps she would only slow them down. At this point, she could not be allowed to live if she sought to leave them, that was for sure. NoLove's thoughts were interrupted by one of the new guys they had taken on.

"Hey, NoLove," he said, approaching from behind.

NoLove turned around to face him, noticing that the rest of his crew was behind him, hands on their gun handles.

"'What's up, new guys?" NoLove spoke, seeing TwoFace was on point and ready if need be.

"My guys and I were talkin', and we've decided this is where we part ways. The way you guys roll, the hangman will be at you soon enough. So, let's divvy up the loot, and we can be on our way."

NoLove and TwoFace smiled at the new guys, taking it all in.

"Bruh, you just spent your share of the loot," NoLove responded.

"What are you talkin' 'bout?" said the new guy, half drawing his pistol.

NoLove shook his head in disappointment. "Well, New Guy, me and TwoFace here..." NoLove held out his hand towards TwoFace. "...we made a bet. A bet that maybe you and your crew would be worthy of wearing the stamp...*our* stamp."

Goon and Swindle took their place next to NoLove as he gesticulated with his hands.

"At least, *I* thought you would, but TwoFace called it. He said you'd take the money and run. He said you'd skin out, said you guys ain't got the steel in your veins to be a part of the Mob or our future. I reckons you guys are conscious killers, whereas the Mob kills without conscience."

"What's that got to do with our share of the loot?" the new guy interrupted.

"Don't you get it, New Guy? Your share of the loot is what I bet, and I lost. So, *you* lose. Did you really think this was purely about the money?" NoLove asked. "The money is only a means, New Guy. We are the Mob."

"Mob shit," barked Goon over NoLove's shoulder.

"That's right, Goon. Mob shit is what we are about," NoLove added. "The Mob is the name of change. We're a group of men who have come together for a common cause…a belief in the betterment of ourselves and the prosperity of our fellow men and family. We are men who, by oath and obligation and acts of allegiance, are willing to do any and everything to achieve our goals, as long as it falls within the moral perimeters we are willing to accept. Yet, at no time will we ever let our love and lust for material gains come before our love and loyalty for our fellow brother. This is the fraternity we are a part of," NoLove stated proudly and slammed his fist against his chest while Goon, Swindle, and TwoFace nodding enthusiastically.

"And for all acts that we undertake to see our aims manifested," NoLove continued, "we envelop ourselves in the code of *Omerta,* meaning everything said or done among us is never revealed to those who are not of us. And even though some of us may die, be locked down in The Fort, or even get The Worm, we will never snitch or betray the code—for even though death and prison walls may separate us from our brothers, our brotherhood will live on. And you, new guys, had a chance to be a part of this. You had a chance to be legends. But now, you will die lame and nameless."

He looked at the guy and his crew, shaking his head in disgust.

At this, the new guys began drawing their weapons, aimed, and started pulling the triggers, only to hear the clicks and clunks as their guns dry fired to their shock.

"Looking for these?" asked Goon, tossing a pouch of bullets on the ground between them.

"On your knees, cocksuckers," said NoLove callously as he and the Mob drew their much-loaded guns and stepped forward. "If you bitches had shown that same killer instinct when we robbed that train, you all might not be dying now."

Swindle grabbed the dame by the arm and pulled her into the gathering. "What about this chick?"

"Yeah, what about her?" NoLove asked, turning to TwoFace. "Double or nothing. I say the lady has steel enough in her veins."

He took possession of her, waiting for TwoFace to respond.

TwoFace nodded and replied, "Bet."

The new guys were now on their knees, held in place at gunpoint. After the lady was brought before them, a pistol was placed in her hands.

"Okay, lady, what will it be?" asked NoLove. "Destiny or death?"

He stepped back, leaving her to decide.

Boom!

A thunderous blast sounded through the trees of the wooded area, sending birds fluttering into the morning sky, followed by three more loud shots as the four men were sent to their maker and the woman embraced her destiny.

***

Foot stepped into the restaurant and awaited his guest. He was in Republic City, and things were happening via the Mob murders, massacres, and mayhem. Of course, that was if you were on the outside looking in. However, if you were on the inside looking out, things looked colossal. Everything was coming together, and the meeting he was about to have would only further that.

Foot took a seat at his table, a window seat. He ordered a paper and cigar and looked out the window as he waited, watching the comings and goings of the people of Republic City as they were shopping, living, and thriving. They were oblivious of the things to come, of the very wolf now among them.

He was brought a copy of the *Republic Speaks* and was shocked to see the front-page story.

Diamond Mogul's daughter disappears, believed to have been on the train that was the scene of a bloody massacre in Reach Providence. However, sources close to the investigation revealed she was not among the dead.

Foot smiled to himself, secure in knowing he was one of the few men on the planet who knew who had her…if she was even still alive. And that in itself could be worth something.

Yes, things are indeed coming together, he thought, satisfied.

He signaled to the waitress that he was ready to order.

"What will you be having?"

"Just bring me your best," he answered.

"Excuse me," the waitress countered.

"Listen here, love, bring me the best of everything. Your best steak, your best wine, and if you fancy yourself, the best waitress. I'm staying at the Republic Plaza Hotel."

He handed the woman several folded notes before shooing her away with his hand. His thoughts then returned to the here and now, again knowing the future was shaping up, and he was one of the shapers.

***

Simon Thorn, also known as The Weasel, had just arrived in Republic City on the Bullet Express out of Noble Haven. He was a slim man of pale complexion, standing about five-eleven with slicked-back black hair. He looked more like a preacher than a lawyer, and with the gold-rimmed glasses he constantly kept sitting on the bridge of his narrow nose, he gave off the appearance that there wasn't a question he could not answer. The kind of guy who could get God and the Devil to shake hands.

He hated trains, especially in light of the recent train massacre, but he loved money, and for the money, he was in Republic City. He would've put a saddle on his wife's back and rode her into town all the way from Noble Haven if he had to. What his client wanted was not impossible, albeit a little tricky and perhaps somewhat questionable. Nonetheless, it was doable. El Chablo had proven that. In fact, Simon had already put out feelers weeks before when Foot first contacted him about what he wanted to do, and the response was favorable. The ticket was 7.5 million and would only be discussed further with money on the wood.

The wood is there, so it's time to put the money on it, thought The Weasel as he entered the restaurant and immediately spotted his client in the crowded establishment.

***

Foot waved to Simon as he stepped into the restaurant and was immediately guided to his table. Simon looked at Foot, remembering their first encounter years before when he helped Foot dodge a twenty-year bid due to a technicality. A technicality Simon was able to implant into Foot's case retroactively and charge it to Foot's bill, which he paid without any qualms. Simon was a good lawyer, but he was a magnificent negotiator. Simon laughed to himself. They didn't call him The Weasel for nothing, but the stakes were much higher now, and so was the bill.

The two men shook hands and sat down.

"What's up, Foot?"

"Nothing much, Simon. I'm good. Hoping you got some good news for me."

The Weasel nodded as the waitress returned and stood between them while he placed his briefcase down.

"What will you be having, sir?"

"Go ahead and order whatever you like," Foot cut in. "It will be the best unless you order her; then it will just be sloppy seconds," he added, laughing.

The waitress turned beet red but kept smiling, for she knew she was in the presence of made men with money to burn, and she was hoping to get some.

Simon chuckled as he admired the waitress, who was very appealing to the eye.

"Aside from you, I'll just have whatever he's having."

The waitress smiled, then pinched Foot on the arm before

fluttering off.

Simon sorted the glasses on his face and looked at Foot, ready to split the middle. Foot took notice and got started.

"Okay, Simon, let's get to the hammer and nails. Can it be done?"

Simon picked up his briefcase, placed it on the table between them, popped the latches, and pulled out a piece of paper, a quill, and a small jar of blue ink. Then he closed the briefcase and placed it back on the floor beside him. He wrote down something on the paper and slid it across the table to Foot.

Foot grabbed the paper, looked at it, nodded, and reached for the quill, which he re-dipped into the ink.

Right under Simon's note, which read *$7.5 million cash*, he wrote his response: *1–week.* Then he smoothly slid the slip of paper back to him.

They shook hands, and Simon again signaled for the waitress. When she came, Simon was all finesse now. He told her that he'd have a cigar and her best friend, slyly mentioning that he was staying at the Plaza, as well. The waitress smiled and immediately sauntered off to another waitress—a blonde with blue eyes and big tits. They looked like sisters.

The waitress whispered in the ear of the other woman while pointing back to Simon. The blonde's face instantly lit up as she smiled and waved at Simon, already knowing he would pay to play, and she was more than willing to be his toy.

Simon waved back and winked. Yes, this trip was already proving its worth despite the apprehension Simon initially felt about traveling by train. Simon never asked questions about where the money came from. As long as his client paid, Simon would find a way. He had just come up on a major meal ticket—

7.5 million for being a middleman. It was no doubt in Simon Thorn's mind that he truly was The Weasel.

Chapter Ten

Marshall Stryfe sat behind his desk in his massive office, brooding over recent events. Too much blood was being spilled; this was true. However, his real issue was that it wasn't the Republic doing the spilling. The defiance would not go unanswered. Stryfe had an ax to grind, and that grinding would start with General Lynch and Captain Hammer, who were now en route to his office. He would apply pressure on them and then set them loose. It was time to restore order to the Plains.

The Death Sagas had people of the Barren Plains thinking they were untouchable and unreachable. But, most notably to Marshall Stryfe, they felt they were *unleash*-able, and it was time to shake the foundations of their arrogant feelings.

There was a knock at his door.

"Enter," Stryfe sounded as the door cracked.

Mr. Happy stepped in, holding the door wide open.

"Sir, General Lynch and Captain Hammer are here to see you."

Marshall Stryfe simply nodded as the two men entered the room. Mr. Happy left, closing the door behind him. General Lynch and Captain Hammer approached Marshall Stryfe. They both saluted and took seats before his desk. The marshall ignored the salutes and started the meeting immediately, going straight for their necks.

"General Lynch, Captain Hammer, explain to me *what* is going on in the Plains and why we are on the receiving end of it!"

Time ticked away in total silence for a few moments as both men pondered an appropriate answer. Yet, it was Captain Hammer, fixing his one-eyed stare on Stryfe, who was first to respond.

"Sir, I've been to Keystone, and from what I was able to ascertain, it was a robbery, pure and simple. However, the high rollers robbed were not the type you leave alive, hence the killings. As for the tamers killed… unfortunately, they were just in the wrong place at the wrong time and lost their lives for their efforts to stop it."

"Captain Hammer," Stryfe cut in, aiming all five fingers of his right hand at the captain's face before going on. "There is no wrong place or wrong time for any representative of the Republic. Despite what the people south of the Republic border seem to think, we make the law, we *are* the law, and we bring death to the lawless wherever they may huddle and hide. Now, proceed with your report."

Captain Hammer was on the verge of challenging Stryfe but thought better of it. Those who rose a fist to Stryfe often seemed to disappear, and Captain Hammer was not strong enough to go against Stryfe, at least not openly and not now. Therefore, he took his tongue-lashing and spoke on.

"I then proceeded to Reach Providence to investigate the train massacre, and a few things were made apparent. First, the men who did this are the same men responsible for the killings in Keystone, and they're a small cluster of about four to eight men, judging by the tracks left behind. And once the decision is made by one to kill, it is indulged and embraced by all. Second, on that train, everyone killed was dome called at point-blank range, and as I'm sure you've heard, none were spared. I can't see much reason in killing babies unless you're a black-hearted son of a bitch, but sure as there's one eye left in my head, there were dead babies and children."

"Perhaps it was Shynes," offered General Lynch, knowing the mere mention of Shynes would rile Captain Hammer up.

Captain Hammer turned to Lynch. "This wasn't Shynes."

"How do you know? They had no problem killing your brothers. Perhaps this is more of that."

"You're right; they did kill my brothers. But blood flowed on both sides. Besides that, killers that the Shynes may be, their killing is more fashioned by the belief of an eye for an eye. And as I've been given to know, Shynes don't kill babies. Also, any Shyne caught outside of Red Rock knows it's a death sentence if they're caught. So, for them to come this far north for a robbery makes no sense," said Hammer.

"Then who was it?" countered Lynch.

"The motive will establish the who," stated Marshall Stryfe, followed by a look for Lynch to be quiet and let Hammer proceed.

"The motive can simply be robbery. As for the killings… unlike the murders in Keystone, where the bandits couldn't afford to leave anyone alive, the killings on the train were purely sadistic. There wasn't a single armed person among the dead. So, they couldn't have killed them for any threat they presented to the killers. I think once they killed one passenger, they said fuck it, let's kill 'em all. Not to mention the cargo of money and gold was gone. So, whoever these bastards are, they have connections putting them on to these takedowns. A sole witness from the Keystone affair says they referred to themselves as the Mob, and they are a pack of mad dogs. And unless I miss my guess, we will be hearing a lot more from them in the future," Captain Hammer said grimly.

"Captain Hammer, we are not asking you to guess. We need you to get results," stated General Lynch, second only to Marshall Strife.

Lynch was a massive man who stood six-foot-three, with a barrel frame, a head full of grey hair, and a grey beard that contrasted starkly against his white skin. He was often called the Grey Grizzly, albeit behind his back and when speaking, he overwhelmed weaker men. However, there were no weak men present.

Captain Hammer turned to General Lynch, sitting next to him, and remarked, "General, Marshall Stryfe was asking *me* for a report, and *I* was reporting to him. Trust, the next time I cross paths with this Mob, there *will* be results."

As both men stared at each other with distaste, Marshall Stryfe studied them from across his desk. Captain Hammer pushed Stryfe's agenda, and General Lynch enforced those agendas with the Republic Army. They were both good and loyal men, but they detested each other to the core. And as long as Marshall Stryfe played them against each other, he wouldn't have to worry about either of them wanting to sit on his side of the desk. He had started with Hammer, and now it was Lynch's turn.

Stryfe spoke, breaking the stillness of the moment.

"Gentlemen, we are all on the same side. Captain Hammer, you have done well, but you must do better. I will not have bandits running rampant, doing as they please. First, it was Keystone, then Reach Providence. How long before they build their nuts up enough to try us right here in Independence? I want those results you just spoke of. Do you understand me, Captain Hammer?"

"Yes, sir," Hammer answered.

Stryfe nodded, then turned to Lynch. "General, how goes the expansion of the Republic into the Barren Plains? Are we any closer to catching Baron Black?"

Captain Hammer grinned, already knowing the answer since Baron Black was proving to be as elusive as El Chablo or Alkada.

"We've located his compound," General Lynch responded. "However, a major assault would be ill-advised at this time."

"General, we've long known where his compound is. So, why can't we get him? And why is it ill-advised for us to attack now?" Stryfe countered.

"Well, sir, Baron Black's compound is strategically positioned against most attacks," answered the general.

The irritation of the general's answer was apparent on Marshall Stryfe's face and even more so in his line of continued questioning.

"Explain to me, General, how is it that this desert dweller can outthink *you*, a general of the Republic Army, into believing that he is impervious to attack? And keep in mind, General, that your answer had best be one that nobody else can find a solution to," stated Stryfe, cutting a glance at Captain Hammer.

The general did not miss the underlying threat nor the wolfish grin on Captain Hammer's face at hearing it.

"Well, sir, for starters, Baron Black's compound can't be approached by sea from his rear due to the fact his compound sits on the part of a cliff face of sheer rock that cannot be climbed, and to try this would leave our ships open to all manner of attacks from above—from everything like rocks to fire. We'd be helpless to defend against this and helpless to retaliate. Thus, our naval strength would be irrelevant and useless. He's protected on his eastern borders by the Barren Hills and the residents that live there who have aligned themselves with him. The guerrilla-type warfare that would ensue if we were to try and come at him from the west would pose a risk greater than any reward we'd stand to gain. Not only would we be fighting Baron Black, but we would also be fighting the very land and terrain. As for his open flanks, he's protected by the Snake Mountains in Sanchie Territory. To approach from that way, which would be most effective, would take the help of Diablo Vasa, and he's no friend of the Republic," Lynch concluded.

"Well, what about a frontal attack down from the north out of the wooded pines?" asked Captain Hammer with a sly grin.

"Yes, what about that?" seconded Stryfe.

General Lynch turned to Captain Hammer and began to address him in a voice of pure acid.

"Captain Hammer, I do not tell you how to fight battles, so please do not think to tell me how to fight wars."

He then turned back to Marshall Stryfe, stern but respectful as he continued.

"Well, I guess a frontal assault is plausible. However, it will be a very involved campaign, especially once winter sets in on our routes, and our means of communication. We will know no end to the harassment on our supply lines. Nonetheless, I have also thought of this." Lynch paused, only to sneer at Captain Hammer before continuing. "I've sent out several scouts into the wooded pines as well as the Barren Hills for this purpose. However, none have yet to return, so I'm guessing they have all been captured or killed."

"You guess?!" barked Marshall Stryfe, standing up to look down on General Lynch and Captain Hammer, further bolstering his authority. "You now guess? Captain Hammer guesses! Well, I have a guess for both of you! You both have two weeks to make good on your guesses, and the next time we meet, you'd best have something good to tell me, or I'll start doing some guessing of my own. Guesses that start with: I guess I can find men to do what you two can't," Stryfe said, stopping only so Lynch and Hammer could fully grasp the enormity of his statement. "I've also implemented agents to aid our efforts, and I await word within the passing of days. So, I suggest you be ready to move on your given objectives at a moment's notice. Good day, gentlemen. You are dismissed," said Stryfe as he sat back down.

Both men rose, saluted him, and left.

Marshall Stryfe then spun around in his chair, gazing out the window at the streets of Independence beneath him. He focused on the square below his window and thought to himself, *Right there. That is the place you will hang, Baron Black, for all to see. And I will be the one to string you up from the gallows tree.*

***

"Lil BB…I mean, Captain. The prisoners are ready for execution…I mean, interrogation, sir," said the soldier as he saluted his captain respectfully, even though he was at least two decades older than the young captain.

"Good," responded Captain BB. "How many of them are there?"

"Five, Lil B...I mean, Captain BB. Please forgive me, sir," the soldier stressed.

Captain BB nodded at the slight of his soldier's words, gripping no anger at his mistake.

"Five prisoners?"

"Yes, and they were carrying this," said the soldier, handing over several papers and sketches confiscated from the prisoners.

"Five? I wonder why so many," Captain BB uttered to himself. Then he faced the soldier and said, "Nonetheless, our leader will be here shortly. Well done, soldier."

Captain BB dismissed the soldier and began walking toward the stable's holding pen where the captives had been placed.

It was the middle of the day, and the heat was starting to push down on the Plains. It was a draining heat that zapped the energy of those unaccustomed to the day-to-day lifestyle on the Plains, which were part desert, mountain ranges, woodlands, grasslands, great lakes, and rivers. This was the Barren Plains, and the people who lived here were soldiers, builders, and cultivators who would kill and die for the lands they lived and thrived on.

These were the thoughts going through Captain BB's head as he entered the pen. He hated to be called Lil BB, but it was a name given to him nearly from birth. It was a name that described him as much as it paid homage to his father. Most of the men who addressed him as Lil BB had fought for this land alongside his father in the Death Sagas, and now he fought with them. They were hearty men, loyal men, and men of grit.

They were the Barren Brigade, and at five-foot-four, a

hundred and eighty solid pounds of lean muscle, Lil BB was their captain. Although short in stature, he was big on heart and honor to his people. He had murderous hate for anything of the Republic, and aside from his slight in height, he was the spitting image of his father.

"Lil BB," a voice shouted from behind him, thick and robust, full of passion and authority.

"Glad to see you," said Captain BB, turning around to greet the one man who gave Captain BB a sure swelling of pride when he called him Lil BB.

"Just as I am always glad to see you and be seen by you, which means neither of us is dead yet," the man responded as he patted the captain on the back.

The two men then entered the stable that housed their horses.

A section had been cleared out for the five prisoners being held there—hands tied behind their backs, on their knees, and under the watch of armed guards.

"Report," the man ordered Captain BB.

"We caught three Republic scouts out in the wooded pines coming down from the north, and two were caught trolling around in the Barren Hills. I'm sure they were gathering information and different routes to our compound to report back to the Republic. We confiscated these drawings from them," said Captain BB, handing over the documents to the man.

The man studied the documents for several moments and then nodded appraisingly.

"Well done. Has any attempt been made to get them to talk?"

"No. I figured you would want to handle the interrogation yourself," answered Captain BB.

"Good assessment," the man said as he approached the first

prisoner, towering over him while the other prisoners looked on at the man who had nearly a foot on Captain BB.

The man had wild salt and pepper unkempt hair, with brown piercing eyes of pure intelligence that made you feel as though you were in the presence of a savage intellectual. His black skin was toned and muscular from the decades of plains survival. And his aura was magnetic.

"Now, let's see which one of you Republic pigs will squeal the loudest," the man said, reaching down and pulling the first prisoner to his feet by the scruff of his neck as if he were little more than a stray cat. "Why were you spying on us? What were your orders?"

When the scout didn't respond, the man threw him to the ground and turned to Captain BB.

"Captain, give me your knife."

Captain BB pulled a buck knife from his waist and handed it to the man.

All the prisoners looked on in horror, fearful of what was to come. The man grabbed the prisoner, pushed him down on his back, and straddled his chest. With his hands tied behind his back, the prisoner was helpless to stop what came next.

"Republic pig, since you cannot speak, you have no need for your tongue!"

"No! No! Stop!" the prisoner shouted as he squirmed underneath the man.

"Ahh, now you speak," said the man as he pressed his forearm into the man's neck, choking him, and jabbed the knife into his mouth to saw out his tongue.

The blade's sharp edge cut through teeth and jawbone. The man then grabbed the prisoner's torn tongue, ripped it out of his mouth, and tossed it aside.

"Now, dog, I will have your eyes," said the man as he gripped the prisoner's neck with his hand, squeezing his Adam's apple. Then, with his free hand, he stuck the knife into the prisoner's eye socket and gauged around it, cutting the eye from its home and plucking it right out of his face. Then flung it aside. He repeated the process on the other eye, watching emotionless as blood filled his eyeless sockets.

The man stood up, looking down at his mutilated victim as he thrashed about, unable to verbally express the pain he was in and helpless to do anything about the world of darkness that had now engulfed him.

The man handed the blood-slicked knife back to Captain BB and turned to another soldier.

"Soldier, strip this prisoner naked, tie him by his feet to a horse, then set the horse running for the Roughs."

"Okay, Captain. Who's next?"

Another prisoner was lifted to his feet and brought before the man.

"Okay, Republic pig, what were your orders?" the man asked.

The prisoner was barely a man and could hardly stand up as tears swelled up in his eyes at the butchery he had just witnessed. He whimpered as the tears ran down his face.

"You fucking coward, there are no tears for us engaged in war! Tears are for the affairs of women, daughters, and babies. For men, there is only blood and death! Strip him naked and put him on his belly," the man instructed his soldiers.

The soldiers immediately did as they were told. Then the man kneeled close to the prisoner, grabbing him by the hair and pulling his head back.

"I hear in Independence, Marshall Stryfe is now putting men to death by a method called *The Worm*," the man said, speaking into the prisoner's ear. "Well, here in the Barren Plains, we have *The Snakes*—a little something I learned from the Sanchies." The man pulled a tubular object from his garment, stood up, and passed the tube to another soldier. "Stuff him."

Several soldiers held the prisoner down as the tube was forced into his rectum. It contained small, worm-like creatures that secreted toxins more poisonous than any snake's venom. Within minutes, the prisoner started to convulse in a full-body hemorrhage, unable to stop the pain and poison coursing through his body.

The man gave another nod, and a soldier stepped forward and doused the prisoner in kerosene. Again, the man nodded, and the prisoner was set on fire. Screams of agony emerged from the prisoner as his flesh began to smolder and burn. The man then stepped forward and fired a single shot into his skull, killing him.

"Next!" the man barked, and a third prisoner was brought before him.

The prisoner immediately began spilling his guts.

"Please, please! I will tell you everything, anything! Please just don't kill me!"

"That's because you are a coward and a rat," the man said and back-smacked the prisoner. "With five scouts, I do not need you to tell me the obvious because what is understood does not need to be explained. But let *me* explain what is about to happen to *you*. You are about to be eaten alive, you Republic pig. Dip him," the man ordered coldly.

Several soldiers dragged the prisoner off to an outside pen that contained a pack of feral and food-deprived dogs. The prisoner was covered in chicken blood and guts, then flung into the pen. Instantly, the dogs attacked the prisoner—ripping, biting, and tearing the skin from his bones as they brought him down to the ground and devoured him, ignoring his shouts of anguish.

The heartless man cocked his head to the side as he relished the sounds of the slaughter. When he was satisfied enough, he turned to the last two prisoners, who were visibly shaking at the madness of all they had witnessed. Before they could speak, the man lifted his fingers to his soldiers, indicating he wanted the last two prisoners to stand up.

"Untie them."

As the two captives were cut out of their bonds, a look of relief washed over their faces. There was a glimmer of hope that the man would spare their lives.

The man stepped before them, placing his hands on their shoulders. He studied them both, noticing and delighting in the visible apprehension he saw in their eyes.

"I have good news and bad news for you two," he said. "The good news is that one of you will live to go back to Independence and tell that fascist pig, Marshall Stryfe, what you have seen here today. You will let him know I do not fear him, and if he encroaches here again, I will encroach there with blood in my wake."

He watched as both men nodded desperately, eager to hear the bad news.

"The bad news is that one of you will die. I will let you decide which one," the man said as he stepped back, snapped his fingers, and was quickly handed a knife.

He tossed the knife on the ground between the two men and walked away as his soldiers surrounded the two prisoners, cheering and urging the two prisoners to fight to the death.

As the man walked away from the barbarous scene of which he was the anarchical architect, he was followed by Captain BB. The man knew it was time to prepare. Five scouts so deep in his lands and at approximately the same time could only mean one thing—the Republic was preparing for an invasion and war. One would surely lead to the other, and there would be no negotiations or peace talks this time. He had learned that from the Death Sagas. The Republic's first great expansion into the uppermost part of the Barren Plains—now called the Civilized Republic.

But the rules would not be muddied as they were back then. It was simple in the man's mind. If you were not with him, you were against him. So, it was time to see how the pieces would position themselves on the board in the game to be played.

The man turned to his captain and said, "Captain, send for a scribe and messengers and meet me in my private quarters."

Within an hour, the message was written and sent. The only thing that mattered now was the responses.

THE TIME HAS COME FOR US TO UNITE AND, FOR SOME OF US, RE-UNITE, PUTTING ASIDE OUR PETTY DIFFERENCES AND STAND TOGETHER AGAINST THE REPUBLIC OR DIE DIVIDED BY REPUBLIC OPPRESSION! TWO WEEKS WE MEET AT FREEDOM COMPOUND.
— BARON BLACK

Chapter Eleven

Alkada and his men rode hard through the Benta Lands of El Chablo and were now crossing the Sanchie border into A-Town, a hamlet within the Sanchie Plains that bordered the Barren Plains. They were about three days out from Shameless, a haven for men on the run. By all accounts, Alkada figured to settle up there or at least pick up the trail on their quarry.

Either way, Alkada was sure things would get lively. There was still a "kill on sight" order out on any Shyne caught out of Red Rock, and the faces of Alkada and HardBody were well known. So long as they didn't set foot on Republic land, Alkada wasn't too worried about the order. Most folks knew Shynes were not to be fucked with, and those who didn't often lost their heads for not knowing.

Once the sun had set, they set up camp in the woods on the edge of A-Town rather than lodging in town and risk having Republic tamers pounce on them.

StreetLife, A1, and London got a fire going to push back the night chill and roast some pheasant they had flushed out. Meanwhile, HardBody tended to the horses, tying them down for the night. He then joined them around the fire.

Alkada momentarily sat apart from them to consult with Skully—reaching out through his sense of connection and awareness to the bird, seeing what he saw, feeling what he felt, and knowing what he knew. Sensing no imminent danger or gawking eyes on them, Alkada broke the connection and began praying to Dempaku. After a few moments, he rose and joined the others, reaching for the spitted pheasant as he sat down.

London stared at Alkada through the flames like he was in the presence of an ancestor.

Alkada noticed and said, "I remind you of somebody, kid?"

He earlier sensed Dempaku in him, and now he'd reckon to know why.

"You walk the path of Dempaku?" London asked as HardBody, StreetLife, and A1 tuned in curiously to the conversation—all aware of Alkada's mystical and spiritual abilities.

Alkada looked at London now in earnest and asked deadpan, "What do you know of Dempaku or those who walk that path?"

"I know the walkers of the path know things that non-walkers don't and can hear things that non-walkers can't. I heard your prayers a few moments ago, and I'm sure nobody else here did," London replied as he glanced at A1 and StreetLife, then cocked his head to the side when his gaze fell on Hardbody like he was seeing him for the first time.

"I know that you, too, walked the path of Dempaku, but you've lost your way. Yet, Dempaku refuses to release you, knowing Mugasa will come to claim you. Death is the purpose of your life, but know that even in righteous killing, one can still be taken by the maddening," said London to HardBody before returning his attention to Alkada.

"I know that Dempaku is the spirit of life and that the energy of life is the essence of all things in the living universe—seen and unseen. And in being connected to Dempaku, you are connected to this omni flow of energy… just as you are connected to him," said London, pointing back to HardBody. "And just as you are connected to the bird that flies above us, seeing what he sees."

All eyes were now on Alkada, waiting for him to admit or deny what London had said.

Alkada studied the boy, as would a father to a son, and nodded his head in agreement. *So, you are a knower*, Alkada thought to himself before speaking to him a single word: "Safu."

"Alkada, Safu," the boy responded, feeling a mutual acceptance now settle amongst them. At least spiritually.

"Okay, scrap," StreetLife said to London, taking the focus off the moment. "I've been all through Republic and even up through Noble Haven, and I've never heard that accent before. So, where exactly are you from, and what's your story? I mean, it's obvious you know about Dempaku, but we don't know about you," StreetLife claimed as everybody sat waiting in anticipation of London's answer.

Only at this did the gaze between Alkada and London break—as if they were looking in a mirror from two different eras. London nodded, looking towards StreetLife as the fire crackled between them.

"You saved my life, and I am grateful. Now I will tell you of the life you saved. I am from a village called Ooganvee in a land many steps across the water called Fumah."

Alkada's eyes narrowed at hearing his homeland mentioned

as told to him by his grandfather when he was a child. He couldn't help but feel a moment of envy for the boy knowing of a place he had only heard about.

London felt Alkada's spark of interest and paused before he continued.

"Ooganvee is a place of luscious greenery and vibrant life, and for the most part, we live in peace, love, and happiness. Nearly all walk the path of Dempaku there from birth. We are taught the blessings of life from Dempaku, the cultivation of our lands, and the continuity of our ways. Some believed this is the point from which all life sparked into existence, favored by Dempaku and contested by Mugasa. So, old and favored were the elders of this land that they were blessed with all sight, which is the ability to see, hear, and know what others do not—a gift given by Dempaku. A gift I sense Alkada and I share, but myself to a much lesser degree."

Again, London paused, this time looking at HardBody.

"It is in our blood, and what is in the blood cannot be taken out. Yet, the further away one gets from the source, the weaker the connection becomes to this power. The elders of my village and others throughout the land were entrusted with many secrets of creation and life passed down through the ages. As I've heard, different tribes were charged with looking after certain secrets, although we shared secrets among each other. My people were the protectors of the sky water—a pure nectar of Mother Earth with the power to heal all ailments, prolong life, and even make the barren fertile. But, after many generations, word began to spread of the people who never got sick and the people who never seemed to age like most people do, and this brought invaders. They came with their lust and desires for our ways but lacked the

138

respect and patience it took to receive it. Thus, they were refused the secrets they sought from my people, and war ensued. Much blood was spilled on both sides as we fought. But ultimately, their guns, such as the ones you carry—cannons and all manner of other exploding weapons—allowed them to overrun us, forcing us from our rooted grounds into different pockets of the land. Thriving when we could and running when we must. This is how it has been for my people for some time now."

"So, how did you get here?" Alkada cut in, eager to know more about the people London spoke about—his people.

"Just recently, my people were set upon by those still eager for our secrets. My mother, father, and brothers were killed in the battle. My sister and I were captured, separated, placed on ships, and brought here."

"How do you know your sister is here?" StreetLife asked.

"Because she touches my dreams—a power she's long had."

"So, what is your true name, the name given to you at birth, because you made no mention of a place called London?"

"My name is Rasun," answered London.

"So why the fuck are you called London?" asked HardBody while cleaning his guns.

"Because the captain of the ship that brought us here was called London Jack, and many times, while stopping on the water to get here, I helped navigate the rough waters by knowing the stars and the winds. And for this help, I was taken under his wing and allowed to move about the ship freely and sleep in his quarters like I was his pet. So, the crew just took to calling me London."

"Why are you not still with him?" StreetLife inquired.

"Because he was a part of the slaughter of my family and people. Many of the other children were sold off when we got here, but I was kept for my talents at sea. So, one night, we were docked in the harbor of a place called Keystone, and while London Jack slept, I slit his throat, carved out his heart, and fled the ship. I've since then been trying to find my sister, guided by dreams and the need to find a woman named Petra. A woman who I sense you know well," said London, looking directly at Alkada before looking back at StreetLife. "I am grateful to you for saving my life, and I owe you a life for my own. And to you, Alkada, I am loyal through our link to Dempaku. I was caught stealing bread, as you know, but only because I'd gone days without eating. But trust that I am no thief."

"Well, London, I'm pretty sure I can get you to meet Petra, and perhaps she will know how to reunite you with your sister. Just as soon as we catch up to those eight men you spoke of in Shameless," Alkada said as he spread out his bedroll.

"I got first watch," said HardBody as StreetLife and A1 pulled out their bedrolls.

London looked at Alkada across the dying fire and said, "I thank you for letting me join you. And the eight men you seek are now four and a woman who now has the same blood on her hands as the men."

***

Sheldon Drake had a lot to think about. He'd been offered the keys to Keystone to run it as he wished. Keystone was surely one of the crown jewels as far as cities went, but the price was high. Killing Baron Black would not be easy—if even possible. Yet, Drake would always find a way to make the impossible possible.

He had killed many men, women, and even children that one

time. He followed the motto: *Kill one, kill one hundred. It's all the same because they can only hang you once*—a motto followed by many among the plains. To him, it was all business—cut the check, and he'd cut the neck.

He chuckled at his little rhyme, but this was no laughing matter. It was the coming of anarchy on the high plains, and Drake would be an acting agent in the chaos.

Marshall Stryfe and Baron Black both offered change, and it was the rolling of the dice that would decide who would win.

Which side should I take? was the question that spun like a whirlpool in Drake's mind.

However, there was no doubt that for the ruling of Keystone, Drake would murder his own mother and fuck the corpse. He knew he was a despicable man, and he was certain all his dead partners would have thought so, too. Backstabbing was what he did best, and he would accomplish the feat no matter the circumstance—even if it meant having to lie to himself.

Yes, Baron Black would die. This was the real deal, so Drake would have to play his cards just right because the game at hand was death, and all the players were playing for keeps.

Well, let the games begin, thought Drake as he sauntered into the town of Shameless.

Chapter Twelve

Fat Pockets sat in his office at his desk, pondering the turn of events, getting things in order for his trip into the Barren Plains. He was thankful he had received Baron Black's message before sending one of his own. He didn't want to seem too thirsty for aid; it was always better to be seen as an equal partner rather than an underling. Marshall Stryfe had made him cruelly aware of how insignificant he was in the grand scheme of things, but perhaps he could show Baron Black how useful he could be to him. *"Getting cherries for strawberries wasn't a bad thing,"* his daddy used to say.

But Fat Pockets wasn't a gambling man. He preferred to put his money on a sure thing, and to go against Marshall Stryfe, he had to be as sure as possible.

Knock, knock, knock.

"What?" yelled an agitated Fat Pockets as his secretary stepped into his office.

"Fat Pockets, everything is ready for your trip, sir. Your

horses and carriage will be at your manor at dawn, leaving through Key West into the Barren Plains," she said, now standing before his desk, her hands fiddling behind her back.

Fat Pockets looked at her with a raised eyebrow and exploded as only he could.

"Bitch, what the fuck you mean *your* trip? Hoe, you best get your mind right and make that *our* trip. You think I'm leaving you in Keystone while I'm gone so you can get your fuck on?! Bitch, where I go, you go. You are a part of *my* show. Must I remind you, I remember when you were Nasty Nancy? I had to stop a knife fight over your asshole. Bitch, I ain't save you; I slaved you, and that came at a price. So, you best stop running 'round here like you something sweet to eat. You sour milk, bitch. Where I go, you follow. So, get a mouthful tonight because *we* leave tomorrow," roared Fat Pockets.

His secretary stood there in a state of shock. She started to respond but was cut short as he continued his verbal abuse.

"Bitch, you starin' at me like you want some smoke. Just let me know. Let Fat Pockets know if I need to get up and slap all types of shit outta you where you stand. Hoe, you know I don't give a fuck 'bout a bitch. I twerk 'em, work 'em, and jerk 'em, and don't give a fuck when and how I hurt 'em. So, go home, pack your clothes, and be at my house in the morning with a rose. Now, get outta my sight, and tell Sergeant Grimble to come take your place," said Fat Pockets, dismissing his secretary with a fluttering of his fingers toward the door.

"Yes, sir, Mayor Fat Pockets," his secretary disdainfully responded as she left his office.

Nancy hated Fat Pockets to his core, but she knew she would still be wearing alley cat coats and sleeping on the docks, surviving on crumb cakes and soups, if it weren't for him. Of course, he wasn't the worst she ever had to endure, but she knew there was always better, and perhaps this trip would prove it. At least that's what she hoped.

Sergeant Grimble entered Fat Pockets' office a few minutes later.

"You wanted to see me, Mayor Fat Pockets?" asked Grimble as he closed the door behind him and walked to Fat Pockets' desk.

Fat Pockets had been writing in his ledgers and stopped at Sergeant Grimble's question, looking up at him and shaking his head in disbelief.

"Bitch, is that a rhetorical question? I sent for you, didn't I? Now sit down, clown, and listen up."

Fat Pockets leaned back in his chair, studying Sergeant Grimble, thinking about what exactly he should tell him. He knew from a past experience that a little information could be dangerous with this fool. So, Fat Pockets decided it would be better not to tell him anything of value.

"Look here, I'm going outta town for 'bout a week or two, and I'm going to need you to hold shit down in Keystone till I get back. And when I get back, shit better still be intact. Because I swear on my dead daddy if it's not—I'm telling you right now, man to bitch—I will have you cut wide open and set on fire in the middle of the city by the man I replace you with. You understand me?"

"Yes, sir, Mayor Fat Pockets. Where are you going?"

"Bitch, is the answer to that question worth your life?"

"No, sir," Grimble answered.

"Good. Then get the fuck out my office and beat them streets till you got blood on the bottom of your feet," Pockets ordered.

Already making plans to go to his favorite brothel, Sergeant

Grimble left out the door looking forward to flexing his muscle on Keystone during Fat Pockets' absence.

***

Elvira Vasa was vibrating with excitement as she walked through the corridors of her fortress stronghold in the Hidden Mountains of the Sanchie Lands. A message had just arrived from Baron Black, and she knew the time was drawing near for a war. She could feel it.

A massacre in Keystone, then a mass murder in Civilized Republic—a direct defiance to the capitalism of Marshall Stryfe. Somebody was making a statement, but who and why were the questions that eluded her. Elvira Vasa didn't like not knowing, but one thing was for sure: whoever they were, their impact was being felt.

All these thoughts raced through her mind as she made her way to her father's quarters, eager to know what his response would be. She was second in command of the Sanchie Raiders, answering only to her father, Diablo Vasa. Even this protocol was tentative, for Elvira was known to react without thinking when enraged. And this was a rage quite familiar to all those who knew her. A rage that had been handed down from one generation to the next, dating back to her ancestors who first laid claim to this mountainous land her father now ruled over, to which she was thee only apparent heir.

A powerful woman, she stood five-foot-eight and had olive skin tinged with red, a trait she inherited from her deceased mother. Her deep brown eyes emanated sex, sin, and seduction. Her long black hair and full, luscious lips completed her alluring aura. This was Elvira Vasa, but she preferred to be called Evila.

Walking through the halls, she looked out at the grand view of the mountains surrounding them. The constant fresh mountain air always seemed to clear her mind. Approaching her father's bed chambers, she noticed the door guarded by two soldiers, indicating her father was engaged with one of the many whores who roamed the castle fortress.

As she reached for the doorknob, one of the soldiers halted her hand.

"Mistress Elvira, Diablo is not to be disturbed at this moment."

Thwack!

The back smack was immediate, sending the soldier staggering back against the door. He struggled to regain composure as he raised his fingers to his bleeding lips. Elvira advanced on him, pointing her index finger at his face and speaking with a voice of honey and violence.

"Do-boy, you do as my father says. I do as my father does. You follow the rules that will save his life, and for me, you bend the rules that will save yours. Remember that," she said before spitting in his face.

She then turned from him and reached for the doorknob again, but the other soldier was faster, opening the door to Diablo Vasa's chambers for her.

Elvira nodded, stepped closer to him, and lightly placed her hand on his face.

"I like you," she whispered into his ear while still caressing the side of his face. Then she kissed his cheek. "Know your place, and I will always have a place for you," she added before stepping into the room.

After closing the door behind her, the soldier looked at the other soldier who was still furious about being slapped. He smirked to himself, knowing he would be favored by Elvira in the times to come.

The bedchamber was a massive and elegant room. Rare paintings and exquisite sculptures were placed throughout. Scented candles constantly flickered from the high mountain breezes that blew through the open windows, protected only by delicate silk veils. A terrace veranda provided a beautiful view of the mixed mountains, which boasted every terrain, from snowcaps and rocky tips to lush greenery—a true mystery of nature.

Elvira pushed through the veils of her father's bed, only to see him lying in a state of ecstasy with a woman's head bobbing up and down between his legs. His hand was enmeshed in her hair, controlling the tempo of the woman's head—a head that looked all too familiar to Elvira.

"Ahh, Salise, so now I see the truth of you," said Elvira, now standing at the edge of the bed.

The woman immediately froze. Completely naked and afraid, she slowly turned to face Elvira, who stood there with her hand held out to the activities that were going on.

"So, you spend your days sucking my father's dick and your nights eating his daughter's pussy," she said to the woman.

"Mistress Elvira, I only—"

"Silence!" Elvira barked. "And be thankful you have such a magical tongue. That is the only reason I won't have your head cut from your shoulders. Now, leave, for I must speak with my father," she ordered.

The woman looked at Diablo for direction, and he nodded,

waving her off with the pointing of his head.

As the woman left, Elvira threw a robe to her father and then went to the nightstand to pour herself a goblet of dark red wine before stepping out onto the terrace. She wanted to watch the sun turn the mountain peaks into diamond tops as it reflected off the snow. A moment later, Diablo Vasa stepped out to join her.

"My dearest daughter, tell me, what is so urgent that you had to interrupt me from getting the best head in all of Sanchie?" Diablo asked, reaching for the goblet of wine she was drinking.

Elvira started laughing; her father could always make her laugh. She had never met her mother because she died while giving birth to Elvira, but for all her stubbornness, Elvira loved her father dearly.

Elvira handed her father the message, then watched as he read it in silence and sighed. He looked out at the expanse of the mountains, a slight look of apprehension in his eyes as he pondered the events to come.

"So, the stage is finally being set for the showdown. A man of vision versus a man of ambition. And we all are the ones caught between," said Diablo, more to himself than anyone else.

Elvira watched her father, studying him, learning from him. No matter what news came to the mountains, Diablo always seemed ahead of it. He was a man of decisiveness, and he was as sophisticated as he was elegant—towering, strong with smooth, copper-toned skin that defied belief of his more than sixty years on the planet, exuding power and pride at all times. This was Diablo Vasa, ruler of the Sanchie Lands.

"So, what is our position, Father?" asked Elvira, eager to hear her father's thoughts.

Diablo looked at his daughter, briefly reminiscing and

yearning for her departed mother, Helen—his beloved wife. Elvira was the spitting image of her in every way except temperament. As Diablo thought of his daughter's frequent fits of rage, he placed his hand on her cheek and adjusted strands of her hair, again reminded of his wife.

"Our position, my sweet Evila, is what it has always been, even in the days of the Death Sagas when I fought beside Baron Black. We will side with the side that best benefits us. Unfortunately, this is a battle of wills that we'll have to take part in. Nonetheless, prepare for travel. It has been a while since we last visited Baron Black. It will be good to know the vibes on the Plains and see which devil offers the best change."

***

El Chablo was in a good mood. He was back in his homeland after a second daring escape from The Fort. Yet, he knew there would not be a third escape. A magician can only fool a crowd with the same trick but for so long. It was his indulgence of hubris that allowed him to be caught at all, and El Chablo decided this was a burden he would suffer from no longer. He governed his own lands. There was no need for him to travel beyond his borders.

For what I have, people will come to me from miles around, he thought to himself as he walked through his fields of weed and skarab seed.

El Chablo produced the best weed the world over. So potent was the strain of weed he grew that it was nicknamed Loud because it caused one to feel an amazingly euphoric high and momentarily amplified one's natural senses, especially hearing.

150

And for this weed, El Chablo was highly sought after since he was the only man who had it. But this was not all El Chablo had, for he was also known for smack—a darker, more potent, sinister, and physically-gripping drug produced by his fields and his fields alone. A powder made from the skarab seed that was sniffed into the nose and known to take away any suffering one felt. However, the absence of pain was only temporary. One had to keep taking it to keep the pain away, be it mental or physical, and often enough, one that fell victim to the clutches of smack often stayed hooked till death.

So devastating was smack that it was mostly outlawed throughout the plains, and in some places, it was fatal to be caught pushing it. But there were always ways to get it for those who needed it, and El Chablo was known for saying he did not make anyone take smack; he only made them pay for it.

These payments made El Chablo rich beyond measure, a boss of bosses, yet always caught in the snare of this gift and a curse. Whereas weed made him famous, it was smack that made him infamous—dreaded and wanted.

Twice he was captured, and twice money, power, and respect freed him. But El Chablo knew there would be no more courts or cells for him. He would not allow it, nor would the Republic. El Chablo had been on defense too long. It was perhaps time to take an offensive approach to Marshall Stryfe and his regime.

The afternoon wind was blowing a strong-scented breeze across the fields. El Chablo reached down, plucked one of the weed buds, brought it to his nose, and inhaled.

"Ahhh, smells like money," he said to himself.

A moment later, El Chablo turned around to the sound of footsteps coming up from behind him, only to see his lieutenant approaching him with a look of urgency on his face.

When he reached El Chablo, he saluted before saying, "Sir, a messenger has brought you word from the Barren Plains."

El Chablo took the message and read it, reflecting on what he knew of the man. He knew Baron Black was the most wanted man of all the Plains—a title El Chablo had not too long ago held——and that Baron Black had openly defied the expansion of the Republic into the Barren Plains since the days of the Death Sagas, which El Chablo applauded. However, he also knew Baron Black was motivated by ideals, whereas El Chablo was about getting to the money.

But isn't the enemy of my enemy my friend? he thought slyly.

"Lieutenant, prepare a small troop for travel. It is time to meet a friend," El Chablo said, saluting the lieutenant and sending him off as he went back to perusing his fields.

***

Alexander Wolfgang sat in his study, still brooding over his daughter's disappearance. It had been well over a week, and still nothing: no ransom demand, extortion attempt, or anything. Over forty people were killed on that train his daughter was on, yet she was not among the dead.

Wolfgang thought this whole ordeal reeked of Diablo Vasa and his daughter, with their kidnapping and blackmailing ways. Yet, he had not received any demand for money, which would be customary in this situation.

From the mining, exporting, and importing of diamonds, Alexander Wolfgang was one of the richest men alive. He was sent here by the Imperium, the Empire, across the water because he was a pioneer, mover, and shaker. He was also a part of the forge that brought the Republic to economic maturity. And he was protected from Republic encroachment due to the sovereignty status of Noble Haven. Despite all of this, his daughter had just vanished.

Wolfgang was a self-made man, and heads would indeed roll when he found out who was behind this. And all of a sudden, he received a message from Baron Black about Republic oppression—an oppression that would not reach Noble Haven. Was it a subliminal message, a hint of some sort to force him into an alliance? Wolfgang would not be muscled, yet he would attend this meeting. Alexander Wolfgang was a stout and robust man of foreign complexion and in his mid-sixties who still had a bit of spark in him. So, by all means, he would go out fighting.

"Mr. Andrews," he called for his servant.

A few moments later, a sturdy middle-aged black man entered the study.

"Yes, sir?"

"I am going on a trip," started Wolfgang as he rose to his feet. "I refuse to sit here in Noble Haven like some stooge waiting on bad news. I will get answers with the business end of my guns," he declared to the open air, heading out of his study.

"Yes, of course, sir. Will your wife be going with you?" asked the servant.

"No," Wolfgang answered, pausing his step. "She's in no condition to travel. Besides, things are bound to get lively. It is high time people were reminded of the name Wolfgang and how I represent it. Ready my guns and rifles and prepare my horses and carriage. Wolfgang is back on the prowl," he concluded, then lumbered out of the room.

Chapter Thirteen

NoLove had just returned to Republic City to link up with Foot for the next phase of the events. Leaving his crew back in Shameless with the broad, who was now all in with them. They all wanted to come, but he knew in light of the heist they had recently put down in Reach Providence, they'd attract way too much attention traveling five deep through Republic territory.

NoLove was sure by now that the connection had been made between the slayings in Keystone and the train massacre and that they were responsible on both accounts.

Things were surely about to change, and a lot more blood would hit the ground before it was over. Nonetheless, he had to move smart. He was traveling with enough drugs, cash, and gold to get him killed or thrown back in The Fort if caught by Republic soldiers, especially since part of the take was lifted from the Republic. But The Fort was a distant memory for him. NoLove had promised himself court would be held in the streets from here on out. A cell or a hangman's rope was no longer an option.

Republic City was on a much different page from Keystone and Shameless, not to mention bigger than both combined. People flooded the streets, and there was a lot of hustling and bustling. Curious onlookers and consumers filled the shops, and merchants stood behind their stands calling to pedestrians that passed by. As NoLove looked around, he saw clusters of men and women gossiping together on the topic of the day. They sported the newest fashions from all over. NoLove spotted Noble Haven aristocrats, Republic rich, and upper-class Plains people collectively moving about as his horses pulled his wagon through the city streets.

The sun was reaching its zenith, taking the heat up with it. NoLove approached the front of the Plaza Hotel, only to see Foot standing out front. When the two made eye contact, they began to grin, knowing they were the two men in possession of a secret everybody around them wanted to know.

NoLove brought his wagon to a stop as Foot started towards the wagon to meet him.

"Mob shit," NoLove said as he jumped down from the wagon and embraced Foot.

"Mob shit," Foot responded, glad to see his brother alive and well.

"What's good, bro?" NoLove asked as he and Foot walked to the rear of the wagon.

"Me, you, and the Mob," Foot responded, nodding at the chests loaded on the wagon.

The bellhops immediately approached the wagon and started unloading the wagon, reaching for the chest containing the loot.

"Man, these chests sure are heavy," one commented.

Foot reached into his pocket and pulled out a roll of bills, handing each bellhop several while issuing orders.

"Make it light and take 'em to Room 112."

Now properly motivated, the bellhops eagerly began to lift the chests as NoLove and Foot watched over them.

Once the bellhops left the room, Foot asked, "So how did everything go?"

NoLove grinned, walked over to the chests on the floor, and began opening them. One contained gold, the other cash, and the final one was full of drugs. He then looked at Foot, who came to stand next to him.

"You tell me," NoLove said.

Foot looked into the chest and shook his head in disbelief as he rubbed his hands together, knowing what the take would accomplish.

"Mob shit," Foot uttered, bending down to inspect the haul.

"So, can it be done?" NoLove asked, standing over Foot's shoulder.

"You fuckin' right it can be done," answered Foot, standing up to face NoLove. "I met with The Weasel, and he guaranteed the rest will be easy as soon as the bag is passed."

"What's the ticket?" NoLove questioned.

"7.5," Foot responded.

"That's a lotta bread, bro. Damn near eight mill. Are you sure he can be trusted with that much bread?"

"Hell no, I don't trust anybody but us, and I for damn sure don't trust no muthafucka called The Weasel, but he's too big to hide from us if he crosses us. And for all my mistrust, I know he does straight business. My mistrust is only in the price. If he chargin' us 7.5 mill, it's really about 4 or 5. But you know how that middleman shit goes. Without The Weasel, we wouldn't even have a hope of getting this done, and for what he's promising to do, I see it as money well spent. Remember, it's love and loyalty over lust and anything for any one of us. Mob shit," Foot stated.

"Mob shit," NoLove responded. "So, what's the word on the Plains?"

"Bro, they got you and TwoFace's name on the Keystone lick—meager descriptions, though. And everybody wants to know who the Mob is. With that train rip, the heat is really on. Got the Republic logic sayin' somebody gotta die, but they not sure if it's El Chablo wagin' a drug war or Baron Black pushing back at the Republic. Either way, it's time to make the Mob a household name and come out of the shadows. I hear a big meeting will be held in the Barren Plains at Freedom Compound. I want you to attend that meeting and represent us and our introduction. Let it be known that the Bluff is now the Mob's territory," said Foot.

"Is that smart, bro?" countered NoLove, sitting down at the table and pouring himself a shot of whiskey.

He downed the spirits, then poured another shot and passed it to Foot, who also downed the liquor in one gulp. Shaking off the burn, Foot started pacing back and forth as he spoke.

"Bruh, dig, we not 'bout to be runnin' 'round this bitch scurryin' like roaches from town to town every time the Republic wanna push down!" said Foot, now fully animated as he stopped at the table, pointing for NoLove to pass him another shot.

Foot downed it, oblivious to the liquid heat in his chest. He embraced the nature of his thoughts but was careful not to let his emotions supersede his intelligence.

"Brother, real talk, you already know how we started. From a few of us in prison against all odds, and we survived. We endured and even thrived. Now, out here in the free world, we will be the same force to be reckoned with, just like in prison. Baron Black doesn't back down from the Republic, so why should we? The Republic wants Diablo, El Chablo, and the Shynes. Yet, all of them have their own lands, and the Republic don't fuck with them because they know it's guns up. So, why should the Mob be looked at any differently? Look, bruh, fuck waitin' for the moment. We gon' make the moment, and if all else fails, we'll *take* the moment. Besides, once I flip this work, double its worth, and convert the gold at double, we gon' be new money 'round this bitch, bro. We pay The Weasel to handle the move, stockpile on weapons, bring in our brothers, start pushin' the work, and the rest is Mob shit. It's all *we* shit, no *I*," said Foot, placing his hand on NoLove's shoulder, emphasizing their brotherhood and bond before continuing. "Besides, once we fortify the Bluff, we will be strategically in a gravy position for news, convoys, trades, and transactions. We will literally be in the middle of all kinds of shit, and once a railroad pops through, there ain't no stopping us. This is the coming of our glory, and you know what they say: No guts, no glory!"

NoLove nodded in agreement and poured himself another shot.

After seeing he'd gotten his point across, Foot reached for a copy of *The Republic Speaks* and handed it to NoLove, then watched as NoLove connected the dots of reality when he zeroed in on the front page.

Diamond Princess Disappears from Train Massacre – Body Not Found Among the Dead.

It went on to say more, but NoLove had already stopped reading and was looking at Foot, his eyes bulging from their sockets.

"Bro, that bitch is the Diamond King's daughter? I knew there was a reason I took that hoe."

Foot nodded his answer, grinning wide before adding, "Alexander Wolfgang, King of Apex Diamonds. Bitch is definitely worth a meal ticket. Where is she now?"

"I left her in Shameless with the bros. I'm glad I didn't kill her on that train. I reckons she may come in handy. We're keeping a low pro at the Danforth Hotel."

"I agree. Keep her around just so long as we can use her. Give the bros my love and loyalty. We'll all link up soon, but not a word to them about our plans with this money. It's levels to this shit, and plans known are plans that can be blown."

"True dat," said NoLove, rising to his feet, getting ready to get back on the road. "One more thing," started NoLove, looking Foot dead in the face. "If you need to reach me, I'm using the name Carter, room 235. Oh, and when we hit that lick in Keystone, we had to kill a Shyne."

Foot raised his eyebrow, now alert in another way altogether. "Do you mean like Alkada Shyne that was with us in The Fort?"

"Exactly. It couldn't be helped, and if the Republic got our names for it, you best believe the Shynes do, too, and they gonna want blood back for it."

"Yeah, they are. I last heard they went at the Republic for killin' the big homey S.I. Heard they killed some soldiers or a captain or something. Got them all outlawed to be killed on sight, but fuck it," Foot said, shrugging his shoulders indifferently.

"You wanna be the best. So, you go against the best. You

know they play for keeps, so don't slip or sleep on 'em 'cause it can cost you your head," Foot cautioned. "Now, go ahead and get back to Shameless. Knowing Goon, he might be done killed the diamond princess and still fuckin' her dead body," he added as both men started laughing.

"What about you? What are you gonna do?" NoLove asked.

"I'm gonna handle business here with The Weasel. Once everything is finalized, I'm headed to the Bluff. I'll be stayin' at the Rose Hotel, layin' shit down for us and linkin' in with more of our bros. So, soon as you get done with the meetin', make your way to the Bluff. Let's say three weeks from today."

"Gotcha," NoLove said as the two men embraced each other.

"Mob shit," NoLove said, heading for the door.

"Mob shit," Foot responded as his brother left.

***

Sheldon Drake sat at an outside eatery in the city of Shameless, pondering his options. He was being given a chance to come up in a major way, but it was not without a major risk on his part. Killing Baron Black was one thing, but getting away with it and surviving the aftermath was an altogether different matter. Yet, if the risk justified the reward, it was a risk he was willing to take.

It was early morning, and the city of Shameless was already alive with activity. Business was being conducted, gossip flowed from mouths to ears, and the smells of breakfast aromas scented the air as people began their day.

Drake was raising a cup of coffee to his lips when a woman caught his eye in passing. It wasn't so much her look or dress that snatched his attention as much as it was her confidence and the sophistication of her walk and mannerisms. Drake studied the woman a second longer, and in that second, he knew she was from Noble Haven. He immediately set down his coffee, tossed a few coins on the table, and got up to follow her.

A woman from Noble Haven this far south and alone without protection could not be a coincidence. He started to approach her but decided to follow at a distance for a while. It was always better to move like a fox before revealing oneself as a wolf. From a glance, he was only about fifty percent sure, and that was not enough. He had to be one hundred percent.

He followed her as she walked with purpose, window-shopping as she went along. While observing what caught her eyes, he concluded she was indeed Noble Haven elite. She suddenly turned into a man's tailor shop. Drake waited about ten minutes before entering the shop himself.

He spotted her talking to a tailor. She then stepped to the store counter and spoke with the shop owner. Drake took that opportunity to flag down the tailor who had been helping her moments earlier.

"How can I help you?"

"The woman at the register, what was her purchase?" asked Drake as he pressed a bill into the man's hand.

The tailor looked back at the woman, then back down to his hand and retracted his fingers several times. Drake took the hint and placed two more bills into the tailor's outstretched hand. The tailor quickly put the money into his pocket before answering.

"She ordered four black suits in different styles and sizes, as well as four pairs of black boots, also in different sizes, to be delivered to her hotel," he told Drake, deliberately leaving out the name of the hotel as he again held out his hand.

On cue, Drake placed a few more bills into his hand. "What hotel?"

"The Danforth," answered the tailor.

Sheldon Drake nodded and glanced one final time at the woman who was still talking at the register. He stepped back out into the street, thinking to himself he was at one hundred percent certainty now.

***

Marshall Stryfe was in his office when the message came to him, delivered by his assistant, Mr. Happy.

I'VE CONFIRMED THE LOCALE AND IDENTITY OF THE MEN RESPONSIBLE FOR THE KEYSTONE KILLINGS AND POSSIBLY THE TRAIN MASSACRE. FACT BEING, THE DIAMOND HEIRESS IS WITH THEM AND OF HER OWN FREE WILL. SEND YOUR MEN TO SHAMELESS. I WILL MAINTAIN SURVEILLANCE UNTIL YOUR MEN ARRIVE. ALL HAIL THE REPUBLIC. —DRAKE

All hail the Republic indeed, Marshall Stryfe thought to himself. This Sheldon Drake was one to watch. Whereas Captain Hammer and General Lynch had no desire to sit on his side of the desk, the same could not be said for Drake. His ambition was as solid as his cunning. Already, he had proven productive where his general and captain proved lacking.

Stryfe had forgotten Mr. Happy was standing in front of him as he read the message a second time, thinking of his response.

"Mr. Happy," said Stryfe, looking up at him while forming a response in his mind.

"Yes, sir," said Happy.

"I have a message I want you to take directly to Captain Hammer," Stryfe ordered.

"Yes, sir."

Stryfe wrote down the message to be delivered, then ushered Mr. Happy out of his office so he could contemplate this turn of events.

The Diamond King's daughter is in cahoots with terrorists and murderers. Stryfe sat back in his chair, pondering the ramifications.

Depending on how one looked at this, or rather how Stryfe looked at it, her actions could be considered an act of treason to the Republic, thereby bringing an end to the sovereignty of Noble Haven—a sovereignty that had long since irked Marshall Stryfe. He had been waiting for an opportunity to end it and expand Republic control over Noble Haven. And that opportunity appeared to be finally at his doorstep, and the very bandits he hunted made it possible.

***

The men responsible for the murders in Keystone and Reach Providence are in Shameless. You are to leave immediately by train for Shameless. Capture them if possible. Kill them if not. Should you find the Diamond Heiress there in league with them, she is to be detained and brought back to Independence. Your contact there is Sheldon Drake. Failure will not be tolerated.

— M. Stryfe

Captain Hammer read the message and then reread it—all too eager to get some action and one up General Lynch for the doubt he voiced in his abilities at their last meeting. He was less concerned with the implications of the Diamond Heiress' involvement. Hammer was a soldier, not a politician. He had already prepared a fifty-man troop to mobilize and move at a moment's notice by train. He could be in Shameless in less than two days, and he would be ready.

***

Foot entered the lobby of the Plaza Hotel and was flagged to the desk. The clerk told him that he had an urgent message delivered via telegraph, one of the modern marvels of communication in Republic City. Foot took the note, opened it, and read the message. Although coded, it was loud and clear.

Shameless is no place for a good fella!!!

Foot already knew what he had to do. He just hoped there would be enough time to save his brothers.

Chapter Fourteen

Alkada and his band had just entered the Bluff, about another day's ride from Shameless. They were making good time, and he felt confident in the men he rode with as far as their hearts being true to the cause they were riding for. However, he knew they all needed to possess the intrinsic killer instinct to take life without caring, like HardBody and himself. There was a big difference between being able to kill and committing murder, and Alkada would have to put the difference in them for those who didn't have it.

As the sun began to set again, they pushed deep into the woods, away from traveled paths. Finding a brook, they made camp and tended to their horses.

"Keep the fire low, and don't eat until I get back," said Alkada, walking away from his men, pushing deeper into the woods until he was sure no eyes could see what he was about to do. He carried with him only a bottle of spirits.

He called out to Skully, then held out his arm as Skully

descended from the night sky and landed skillfully on his forearm. He brought him in front of his eyes and spoke two words. "Snake, rabbit."

"Rahhh," Skully shrieked and once again became a part of the night sky, off to do Alkada's bidding while Alkada made ready for the ritual he was about to invoke.

Alkada thought about how much time had passed since he last sought out Mugasa. Just as Dempaku was the embodiment of all things alive and bright, Mugasa was the other half of the balance—the manifestation of death and darkness. It was this energy Alkada now sought to consort with.

Alkada found a small clearing among the trees, perfect for what he needed to do. He began the ritual by removing his shirt and boots, acquainting himself with the natural elements—feeling the breeze against his skin, the dirt under his feet, connecting his mind and body to the planet. He picked up a nearby stick and drew a circle around himself in the soft soil. He grabbed several more sticks and branches, gathered them before him just outside the circle line, and set the pile ablaze with his flint. He then sat in the lotus position. Reaching for the bottle of spirits, he brought the bottle to his lips and took a long swig, feeling the burn deep in his chest.

The sound of Skully's massive flapping wings signaled he was back, and it was time to begin. After filling his mouth with another swig and setting the bottle down, he spat the liquid into the flames. The fire rose as Alkada closed his eyes and began speaking the words that would open up his soul to the spirit of Mugasa.

"*Ohfway-dunahga-conga,*" he chanted, opening himself, preparing for what was to come.

He spoke the words a few more times and opened his eyes, which were now all-white orbs.

"*Ohfway-dunahga-conga*," he chanted a final time, feeling the fire had become a living thing as forceful winds announced the unseen presence of Mugasa.

"Ahhh, Alkada, so long has it been since you've called upon me," said the mellifluous voice.

"Yes, it has been many years," Alkada responded, now feeling engulfed by the night.

"Too many years, Alkada. Too many years since you've paid homage to death and darkness. Tell me, Alkada, have you lost your taste for my wine?"

"Forgive me, Mugasa."

"Alkada, you know there is no forgiveness here, only the absolution of death and darkness. And there is no forgiveness to be given for what is the natural order. Is this not why you now call upon me—for my aid in dealing death?"

"This is true."

"This is all, Alkada? Do not seek to play games with me or find that I may play a game with you that only I can win."

"Mugasa, trust, I know better than to play with you. I need your help and blessings in killing."

"Ahhh, yes, now we are to the root of it. You, Alkada, a walker of the path of life and brightness, seek me to bring souls to death and darkness. Such a hypocrite to the path you have chosen. Killing time is the only time you bow to me," the voice hissed.

"Killing time is the only time I have need of you. Dempaku sees to all my other needs."

At the mention of Dempaku, the fire erupted, and the wind

pelted lashes of dirt against Alkada's face in a violent gust.

"How dare you mention that name in my presence, Alkada," the voice spewed with ire, and again dirt lashed Alkada, causing him to wince in pain.

"Rahhhhh," Skully shrieked in defiance at hearing Alkada's indication of pain.

"Still your familiar before I do," the voice ordered.

At this, Alkada reached out to Skully's mind to calm him.

"Forgive me, Mugasa. I meant no disrespect in mentioning the other."

At this appeasement, the wind died down.

"Spare me your homage, Alkada. I know you have been warned not to call upon me or be played for a fool."

"Yes, I have. Yet, here I am," Alkada responded.

"Yes, here you are—a fool seeking favor from the fooler. Speak your request, Alkada."

"Your help in killing."

"Who, Alkada?"

"Many," Alkada answered, thinking not only of the Mob but whoever else they would encounter along the way.

"Why, Alkada?"

"Because I was put to an oath that I must fulfill."

"What do you offer in trade for my help?"

"For every life, I claim to be taken in your name," Alkada answered.

"Ahhh, Alkada, my domain is full of dead souls. I require no more. I require one to bring my name to life in your domain—to be mentioned with the same prominence of the other."

"Then what can I offer?"

"A promise, Alkada," the voice purred.

Alkada was instantly aware of a play of guile by Mugasa, and he knew to watch his words.

"What do you want a promise of?"

"I want the promise of a voice, a child's voice."

At this, Alkada knew what was coming and sought to cut it short.

"Mugasa, as you know, my daughter not only walks the path of the other but has been personally claimed by the other. As for my unborn, it has already been predicted when the child is born to be claimed by Dempaku, as well," said Alkada, absent-mindedly speaking the name of the other.

A mistake that would cost him as the wind whipped lashes of dirt across his back, causing streams of blood flow. Alkada stilled himself against the pain and stilled the rage swelling up in Skully at Alkada's lashing.

"I do not ask you for your daughter, living or yet to be. I ask you for a promise. The voice of a child in this realm to represent me as does your daughter represents the other."

"But I know of no other child," Alkada said.

"Do you doubt me, Alkada?"

"No, Mugasa, I do not doubt you, but I'd be a fool to lie to you," Alkada countered.

The voice belted out an echoing laugh that seemed to come from everywhere at once.

"Alkada, we already know the roles we are playing. You are the fool, and I the fooler. The game is set. Now, answer me. Do you promise to give me what I ask, be it within your power to give?"

"Is this the only offer you will accept? Is there no other sacrifice I can give?"

Again, wind and fire rose to answer, the blaze reaching out to sear Alkada's skin with its flame, dirt spraying his face.

"You dare question me, Alkada? Do you ever question the other?"

"No, I do not question you, Mugasa, and the promise you ask of me will be given be it in my power to give."

"And how do you honor our pact, Alkada?"

"By my word and my blood, I honor our pact."

"Then what you ask will be given, and what you have promised is now mine."

"What do you mean?" Alkada asked, alarm in his voice.

"Farewell, Dear Alkada. You remain my greatest fool," said the voice as laughter began to fade around him and, with it, Mugasa's presence.

Finally, Alkada called out to Skully and uttered a simple word. "Rabbit."

Skully leaped up, hovering above Alkada, a rabbit clutched in his talons and a snake in his mouth. He dropped the rabbit into the circle with Alkada. With a quickness, Alkada reached out, taking the rabbit into his hands, and pinned it down next to him, holding it still with one hand and drawing his knife with the other. He slit the rabbit's throat in one deft movement, then held it up, tracing the circle he sat in with the rabbit's blood. At this, the fire again blazed up in response. He finally held the rabbit over the bottle of spirits, letting its blood mingle with the liquid. Now done with the rabbit, he tossed it into the flames, and the fire crackled as it consumed the dead animal.

He then rolled up his sleeve and spoke another word into the night. "Snake."

Skully now flung the snake from its beak into the circle.

Alkada grabbed the snake as it began to coil around his forearm and plunge its fangs into his wrist. Instantly, Alkada felt the snake spew venom into his veins as he pumped his hand rapidly to ensure the poison flowed through him. Next, he cut the head off the snake and let its blood and venom pour into the same bottle as the rabbit's blood. Afterward, he also tossed the headless snake into the fire.

Alkada then chanted more words, opening himself up to the death and darkness he wanted to inflict on the men he hunted.

"*Bohndo wah esa,*" he chanted, evoking Mugasa's energy into his body.

"*Bohndo wah esa,*" he repeated, feeling the death and darkness consume him, the tightening of his limbs, the snake venom burning his blood.

"*Bohndo wah esa,*" he chanted a final time.

In that moment, he felt the connection of life and brightness leave him to be replaced by death and darkness—the death all living things will one day come to know—along with its coldness and totality. This was now the sensation gripping Alkada's soul. He felt a blackness so deep within himself that he released a bloodcurdling scream of the horror and killings to come. The inhuman howl echoed and reverberated through the woods, sending shivers through all that heard it, man and beast alike.

The horses heard the shriek and felt its ungodliness, sending their animal instincts into fright-and-flight mode as they bristled and whined, pulling at the ropes that held them tied to the trees.

StreetLife heard it, as well, and lit a cigar while scanning the woods around them. HardBody was cleaning his guns and only smiled at the scream. A1 drew both his pistols and pointed them into the darkness of the woods.

"What the fuck was that?!" he shouted, waving his guns blindly into the night.

"A declaration of death," answered London as he came to stand beside A1, also looking into the woods.

***

Back in Shynetown, Nefertiti awoke from her slumber as if by a hair being pulled across her face and the whisper of a name that was already fading from her memory. She got up out of her bed and went to the window, looking out to the north star-filled night, whispering one word as a tear rolled down her face: "Daddy."

***

Many miles away from Shynetown in Noble Haven, a young boy, barely a teenager, awoke gasping from a dream. While trying to catch his breath, he also tried to hold on to the flashing images in his mind that were already starting to disappear. The sudden knowledge of a father and sister he had never heard of, along with a name, felt more like a force pushing into his soul—a name he didn't know. He laid back down, trying to understand, wanting to know, but the only thing that remained was the name Mugasa.

***

After coming out of the trance, Alkada grabbed the bottle, slit his wrist with the knife, and let some of his blood drip into the bottle. He then corked the bottle, shook it up, and tossed it into the embers of the dying fire while he got dressed. The only witness to his coquetting with Mugasa was Skully. He looked at the bird, and with a "*fsk*" of his teeth and lifting of his head, Skully leapt up into the night sky again.

Alkada then bandaged his wrist, reached for the hot bottle of spirits now turned potion, and headed back to the others, making sure not to look back at the evidence of his indulgence with the dark side of nature.

***

Alkada walked back into the camp, bringing a wholly different aura. No less powerful but a lot more malevolent, an emanation of maliciousness and eagerness to commit violence radiated from him. StreetLife had seen glimpses of it when they were locked down in The Fort, and HardBody knew it from the brother-like bond he shared with Alkada all his life. But for A1 and London, it was completely new.

Alkada came to stand before them, his eyes glaring, reflecting the flames of the fire, his visage grim as granite.

"Listen up. Everything up to now has been light. But heavy metal is coming, and I ain't 'bout to force you all to it or hold your hand through it. The oath on Leggs was put to me, so with or without ya, I aim to collect heads. But the oath I put to you all, should you decide to ride, is this: I will never betray you, abandon you, or snitch on you if caught or otherwise under penalty of death. But if any of you are having second thoughts, now would be the time to skin out," he said, awaiting their response.

They looked at Alkada and then at each other, all waiting for somebody to break the silence, and HardBody didn't disappoint.

"Bruh, are you done? If so, where's the drink?" HardBody asked as everybody else looked on, confused.

Alkada grinned, tossing the bottle he held to HardBody and stating, "You don't need it."

"I know. I just like the taste," HardBody said as he shook the bottle, uncorked it, and took three long gulps.

He then passed it to StreetLife, who raised the bottle to look at it in the light of the fire. StreetLife shook his head in a brief moment of hesitation before downing several gulps and passing it to A1.

"Whoo-haa!" StreetLife shouted. "Now that is firewater!"

Finally, A1 took control of the bottle. Looking at it like another rite of passage, he took a few swallows and passed it to London.

London took possession of the bottle and looked at Alkada, knowing Alkada had invoked spirits of darkness and death in the drink that he only heard about as a child in his village. He never dreamed he would take part in such a ritual. But this man was a man to be followed. His men saved his life, and he now ran with their clan. London made his decision and began to drink down the liquid, gulping the final contents of the nearly empty bottle. But right before he could finish, Skully swooped down with an ear-splitting shriek.

"Rahhhhh," he squawked at Alkada as if feeling slighted at being left out of the drinking ceremony. He landed on Alkada's shoulder, now shrieking his anger at London.

Alkada reached for the bottle and raised it to Skully, pouring the final drops of the dark nectar into Skully's beak. Skully again shrieked, spreading his massive wings, and disappeared into the night sky.

"What was that?" asked A1, already feeling the effects of the firewater pulsating through his body.

Alkada looked at them all in turn. "It's the best of the worst in me that will bring out the best of the worst in you," he said just as the wind began to blow around them.

***

At that very moment, Petra sat looking at the bones she had just rolled, content with the camaraderie she saw that surrounded Alkada and his men. Yet, she was angered that Alkada sought to drink Mugasa's wine on this endeavor. Something was being set in motion, much deeper than fulfilling blood oaths. Petra could feel it, almost touch it as if it were a living thing. Pieces were stepping onto the board, and they were being pushed by the greatest players of all: Dempaku and Mugasa.

Chapter Fifteen

NoLove had just arrived back in Shameless after two days of riding down from Republic City. Based on what Foot told him, they had about a day or two before they needed to start heading for Freedom Compound to attend the meeting called by Baron Black. It was a meeting that couldn't be missed, and thus, they wouldn't miss it. But as NoLove rolled through the streets of Shameless, the sun was only beginning to rise on this Saturday morning, and he decided he would enjoy the weekend and embrace some downtime with his brothers.

He left them posted with enough money to maneuver and hold them down till he got back, and with the dame to run errands, he didn't anticipate much trouble, if any. Nonetheless, as he brought the wagon to a stop in front of the Danforth Hotel, he was unaware that his brothers were being watched, and he just stepped into the picture.

Roosters were starting to crow, echoing throughout Shameless as NoLove entered the Danforth. He crept up the stairs to his room, nodding at the clerk on the way up. Then, pulling a key from his pocket, he quickly stuck it in the lock and entered the room unannounced. Before he was even two steps inside, two pistols and a rifle were aimed at his head. NoLove smiled to himself; their reflexes were sharp. They all had the killer instinct, and they would need it for what was to come.

"Mob shit!" greeted NoLove as he stepped fully into the room and closed the door behind him.

"Mob shit!" the men responded while lowering and re-holstering their weapons.

"Bruh, you almost got your top popped," TwoFace said, stepping forward to embrace NoLove, followed by the rest of the crew.

NoLove laughed at the comment, knowing it was entirely true.

"Well, bruh, if you had killed me, you would've been the leader of the gang by default, and we'd go from being the Mob to being the Grim Reaper Gang. And it's a lot more to us than killing, Face!"

"Yeah, I know, but killing is one of the job's perks," TwoFace responded.

At this, they all laughed.

NoLove took a seat at the table so he could explain everything as his bros gathered around.

"I just left Foot, and everything is in motion. He sends his love and loyalty and says we'll all link up soon."

"What's the word on the Plains?" Goon asked.

"Shit is sweet. I mean, they got our descriptions for the Keystone lick, and my name and TwoFace's. Really, they just puttin' the train heist on us, but nobody is for sure. You got the tongue waggers saying El Chablo and the law dogs shouting Baron Black, but really, it's a buncha goofies talkin' 'cause they got lips," NoLove reported as they all nodded. "There's a big meetin' goin' down deep in the Barren Plains at Freedom Compound. All the bosses and shot callers of the territories will be in attendance. Foot says we are to make that meetin' and formally introduce ourselves to the chessboard and not as pawns. But, at the same time, lettin' it be known, the Bluff is under Mob control. So, the word is bein' sent out to all the bros to meet there."

"That's what the fuck I'm talkin' 'bout. It's time everybody knows our name and respects it when they say it," Goon said excitedly.

NoLove took in all their expressions to the news. The love was there, the loyalty was there, and the vision was being manifested. The moment had arrived, and they were living in it.

"Where's the dame?" questioned NoLove.

"She's in the room," Swindle answered, motioning with his head toward the door.

NoLove nodded, adding, "How's the pussy?"

"Bruh, the pussy is flawless," TwoFace answered.

NoLove burst out in laughter.

"What's so funny?" TwoFace asked him.

"Bruh, you said the pussy is *flawless*."

NoLove continued to laugh as he stood up and pulled out a copy of *The Republic Speaks* that he got from Foot.

"It should be flawless," said NoLove as he walked toward the room. "That bitch is the Diamond Princess."

***

NoLove entered the plush room to find the Diamond Princess looking out of the window at the sunrise, deep in thought.

"Bianca."

She turned around to face him, shocked he knew her true identity. Her secret now revealed, she approached him tentatively, speaking softly.

"They all had their way with me."

NoLove responded by smacking her to the ground.

Swack!

"Bianca Wolfgang," NoLove said as he stood over her.

She looked up at NoLove, searching his eyes for mercy but finding none.

"That's who I was before you," she said, getting to her feet, "but that's not who I am now."

"Then who are you?" he demanded.

"I'm whoever you want or need me to be," she answered.

NoLove looked at her and again slapped her face.

Swack!

"Then be a good bitch and get naked. Show me you're worthy to be a Mob bitch," he said, watching as the trickle of blood streamed down her chin from her lip.

Bianca wiped the blood from her face with her fingertips, then looked back at NoLove and licked her fingers clean. She stepped toward the dresser in the room and reached for a ring box. She opened it and produced a gold ring circled with ten princess-cut diamonds with black baguettes in its center. She slipped the ring on the middle finger of his right hand and then went to her knees before him. Still holding his hand, she balled his hand into a fist, and while holding it in both of hers, she brought his fist to her lips and kissed his ring as she looked up into his eyes.

"The next time you slap me, do it right," she told him.

Mob shit, NoLove thought to himself as Bianca stood up and backed away from him, stepping out of her dress.

Now completely naked, she stepped to the bed, got on her hands and knees, and then laid her face down on the pillow. Reaching her hands back behind her, she pulled her ass cheeks apart.

"Make me a Mob bitch."

***

The night had begun to fall over Shameless, and true to its name, the decadence, depravity, and debauchery knew no shame. It was as if the night sky transformed Shameless into a wanderlust of the most wicked sexual desires. While NoLove was away, they had all witnessed it from the window as they stayed low, waiting for him to return. But now that he was back, they all wanted to partake in what they'd witnessed.

There were gambling houses, saloons, brothels, restaurants, theaters, smack dens, and weed houses. The streets were full of people everywhere one looked, all in total concord with the hedonism that consumed them—a complete disregard for any conscious morality. And for all the merriment to be had, one knew the potential for violence was ever-present since holstered guns were openly displayed.

This was the atmosphere the Mob now found themselves in. Four men and a woman dressed in the finest black fabrics good taste could appreciate. They all sported a single diamond ring on the middle finger of their right hand that served as a testament to their solidarity and loyalty to each other.

Bianca stood amongst them, dressed in an all-black gown with a see-through lace veil that came down over her face but allowed her green eyes to show—eyes that matched the emerald necklace adorning her neck, revealing she was a woman of class, wealth, and sophistication. She clung to NoLove's arm as they all stood in front of the Danforth Hotel.

NoLove was first to speak.

"So, what are we doin' t'night, fellas? We got a day or so before we need to be headin' west. I reckons we all could use some downtime."

"I'm 'bout to snatch up a Lucy," TwoFace announced.

"Me, too," added Goon.

"What about you, Swindle?" NoLove asked.

"I'm 'bout to hit the gamblin' spot and see if I can shake somethin' wit' the dice," he answered.

"What about you, bro?" TwoFace asked NoLove.

"Well, I reckons me and the Diamond Princess here will have us a nice dinner and take in a show," NoLove said. "We'll all meet back at the suite no later than noon tomorrow. If any smoke pops up, go guns up and hightail it for Freedom Compound. Keep the drinkin' to what you can handle. Mob shit!" he finished.

"Mob shit!" they all replied before going their separate ways.

***

Sheldon Drake watched as his quarry split up and went in four different directions. Sheldon decided he'd stay with the one who had arrived that morning. He appeared to be the shot caller out of the bunch, and sooner or later, the rest would come back together around him. And what a sight. He was arm-in-arm with the

Diamond Princess.

Well, if there is any place in the world one would expect to see an heiress with a wanted man as a couple, Shameless is the place, thought Drake. *Whoa, how the mighty have fallen.*

Shaking his head, he reached into his pocket and reread the message he had received earlier that day.

CAPTAIN HAMMER TO ARRIVE WITH THE DAWN. MAINTAIN OBSERVATION. TILL THEN, LOYALTY IS NOT FORGOTTEN, NOR IS FAILURE FORGIVEN. HAIL THE REPUBLIC.

—M. STRYFE

Drake was not naïve by any means. In fact, he was a very pragmatic man. He knew he was little more than a tool in the aspirations of Marshall Stryfe. However, of all the tools in the drawer, Drake considered himself a pretty sharp knife, and if he played his cards just right, he could cut out a nice future for himself.

***

NoLove and Bianca entered a restaurant called The Roast. The dimly lit yet very crowded place featured live music and displayed its kitchen in the middle of the restaurant as chefs dazzled and amazed patrons with spectacular displays of culinary craftsmanship.

As NoLove and Bianca took a seat, a waiter appeared at their table.

"Welcome to The Roast. I'll be your server for tonight. Allow me to get you some menus," he offered, but NoLove halted him with a raise of his hand.

"No need. We'll have the crescent duck, well-seasoned and lightly singed, with garlic mashed potatoes and pan-flashed asparagus, salt dusted with the ends snipped," NoLove ordered.

The server smiled and nodded his respect for NoLove, recognizing he was a man with a discerning palate.

"May I recommend an effervescence or spumante?" asked the server.

"No, but we will have a bottle of wine, and be sure it's been aged and not just an age," added NoLove before he waved the server off, flashing his diamond ring.

Bianca was already enthralled in the violence and single-minded determination of NoLove. So much so that she wholeheartedly embraced the vision of the Mob by taking lives herself, although she knew she would now be buried with them herself had she not killed those men. But why did she like killing them was the question plaguing her mind. The pulling of the trigger, feeling the weapon kick back in her hands, watching as a man's body instantly crumbled, and feeling the blood splashback on her face filled her with a sexually demented euphoria. Covering the four dead bodies with dirt, knowing they all died by her hand, made her pussy wet with lust for more.

She already proved she'd kill for these men, but now, in the twilight of events, she knew she would be willing to die for them, too. And now, being here with NoLove and hearing the eloquence with which he placed their orders impressed upon her his ability to play strong on any stage.

Here she was, the Diamond Princess—a woman wanted by any man who saw her. Yet, she found herself wanting a wanted man. She had chosen him and the life he lived.

I wonder what my father would think of me now? Bianca thought to herself.

As if he read her mind, NoLove pressed her, "Tell me, love, what do you think your daddy would say if he could see you now?"

She looked him dead in the eyes and replied, "I don't know. Why don't you tell me…." She paused briefly before adding, "Daddy."

NoLove studied Bianca, his poker face giving away nothing of what he felt.

"Is that how you feel?" he asked.

"What's understood doesn't need to be explained," she answered, then elaborated further. "As long as I have you in my life, the world can die. Some women live to serve God. I'd much rather please the devil."

This broad is fire and ice for sure, thought NoLove.

If her actions kept pace with her words, he could see a place for her in the grand scheme of things.

Just then, their food arrived as an additional server accompanied the first, carrying a bottle of wine. After he uncorked the bottle and began explaining the year of its vintage, Bianca took hold of it and fanned him away along with the other server. She then poured the wine for NoLove.

"I told you when we met, take me with you, and I promised you many things. My submission is only the beginning," Bianca said as she served him.

***

Drake was right to follow the man with the Diamond Princess. He returned to the hotel, and just as he had anticipated, the other men began to return to the Danforth, as well. Yes, things looked promising for a very lively morning, and Drake would have a front-row seat. He smiled to himself just as the last man arrived with two women in tow, who appeared to be Lucys. Secure in the whereabouts of his quarry, Drake would now await the arrival of Captain Hammer to brief him on the situation, knowing they weren't going anywhere soon.

***

TwoFace entered the room with two Lucys, only to be greeted by Goon sitting at the table working on his Flesh-Eater.

"What's good, bro? I brought some Lucys through," said TwoFace as he smacked their plump asses, causing them to squeal with delight.

"Man, fuck them hoes. I done lost a sack at the dice tables fuckin' 'round with Swindle. And now he's passed out on the firewater, and NoLove is cozied up in the room with the dame," spat Goon in frustration.

"Well, I guess it's two against one," TwoFace said as he took both women under his arms.

"I have a room right across the street at the Belmont," one of the women chirped.

With that, the trio left just as quickly as they came—a crucial detail that escaped Drake.

Chapter Sixteen

The clear blue skies over Shameless promised a beautiful day ahead. But little did anyone know it would end up being one of the bloodiest days in Shameless history.

The early morning quiet was deafening, except for the crowing of roosters trying to wake up a town that had only just gone to sleep. It had been a night of festive jamboree and sexual revelry.

Drake arose at sunrise just as he planned, eager to start the day. The Republic would not be late in their arrival, nor would he be late to meet them.

After freshening up, Drake left the hotel to make a beeline for the station, arriving just as the telltale puffs of smoke could be seen, announcing the train's approach.

As the train came to a complete stop, Republic soldiers immediately began to exit the train, unloading all styles of weapons.

While Drake watched with anticipation, a soldier approached

him and asked, "Are you Sheldon Drake?"

"Yes," answered Drake.

"Come with me, sir. Captain Hammer awaits you."

The soldier turned on his heel, stepping as Drake followed.

He led Drake to a man overseeing the soldiers and speaking to several officers. As Drake watched the captain, his first impression was one of great respect. Captain Hammer was a powerful-looking man with silver hair, a greyish beard, and a black eye patch that in no way took away from his aura of power and grit.

Noticing Drake, Captain Hammer stopped his conversation with an officer to greet him as both men reached out for a firm handshake—assessing, testing, and gauging each other as they did so.

This man has the look of a man who has fought many wars and led many battle campaigns. A Republic attack dog, thought Drake.

Drake was a younger man in his mid to late thirties, dapper, and sophisticated with the feel of a man who had started or instigated many battles through espionage or manipulation.

A political snake, thought Captain Hammer as the two men released hands.

"Captain Hammer, I presume," said Drake.

"And your presumption would be correct, Sheldon Drake. Now, let's say we cut the fat and get right to the innards of the matter," said Captain Hammer.

"Yes, of course," Drake answered, seeing that the captain was a shrewd and perspicacious man of action. "The men you seek are laid up at the Danforth Hotel, room two-thirty-five, on the third floor. Their suite faces the street, so an approach of stealth would be advised. There is one main entrance to the hotel and a fire escape on the side. It starts from the fourth floor down into the alley with no back entrance. As of last night, there are four men and three women in the room, and all the men are armed," reported Drake.

Captain Hammer nodded, taking in the information.

"And the Diamond Heiress?" asked the captain.

"She's among the three women. I saw her the one time and never again, other than passing by the window. She is in there, but under what condition, I can't say," Drake answered, thinking it was better to keep the full story of the Diamond Heiress to himself for now and wait to see how things played out. What he held back could be leveraged later for blackmail purposes.

Again, Captain Hammer nodded, then turned to his men.

"Lieutenant Hayes," he barked, and immediately an officer stepped before him and saluted.

"Yes, Captain," said the lieutenant.

"Set up a perimeter around the Danforth Hotel. Room two-thirty-five is our focus on the third floor. I want soldiers covering the side alley with a Gatling in case the bandits try to escape. I want another Gatling facing the front of the hotel, with sharpshooters on the roofs across the street from the hotel. Then, I want the hotel evacuated quietly. After that, we will approach and do a door kick. There are four men and possibly three women, one being the Diamond Heiress, also to be taken," the captain cut a glance at Drake to assure he didn't miss anything, to which Drake only nodded.

"And our rules of engagement, Captain?"

Captain Hammer fixed his one eye on the lieutenant, smiling as he flashed two gold canines, and answered, "The rules are simple, Lieutenant. Weapons free, and the options are surrender or death."

Lieutenant Hayes nodded and immediately began to carry out his orders.

Captain Hammer then returned his attention to Drake.

"Mr. Drake, your assistance has been duly noted and appreciated. We will handle it from here."

"Yes, of course. I'll be right across the street at the Belmont should you need me for anything further. Hail the Republic," ended Drake.

Captain Hammer looked at Drake as though he was looking at a smiling wolf. Then, finally, he nodded and walked off.

Yes, things were about to erupt, and Drake was in the middle of it all. He walked toward the Belmont as the soldiers moved about. Reaching the lobby, he took a seat. It was early, and the lobby was empty. He had a bird's eye view of the Danforth. Now all he had to do was wait for the pandemonium that was surely about to ensue. Drake felt smug in knowing he was the author of it all.

Civilized Republic, he thought to himself. *Republic of Chaos sounds so much better.*

"Let the games begin," he whispered with a wolfish smile.

***

The next few moments would reverberate in Shameless and throughout the Plains for years to come. Although the details and reasons would become blurred over time, depending on who told the tale, one thing would always be remembered: this was a battle that would lead to the Great War between the Barren Plains and the Civilized Republic—a war that would rival even the atrocities of the Death Sagas. Many would rise, and many more would fall, but only time would tell who would win.

***

"Get the fuck up!" Swindle yelled as he kicked open the door to the room where NoLove and Bianca lay in the bed.

While clumsily holding a rifle under his arm, Swindle slammed a fully loaded cylinder into his revolver. When NoLove and Bianca looked up at him in confusion, he headed straight for the window and pulled back the curtain.

"Look!" he yelled.

After grabbing his guns, NoLove sleepily stepped to the window to find a battalion of Republic soldiers lining the streets and rooftops right across from them, all setting their aim on their room.

Goon rushed into the room next, seeing NoLove and Swindle looking out the window with Bianca trying to look over their shoulders.

"If ya finished with ya fucking, somebody tell me what the fuck the plan is," Goon shouted, toting the Flesh-Eater.

NoLove took it all in. This was a moment—a moment that would either make them or break them. There was no in-between.

NoLove stepped away from the window, taking a deep breath and surrendering to the adrenaline coursing through his veins, getting it under control so he could take control of the situation. Finally getting his mind right, he was ready to embrace the moment. He looked at Goon and Swindle, but he saw no fear. On the contrary, they would feed off of whatever energy he radiated.

Even Bianca, half-naked, seemed ready for whatever was to come.

"Where's TwoFace?" shouted NoLove.

"He ain't fuckin' here! Next fuckin' question," Goon spat.

"Calm the fuck down, Goon," NoLove barked.

He had to get control of the situation before panic set in. Guns in hand, NoLove grabbed Goon and Swindle at the shoulders.

"Look, bruh, ya already know what's out that window. For them, it's just another day at the job. For us, it's life in the Mob, and I'm not ready to die. Are you?" NoLove asked.

"Fuck no," Goon said, jutting his weapon out in front of him for emphasis.

"And what about you, Swindle?"

"Mob life! Mob death! Mob shit!" Swindle answered, cocking his guns.

"That's right! Mob shit! This is it!" NoLove said, then turned to look at Bianca.

"I'm with you, Daddy," she said.

Just then, a voice yelled up to their room from the street below.

"Attention! There is no escape! You are surrounded! Surrender and come out with your hands high, and you won't be killed! This is Sergeant Smith of the Republic army! You and your men are to be brought back to Independence for trial in Independence courts," shouted the sergeant, standing in the middle of the street.

NoLove went to the window. This was his moment, and he would own it.

Looking out the window, NoLove shouted back, "Bruh, why drag us back to Independence for court when we can hold court right here!" Then he ducked out of sight again.

"Well, I reckons if that's the way you want it, that's the way it will be. And who am I talking to?" the sergeant shouted back.

At that moment, there was loud knocking at the door of their suite. NoLove cocked both guns and answered the sergeant's question as he shouted out the window.

"It's the Mob, stupid!" he barked, banging the hammers on his guns.

Boom! Boom! Boom!

He fired into the sergeant, causing his body to jump sporadically as the bone-cracker slugs punched into his face and chest, blowing him away in puzzle-type pieces of flesh.

At the same time, Goon stepped to the suite's door, raising the Flesh-Eater to fire through the door at whoever was knocking.

Boom!

The Flesh-Eater blew a hole through the door.

"Who is it? Didn't you see the *Do Not Disturb* sign on the door?" Goon barked, kicking what was left of the door open to step into the hallway, where the face and chest of a soldier were blown on the wall across from him.

Goon turned to the right to see three more Republic soldiers attempting to aim their weapons.

Boom!

The Flesh-Eater roared, ripping through the soldier's stomach, blowing his guts out the sides, and crumbling his body. The remaining two soldiers turned to run as Goon chased after them.

They headed for the side exit stairway that led to the alley.

Boom!

Goon fired, turning the back of the soldier's head into an explosion of brain and bone matter as the headless body ran on a few more steps before collapsing. Goon quickly reloaded, still on the heels of the final soldier, raising his gun just as the soldier reached the exit door. He pushed it open, and sunlight flooded into the hallway from outside as the soldier started down the steps.

Goon rushed through the door right behind him, aiming at the soldier's back. At that moment, Goon saw the Gatling gun manned by two soldiers aimed right at him. The Gatling erupted, ripping through the steps right below Goon's feet. Goon quickly turned around and raced back up the steps, diving into the hallway just as a bullet ripped through the back of his thigh.

"You sons of bitches! Ya gonna pay for that!" he yelled back through the door as the shots continued to cut through the doorway.

Goon pushed himself up, grabbing his dropped Flesh-Eater. The pain was brief and no match for the adrenaline pushing him on. He stumbled back down the hall to the room transformed into a scene of pure chaos—deafening sounds of gunfire, shattering windows, and whizzing bullets. Swindle was in the window with a sharp-eye rifle, aiming and banging before ducking as shots came for him.

"That's four, NoLove. Where you at?" shouted Swindle as he reloaded his rifle.

Blam! Blam! Blam!

He fired, then immediately hunkered down as bullets ripped into the suite.

"Stop cheating, Swindle. I'm at six, so catch up," NoLove shouted back out of the bedroom.

Swindle turned to see Goon holding his leg as he limped into the suite.

"Goon's back," he shouted over the sound of gunfire.

"Bout fuckin' time. Bianca, load me!" NoLove ordered.

Bianca crawled on her hands and knees, dodging shattered glass and bullets. Grabbing NoLove's revolvers, she began to load them as NoLove picked up a rifle, took aim at one of the soldiers on the roof across the street, and fired. His bullseye was apparent as the soldier plummeted to the street below, smacking the ground with his body as a puff of dirt rose around him.

"That's seven, Swindle," NoLove shouted from the back room. "Goon, how was your walk?" he yelled as a barrage of bullets ripped through the window he'd just shot from.

"Short," Goon answered, ducking down, putting his back to a wall. "The side exit is blocked off. They got a fucking Gatling that way. Almost tore my motherfucking leg off," Goon shouted, showing the wound where the bullet hit him. "Toss me a rifle!" he then barked. "And, bitch, come wrap my muthafuckin' leg!"

NoLove flung Goon the Sharp-Eye, as he now had two fully loaded revolvers. Bianca crawled to Goon, tearing part of a bedsheet to wrap his leg.

"Good," said NoLove, "because we're goin' out the front door anyway. Same way we came in. Dead or alive."

Just then, an onslaught of bullets ripped through the suite windows, forcing everyone to their bellies.

"Sounds like they got a Gatling out front, too," Swindle shouted.

"No fuckin' kiddin'!" Goon shouted back as they all started laughing.

***

Captain Hammer stood behind the ranks of his soldiers,

watching as the scene unfolded before him, rage apparent in his one good eye as he saw his sergeant blown away, face first.

He turned to Lieutenant Hayes, grabbing him by his collar with an iron grip and pulling him close until they were face-to-face.

"Get that fucking Gatling up now!" he roared, spittle flying in the lieutenant's face as he shoved him away.

Captain Hammer then broke from behind the ranks and headed for the very front of the Danforth.

"Fire at will! Fire at goddamn will!" he shouted to his men. "And by God's aim, shoot to kill!" he ordered.

This was what Captain Hammer lived for. He stepped to the front of the Danforth Hotel—as if he were impervious or immune to lead and heedless of death—to the very spot where his sergeant lay slain. Reaching down, he grabbed the guns from the dead man's waist, turned around, and aimed upward towards the suite, firing into it himself.

***

Drake watched excitedly from the lobby of the Belmont, reveling in the carnage of it all, totally taken by the turn of events. The sound of gunfire and the bodies dropping everywhere—he was the one who had brought this about, and he was delighted by his handiwork. Then another twist occurred. The last man he had seen arrive that evening flashed past him at less than an arm's length away.

Drake reached for his sidearm and was about to shoot the man down from the back but stopped when he saw one of the horse tenders standing nearby. As TwoFace hurried to unhitch the reins of several horses fettered there, he was approached by the horse tender, who had only been watching the fiasco at the Danforth up until then. TwoFace began snatching the reins, and when the horse tender attempted to grab them back from him, the quick-handed bandit pulled his gun faster than Drake's eyes could process. Placing the metal against the man's face, TwoFace pulled the trigger, blowing him away without hesitation.

Upon seeing this, Drake decided not to intervene. Better to see what would happen next. Drake looked up at the Danforth to see a white flag waving out the window of the bandits' room.

***

Captain Hammer saw the white flag waving from the shattered window of the suite and announced a cease-fire.

"Surrender now, or there will be no surrendering later," he yelled up to the suite.

"You got us fucked up, bruh," NoLove answered back. "The Mob doesn't surrender. We just tryna send a woman out."

"By woman, do you mean the Diamond Heiress?" Hammer shouted, still standing in the street, guns in hand.

"One and the same," answered NoLove.

"Then do so now!" Hammer barked.

Bianca heard the exchange of words, knowing she was at the center of it and knew what was expected of her. She didn't want to leave them but would do as she was told.

"The bitch is on the way," NoLove yelled out through what was left of the window, then looked at Bianca and nodded her towards the door.

She nodded to Swindle and Goon before turning to NoLove

and saying, "I love you."

"Then now is your chance to prove it," he replied.

Having already been told what to do, she headed for the door. Stopping short, she turned back around to NoLove. Reaching for his hand, she kissed his ring and left the suite.

***

Bianca Wolfgang exited the Danforth Hotel, bleeding from a graze to the head, her hair a mess, and crying uncontrollably. She ran to the soldiers and was immediately taken behind the perimeter.

"Are you all right, ma'am?" asked Hammer, looking at her from where he stood.

Bianca began to scream and shriek unintelligible words.

"Set her aside," said Hammer, pointing to an area out of the line of fire.

NoLove then popped back into the bullet-ridden window, aiming his two guns.

"Recess is over, bitches," he shouted and commenced firing.

He grazed the captain but killed the soldier behind him. The Gatling instantly roared back to life, eating away at the suite and forcing NoLove, Goon, and Swindle to the floor again.

Then the distinctive sound of the Flesh-Eater went off, and the Gatling stopped. When Swindle looked out the window, he saw the man who had been manning the Gatling was now headless—his lifeless body slumped over the monster gun. Then an even crazier sight greeted Swindle as he looked closely to be sure. The fire rose into his chest as he observed TwoFace charging up the street with horses in tow. Swindle couldn't believe what he saw, and his excitement showed when he relayed it to the others.

"It's TwoFace! TwoFace is out there!" yelled Swindle, loading his guns and getting amped up.

Hearing this was the second wind they needed. Lock and loaded, they exited the room and headed hastily down to the lobby, taking full advantage of the chance Bianca had given them.

***

TwoFace came from behind the line of soldiers, horses charging and guns blazing. He spotted Bianca as she stood behind the officer shooting the Gatling gun and fired the Flesh-Eater into the back of his head, causing his skull to explode into a thousand pieces. TwoFace followed suit, taking aim and firing into the backs of the soldiers' heads, watching as they died, not even knowing where the death came from.

Captain Hammer dove out of the way just as the small stampede barreled past him into the lobby of the Danforth Hotel.

Captain Hammer's line had been broken. His soldiers lay dead, dying, and scattered, but he would rise. He picked himself up from the dirt and moved towards the Gatling gun.

***

TwoFace entered the lobby, the horses rearing and bucking as he pulled their reins amongst the chaos.

"Where the fuck was you at?" NoLove asked, shouting as he approached the stairs that led into the open lobby, followed by Swindle and a limping Goon.

"Does it fuckin' matter?!" shouted TwoFace. "Had I fuckin' been here, we'd all still be up in that fuckin' room waitin' to be fed to that Gatling. Now, let's go!"

They all jumped on the horses and started for the entrance. TwoFace was out first, killing two tamers as he busted out of the lobby, making a lane for his brothers to follow. Next came NoLove with Goon right behind him. Then, the Gatling sounded.

Captain Hammer had thrown the lieutenant's dead body off the wagon and took control of the Gatling, immediately firing a barrage of bullets into the lobby. He could not stop the first three men from escaping, but the final horse reared up as bullets ripped into its body, causing the horse to throw his rider.

Swindle was coming up behind Goon when the Gatling made his horse buck up. As shots hit the animal, Swindle was thrown off the horse. Bianca jumping on the back of NoLove's horse was the last thing he saw before his world went black.

***

TwoFace and the gang raced out of Shameless, heading west into the Barren Canyons. After seeing there was no pursuit, they pulled up. TwoFace immediately noticed Swindle wasn't with them.

"Where's Swindle?" he shouted, looking back to see if he was coming.

"He was right behind me," Goon answered, turning around to look.

"We gotta go back. We gotta get Swindle!" TwoFace said, pulling the reins of his horse to turn it around.

"No, we can't go back," NoLove told him, grabbing

TwoFace's arm.

"What the fuck you mean, bruh?! I didn't leave y'all, and we not leavin' him," TwoFace spat.

"TwoFace, don't be fuckin' stupid! Listen, bruh, if we go back now, we all get dead. The Mob is bigger than one man," NoLove stated.

TwoFace snatched his arm away from NoLove.

"Fuck all that and fuck you! Goon, you with me?" asked TwoFace over his shoulder, his eyes never leaving NoLove's.

"No, he's not, bruh," NoLove answered. "Bruh, listen, get outta your feelings. You're lettin' your anger and emotions supersede your intelligence," NoLove said, now grabbing the reins of TwoFace's horse as Bianca and Goon looked on.

TwoFace glanced at Goon, then looked back at NoLove and said, "Get out of my way or be put out of my way." He let his hand fall to one of his guns. "Ain't no way I'm leavin' my cousin behind. Alive with you or dead without you, I'm goin' back."

With no warning, Goon banged the back of TwoFace's skull with the Flesh-Eater, knocking him out cold. Then NoLove and Goon fastened TwoFace to his saddle, took the reins of his horse, and continued west.

NoLove hated to leave Swindle behind, but he made his decision based on the odds that faced them. Yet, he had no way of knowing that what started as twelve-to-one odds was now three-to-one. For had he known, he would've surely gone back.

Chapter Seventeen

Captain Hammer walked among the wreckage that was once the lobby of the Danforth Hotel, still mystified at how it all went so wrong. The bullet-riddled wood, the crunching of shattered glass that sounded with every step he took.

Nothing but death and destruction, he thought.

Things had not gone as anticipated. His forces were cut down to less than half, their bodies a gruesome display of disregard for their lives and authority. These bandits were a different kind of evil. They were mad dogs, killing like they had rabies.

First Keystone, then Reach Providence, and now here.

Yes, they would have to be put down, and Captain Hammer knew he was the man for the job.

He had his nose wiped today, but he would be ready next time. He killed many men, even his own if they proved to be cowards. He killed Bentas, Sanchies, and even the infamous Shynes in the Death Sagas, whom were feared all over. It had cost him an eye and the lives of his brothers, but nonetheless, he killed them. And now, these upstarts—The Mob, as they called themselves—he would kill them, too…in time. Unfortunately, he underestimated them today, and that mistake cost him dearly. But it was a lesson learned and a mistake he would never make again.

"Captain, the prisoner is awake," said a soldier who had come to stand at Hammer's side, saluting after giving Captain Hammer the news.

"Bring him to me," Captain Hammer snapped. It was time to meet and know the measure of the men who he was up against.

A shackled Swindle was brought before Captain Hammer. At first glance, Hammer could tell he was young, which now accounted for all the blatant killing, but most acutely, he noticed there was no fear in his eyes. He was not yet old enough to appreciate life, but he was definitely a soldier.

"Okay, prisoner, any idea where your partners be getting to?" asked Captain Hammer.

Swindle mumbled something but the captain couldn't hear.

"Speak up, boy," Captain Hammer said, leaning in closer to hear him, putting his ear to Swindle's mouth.

Swindle snapped to life, striking out with his mouth and biting the captain's ear, locking on it as if he were a dog.

"Arrggh!" the captain gritted and growled, embracing the pain and punching Swindle in the gut, forcing him to release his lockjaw hold on his ear.

Swindle was immediately pummeled to the ground by surrounding soldiers.

"Mob shit, bitch!" Swindle shouted as he took blows from boots and gun handles.

Hammer grinned as he stepped forward, bringing a stop to the beating while wiping the blood from his ear as if it were little more than a mosquito bite. Captain Hammer kneeled to speak to the prisoner, who was face down on his belly.

"You have grit to you, boy. I like that. Ain't much grit left around these days. I'm glad to see you mobsters come from sterner stock. I look forward to killing ya. Now, I'm gonna ask you one more time, where is your gang off to?"

Swindle was unable to do anything but lift his head.

"Fuck you," he said, then tried to spit on the captain.

Captain Hammer stood up, wiping the spittle from his chest with his hand and then on the soldier standing next to him.

"Mark my word, boys, this here is a soldier," Hammer announced to his men. "But we'll see what he's really made of when we get him back to Independence and put him to the testing of truth."

Captain Hammer then positioned his boot up at the side of the prisoner's face and pulled his spur across his jaw, scarring him. He smiled as blood appeared in the sliver of open flesh.

"Take him to the pokey and prepare him for transport to Independence," ordered Captain Hammer.

Lifted to his feet, Swindle was taken away. Drake was entering the lobby as the prisoner was being carried out, giving him only a glance. Drake was delighted more by all the carnage he saw. He approached the captain, who was now standing at what used to be the hotel's front desk.

Captain Hammer looked at Drake with a suspect eye and said, "It would appear your information was somewhat flawed, Mr. Drake, and because of this flawing, I lost officers and soldiers."

"Yes, it appears you have," countered Drake with an air of arrogance that Hammer didn't like.

As Drake stepped around the splintered desk counter, he

started perusing the message boxes, stopping when he got to the one for Room 235. Grabbing the paper inside, he unfolded it and read it as Captain Hammer continued to talk.

"A flaw like this could land a man in the worm room when Marshall Stryfe finds out."

Despite the gravity of his tone, Hammer saw no sign of fear in Drake at his words.

"Perhaps, perhaps not," Drake responded. "Besides, who ends up in the worm room when Marshall Stryfe reads this is a question you may want to ask yourself," he added while handing Captain Hammer the message.

Drake watched Captain Hammer as the implications of the note set in.

LEAVE IMMEDIATELY! WOLVES COME WITH THE DAWN THAT HAVE YOUR SCENT. MAKE THE MEETING AT FREEDOM COMPOUND. THEN MEET ME AT THE ROSE.

— FOOT

"Well, Captain Hammer, it would appear the flaw in the matter comes from the very Capitol itself and therefore excludes me from any blame for today's calamity," smiled Drake. "So, may I suggest that what Marshall Stryfe finds out about today's events is only what *we* want him to know as told by us, assuring neither you nor myself need be concerned with the worm room other than to decide who should be in it," said Drake, pausing to allow the captain to ponder his statement.

Captain Hammer nodded in agreement with Drake, already conceding that what he implied was true. There was obviously a spy in Independence close to the top, and he and his men were ambushed because of it.

It wasn't the total truth, nor was it a complete lie. As Hammer saw it, it was politics—politics indeed.

***

Foot sat in his hotel room, hoping NoLove had gotten his message. There was no way of knowing for sure. He had only just gotten the word from his mole in Independence the day before. However, everything he had gotten from him thus far was grade-A information and spot-on, from the train heist to the fact that what he was attempting to get done with the Weasel was even possible. So, if Tamers were about to bite down on his bros as the mole said, it had to be facts, especially since the mole had no way of knowing his bros were actually in Shameless.

Foot hated not knowing, but he did know that NoLove would handle himself or die killing—of that, he was sure. They were all in motion now, and all had moves to make. No matter what, the Mob would march on. In a few days, the gold and drugs would be converted into cash, The Weasel would be paid, history would be made, and the message would be loud and clear: Make way for the Mob!

***

Fat Pockets had just ridden out of the Bluff from the east and was about to enter the Barren canyons. He was about four days out from Freedom Compound. The fact that he was headed to Freedom Compound assured his safe passage through the Barren Plains. The view was amazing, but the route wasn't the smoothest as his coach traveled along, bumping, shaking, and tilting through the rugged terrain.

He ordered Nancy to fix him something to eat, and as she attempted to, she accidentally dropped some food on Fat Pockets when the wagon hit a bump in the road.

"Bitch, pay attention to what you doin'," Fat Pockets snapped at Nancy, who was momentarily distracted while looking out the carriage window at the beauty around her.

Nancy had never been out of Keystone, so everything she saw was new to her eyes.

"Bitch, ain't nothin' out them windows but mountains. You got your eyes glued to the glass like you looking for tricks, but I tell you what… Drop, spill, or waste one more thing on me, and I'ma slap your day away! I bet you don't spill a drop when you suckin' cock. Now, get your mind right, hoe, before I let you go."

"Yes, sir, Mayor Fat Pockets. It won't happen again," she said pleadingly, then focused solely on getting his food ready.

"Well, be sure it doesn't. You know I'll slap you if I have to," Fat Pockets warned, leaning his head toward the window to take in the natural majesty of the landscape around him.

***

At the same time, Alexander Wolfgang was crossing the border into the Barren Plains from Reach Providence, headed towards Freedom Compound. In the twilight of his life, he felt strong and ready to take on the world to find his daughter. Little did he know that very daughter had just taken the Wolfgang name from its plateau of prestige and wealth to the heights of infamy.

***

El Chablo was also making his way to Freedom Compound with a small escort of soldiers; he didn't feel the need for more than that. Showing up at the meeting with more than his selected handful might imply he was a little nervous or fearful, which was not El Chablo's way.

It would be a few days before he reached Freedom Compound down through the Barren Hills. The last time he'd been through these lands was when he escaped The Fort. But now, he found himself going back through these parts for a much different reason. He was sure Diablo Vasa wouldn't mind him passing through his lands, given the purpose of his passing. They were, after all, courteous neighbors, but perhaps this meeting would now make them allies.

***

Diablo Vasa sat on the terrace of his room, overlooking the beautiful mountains of his land. Feeling the breeze, he sipped on his wine and contemplated while looking in the direction he would soon be traveling.

For him, the choosing of a side was a very simple matter. Diablo was a commonsensical man. He would side with the devil he knew, which was Baron Black and the people of the Barren Plains. Yet, Diablo would make it perfectly clear that all knew he had options, and he would not be forced to choose anyone's side. And the side he did choose would know they needed him as much as he needed them. This was the angle he would negotiate from. The Death Sagas had been bloody, and should the smoke kick off again, things would be a lot bloodier this time around.

***

AMBUSHED IN SHAMELESS! I DARE SAY BUSHWACKED! WE KILLED THREE AND CAPTURED ONE. NOW EN ROUTE TO INDEPENDENCE FOR THE TESTING OF TRUTH. AS WELL, THE DIAMOND HEIRESS IS IN LEAGUE WITH THE BANDITS. WE ARE NOW IN PURSUIT OF THE ONES THAT GOT AWAY. MORE TO REPORT, BUT ONLY FACE-TO-FACE. HAIL THE REPUBLIC.

— CAPTAIN HAMMER

Marshall Stryfe read the communique several times, trying to decipher the hidden message. Something had gone wrong in Shameless that could only be spoken about once they were face-to-face.

How peculiar, thought Stryfe. *There's obviously a snake about, but time and patience will flush him out. And then let's see how the snake stands up against The Worm.*

And imagine that, the Diamond Princess roving with outlaws. Surely the penalty inflicted on her can be extended to all of Noble Haven. Finally, Stryfe thought, grinning, his mind already lit with a scheme.

Chapter Eighteen

Alkada and his men entered into Shameless grim, determined, and eager to add to the death already in the air. After bringing their horses to a stop, London was the first to speak on what they all felt as they unsaddled.

"There has been much killing here today."

"Yeah, I feel it, as well. So, be on point," Alkada said to everyone, then transcended an unspoken message from his mind into Skully's—a word of instruction: *Watch.*

Flying overhead, Skully shrieked back in response to receiving the mental message, indicating his understanding and compliance.

The way people were running and scampering about, it was apparent something had taken place in Shameless. Everywhere they looked, they saw somebody leaning down into somebody else's ear, spreading the word, or somebody cocking their head to catch a bit of gossip. Alkada was sure he and his men would soon find out what had taken place. After tying up their horses and entering a saloon, the men took a seat as StreetLife went to the bar.

"What'll it be?" asked the bartender as he wiped clean some shot glasses in preparation for their orders.

"Let me get a round of whiskey for my friends and me," said StreetLife, waving a hand back to his men.

The bartender looked at all the men and instantly marked them as gunslingers, especially when he looked at HardBody and Alkada.

"A round of whiskey comin' up. I gather you aren't from 'round these parts. So I reckons you ain't heard. You best be careful flashing those sidearms as you are, especially the scarfaces," said the bartender, cutting an eye at Alkada and HardBody, knowing their scars marked them as Shyne. "Yeah, a big ruckus on the other side of town, as I be hearin' it. Say Republic tamers was involved, lot'a shootin'. Say a posse went off chasin' the people involved, but still may be some lingerin' around. I'm sure you wouldn't want to be crossed up in any of it," the bartender offered as he poured their drinks.

"Is that right?" said StreetLife, passing drinks to his comrades, then returning to the bar. "What was—"

StreetLife was cut off mid-sentence by a man who came barging through the saloon doors, unaware that several guns were trained on his skull.

"Ben, fix me a drink and make it strong!" the man said, slapping his palm repeatedly on the bar in impatience.

"Jesse, don't you see me tendin' to a customer? Show some goddamn respect," the bartender snapped back.

The man then turned to StreetLife, just noticing him.

"I beg your pardon, partner, but I just seen killin's like no other and on the Lord's day. And I means to forget it with a drink," said the man.

StreetLife looked at the bartender and nodded for him to give the man what he wanted as he slid the bartender a few bills.

"Much obliged, stranger," the man said, then turned to the bartender, harping, "Get me that good shit, Ben. That's high dollar this man just passed you!"

The bartender grabbed the money before ducking down beneath the bar. He reappeared a few seconds later, holding a bottle of clear liquid with gold flakes floating inside.

"Whoo-wee, sweet glory," the man whistled, knowing this was not the rotgut he was used to.

"Don't you try joshin' me, Ben. Get a tall glass," the man said.

"Calm your thirsty ass down, Jesse. I'll fix you good and proper," countered the bartender, placing a tall glass on the bar and filling it up.

Jesse grabbed the glass almost before Ben could fill it and downed the firewater with a series of loud gulps.

"Clear," said Jesse, pushing the glass back to Ben to be refilled.

StreetLife tapped the man on the shoulder to get his attention.

"Say, Jesse, why don't you tell me what you saw that you aims to forget?" StreetLife pressed.

Jesse downed a second glass, again announcing, "Clear."

When he was done, he wiped his beard and turned around, putting his back to the bar. He noticed an audience waiting to hear what he wanted to forget. He looked up at all the faces, pausing on Alkada's and HardBody's.

"Shynes," the man whispered under his breath, but the respect and fear were loud and clear. "Well, I was up at the Danforth

Hotel tending horseshoe, me and Chip—like we always do for leavin' guests on Sunday mornings—when I looks up and notice a bunch of Republic soldiers—all-black fashioned, as you know 'em to be—across the street up at the Belmont. You would've thought Marshall Stryfe himself was in town the way they started evacuating the Danforth, setting up Gatling guns right in the middle of the street, and posting soldiers all around and on rooftops. I ain't never seen the likes of such soldiering. But then some soldier—I reckons an officer—hits the middle of the street in front of the Danforth and gets to telling somebody to come out. And that was the last time he'd be telling anybody anything. You understand me? 'Cause them bastards came out the window guns up with no forgiveness!" Jesse squealed, looking again at HardBody and Alkada.

Although Jesse didn't say it this time, one could tell the thought in his mind again was *Shynes*.

"What happened next?" StreetLife asked, snapping the man from his trance.

"Fix me, Ben," the man said, shoving his glass to the bartender.

Ben fixed him a shot, and the man quickly downed it before he went on.

"Well, all the sudden, a man comes out the window, gunnin' and firin' right down into that officer, putting his brain behind him, making it no more useful than the dirt on the ground. Then, all hell broke loose—all hell on a Sunday. Guns firing and men dying. I can't say for sure what was going on in the room the soldiers were shooting into, but I'll be damned if it wasn't blood on the streets. Every time you looked around, a soldier's head would explode, or a body would just crumble like a sack of potatoes. I even saw a man swan dive off a roof, but I swear when them soldiers fired up that Gatling, it was the devil's laughter as they started ripping shots into the hotel room getting at them bandits. Then the darndest thing happens. All the shootin' stops, and I see a white flag wavin' out the window as if the varmints were givin' up, and I'd be a fool by my thoughts as another officer gets to exchangin' words. I can't rightly say what, but it wasn't a surrender. Next thing I see is a woman come out, and then they get right back to shootin'. And right as Chip and I are watchin' it all, a bandit comes outta the Belmont and starts unhitchin' horses behind us like we weren't even standin' there. So, Chip pulls up like, 'Partner, what you think you doin' wit' these horses?' And then grabs at his arm."

The man paused in his story, shaking his head at the dreadful memory, and then looked again at the bartender, trigger-fingering at his glass for the bartender to fill it. After receiving and downing another drink, he continued.

"Well, Chip reached for the bastard's arm, and quick as lightnin', this bastard pulls a gun, put it to Chip's head, and blew his goddamn top off, and had the gun back in his holster before Chip's body dropped. Then, he looked me right in the eye and said, 'Mob shit. You want it?' Boy, I tell you, I had my hands so high in the air, I could've scratched God's ass. This bitch was a real rattlesnake, but had I an iron, I coulda took 'em," the man boasted unconvincingly.

At this, HardBody chuckled, knowing the man he was talking about was TwoFace, making him lucky even to be there telling his story.

StreetLife could tell the liquor was starting to take effect, and they needed as much accurate information as possible.

"What happened next?" StreetLife urged him on as Alkada and the rest of the band listened intently.

"Easy now, stranger," the man said, looking at StreetLife. "I just told you my buddy got his face canoed, so ain't no needs you be rushin' me along. Mind you, ain't no happy endin's to come with this story."

The man gained back a little control of the moment, enjoying the attention from his captive audience.

"Well, after that bastard killed Chip and took the horses, he heads straight toward the fray, gallopin' right at them soldiers. I think maybe to yell out a warnin' or something, there being women about. But they wouldn'a heard me over the Gatling's rattlings. But then, I notice the same woman that came out of the Danforth walk up right behind the soldier on the Gatling and fire up a shiny, black Flesh-Eater and put his brains in the sky, thoughts and all. Nasty sight, I swear. Even worse than poor Chip. And now, that horse thief… He was no slouch by far. First, he pulled up on them soldiers' backsides, doin' the devil's work indeed. On horseback killin' everything he came upon. Then he rushed into the lobby."

At this, the bartender interrupted.

"Jesse, you best not be lyin' none to these men. I think the liquor got your tongue dancin' with your words."

Taken aback, Jesse stopped talking mid-sentence and looked at the bartender.

"Ben, you callin' me a liar? I know you ain't callin' me a liar, Ben. But, listen here, Ben… You've known me since I've been a jit off my pa's knee, but just as sure as I got Chip's blood and brains on my boots, I'll wrap you 'round the jaw and bring a kickin' to your ass if you sayin' I'm lyin' 'bout what I saw. Now fix me before I give you a tastin' of a slap just for measure," ordered Jesse, holding his glass in the air as the bartender filled it.

Having properly checked the detractor, the man got back to it.

"Now, as I told you, fellas, ain't no tellin' what was going on in the hotel, but I reckons the horse thief was in real proper with them because the next thing you know, a bunch of them come busting out the hotel lobby on horseback, guns blazing. 'Bout two or three of 'em get away before that Gatling came back to life like termites on virgin wood. The bullets were going, and that bitch on the Gatling wasn't bullshitting, put one of them bandits on his back. Although I'm surprised the bastard hit anything, seeing how he had one eye," the man reported.

Alkada and HardBody exchanged a knowing look at hearing that Captain Hammer was about.

"I see the woman jump on the back of one of the horses, and they and two more bastards rode right past me, heading west toward the Barren Canyons. I tell you, fellas, ain't nothin' to be seein' on no Sunday, or any other day for that matter," the man concluded.

"What did the soldiers do next?" StreetLife pushed.

"Well, they tended to their wounded, and it was a lot of tending because them Republic boys got their nose wiped real good. The man with one eye got a posse up of what was left of his soldiers and skinned out after the bandits. They took the prisoner they caught to the town pokey, saying they gonna ship him off to Independence," he answered.

"What prisoner?" asked Alkada, getting to his feet, followed by A1 and London as HardBody headed out the saloon doors.

The man turned to Alkada, focusing on his scarred face. He

now felt emboldened by the liquor, as was apparent in his answer.

"Look here, big fella, I know you're a Shyne, but if you'd let me get through with my story, I was getting to that part," he slurred.

Alkada stepped forward, pulling his gun with no hesitation, and placed it on the man's chest, cocking back the hammer.

"Finish now or be finished!" said Alkada, his voice all steel.

A1 and London drew their guns, too, throwing their aim at the bartender.

"Well, since you put it that way. They say he's to be leaving by sundown. Gonna ship him to Independence and put him to the testing of truth, they say. Words in the wind say he was part of the killings in Keystone and the train massacre up north."

"So, there are no other soldiers around?" asked Alkada, his gun still pressed against the man's chest.

"Just the two or three that carried the prisoner off. The rest are dead or left with the posse," he responded hesitantly.

Alkada nodded and holstered his gun, followed by A1 and London as they all turned and exited the saloon.

"Fix me, Ben," said Jesse, shaken but relieved they had left.

"Fix it yourself, Jesse. I done shit my pants thinkin' we were 'bout to join Chip," said the bartender, taking a swig straight from the bottle himself.

"Yeah, Ben, them were some mean sons'a bitches right there. It was like lookin' at the twin brothers of them bandits from earlier."

***

Alkada and his band pushed their way through Shameless,

and it was just as the man in the saloon had said. The Republic for sure had their nose wiped. It was evident from the dead bodies of Republic soldiers sprawled out everywhere. Skulls were blown open and faces blasted off. Plenty of work for the undertaker or food for the buzzards that started to form overhead, attracted by the smell of death.

Alkada reached out to Skully with connection and awareness. NoLove was too far gone, but through Skully, Alkada saw the posse giving chase. Alkada focused on the leader and urged Skully with a simple command: *Closer.*

Skully received the command and obeyed, swooping down on the riders—the leader, in particular. Flying over their heads, Skully looked in on the white-haired man with the black eye patch, making sure Alkada saw the man as clearly as he did. In an instant, Alkada knew beyond a doubt that Captain Hammer was about.

Return, Alkada told Skully and severed the bond as he continued to take in the carnage he saw as they passed the front of the Danforth Hotel.

Playing back what the drunkard had told them in the saloon, he had to admit it was a very accurate account of events. Four men had slain over half a troop of Republic soldiers and, by the look of things, had taken no losses other than the captured prisoner, which was probably a hard choice split decision on the leader to get away with some or all die together.

The front of the Danforth was in shambles. Alkada looked up to the room NoLove had to be in, then looked around where the soldiers had fallen. The soldiers on the street were fighting men with an elevated position and the added advantage of shooting from cover. They didn't stand a chance, though. The soldiers were sitting ducks for four men with Sharp-Eye rifles or even revolvers at such close ranges. Although the Gatling would've made a difference, that's why they took it out of the fight.

Smart move, thought Alkada. *That's exactly what I would've done.*

They rode on through the streets of Shameless, watching as they were being watched. The people in town scurried about gossiping, trying to make sense of the senselessness that had taken place, and inventing pieces of the story to fit whatever they couldn't understand or explain.

HardBody had checked out the pokey and caught up to them.

"What's it look like?" asked Alkada. "Can we get the prisoner?"

"Pretty solid one-level structure. Bunch of townsfolk guarding him. Three Republic soldiers are getting him ready for transport. It wouldn't be sensible to bust him out of there. It'd be too much of a performance. Better we take him en route to Independence. I scouted out the path they'll be taking, and there's a nice ambush spot that will make it real easy like," said HardBody.

"Then I reckons we're 'bout to be some rattlers in the road," responded Alkada as they all rode off, following HardBody's lead.

***

Just as HardBody said, the spot was perfect for an ambush. There was a small clearing of land in the trail, about an acre covered by trees on both sides. They would have the transport in a bottleneck.

StreetLife and London posted off to the side of the trail with a Sharp-Eye rifle, while HardBody and A1 posted up ahead in the brush to be facing them when they approached. Alkada sat directly in the middle of the trail and waited. Once again, he reached out to Skully with connection and awareness: *Be watchful.*

Skully shrieked back acknowledgment, soaring above them as the sun began to set.

Just as planned, Alkada spotted the wagon bending into the clearing. There were only three soldiers in the transport: the driver holding the horses' reins, a soldier beside him riding shotgun, and a soldier behind on a single horse.

Alkada surmised that their heading into Republic land gave them the confidence to travel so lightly with a prisoner. The soldiers on the wagon were passing a bottle between them when they spotted Alkada in the middle of the trail, hands resting on his saddle as if he were enjoying the ending of the day.

The soldier riding shotgun was first to speak.

"Howdy, partner. I reckons you must be lost," he said to Alkada as the soldier holding the reins brought the wagon to a halt.

"Not at all," responded Alkada nonchalantly. "In fact, I believe I'm right where I needs to be, seein' how I'm here to collect that prisoner you're transporting."

The soldier riding behind galloped up to the side of the wagon. Reaching the forefront, he looked to his comrades with a befuddled expression.

"What's going on? Why are we stopping?"

Again, the soldier riding shotgun spoke up.

"Well, this man here…" He paused, pointing his chin towards Alkada. "…he says our prisoner belongs to him."

"Is that right?" answered the rider, just noticing Alkada. He kicked his horse forward, pulling right up to him. "I believe you got it twisted. This man is headed to Independence as our prisoner for the testing of truth and then to the worm room," stated the soldier before letting his hand drop to his gun. "Now, I suggest you best step aside or be put aside."

"That's telling him!" sang the driver of the wagon.

"Yes, sir, this prisoner is worm food," added the shotgun rider as he cocked his rifle after passing the liquor bottle.

Alkada smiled, now turning to fully face the three soldiers, revealing his whole face and the telltale scars that marked him as a Shyne.

Reality dawned on the soldiers too late to matter as Alkada dipped his head and gave the sign.

Blam!

A shot rang out, turning the horse's rider into a headless horseman as the horse jumped up and trotted off, leaving its' rider's body to fall into the brush.

Blam!

Another shot went right through the eye of the soldier riding shotgun. The way his body slumped to the side on the driver's shoulder made it look like he had decided to take a nap, the back of his head gone. The driver shoved the soldier's body to the ground and quickly raised his hands to surrender.

"Shynes," he uttered as he dropped the reins of his horses.

Blam!

Another shot blew the bottom half of the bottle away that he held; liquor splashed with the shattered glass.

Tossing the top part of the bottle to the ground, the soldier immediately began shouting, "Take him! Take him! He's all yours!"

"I know that's right. Now get down off the wagon and get on your knees," Alkada ordered as he unsaddled.

When Alkada's men came out of cover, the soldier's head swiveled in confusion. He realized they never had a chance. The fact that he went from captor to captive in a matter of seconds sent him into a panic.

He fell onto his knees, pleading, "Please don't kill me. Please. I'll do anything! I ain't know there was Shynes to be meddled with in all this."

"Shut the fuck up!" Alkada barked, pulling his gun and placing it on the soldier's forehead. "Tell me everything I want to know, and I won't kill ya."

At this, the soldier became dog-like in his effort to please, ready to tell Alkada all that he knew.

"Now, why do you have this prisoner?" Alkada demanded.

"Because he's one of them bandits involved in the train massacre up north in Reach Providence and them killings back east in Keystone, not to mention the hell-raising he done today in Shameless," answered the soldier.

Hearing this, Alkada was satisfied that whoever was in the wagon had a hand in Leggs' killing.

"Where's the rest of your troops?" Alkada pressed.

"Captain Hammer took what was left and went after the ones who got away. Says there's a big meeting in the Barren Plains, and all the shot callers of the Plains will be attending. Hammer figures that's where the bandits be gettin' to. A place called the Freedom Compound."

Alkada nodded briefly, remembering the days when Baron Black fought alongside his father in the Death Sagas.

At the mention of Captain Hammer, HardBody and Alkada held eye contact before HardBody said, "So, old one-eye is back behind the gun, huh? This is going to be a good one."

That was a fact Alkada already knew, given their history.

The soldier looked at HardBody, shock on his face as he noticed the number of scars. He instantly knew who this man was and that his chances of survival plummeted.

"How many got away, and how many went after?" questioned Alkada.

"Three men got away, and one woman says she's the Diamond Heiress from the train massacre. Captain Hammer and 'bout eighteen men are on their heels," the soldier answered carefully, hoping his answers would save his life.

But, when he reached into his pocket, several guns were cocked and aimed at his face in a flash.

"I'm just giving you the keys to the wagon," said the soldier, his hand trembling as he handed the keys to Alkada.

"Well, I suppose you take a second and get ready to greet whoever you believe in," Alkada said, reholstering his gun.

Panic again gripped the soldier at hearing those words.

"Wait, I told you what you wanted to know. You said you would let me live!" pleaded the soldier, bringing his hands together as if praying while tearing up at the thought of death coming for him.

Grinning, Alkada looked down at the soldier.

"And I am a man of my given word. I ain't gonna kill you, and I'm going to let you go. It's my scrap you needs be worried about," said Alkada, nodding toward London.

London looked at Alkada puzzled until StreetLife stepped forward and said, "Aye, bruh, ain't no vegans in this crowd. So, I reckons now's the time for us all to *see* you eat food."

"Or be food!" added HardBody, cocking both his guns, followed by A1 as they all looked at London.

"But why ya doing this?" the soldier asked, looking from face to face, hoping to find sympathy or pity in one. "The man in this wagon is a killer and wanted man."

Alkada spun and snickered at the soldier.

"You say he's a wanted man, but every Shyne is wanted—whether man, woman, or child—by your Republic just for being born. And you soldiers are fools and tools the Republic uses to its end until you are rendered useless. So, it should be no wonder to you how you now find yourself on your knees with Shynes deciding what to do with your life. Whatever that man's done to be wanted is his business. No man on earth is without sin or secret. My salts with him are soldier to soldier, but my salts with the law are forever and more," Alkada preached, then stepped aside to clear the pathway for London.

The man immediately turned on his knees, his hands still clasped.

"Please don't," started the soldier as London approached him and raised his gun.

Blam! Blam! Blam!

London fired three shots into his face, folding him backward.

StreetLife, Alkada, and HardBody all nodded in approval. Thus, London ascended in their eyes and was no longer a vegan.

London looked at them all in turn, knowing now he was accepted, at least to some degree. He also knew had he not risen to the occasion, he would now be dead.

"Raaaaawk," Skully shrieked overhead.

Alkada immediately reached out with connection and

awareness. After Skully alerted him to what he saw, Alkada severed the connection.

"Riders coming from the east. Let's get on with this," he said as they all approached the wagon.

Once Alkada unlocked the door and pulled it open, Swindle stepped in the doorway. He'd heard enough to know it was over. His hands were clamped in wrist irons with a chain leading down to his feet and shackles around his ankles.

Alkada looked to StreetLife.

"He's one of them," StreetLife said, reflecting on the night in Keystone.

Alkada nodded, then looked back to Swindle.

"It's time to pay the bills, son," Alkada said, looking at the kid who wasn't much older than A1 or London.

Upon seeing Alkada and HardBody's scarred faces along with three pairs of other eyes that wanted him dead, reality set in on Swindle. He looked up at the setting sun, knowing it would be his last. Then he took a deep breath and stepped down from the wagon.

Alkada spoke, knowing full well what was on Swindle's mind. He d seen this look many times before.

"That's right, kid. We're Shynes, and we're here to collect your head. Seems you and NoLove killed one of my bros back in Keystone, and we just can't let that slide," Alkada told him.

Swindle shrugged his shoulders and uttered two words: "Mob shit."

"Man, fuck all that," A1 said, stepping to the forefront, raising his gun, and firing.

Blam! Blam! Blam! Blam!

He fired the shots directly into Swindle's chest, point-blank range. The impact blew him back against the wagon. Startled, the horses bucked up and pulled the wagon forward a few feet, causing Swindle's body to fall to the side. A1 then kicked him on his back and, while standing over his body, fired a fifth and final shot into him.

"Ain't nothing to talk about. Dudes killed my pops," A1 stated as he quickly knelt to claim his prize. Holstering his gun and unsheathing his knife, he pointed to London and said, "Hold his body straight while I cut his fucking head off."

A1 placed his left palm on Swindle's forehead, and with his right hand, he began sawing his head off. The sharp serrated edges of the knife were designed for such grizzly work—cutting through flesh and cartilage. The sound of bone cracking and crunching could be heard as steel bit into it. Blood began to slick his hand and blade, causing London to gasp at the scene.

"What you doin'? Hold him straight," A1 stammered to London as he continued to cut.

HardBody looked down on the two, smiling as he remembered the first time he took a man's head while Alkada stood over him. Even Alkada watched A1, reminiscing the first time he had taken a man's head as HardBody's father watched over his shoulder. This was tradition. They were Shynes, and this act was regarded as proof of Shynes showing how it never ends.

StreetLife took it all in, then looked at Alkada and HardBody, shaking his head in disbelief and remembering the note Alkada's daughter had written him.

"Bruh, y'all some sick muthafuckas!" he said and started for his horse.

"Don't forget that ring," said HardBody, pointing to the diamond ring still on Swindle's hand. "I reckons it will make a nice little keepsake."

"Already," A1 responded.

Finally done, A1 picked up the severed head and dropped it in his sack. He then pulled the ring from Swindle's hand and dropped it in his pocket.

"Where to now?" StreetLife asked after they saddled up.

"West," said London. "The men we seek are headed west."

"You heard the man. We head west to collect the rest of the heads owed to us, and I reckons we got a meeting to attend, as well," Alkada finished, choking up on the reins of his horse and leading out, leaving the mutilated bodies as a testament to their actions.

Chapter Nineteen

General Lynch entered the office of Marshall Stryfe to find him reading a telegraph that he folded upon the general's arrival.

"Commander, you wanted to see me?" asked the general as he stood before Marshall Stryfe.

"Yes, General, at ease and have a seat," Stryfe responded as he studied the general.

Marshall Stryfe knew there was a spy among them, but he couldn't pinpoint who it was just yet. Nonetheless, he proceeded with caution.

"General, have you debriefed the soldier who has returned from Baron Black's compound?"

"Yes, sir."

"And your report?" pressed Stryfe.

"Well, Commander, it's pretty much what we already suspected. All our scouts were captured and tortured to death at the hands of Baron Black himself, and the message is clear that he will suffer no further encroachment into his lands."

"His lands?" interrupted Stryfe, raising a questioning eyebrow to the general.

"Forgive me, sir. I meant the Barren Plains. And as we have surmised, he has pretty much secured and fortified most of the lands around him either by force or finesse."

"And you say this to say what, General?"

"That more of the native people of the Plains are with him than against him, and those who are not with him are not with us," said the general.

"And our conundrum being, in your opinion, that a full-frontal assault, as Captain Hammer suggests, would be ill-advised?" asked Stryfe.

General Lynch momentarily hated Captain Hammer for putting this thought in Marshall Stryfe's head because he now seemed ensnared by this asinine idea.

"Again, sir," the general responded, "I want you to be aware that it will be a very costly and engaging undertaking. We would need supply routes for our soldiers to sustain a prolonged campaign throughout the harsh winters of the Barren Plains. Mind you, those supply routes would have to go through lands Baron Black has under his partial, if not total, control. We would be constantly attacked, and vital resources and munitions would fall into Baron Black's hands. In all reality, sir, we need an ally in the Barren Plains and preferably one at Baron Black's back."

"Well, I guess we'll have to find one because I will not sit here in the Civilized Republic knowing everything south of us lives by the rule of anarchy."

"Has there been any word from Captain Hammer?" asked Lynch, attempting to deflect.

"None worth mentioning," answered Stryfe with a wave of

his hand, making it clear there would be no more questions on that particular matter. "Now, as for this soldier, do you believe all he has told you to be true?" asked Stryfe, intentionally controlling the flow of the meeting.

"Yes, I could see no reason for him to lie, and given what we know of Baron Black, I would expect no less," answered the general.

"Duly noted, General, and you may well be right. However, if you're wrong, having now been in the clutches of Baron Black, it's no telling if this soldier may now be a sympathizer to his cause. We can't take a chance of him spreading this sympathy among the ranks and undermining the morale of our soldiers with his experience at the hands of the enemy that he may now view as a victim. You know the saying: *One bad apple.* Nonetheless, have the soldier put to the testing of truth, then quietly execute him and dispose of the body."

The general was a bit taken aback by the orders he had just been given, but at the same time, he knew they would be carried out. Marshall Stryfe had not become the leader of the Republic by being timid or second-guessing himself. Besides that, General Lynch was for the Republic at all costs.

Not one to miss any detail, Marshall Stryfe took in the general's reaction and unspoken meaning behind it—now confident the general was not a spy.

"General, I gather you may be distressed by my orders. Well, you needn't be. We—and by that, I mean you, me, and Captain Hammer—are building a nation of greatness, and as long as everybody plays their part, we can't be torn apart. Issues such as antagonism or dissension have no place in our building plans. Do you understand me, General?"

"Yes, sir!" General Lynch responded firmly.

"Good. General, you know like I do, you must break a few eggs to make an omelet. Unfortunately, sometimes, the eggs to be broken are our own. Good day, General. You have your orders."

With this, the general stood up, saluted, and left. When the general was gone, Stryfe again read the last telegraph he received from Captain Hammer.

I'VE PURSUED MY QUARRY INTO THE BARREN CANYONS BUT AM UNABLE TO PROCEED WITHOUT REINFORCEMENTS. GATHERED INTEL. SAYS BIG MEETING TAKING PLACE AT FREEDOM COMPOUND. REPORTS SAY FOREMOST SHOT CALLERS TO BE IN ATTENDANCE. HAIL THE REPUBLIC.!

— CAPTAIN HAMMER

Marshall Stryfe digested the message, his thoughts racing. He would not be deterred. He would have his omelet no matter how many eggs had to be broken. The dogs were being called to gather, but he didn't care.

By the time I'm done, the dogs will be groveling at my feet, Stryfe thought to himself.

"Mr. Happy," he barked from his desk, and in a moment, Mr. Happy stepped into the office, eager to do his master's bidding.

"I have an urgent message of the utmost importance I need you to send."

"Yes, of course, sir," answered Mr. Happy, oblivious of the spider's web he was about to step in.

***

234

CAPTAIN HAMMER, IN ACCORDANCE WITH YOUR LAST REQUEST, REINFORCEMENTS HAVE BEEN SENT. PROCEED WITH CAUTION AND AT YOUR DISCRETION. ASCERTAIN PURPOSE OF MEETING AND "ALL" WHO ATTEND. CAPTURE WHO YOU CAN FOR THE TESTING OF TRUTH. I AWAIT OUR FACE-TO-FACE. HAIL THE REPUBLIC!

— M. STRYFE

Captain Hammer read the telegraph, knowing Stryfe realized a spy was amongst them. Sooner or later, he would be caught, and by hell, his flesh would burn. But he was on assignment right now. A lot was going on in the Barren Plains, but he dared not venture beyond the Barren Canyons with such a paltry force of soldiers, for they would surely be swallowed up to the last man by Baron Black's men if they got too close with too little.

Nonetheless, he needed to know what was going on. There were sightings and whispers of El Chablo, Diablo Vasa, that pig Fat Pockets, the Diamond King Alexander Wolfgang, and his now-infamous daughter in league with the very men he was chasing—all headed into the Barren Plains.

***

These are some of the most nefarious characters around... and all are meeting at the same location. Why is that? There's something major going down—no doubt about that—and the script is being written before my very eyes, thought Drake.

Things were shaping up, and Drake needed to know with whom he would ultimately align himself. The promise of

Keystone meant nothing if he weren't alive to take hold of it. So many players, so many possibilities. Marshall Stryfe offered civilization, but a civilization of his own design and direction—in earnest, a civilized dictator.

How foolish, he thought. *How long before the civilized totalitarian conformed to a total despot?*

Drake was certain Marshall Stryfe feared Baron Black, and the fact that Drake had been hired to assassinate him was proof of that.

But for all Baron Black's talk of freedom and democracy, what if he is merely the opposite side of the same coin yet to be flipped over? One thing's for sure: I won't find the answers closeted among the rocks and cliffs of the Barren Canyons, Drake thought, letting his inner monologue reign free.

"Captain Hammer!" called Drake as he approached the captain standing on a ridge, pulling his horse behind him.

"Yes, what is it?" asked the captain as he turned to face Drake, irritated that his thoughts were disturbed by this dandy.

"It is time for me to take my leave," said Drake as he pulled his saddle tight again.

"What do you mean?" pressed Hammer. "Are you not with the Republic?"

"Dear Captain, how can you ask such a question? Am I not here scuttled among the rocks with the Republic? Have I not brought you the scent of the men you now hunt with information I gave the Republic? But I digress," said Drake, grinning as he tilted his head to one side. "Captain Hammer, let me answer your question with perfect clarity. While you may trust that my actions surely merit that I work with the Republic, unlike you, I do not work for the Republic. Events are unfolding in the Barren Plains."

Drake paused and pointed his finger to the distant mountains. "And the elements being placed in the cauldron imply that a dish most sinister is being prepared. Captain Hammer, I am of a mind most curious with many questions, and Freedom Compound has the answers."

"Well, how do you know you won't be shot dead as a Republic spy?" asked Hammer, staring daggers at Drake with his one good eye.

Drake flashed his wolfish grin as he leaped on his horse and looked down at the captain, preparing to ride out in the direction of the setting sun.

"Well, Captain, I guess my being marked for a spy is dependent on the fact of one determining if it can actually be determined whom I'm spying for." Drake slapped the reins on his horse's behind, causing him to jump into a gallop. "Yah! Yah! Hail the Republic!" Drake shouted as he began to laugh while riding away.

Captain Hammer looked at Drake, hearing the cross in his laughter and knowing exactly where his loyalties lie.

***

UNSURE WHAT HAS TAKEN PLACE, BUT A BATTALION OF REPUBLIC SOLDIERS ARE EN ROUTE TO BARREN CANYONS AT THE REQUEST OF CAPTAIN HAMMER. YOU HAVE BEEN WARNED.

Foot finished reading the message, crumbled it up, and threw it into the street. Based on the last message he received, he was now sure the Republic was on to the Mob. But for all the talk in the streets, he was equally sure his brothers had gotten away, or at least some of them. The latest copy of *Republic Speaks* assured him of that, stating, *Another Massacre in Shameless. Bandits are still on the loose. Three major slayings in as many weeks. When will it end?*

Foot smiled to himself, thinking back on the article. *When will it end?* As far as he and his brothers were concerned, the Mob was just beginning.

The dots, however, were being connected. Then again, he thought of another description in the article: *Baron Black, the Shynes, Diablo Vasa, and the Mob. Murder and anarchy on the Plains. People in fear of the return of the "Death Sagas."*

The Mob had arrived and—as expected—was being felt by way of the gun. The plan was never to remain in the shadows but rather to establish a seat at the table with the big dawgs. These events were only the catalysts of their ultimate introduction to the world stage, and the meeting at Freedom Compound would dictate exactly how they were to be received by the world.

He would've preferred to have been at the meeting himself. However, the business at hand was of equal importance, if not more so. Besides, he was sure NoLove would put it down the Mob way. In the meantime, he would handle his end.

He'd just given the Weasel a *hellafied* meal ticket, and he expected it would be money well spent. Big moves didn't come cheap, and this was a whopper. But no guts, no glory.

Foot had a few errands to tend to, and since he had a little downtime while he awaited confirmation from the Weasel, he would get the minor issues out of the way. He'd head for the Bluff as soon as he got word back from the Weasel. By now, bros were sure to have gotten the word that it was time to build.

It was early afternoon, and the city streets were crowded. He stopped at numerous stands, buying books, tobacco, coffee, and such. When he got everything he needed, he proceeded to have it boxed up and sent.

It would take a while to get to its final destination, but it would be greatly appreciated when it finally arrived.

***

With a briefcase full of freshly minted currency and a mission, Simon Thorn, aka The Weasel, had just arrived in Independence by train, which was a method of transportation he truly hated. But money was a great motivator for getting one to do what one didn't like, and if he pulled this lick off, he could sit pretty for a minute.

It occurred to him that it had been a minute since he'd been to Independence, a massive citadel of buildings, great grey-white, constructed representations of the Civilized Republic. There were buildings of colossal designs and modern architecture where all major decisions regarding the Civilized Republic were made. These decisions involved the value and interest on currency, the law and social mandates of the Republic, and all legal implementations to be respected south of Independence— although the influence seldom crossed the borders of the Republic into the Plains or beyond.

Baron Black and a host of other characters made sure of that, thought the Weasel as he approached the Building of Judgement, a squarish four-story building of grandeur where the fates of many men were decided—if they weren't outright shot first or hung in whatever country, town, or hamlet they committed the transgression that would've brought them there.

Truth be told, Republic law only mattered in the Republic. Most other places applied their own line of justice, and it was this judicial freedom among the Plains that Marshall Stryfe also wanted to bring to an end. The Weasel had done a lot of wheeling and dealing in this building. He had saved a lot of men from the dreaded Fort prison, swapped out others that couldn't pay, and bargained countless deals for those that could afford it.

There were several judges there, and the Weasel knew them all; he even nurtured a friendship with a few. Unfortunately, the judge he was there to see was not one of the few. Judge Grimlock was a well-respected Senior Judge of Independence, the lone wolf of these hallowed halls. He was known to condemn prisoners in only two ways: the ever-popular Worm for those sentenced to death or life in The Fort. Without a doubt, he was the lord of this tribunal, and it was whispered that the strings attached to the backs of all the other judges were tied to his fingers. Judge Grimlock was among one of the most powerful men in the Civilized Republic, to be compared only to the likes of Marshall Stryfe and General Lynch. He was a fixture in Independence from its founding, even before the rising of the draconian upstart Stryfe.

And if the surreptitious murmurs the Weasel heard were true, Grimlock had eyes on Stryfe's back. Just the fact that this meeting was taking place was a clear indication that if they were true, the judge was now filling his coffers to take his shot.

The Weasel entered the building, walking until he reached a large antechamber where massive portraits of the men who founded and solidified Independence hung on the walls of the circular area. He noticed a beautiful woman of foreign descent seated at a large desk before him, and he recalled rumors about

Grimlock's taste for young women.

I guess a man well into his seventies still likes getting good head from young ladies every now and again, he thought humorously.

As if reading his thoughts, the secretary rose with a smile that confirmed the judge had her there for more than her clerical skills.

"Simon Thorn, I presume?" she asked as she stepped from behind her desk to greet him, extending her hand to shake his.

He met her handshake instantly, turning it over and bringing the back of her hand to his lips. Now holding her delicate fingers, he kissed her hand, taking in her amazing body as he bowed.

"Yes, love, I'm Simon Thorn. Very pleased to meet you," he responded. "And what might your name be?"

Before she could respond, the enormous doors of Judge Grimlock's office boomed open.

"Who she is, is of no importance to you, Mr. Thorn," Judge Grimlock said sternly with the voice of an old lion.

He stood in the doorway of his double-doored office, his immense frame filling the entrance. His salt and pepper hair matched his beard, all well-trimmed and cut. He still looked to be very fit and spry—standing there stoic and poised, every bit of what the Weasel remembered of the most prominent and pronounced judge in the Civilized Republic.

"I believe you came to see me and not fantasize about how good my secretary can suck a dick, which given the way you were lusting over her, surely must've been one of your initial thoughts," said the judge, his voice now magnetic and pressing, before turning into his office and vanishing from the entrance of the doorway just as quickly as he appeared.

Simon Thorn and the secretary looked at each other,

momentarily taken aback before quickly recomposing themselves. The secretary swiftly took his arm and ushered him into the judge's chambers.

When both were in the office, the secretary called out to the judge, "Grim, do you need anything?"

"Just privacy," he answered back over his shoulder, staring out the window of his chambers, appreciating the view of Independence from his window.

Books of law filled his shelves, portraits of important dead people hung on the walls, and numerous trophy heads of animals he had hunted were perched in different corners of the room. It was a display intended to clarify that Judge Grimlock was as much an outdoorsman as he was a lawman.

"Simon Thorn, in light of all that is going on, I trust your trip here was uneventful?" asked Grimlock, still looking out of his window.

"Yes, sir," answered the Weasel, still standing at the doors of the judge's chambers.

"Join me, Simon. I'd like to show you something," said Grimlock, gesturing to Simon with a raised hand and pull of his fingers.

The Weasel walked over, briefcase still in hand, and joined the judge at the window. This was a lot different than approaching the bench in Grimlock's courtroom. However, the judge still gave off an air of eminence. Grimlock looked at the Weasel tentatively and sized him up—a routine check that he tended to perform before conducting business with anyone on this level. Satisfied with his gut feeling, he pointed to an oak tree in the park.

"Simon, you see that tree right there?"

"Yes, sir."

"Well, as a boy, I remember when it was only shrubbery, but even then, I knew it would one day be the grand tree you now see before you." He next pointed toward the citadel of buildings off to the right and asked, "You see that square there?"

"Yes, sir," repeated the Weasel.

"Well, I remember it was merely a whistle-stop, but even then, I knew it would be the metropolis we now call Independence. Now, look out there."

The judge directed Simon's attention to the distant mountains south that bordered the Barren Plains.

"Mr. Thorn, there is a great change coming here from there that will affect us all, and I'd advise you to be on the right side of that change. Because mark my words, all those who are on the wrong side of it are not going to last long in this world," said Grimlock, staring Simon Thorn directly in the eyes before he went back to looking out of the window, letting the implications of what he just said take root in the Weasel's mind.

"Now, leave your briefcase on my desk. As to what you request, it will be done by month's end. I'll be in contact with you on the specifics. Go back to Noble Haven and prepare yourself. I feel a change may be coming there sooner than you think, as well. And please send my secretary in on your way out," the judge said, waving the Weasel off.

And just like that, the Weasel placed the briefcase on his desk, handing over 4.5 million dollars with little more than an utterance of *It will be done*, he thought as he proceeded to the door.

As he reached for the doorknob, Judge Grimlock called out to him, stopping him mid-step.

"Mr. Thorn, if you so much as whisper this meeting's occurrence or its undertakings to anyone, I will have you murdered, and your lovely home in Noble Haven burned to the ground with your pretty wife and beautiful twin daughters still inside it. Do you understand me, Mr. Thorn?"

"Yes, sir," answered the Weasel, feeling a wave of anger wash over him at the threat to his life and his family.

The judge, anticipating the impact of his words, went on with his warning and reasoning.

"Excellent, Mr. Thorn, because I'm a man of my word, and once my word is given, I mean business. And it *is* business and *never* personal. Good day, Mr. Thorn," ended the judge as he went back to surveying the landscape.

***

Simon Thorn left the Building of Judgement, and for the first time in a while, the Weasel knew what it was like to be under the wolf's paw. He just forked over a major meal ticket, but he was being paid well to do it. That thought brought a smile to his face and a good feeling to his heart as he walked to the telegraph station.

***

Foot had just entered the lobby of the Plaza when he was hailed down by the desk clerk and handed a message.

DONE! REQUEST TO BE GRANTED! SPECIFICS TO FOLLOW SHORTLY! KEEP ME ABREAST OF YOUR WHEREABOUTS!

— S. THORN, AKA THE WEASEL

Foot read the telegraph and smiled. *There are levels to this shit, and I've reached one of the highest,* he thought proudly. Now, he could head to the Bluff and start getting things in order. The bag he had just passed was heavy. But in the Mob, it was love over lust always, and what he did had to be done. Besides, he had just paid for something that was priceless. The irony of that thought made him chuckle, forgetting he was standing at the desk.

"Is everything all right?" asked the desk clerk.

Foot snapped out of his reverie, looking dumbly at the clerk.

"Yeah, yeah…I'm fine. Um, everything is fine, but it just got better. I'll be checking out in the morning, heading for the Bluff. See to it that horses, a carriage, and a driver are waiting for me," he said, then tossed the desk clerk a gold coin equivalent to ten dollars and headed to his room.

The desk clerk caught the coin, brought it to his mouth, and bit down on it.

Satisfied it was real, he shoved it in his pocket and answered, "Yes, sir," to Foot's back.

Chapter Twenty

Freedom Compound was a monumental establishment of modern engineering. Part fortress, part garrison. A miniature citadel and all stronghold, with a grandeur that couldn't be described—only experienced. There were gardens, crops, and lush plantations with irrigation. Barracks, stables, as well as water conduits for sewage and drainage, villas with verandas, and a winery with a robust vineyard that stretched for miles. The grounds were immaculate, and there were people everywhere going and coming. Soldiers unified in their movement marched with purpose. But what was most obvious was that this was a way of life that the people of Freedom Compound were willing to fight, kill, and die for.

Fat Pockets took note of all this as his carriage rolled downhill, stopping at what appeared to be an entryway into the compound. As far as first impressions went, he was impressed. Freedom Compound displayed a flare of modernism that rivaled Keystone. Yet, Fat Pockets was not one to be swayed by first impressions—he would have to know what lay beneath the surface.

When the carriage came to a halt, Fat Pockets pointed at Nancy and then to the door handle.

Nancy immediately reached over and opened the carriage door, making way for Fat Pockets to step out.

"Mr. Fat Pockets of Keystone, I presume?" Captain BB said as he stepped forward, extending his hand to greet Fat Pockets, who struggled to climb down from the carriage. "I see the name fits the man!" he added, commenting on Fat Pockets' wide girth as he finally got down from the carriage.

Not appreciating the slick mouth comment or the snickering soldiers who chuckled in response, Fat Pockets went on the offensive.

"Yeah, I'm Fat Pockets, the big boss from back East," he replied, holding his hand over his eyes and squinting under the sun's scorching glare. "My luggage is in the back, boy."

Captain BB turned red at the slight, knowing his uniform obviously marked his standing. But he immediately regained his composure.

"Fat Pockets, I am not the luggage boy. I am the captain of the Barren Brigade, Captain BB, and son of our beloved leader, Baron Black…here to welcome you to Freedom Compound."

Unphased by the man's bravado, Fat Pockets proceeded to take him out.

"So, I guess it's *your daddy* that I'm here to see!" he responded with a big grin.

Nancy stepped out of the carriage at that moment, breaking the tension and completely stealing away Captain BB's attention.

"Ah, such a beautiful woman," Captain BB whispered, reaching for Nancy's hand to help her take her last step to the ground. "And what might your name be, my dear?"

He kissed the back of her hand in a true display of chivalry that made Nancy blush.

Fat Pockets smiled slyly and said, "Now, hold on there, BB."

He looked at Nancy and then pointed to the ground, signaling her to cast her gaze to her feet.

"You showin' this hoe way more respect than she deserves to know. Now be glad you kissed her hand and not her mouth, or you'd know what half the dicks in Keystone taste like because this here is Nasty Nancy—nothing at all fancy."

Fat Pockets raised his voice further for all the soldiers clustered around Captain BB to hear.

"See, back East, we call her Miracle Mouth, and if you play your cards right, I might let you try her out and have a miracle performed on you," Fat Pockets teased as he winked at Captain BB. "That's right! Fat Pockets is in the building. Now, where are we putting up at? I'd like to get myself together before I meet your daddy."

Nancy's gaze was locked on the ground—her beet-red complexion and silence a sign that all Fat Pockets said was true.

Captain BB returned his attention to Fat Pockets, his envy apparent that such a beautiful woman was enthralled by such a swine of a man. Yet, despite the bitter introductions, Captain BB would follow protocol and treat Fat Pockets as the guest he was.

"Of course, Fat Pockets, let me have you shown to your quarters. All the other guests should be arriving today, as well. You will be sequestered in your rooms until tonight's gathering when my father will receive you. And lastly, I must relieve you of any weapons you may be carrying while you are here. When you leave, they will be returned to you. In the meantime, rest assured that our guns will protect you from any danger, and you will have runners at your behest should you need anything. Until we meet again, please enjoy our accommodations."

With that, Fat Pockets was led to his quarters with Nancy in tow, her eyes never leaving the ground in front of her, and Captain BB's eyes never leaving her.

***

Alexander Wolfgang was next to arrive with no such fanfare—a simple carriage and rider. Much to his dismay, he was relieved of his weapons and told he would meet with Baron Black at the night's gathering like everyone else. Upon arrival, he was amazed to see such modernization this deep in the Barren Plains; it went against Wolfgang's expectations of Baron Black.

It was apparent Baron Black was assertive, disciplined, and calculating in commanding such a metropolis. Certain parts of Freedom Compound even reminded Alexander of Noble Haven.

One thing was made clear to Wolfgang: Baron Black would surely know where his daughter was with all this power at his disposal.

***

Diablo and Elvira Vasa arrived next. The two raced into Freedom Compound on two mustangs, looking more like brother and sister than father and daughter. They knew these lands well, and if anybody could move around the Barren Plains undetected, it was them.

In fact, Diablo Vasa's land was the only chink in the armor of

Baron Black. An array of caves, caverns, and mountain passages led into the Barren Plains from Diablo's lands that neither Captain BB nor his father could locate. However, mutual respect between Diablo Vasa and Baron Black—born from the Death Sagas—made the hidden routes a minor mention.

"Captain BB, how are you?" asked Diablo as he brought his mighty black mustang to an abrupt stop right before the captain, causing him to pivot out of the way.

Diablo jumped off his horse, handed the reins to a soldier, and approached Captain BB for a soldier's embrace, patting the man on the back.

"I am well, Diablo."

Diablo took a step back, maintaining his grasp on the younger man's shoulders, and admired him like he was the son he always wanted.

"I see you are taking care of yourself, Diablo!" said Captain BB, looking at the older yet robust and energetic man with mutual admiration.

"Ah, it's the mountains, my son. I age as they do, and I see you've grown in height and rank. How's your father?"

"He's well. He'll receive you tonight."

Just then, Elvira pulled up on a horse as grand as her father's, and she carried all the attitude that Captain BB remembered her to have.

"Father, why must you always cheat?" she spat as she pulled her horse to a stop, brushing several of the soldiers aside as she did so.

Her shirt and britches clung to her sweaty body as she swung a leg over the saddle and leaped from the horse in one smooth motion. She looked as sexy as she was deadly.

"Dear daughter, I did not cheat at anything. On the contrary, I gave you the faster horse. It's not my fault he isn't the smartest," laughed Diablo as he winked at Captain BB.

"Whatever, Papa! You knew he had no water and would stop at the first brook he saw," Elvira whined, waving a dismissive hand at her father. Then she approached Captain BB and hugged him as one would a cousin. "My Lil BB, you've grown so much shorter since the last time I saw you!"

Several soldiers began to laugh at the joke, triggering Diablo.

"Elvira!" Diablo snapped. "That is a captain you are speaking to. Show some respect."

"Psst, whatever, Papa," Elvira countered, placing an arm around Captain BB's shoulder. "As long as he is shorter than me, he will always be Lil BB to me."

Her comment prompted more laughter.

"Now, where are we staying? I wish to bathe and have a masseuse and a bottle of chilled wine sent to me immediately."

She unbuttoned her shirt, peeled it off her sweaty skin, and threw it at the face of a soldier who was ogling her. She then grabbed her hair and began to wring it free of sweat as she stood there topless, baring her beautiful, naked breasts for all to see. She walked off, leaving everyone to stare at her back in amazement.

"You will be shown to your quarters," said Captain BB to Diablo as he continued to stare at the brazen woman.

Diablo Vasa stepped forward and snapped his fingers at the captain's ear.

"Captain! Focus. And remember, no matter how beautiful a snake is, it is still a snake," said Diablo as he smiled, nodding to his daughter.

"Yes, of course," responded Captain BB, shaking his head

and snapping back to the moment. "The gathering is tonight. I must relieve you of your weapons, however, while you are here."

Diablo Vasa burst out laughing before placing a hand on the captain's shoulder. "Captain BB, surely you of all people know that this deep in the Plains, my daughter nor I have need of weapons. Our names are weapons enough."

Captain BB nodded and smiled at Diablo Vasa's words. He liked and respected Diablo like an uncle. He reminded him of his father, but where Diablo showed finesse and respect, his daughter was the direct opposite: rude, brash, and facetious. Their rivalry stemmed from childhood, yet Elvira made it apparent that it still carried on.

El Chablo was next to arrive with a small contingent of soldiers. He was allowed to keep two as his personal guards with him; the rest of his troop would be quartered in the garrison along with the Barren Brigade. Naturally, they bristled when told to hand over their weapons, but El Chablo quickly brought his men into compliance with the orders of Captain BB.

This was a meeting of peace. There was no need to rock the boat, at least not until they knew what was in the water—and they would know that by nightfall. Until then, El Chablo was content to go with the flow.

***

NoLove and his crew brought their horses to rest atop a hill, from where they could view Freedom Compound below. For the past few days, they rode non-stop, putting distance between them and Shameless. The Republic had been running them down initially but fell back when the Mob got too deep off in the Plains.

Days had passed since any of them had spoken, although the obvious question wearing on all their minds was: *What happened to Swindle?*

Before making his descent down into Freedom Compound, NoLove emerged from a throng of shaded trees to approach TwoFace with Goon at his side while Bianca watched them.

"Bruh, I reckons you're still mad about us leaving Swindle, and I get that, but it was my choice. I made the call, not Goon nor the dame. So, if you're salting about it, that salt is with me."

TwoFace stared at NoLove blankly.

"Nah, bruh, ain't no salt between us. The call you made was the right one, but that doesn't mean I have to like it," TwoFace admitted.

"Be sure, bruh…because we 'bout to enter this compound for this meeting, and we are gonna do it as brothers or not at all."

"We good, bro. Mob shit this way," TwoFace said.

"Mob shit," NoLove and Goon responded simultaneously.

NoLove then nodded to Goon, and Goon handed TwoFace's guns and gun belt back to him.

TwoFace checked his guns and let out a satisfied grunt. He wrapped his gun belt around his waist and fastened the cross clutch, dropping his weapons into the holsters. He looked back at Goon and NoLove, and in one fluid motion, he drew both guns and planted one apiece on their foreheads.

Bianca leaped forward but was stopped by a hand gesture from NoLove, who knew she would be dead in an instant if TwoFace wanted. TwoFace didn't waver an inch, directing his attention to NoLove first.

"Bruh, from this point on, we all get away or die together. You got that?"

NoLove nodded in agreement.

TwoFace turned to Goon next. "Bruh, I love you, but if you ever put your hands on me again, you die for it. Dig me?"

Goon also nodded in agreement. Then just as quickly as the guns appeared, they disappeared back into the cross clutch.

"Good. Now that we have some clarity, let's go down to Freedom Compound and introduce ourselves," TwoFace announced.

With that, they all saddled up and headed down to Freedom Compound, totally unaware of the eagle that flew overhead.

***

Alkada and his men rode hard and adamantly, circumventing Captain Hammer about two days back in the Barren Canyons. It took every ounce of discipline Alkada possessed not to confront Hammer and settle up on owed blood. However, catching up with NoLove and the Mob took precedence at the moment. *Shyne loyalty must be upheld*, he thought to himself when he made the decision. Besides, they were hot on their quarry's trail by not even a half day's ride behind.

Alkada reached out to Skully. Vexed by what he saw, he signaled for everybody to stop.

"They're already in Freedom Compound," Alkada announced.

"Are you sure? The trail is still fresh," countered StreetLife, pointing down at the newly made hoof marks on the ground.

"Yeah, I'm positive, and there's a lotta activity goin' on. People are movin' all about there. But I'm not sure how this is gonna play out if we gotta rock the bells."

"So, let's post up here and wait them out," StreetLife suggested.

"No, that's no good. Whatever has brought them here has brought many others from all around. I guess that meeting the soldier told us about is pretty big. So, I'm sure our arrival won't be a total surprise. Besides, waiting here may go from laying on three enemies to being greeted by a battalion, and having Republic soldiers at our backside don't sit proper with me. Not to mention, I don't believe Baron Black will take too kindly to us jus' kickin' grass so close to his compound. He and my father go way back, and that alone will warrant me payin' him the respect of a visit. And it's a good bet we're bein' watched right now."

"Rahhhhh," Skully screamed overhead, confirming Alkada's statement.

Alkada reached out to the bird with connection and awareness and saw that several sentries from Freedom Compound were watching them. A moment later, Alkada snapped out of the connection he harbored with the bird.

"Yeah, we're bein' watched. But, right now, it's just curiosity as to why we are clustered here talkin' without proceedin' to the compound. So many others have passed through here recently. We're just one of many, but it won't be much longer before mild curiosity turns to violent interest."

"Well, that definitely kills waitin' 'em out," reiterated StreetLife.

"Facts," agreed HardBody.

"Man, fuck all that!" A1 barked. "Those motherfuckers killed my father, and we up on this hill talking!"

Alkada instantly kicked his horse forward and grabbed A1 by the scruff of his collar.

"Who the fuck you think you talkin' to?!" Alkada's tone was acidic. Pulling A1 closer, he whispered into his ear, "You collect one fuckin' head, and you think you the big bad wolf? Scrap, that's my blood coursin' through veins that got your fangs showin' like that. HardBody and I were takin' heads when you were still swimmin' in your pop's nutsack. It was your father who stood over my shoulder when I took the head of the man who killed my father, the same way I'm here standing over yours. Now, check your emotions and get your mind right. I'm the captain of this ship. You're just on it!" Alkada said, then shoved A1 back into his saddle.

A1 was livid at being handled in such a way; his hand twitched like he wanted to reach.

"Say, kid, it's only feelin's," Hardbody said. "They'll go away, but if you reach for that gun, I'll water the grass with your brains."

A1 looked at HardBody and then back to Alkada, nodding acknowledgment of his mistake and understanding never to draw on a Shyne.

"Now, listen up. Follow my lead when we get down there. Keep your hammers on cock, but don't drop 'em unless I do. We gotta play this close to the chest. Streets and I will take NoLove. TwoFace is your dance, HardBody. A1 and London, y'all deal with the third. Once the killing starts, if anybody gets in your way, blow their top," Alkada ordered.

And with that, they set off for Freedom Compound to collect some heads.

Chapter Twenty-One

General Lynch sat in his office, contemplating the many events taking place, particularly the meeting in the Barren Plains.

Who called it? Who's attending it? What is its purpose? Surely, Captain Hammer is also seeking answers to these questions. And while he's a good captain, he doesn't think outside the box. He is, at best, a soldier and, at worst, a soldier, but always a soldier nonetheless. Yet, in war, one must be a soldier, tinker, tailor, and a spy. I am all these things, and this is war, thought Lynch.

He believed in Marshall Stryfe; he believed in the Republic. Baron Black needed to be eliminated—his followers locked up and scattered, his ideals forgotten, and his lands assimilated. Everybody must be brought to the conformity of the Republic. It should've happened long ago when Black Heart ruled the Republic, but luck favored the underdog. The Republic had the potential to be the most powerful force in the known world, despite beliefs of the contrary by those an ocean away. In due time, even they would be brought to heel. Yes, the Republic would reign, and they would not be thwarted by the defiance of a rebel or a rebel regime for that matter.

Yet, for all his ruminations, General Lynch had to admit—even if only to himself—that Baron Black was no fool and a very formidable adversary. Just how he fortified himself by using the lands around him spoke volumes of his strategic brilliance. He couldn't be attacked by sea nor from the rear, and a full-frontal assault would be costly, if not completely dire. Yet, Stryfe couldn't get his mind around these facts. But were Baron Black to be beaten, all the surrounding lands would topple right along with him, succumbing to the might of the Republic.

Diablo Vasa of the Sanchie, El Chablo in Benta, all the way down to Red Rock—filled with gun-toting fools engulfed in mystic beliefs of ritualism, loyalty, and honor. They were the ones who rose to the occasion during the Death Sagas and the ones who altered the outcome, tipping the scales in Baron Black's favor. But that was when Lynch was not the general. A lot had changed since then, and soon all would know the wrath of the Republic.

It was time to tighten up. Even in Independence, the whispers were beginning to take form that maybe there was a better way to unite the Plains without bloodshed. Undoubtedly, these whispers were orchestrated and spread by Judge Grimlock, who was still feeling the salts about Marshall Stryfe sitting behind the desk that he had his eyes on. Lynch would be sure to keep ears around Grimlock, for he was not a man to be taken lightly.

Knock, knock, knock.

"Who is it?" barked Lynch.

A soldier stepped into the office, saluted, and addressed the general.

"Sir, I bring urgent news from Shameless," said the soldier coming forward, extending his hand with the message.

"What news?" asked the general, getting to his feet.

"A telegraph received from the troop that went to reinforce Captain Hammer, sir," the soldier responded.

"What further calamity is there to be had after the fiasco in Shameless?" the general said, snatching the telegraph from the soldier's outstretched hand.

FOUR FOUND DEAD EN ROUTE TO SHAMELESS, THREE OF WHO WERE REPUBLIC SOLDIERS. ONE PRISONER A BELIEVED SUSPECT IN RECENT MASSACRES. HEADED TO INDEPENDENCE FOR TESTING OF TRUTH. SOLDIERS WERE SHOT DEAD. PRISONER HAD HIS HEAD SEVERED AND TAKEN!

— LT. LADUE

"Thank you, soldier. You're dismissed," said the general, nodding to the door.

After the soldier saluted and left, General Lynch sat back down and returned to the message, rereading it.

Head severed and taken? That had to be Shynes.

The general could care less about the prisoner—beyond whatever information could've been extracted by putting him to the testing of truth—but the murder of three Republic soldiers surely got his attention. Perhaps Red Rock would provide the back door the Republic needed; if the Shynes were involved, maybe the Republic work would be done for them.

Tinker, tailor, soldier, spy indeed, General Lynch thought as he smiled to himself.

***

Captain Hammer was in his tent when he was brought word of the arrival of his reinforcements. It was a contingent of thirty heavily armed infantry soldiers led by Lieutenant LaDue, an up-and-coming officer eager to make a name for himself fighting for the Republic. Hammer had heard the name before but never met the man—as was the case with most of the officers in the Republic Army.

Captain Hammer was a man of action and preferred to roam about the Plains, eager for war and forever hungry for blood, especially where Shynes were involved. He was always seeking blood back for his dead brothers and missing eye.

As Lieutenant LaDue and his troop entered the makeshift camp, he was immediately taken to Captain Hammer. Following protocol, a soldier entered the tent of Captain Hammer and announced the arrival of the lieutenant. Then he stepped back out, holding the tent flap open for the lieutenant to enter.

"Captain Hammer," said the lieutenant as he approached the captain's desk and saluted. "I've heard much about you, Captain, and I consider it an honor to serve alongside you. I was sent here by direct orders from Marshall Stryfe to aid and assist your campaign in any way deemed necessary."

Captain Hammer did not respond; he simply continued to study the man before him, creating an awkward silence between them.

"May I ask about our current situation, sir?" Lieutenant LaDue finally asked.

Captain Hammer pointed to the chair before his desk, indicating the lieutenant to have a seat. He then fixed his one-eye stare on the lieutenant and began to speak without preamble.

"Lieutenant LaDue, our situation is this. I just lost over half my troop in Shameless, tangling with the bandits responsible for the murders in Keystone and the train massacre in Reach Providence. And all I have to show for it is one prisoner taken alive who is now on his way to Independence for the testing of truth. The other four, including the Diamond Heiress, got away and are now in Freedom Compound for a meeting with the most notorious sons of bitches of all the lands. We chased them into the Barren Canyons, where you now sit before me. My orders are to ascertain the purpose of this meeting, figure out who is attending it, and capture whomever I can! I need to find out what the fuck is going on. And I also have my own agenda—to get blood back for my fallen soldiers, a sergeant, and a lieutenant among them. Our rules of engagement are simple; whoever we catch, we will torture for information and kill. There will be no quarter given, no mercy extended, and no more prisoners taken. Do you understand and comply with these rules, Lieutenant?" asked Captain Hammer, letting his hand fall away from the desk and down to the handle of the gun on his hip as he waited for the lieutenant to answer.

"Yes, Captain," the lieutenant immediately answered, knowing a non-affirmative response would most likely count him among the dead.

Captain Hammer was known to put men to death on the spot for what he perceived as cowardice or dereliction of duty. He intentionally paused for a moment and released his grasp on the gun.

"Good, Lieutenant. As it were, I want to push a little deeper into the Plains, but not too close. Just close enough that we can snatch somebody who attended the meeting and be in the know of what took place. We gotta be cautious. A force as small as ours can easily disappear here in the Barren Canyons. And make no mistake, Lieutenant, these are some of the meanest rattlers around. So, if cornered off, my only advice is to save a bullet for yourself, and should the time come, don't hesitate to eat it. Trust me, you do not want to fall into the hands of these enemies. No, you don't, because you will die a slow and painful death."

"Yes, sir. I gathered that much on my way here."

"What do you mean?" asked the captain, his eye alight with a new interest in the lieutenant.

"Well, coming here, we came down through the Southwestern trail, skimming the edge of Shameless, and we came across that prisoner you mentioned. He and his escort had been murdered, with the prisoner bearing the brunt of it, seeing how his head had been taken."

The captain was fully alert now, excitement and hatred apparent in his single eye. As he stood up, his palms plastered flat on the desk, he glared down at the lieutenant.

"Taken how?"

"Taken, like…cut off. Savagely severed, to be more exact."

"And what of the soldiers?"

"Single shots through the head. One soldier was shot at least three times point-blank range in the face."

"Shynes," whispered Captain Hammer into the open air before him, instantly recognizing the Shynes' grisly way of overkilling.

He reminisced on the Death Sagas, S.I.'s murder, discovering the lifeless bodies of his brothers on the streets as headless corpses. Many names floated around in his mind from that time long ago, but one fought to the forefront and stayed there: *Alkada.* Although a man lionized in myth and legend, Alkada was no myth to Captain Hammer. His missing eye was a testament to that. He swore revenge on Alkada and all Shynes, and now it seemed the time was at hand to make good on that revenge. The wolf had wandered out of his lair, and this time, the hunter would be ready.

"Captain? Captain, are you okay?"

The captain looked at the lieutenant like he had been awakened from a stupor.

"Yes, Lieutenant, of course! Yes, I'm okay. I'm a Hammer, and if you want to stay okay, I'd advise you to grow eyes on the back of your head so you don't end up like my last lieutenant. There are Shynes about, so have no doubt there will be blood in this affair, and it only flows two ways. You're either spilling it or giving it. Ain't no in-between to this one, son. So, let all the men know the game we're playing is death, and there are only two moves to make on the board—killing and dying. Now, prepare the men. We march within the hour," Captain Hammer barked with renewed vigor.

"Yes, Captain. And our general direction?" asked the lieutenant, standing up.

"West. Into the Barren Plains."

"Yes, sir," responded the lieutenant as he saluted and left. He'd heard of the Shynes before, and from what he heard, they were all known to be killers down to the last, but the fact that there was an open decree to kill any Shyne on sight meant they very seldom were seen out of Red Rock.

Avery Brown

What brought them back out into the open now?

The question spun around in Captain Hammer's mind as he sat back down, now lost in the history of his memories—the days of the Death Sagas, as they were called. It appeared the good ole days, the buckets of blood days were coming back. And Captain Hammer couldn't wait.

***

The sun was starting to set over The Fort prison. Located in the high north of the Republic, it was the biggest prison known to exist, housing over five thousand inmates with no one exempt over the other—whether they were there for murder, rape, bank robbery, cattle rustling, or grave robbing. The crime didn't matter in The Fort. Only the heart of the inmate did.

Thus, The Fort remained a place of ultra-violence where only the strong survived, and "rats" didn't survive at all, often killed within twenty-four hours of their arrival.

The Fort was a miniature city surrounded by four high grey walls. The only view consisted of the sun and clouds in the sky during the day and the moon and stars at night—and, of course, the sharpshooters who were ready to kill any man who tried to scale the outer walls. Many tried, and many died. The Fort had stood for over seventy years, and to date, nobody had ever escaped, except for one man—and that man didn't go over the wall.

This prison was a world unto itself, a real chain gang. The guards who worked there let the chain gang run itself because the rules were very simple: survival of the fittest. Only the fittest survived and thrived, and those who could not became the

266

minions or sexual slaves of those that could. And in this world, everything was for sale, giving rise to an economy and social dynamic of its own.

Everything from extra food portions to clothes, weapons, and protection was bought and sold. Even a man's flesh and mouth had value; every man had something to trade. But men who bartered their bodies were frowned upon and referred to as lady-boys or lizards—barely above the title of a rat and right below that of a do-boy. Nonetheless, they had their place on the totem pole and were a part of the fabric that made this world go 'round.

The next rung up were the hustlers, transporters, and gatherers—the inmates who could get their hands on whatever one needed, be it contraband or necessities. They moved freely around The Fort and delivered their goods.

Above them were the playmakers and the hit-'em-up kids. Playmakers were usually those individuals who managed to hold onto enough money from their crimes and convince guards to smuggle in contraband, such as drugs, weapons, and free world food. The hit-'em-up kids were knife-wielding killers often paid to make sure everybody else paid what they owed, whether in money or blood.

All in all, it was a lucrative market for all parties involved, and in a prison housing over five thousand inmates, the market was booming in the general population. But at the top of the totem pole, you had the worst of the worst—the men labeled threats to the general population, too dangerous to be allowed around other inmates or even have cellies. These were the men who could have another man killed simply by "flying a kite"—a name written on a piece of paper and sent out to the general population to exterminate the inmate the name belonged to. So influential were these men that the administration sought to silence them by housing them in a prison within the prison formally named The Tier and informally named The Pit—because most men who fell into this category were stuck there. Their names were tagged on The Fort's Top 200 Deadliest Inmates list.

The power and reputation that gang leaders, mob bosses, serial killers, shot callers, and other men had in the free world followed them to the chain gang. Most were lifers; others were on death row. The men with no release date were known as the living dead as each passing day brought them closer to execution. To look at them was to look at a living corpse.

Every man on the tier was locked down for twenty-three and one, meaning they were only allowed out of their tight, dank cells once a day, only to be placed into exterior yard cages smaller than their live-in cells for an hour of fresh air. Even this was a rare occurrence as guards often refused to "run yard" because inmates would often use this time as an opportunity to attack them.

To date, three officers had been stabbed to death by inmates who slipped out of their cuffs and took a shank to a guard's neck for whatever grievance he had committed against the inmate or one of his brothers. These inmates never forgot nor forgave. They just waited, and when the time was right, they struck. And with the score three-to-one in the inmate's favor, yard time was often a disregarded function.

The Pit was a three-story concrete building located within The Fort, built within the walls and fenced off by a black screen to prevent inmates from looking out and the general population from looking in. As soon as one entered The Pit, they were greeted by three stories of cells on each side, listed as odd or even: one, three, five to the right, and two, four, six on the left. Thirty-three cells on each side faced each other. Stepping into The Pit was the equivalent of stepping into a madhouse.

And it was a madhouse that greeted the guard Brownlee as he showed up for work for the sundown to sunrise shift. As soon as he stepped into the cellblock, the shouts for his attention began before he could even set his mailbag down.

"Aye, Brownlee, give out that fuckin' mail!"

"Brownlee, come on wit' the water!"

"Yo' bitch-ass gonna get shitted down today, Brownlee," another inmate shouted from the top tier.

Brownlee ignored them all as he prepared to make his rounds.

A short, portly, white man, he'd been stabbed, assaulted, and had shit and piss thrown at him, but it didn't faze him. After standing his ground for so long, he earned a measure of respect from the inmates in The Pit. Although he wouldn't smuggle anything in for anyone, he wouldn't say anything if an inmate got it in on their own. He was just trying to feed his family and make it home to them at the end of his shift. He let the chain gang be the chain gang.

So, when other guards entered his cellblock and went to certain cells carrying things in their pants pockets or bulges of their shirts, Brownlee paid no mind. Most of the time, he would find something to do to avoid the sight. This was part of the reason he had the respect he had, coupled with the fact that he was one of the few guards who could even work The Pit. Thus, he was given free rein to run it his way for the most part.

He sat at the desk and began writing in the logbook, ignoring the shouts and hollers. The smell of weed and flung shit wafted through the air—evidence of a recent drug drop and an indication that someone had been shitted down.

Finally done, Brownlee closed his logbook, grabbed his mail sack, and started making his rounds to perform count and hand out mail. He started on the bottom range known as The Flats, and the top range loudly voiced their anger at having to wait.

"Aye, Brownlee, why the fuck you always start mail on the bottom?"

"We gon' bust ya bitch-ass t'day, cracka," shouted another prisoner.

"You ain't gonna do shit, Maleek," Brownlee fired back as he passed several cells, stopping here and there to pass out pieces of mail.

When he was done with The Flats, he made his way to the second floor known as The Mids.

"We gon' set you on fire t'night, Brownlee."

"You ain't gone do no such thing, Bat," Brownlee shouted, walking to the back of the range and around to the other side.

"Fuck ya bitch-ass, Brownlee."

"Fuck you, *Chico*! That's why your bitch-ass waiting to die, maggot."

"Brownlee, hurry up with the mail. I need some water."

"Well, stick your head in the toilet or wait till I bring it to you, Willa. Your loud talking don't scare me," Brownlee barked back.

He had been working The Pit for so long that he could easily associate names with voices. He made his way through The Mids, sliding mail through the bars, and kept pushing.

"You gonna get stabbed tonight, Brownlee!"

"You ain't gonna stab shit, KujoShyne!"

Brownlee finally got to the top tier, and just as he reached the floor, he heard a familiar banging that seemed to rattle the whole cell block.

Boom! Boom! Boom! Boom!

"Brownlee, I need to talk to you."

Boom! Boom! Boom! Boom! Boom!

"You know who this is, muthafucka!"

"Forever, would you stop beating that damn gate! If you're all that damn gangsta, take your ass back out there to population. You are the only inmate back here in the top two hundred that's not in the top two hundred. So, don't make me expose your ass, Forever," Brownlee barked into the cellblock.

The banging instantly stopped.

"Expose his bitch-ass," came a voice after a moment of silence.

"Aye, Clownlee, where my mail?" asked an inmate as Brownlee passed his cell.

"You ain't got no mail, Juggernaut. If you had, you'd be reading it instead of looking for it. Now, get off your gate!"

"Hey, Peter Rabbit, I guess somebody loves you out there. Seems you got a nice little package," Brownlee said, reaching into his sack and pushing a parcel through the cell bars.

When he handed out the last piece of mail, he announced, "That's it for the mail. If you ain't get none, don't get mad at me. Get mad at your bitch, or get mad at the man that's fucking your bitch."

"Fuck you, Brownlee, you bitch-ass crack," shouted a voice as Brownlee headed down the stairs back to the The Flats.

"Fuck you back, Santanna. You another bitch back here hiding. You a bitch, your momma's a bitch, your daddy's a bitch. You come from a family of bitches, and word on the Plains is them Billies gone kill your bitch-ass for spitting in the wind."

And with that, Brownlee walked out of the cellblock,

Avery Brown

slamming the main gate behind him.

***

Receiving mail was a blessing in The Pit, but it was especially so for two individuals. The first person was waiting for something specific and hoping this was it as he went through the package. He set the contents on his bed: tobacco, coffee, and books. He reached for the book, *Heaven's Words*, smirking as he opened it and eagerly looking for the message. He grinned as he read:

ALL IS WELL AND HAS BEEN DONE. THE MOMENT SOON APPROACHES.

—FT

Yes, it was the message he had been desperately waiting to receive. He nodded his head as he reread it again and again. In this tiny cell, this hellhole of misery and despair, he now had a reason to smile.

***

Peter Rabbit tore into his package, eager to know what was in it and curious about who had sent it. Looking inside, he saw the usual allotted stuff: books, pencils, paper, tobacco, the usual fanfare. But then, he spied a note.

I KNOW YOU ARE SOON TO TOUCH. JOIN THE FAMILY. THERE'S A SEAT AT THE TABLE FOR YOU. IF YOU TRYING TO EAT, COME TO THE BLUFF. WE AIN'T HARD TO FIND.

—FOOT

Peter Rabbit read the note several times, remembering all those he met during his bid—all those who promised to do "this and that" on their way out the door for the brothers who were still locked down. Few ever made good on their capped-up vows to do this or that, forgetting to reach back for a comrade still behind the wall. For most, it was "out of sight, out of mind." Yet, here it was—proof that a comrade could go against the norm and reach out, soldier to soldier. This note was a testament that not all are forgotten.

Until this moment, Peter Rabbit hadn't given much thought about what he would do or where he would go as a free man, but now he had a destination. And with that, a destiny would follow.

Chapter Twenty-Two

Baron Black sat behind the desk of his private chambers, holding council with his son before the gathering. Everyone had arrived, and he now wanted his captain's perspective on the more major arrivals to Freedom Compound. He already had most—if not all—of the Plains people under his banner either by press, finesse, or respect. But it was these specifically invited individuals and non-conformists that he needed to be in accord with before he could go on.

"Well, Captain, what is your assessment of our guests?" asked Baron Black as he leaned against his chair.

The burning scones hanging on the walls released a crackling sound and cast a dim light in the room.

Captain BB sat across from his father—his leader and mentor—thinking well about his answer. He was tried and proven in battle and loyal beyond belief. Yet, at times like this, his father had a way of making him feel like a child again. But it was a fleeting feeling and momentary at best.

"Well, Father, starting in order of arrival, the first to arrive was Fat Pockets of Keystone."

"Yes, and what are your thoughts on him?"

"To be truthful, I don't like him," started Captain BB.

He knew part of the reason for his bias was because he was enamored by the woman who accompanied him. But that was an emotional answer and an answer his father would disapprove. So, it was better to give an intelligent response fitting for a captain.

"My reason is because he is a weasel and pig of a man who rules by intimidation, and at that, it is the intimidation of the one he serves that he uses to rule."

"Marshall Stryfe?" Baron Black cut in.

"Yes. However, for all his slick mouth blustering, he is as crafty as a fox—the fox that walks before the lion and warns the lion of the traps. In return, the lion scares away all the fox's enemies, and the fox is permitted to do as a fox does."

"So, you believe this Fat Pockets to be a fox?"

"Yes, and he will side with us because he will see that we are the bigger lion approaching the one he now serves. And being that the first law of nature is self-preservation—a law I know he adheres to wholeheartedly, it's also safe to assume he's smart enough to know when he's been outfoxed. For should he refuse our offer to join us, he knows his demise is inevitable, for any number of mishaps could befall him on his way home," said Captain BB with a grin that implied the unspoken.

"Yes, plans known are plans that can be defeated," offered Baron Black, reading in between the lines.

Baron Black felt proud that not only did his captain understand loyalty, courage, and dedication, but he was also astute in the ways of people and politics.

"Who's next?" asked Baron Black.

"Alexander Wolfgang of Noble Haven."

"As expected," stated Baron Black.

"Agreed. However, I don't believe his appearance here is for *our* desired purpose. He was adamant in expressing to me that he believes we know the whereabouts of his daughter who went missing during the train massacre in Reach Providence a few weeks back."

"And why would he think that? That's more Diablo's cup of tea," pointed out Baron Black.

Captain BB shrugged his shoulders and replied, "The timing of our invitation, along with our reputation, would make it easy for him to jump to the conclusion that we kidnapped her as a way to muscle him to our cause. Rest assured, I told him we had no knowledge of who took his daughter or her whereabouts. However, as you know, words tend to travel faster than horses. So, between you and me, I now *do* know who took her and where she is."

Captain BB grinned at his father's apparent puzzlement.

"How so?"

"Patience, Father. I will explain," his son answered, pleased with himself.

"Proceed," uttered Baron Black, again proud of his captain's handling of the matter.

"Alexander Wolfgang is an ominous man, but now, his passions are ignited again in the twilight of his life. The passion of a father bonded to the love and protection of his daughter. Now, if his daughter were to be taken or killed by our enemy, we would surely have an ally in him. His contacts and financial resources would be paramount to our cause. But, alas, that is not the case *yet*. Nonetheless, events are underfoot that may still bring Wolfgang to align himself with us."

"Events such as what, my captain?"

Captain BB smiled at his father's acknowledgment of his title, knowing it was a sign that his father was pleased with his report so far.

"Well, Father, that daughter is now wanted by the Republic for acts of treason. And not even Alexander Wolfgang, a respected patrician he may be, can get her out of the shit she has stepped in! And as luck would have it, this daughter is now in Freedom Compound."

Baron Black smiled at his son, thinking about what this could mean for them.

"A higher power is smiling down on us," Baron Black stated.

"Or grinning up at us, depending on your beliefs," countered the captain with a mischievous chuckle.

"And what would the animal be for this Alexander Wolfgang?" asked Baron Black.

"Oh, he's a grizzly... an old grey grizzly moving towards his final fight before death… when he is most fierce," answered Captain BB.

Baron Black nodded in agreement.

"Who was next?"

"Diablo Vasa. And he rode in like a man who knows his value. He knows that you and Marshall Stryfe know that he knows his value to you both. He's too far from the Republic to be forced into obedience, and he proved during the Death Sagas that he would be a formidable adversary to anyone who would challenge him. Finally, he is equal to us in military might, but his loyalty will be to his own self-interest."

"Good assessment. It would appear my old friend hasn't changed a bit. He fought against the Republic during the Death Sagas, and I don't see him changing now."

"Yes, he did fight against the then ruler of the Republic during the Death Sagas, but he fought for his own personal reasons."

"Yet, he didn't fight against us," pointed out Baron Black.

"Nor did he fight with us. Truth be told, I believe the fact that the Republic was a common enemy to us all kept the hostilities among us at bay on the Barren Plains. But that was then, and this is now," retorted Captain BB.

"And the difference?"

"Back then, the Republic was led by the now-dead Black Heart. He was after all the Plains. It is led by Stryfe now, and he is only after you. I'm certain he hopes everybody else will remain neutral. But who's to say if Diablo may feel as though he can weather the storm no matter how the winds of war blow."

"Duly noted, and as an animal, who would he be?" asked Baron Black, wanting to be sure his son was aware of the only chink in their armor.

"He would be a wolf that wears a fox's mask, but by the time this fox removes its mask and reveals its true self, it is too late for the prey to escape. As far as we are concerned, he is the wolf lurking in the forest, sniffing at the wind and biding his time. A wolf we must watch."

"And what of his daughter, Elvira, whom I'm sure eagerly awaits her turn to rule?"

Captain BB snickered, thinking back to their greeting today.

"She is the opposite side of the same coin."

"But what creature would she be?" Baron Black asked.

"Ah, she would be the spider that promises the fly she would not eat him if he were to land on her web and rest his wings," he answered.

Baron Black was truly pleased with his captain. He learned how to decipher a person upon first impressions and discern the true nature of their character.

"El Chablo was next to arrive."

"So I've heard. And he brought a troop with him, as well—as if that's supposed to matter to us. Anyway, tell me what you think," Baron Black requested as his ire for El Chablo reddened his face.

"Well, Father, keep in mind that El Chablo is the most wanted man alive right now after you, and this in itself puts a mark on his back for bounty hunters, rivals, or any number of people who could and would profit from his death. Basically, anybody could be up to the challenge. I believe this is the reason he travels as he does. Keep in mind, twice he has been in Republic hands, and twice he has escaped under very suspicious circumstances, to say the least, which means he was obviously able to exploit a weakness in the fabric of the Republic. A weakness we know nothing about but may one day need to figure out. His capabilities and contacts are far-reaching as he has proven, not to mention his money, power, and respect rival ours."

"But will he be an enemy or an ally?" cut in Baron Black, lashing an open hand through the air to accentuate his question.

"Father, he is already an enemy of the Republic, but if the essence of your question is if our enemy's enemy will be our friend, then I think that depends on whether we respect his trade."

"Well, how do you feel about his trade, Captain?"

"Truth be told, he doesn't force anybody to use or buy his poison, and the problems of addiction here are minuscule at best.

In places like Shynetown, it is forbidden to indulge in the use of smack under the penalty of death. In fact, El Chablo's plague of poisons is stronger in the Republic than anywhere else and in little hole-in-the-wall towns that don't matter. Besides that, the people who deal with this devil go to his table. So, I believe it would be in our best interest to make him our ally."

"Why?" interjected Baron Black, his tone relaying his anger at the thought of connecting with a drug lord.

"Because as I ponder it, El Chablo would make the perfect insurance policy against any betrayal from Diablo Vasa. Should Diablo at any time choose to backdoor us, he would certainly know that El Chablo's knife would be at his back," the captain concluded.

"Well, this is quite the conundrum, my captain, and your every word was delivered with logic. So, for now, we will tie rags with him for the sake of solidifying our strength against our common enemy. However, I will not have our ideals intertwined with his when the time comes to present our democracy to the world stage."

Captain BB laughed and said, "Father, with all due respect, the world stage is a platform El Chablo is already a star on."

"Indeed, he is," chuckled Baron Black. "I guess it's true what they say that war can make for some strange bedfellows."

"Yes, and it gets even stranger," announced the captain.

"What do you mean?"

"Well, our final two major arrivals really surprised me. One came uninvited, but I welcomed them for what they bring to the table. And the other, I guess you could say, is an honored guest of sorts."

"Okay, Captain, tell me more about the uninvited yet

welcomed guest."

Captain BB grinned, knowing that what he was about to reveal was unforeseeable.

"Whoa." Baron Black raised a finger, stopping him before he could speak. "You neglected to tell me the animal that El Chablo is," he said, pointing his finger scoldingly.

"Yes, forgive me. I assumed it was obvious," said Captain BB, a verbal pivot to his father's jab.

"My captain, nothing is to be taken for granted in times of war."

Captain BB acknowledged his father's wise advice with no further banter and answered, "El Chablo is nothing short of a tiger. A tiger that walks about with his tail in the air, hopeful that somebody will grab it because he is ready for when they do."

Baron Black nodded to his son, pleased by his insight.

"Now, tell me that which you know I know not and am eager to know of," said Baron Black, knowing the captain was saving the best for last.

"Is it that obvious?"

"You are my captain now, but you have always been my son, and I know my son very well." Baron Black waved his hand, urging him to go on.

Captain BB nodded, feeling much pride in the bond he shared with his father.

"Well, the uninvited guests are a small group that calls themselves the Mob, and they have decided to use this gathering as a platform to introduce themselves to everyone. And the missing Diamond Heiress, of who I spoke earlier and whom initially I thought to be their captive, is utterly and totally a cohort."

Baron Black took in the information, pondering the implications. "What do you think of them?"

"They're young and brash. However, if they can be brought under the belief of unity and democracy among the Plains—a unity, mind you, agreed upon by all parties involved—then perhaps they can be an asset to the cause. But, as for now, their purpose is self-serving. In addition, they have also come to announce their claims of the Bluff as their base of operations."

"That's pretty audacious and presumptive, don't you think, Captain?"

"Yes, even laughable, Father. But like I said, they are young."

"And what are their thoughts on the Republic?"

The captain laughed.

"Well, Father, if you are the most wanted, a slot you share with El Chablo, it would appear that soon this Mob will be joining ya. Currently, to their credit are the killings in Keystone, the train massacre in Reach Providence, and a gun-blazing escape out of Shameless over the dead bodies of Republic soldiers. So, I would say their message to the Republic is loud and clear: Fuck 'em! It's guns up," answered Captain BB, matter-of-factly.

"They sound like little more than wild upstarts with a taste for violence," retorted Baron Black.

"But, Father…thirty-five or forty years ago, could not the same thing have been said of you?" Captain BB asked with a crooked smile, knowing he had cornered his father.

"Ah, again, my captain, you back your words with sound logic, and you've studied well on your history. Thirty to forty years ago, you didn't even exist, and to my credit, the lives I took had a purpose in those days. I had a vision," said Baron Black.

"As do the Mob. It would appear their only flaw thus far is

that they have incurred too great an enemy too soon," said Captain BB.

Baron Black looked at his son, puzzled. They were already enemies of the Republic, so what other great enemy could there be? Captain BB saw the befuddlement in his father's eyes.

"Explain, Captain."

"Well, Father, it appears in the Mob's bloody beginning that they murdered a Shyne."

Baron Black sat straight up in his chair, raising an eyebrow in great interest now as he looked at his son and thought back to when he fought side by side with the Shynes against the first push of Black Heart and the Republic in the Death Sagas.

Afterward, the Shynes sought to carve out their own lands and way of life in Red Rock, just wanting to be left alone with their beliefs and loyalty-driven ways. So much history, so much bloodshed, and so much death. Yet, that was then. Baron Black couldn't afford to be bogged down with personal vendettas. If this Mob expected to survive, they would have to be made of sterner stuff.

"Well, Captain, as you said, they are young and brash. I guess time will tell what they are built like. Nonetheless, we will take no sides in their salts with the Shynes. Our position is for the greater good of all who side with us in the free choice of life under the terms that we create together as a democracy…as opposed to the rule of that dictator's so-called Civilized Republic. We are for the many, not the few with self-serving interests here or there. I only hope the Shynes will see the blight coming and see it fit to join us. Either way, trust that the Shynes will do as they have always done: collect the heads of their enemies and return to Red Rock. So, as far as I see it, the Shynes have a legacy to uphold, and this Mob has a legacy that is just beginning. Time will tell who is to prevail. Now, tell me, this Mob, what animal would they be?"

Captain BB thought on it for a second since the question was about them as a collective.

"They are alligators. Alligators that look at the world as their river," he answered and waited.

"Yes, my captain, you are exactly right. So, you already know we must watch ourselves when in deep waters with them."

Captain BB nodded in agreement.

"Now, who is this honored guest you mentioned?" asked Baron Black.

Captain BB smiled and replied, "Alkada."

Baron Black stood up, looking down at his son's crocodile smile, knowing he'd been finessed into giving a point of view before knowing all the facts. He had been verbally trapped. It was clear that son learned from father, and father learned from son.

Baron Black's facial expressions asked his questions for him. Captain BB held up a calming hand to his father, gently patting at the air between them.

"Don't worry, Father. Alkada and his men were relieved of all their weapons and told no bloodshed would be tolerated in our compound under the penalty of death."

"And what was his response to that stipulation?"

"That he would respect you just as his father had and that he would honor the laws of our compound, as well. He would also hear your proposal out. But once he left our lands, he would collect the heads of the men he came for, whether they joined our cause or not. And to his reputation, he has already added one head."

Baron Black began to pace back and forth, contemplating this situation. Alkada here in his compound. It had been a while since he last laid eyes on any Shyne, especially Alkada. And he was barely a jit then, eager to fight at his father's side. Elijah Shyne, a true comrade and friend, gave his life to the cause during the Death Sagas.

"And where are all the guests now?" asked Baron Black.

"They are at the main hall awaiting your arrival, as well as all the guests I just mentioned. Our men are alert and on point. The main guests have been sectioned off and separated with our best men in between."

Captain BB got to his feet as he and his father made for the door to meet their guests.

"I have one more question for you, Captain," said Baron Black, pausing his step. "I remember Alkada as he approached manhood…still in the clutches of adolescence, as loyal to his father as you are to me. But time has a way of changing people. So, now that Alkada is a man—a man of great repute, I might add—tell me what kind of animal he is."

"Father, Alkada strikes me as a patchwork of animals—a fox, a wolf, a bear, and even a rattler. Try as I might, I can't pin any one animal to him with certainty. But I will say he is a man I would embrace as a comrade since he exudes unwavering loyalty."

Baron Black patted his son on the back as they started for the door.

"You have a sharp eye and a true tongue, my captain, for you have just described the son in the same way that I would have described the father. May he rest in peace. You are a loyal son and a supreme captain, and with time, you will make a great general. But in regard to what you said of Alkada, there is a name for a man made of so many animals," said Baron Black.

"What's that?" Captain BB asked in earnest.

Baron Black looked at his son and smiled inwardly.

"He is a monster. And often enough, in times of war, it is the army with the biggest monsters that wins. Now, let's not keep our guests waiting any longer," finished Baron Black as he and his son left his private chambers and headed to the main meeting hall.

Chapter Twenty-Three

Baron Black, flanked by his son and most trusted officers, entered the large atrium. He was draped in full military regalia, and his hair—although wild and unkempt—would lead one to know this was a man in total control of himself and others.

The massive meeting hall was filled with over five hundred people from all over the Plains. So many people had heeded Baron Black's call. They all stood and began to clap as Baron Black made his way to the stage. The shouts and roars from the crowd were deafening.

Baron Black nodded and waved to those in the crowd who he knew and those who he didn't. They were all Plains people, and he was as much the showman as he was a freedom fighter. The energy that radiated from him left no doubt of his sincerity and dedication to his championed cause.

Baron Black stepped onto the stage and looked out into the crowd as his men stood behind him. Looking out over the attendees again, he saw old, new, and raw power. He reached both his arms into the air, palms facing forward, and began lowering his hands, signaling for the crowd to be seated. When the people finally settled down, Baron Black surveyed the room. He took in every aspect of the energy he felt—the curiosity, the vibrance, the anticipation. *Yes, it's time to begin,* he reasoned.

"My gathered guests, ladies and gentlemen, I am Baron Black, and I want to first thank you all for coming at my call. I know some, and perhaps many, of you have traveled from great distances to be here. And again, for this, I want to thank you. I've called this assembly to make you all aware of the tyranny that presses down on us from the North, and the author of this tyranny is Marshall Stryfe and his draconian Republic regime. This tyrant has a vision—a vision that means us no earthly good in that he desires to convert our way of life into a reality of his direction. Either by choice or by force. But I, myself, will not be forced to live by the will of another man. I was born free, so free I shall live and die."

Baron Black paused as the hall erupted in cheers of shouts.

"We are with you!"

"Fuck the Republic!"

"Live free and die free!"

The shouts erupted from the crowd like shots out of a cannon. Baron Black took this turnout to mean it had to be the general sentiment across the land and people from all walks of life across the Plains.

Baron Black raised his hands again for silence, electrifying the crowd as he intended to. Yet, looking out over the attendees again, he saw old, new, and raw power. He wanted to solidify them in solidarity now, but first, he had to expose key players that would face alienation from all those present if they refused to join the movement.

Baron Black smiled, proud of his son's brilliance for placing the key players at the front of the stage with the massive crowd behind them, adding pressure to the moment of their decision. Although these were men who couldn't be bullied, every trick or tactic would help. Baron Black glanced back at his son seated behind him and gave him a wink of praise, to which Captain BB nodded as his father continued his speech.

"As I look among you, I see power. I see revolution. I see myself. Because not only am I with you, I am you."

Again, the crowd raged.

"I see sisters and brothers. I see fathers and mothers. I see people who I will come to call my comrades," said Baron Black as he walked about the stage, absorbing the light.

He then looked down at the crowd to face his first subject.

"Diablo Vasa of the Sanchie Plains and my good friend, surely you see the need for us to all come together as one united front," stated Baron Black, looking intently at Diablo as the crowd fell silent.

Everyone in the audience looked to Diablo Vasa, awaiting his response.

Diablo recognized the gambit for what it was and knew he was being baited. His daughter also recognized the stratagem. Taking advantage of the moment, she leaned over and whispered something into her father's ear, a clear display of her influence in his decision-making. He nodded in adherence to her, showing their unity and that they would not be pressured.

Diablo simply raised his wine glass and nodded at Baron Black to proceed without saying a word.

Stalemate, thought Baron Black as the crowd looked on in

wonder. Yet, Baron Black couldn't afford to lose momentum as he now shifted his attention over to El Chablo.

"El Chablo, your hatred for the Republic is well known, and your escapes from the Fort are renowned. Along with me, you are also the most wanted man alive by Marshall Stryfe. I know you have no love for the Republic, but do you have love for your fellow man that fights against the Republic as you do?"

The two men locked eyes, knowing this was a major moment between them. El Chablo wouldn't be outplayed, nor would he be made into a puppet.

He stood up from his table and responded to everyone, "I have love for any man who will fight and is willing to die for what he believes is his right, no matter what the nature of the affairs by which he conducts his living. Do you not agree, Baron Black?"

Time froze as the crowd held its breath, now awaiting Baron Black's response to what El Chablo had implied with his question—if Baron Black would turn a blind eye to El Chablo's drug trade in order to garner his aid in the war to come.

The moment of silence was everything but silent before Baron Black answered, "Yes, El Chablo, I do agree."

"Then consider El Chablo a comrade to your cause as I now consider you a man of understanding to mine," retorted El Chablo.

The two men again locked eyes, knowing at once this was a pact between devil and demon.

El Chablo raised his wine glass in a toast. "I toast to you, Baron Black, for you are now the Plain's most wanted man alive."

"Ah, but you are right behind me," offered Baron Black.

"No one remembers second place." El Chablo laughed as the hall erupted in cheer, the levity of the moment erasing the tension that threatened to rise only a moment earlier.

As El Chablo seated himself, Baron Black moved on to Fat Pockets. He was a walking ego-man, yet a necessity for the campaign.

"I see now the Mayor of Keystone has graced us with his presence," stated Baron Black, now drawing the crowd's attention to the man. "Fat Pockets, I'm sure you understand the need for freedom of choice. Or does it suit you to deal in your trade of imports and exports with a leash around your neck, held by the hand of the Republic who jerks you back in your place every time you decide to move or think on your own? Does it suit you to live your life in constant fear of your new master?"

Baron Black neared the edge of the stage to look directly into Fat Pockets' resentful eyes. His words were spoken intentionally to sting after discovering the disrespect his son suffered upon Fat Pockets' arrival earlier that day.

Fat Pockets knew when he was being goaded; he also knew when to play his position. Most importantly, he knew how to survive. He knew the game being played well, and he knew he had to be more than a pawn, which he made evident with his response.

"Look here, Baron Black… With all due respect, if you're expecting Fat Pockets to roll with the rush, then you gotta make sure Fat Pockets ain't touched, dig? I already see what's comin', and anybody caught slippin' when the gunslingin' starts is a goner. And me, myself, I'm no sass with the pistols. So, just as sure as I sit safely here, I gotta sit safely everywhere. You guarantee that, and I guarantee me. Because anybody caught half-assin' in this matrix, like I said, ain't gone make it. And I'm no good to you or anyone if I'm dead."

"Often blood is the price to be paid for revolution, and this revolution will be no different, for there will be blood," countered Baron Black.

"True enough, but if the Republic stoves my top, they'll move in, take over Keystone, and that's another issue for you to deal with. So, put it like this. I'm with you, but sure 'nough when this bitch goes ka-boom, I expect you to be with me," Fat Pockets snapped back.

This is good enough, thought Baron Black.

As his son had indicated, this fox saw a bigger lion approaching and acted accordingly. However, Baron Black wanted to impress upon this fox that he was in a fox hole, and there was no way out.

"Fat Pockets, I understand your situation. So, I will guarantee you this: if you are with us, everyone you see here will be with you. I guarantee it. But if you are against us, I also guarantee you that everyone here will be against you, and I cannot guarantee what they will do once you leave Freedom Compound," said Baron Black with just a hint of a grin on his face.

Fat Pockets made his decision in an instant. After all, he was a survivor. Picking his wine glass up from the table, he raised it to Baron Black and confirmed his allegiance.

"Let's get it," he said as the crowd cheered their approval.

For a brief second, Captain BB locked eyes with Nancy. Neither could hide the desire that trickled from their gazes.

Baron Black nodded his acceptance and returned his attention to the crowd.

"The Republic would seek to impose their law on us, their taxes on our trades, and gun control on our culture! This is *our* trade that we conduct on *our* lands. These are *our* lives that we have established and passed down for generations. And the Republic suddenly feels we owe them homage and payment, capitalist pigs!" barked Baron Black as he spat on the stage floor. "They have never set foot down here in peace and offering but would have us give tribute for what goes on down here. But alas, I will pay. I will pay as I paid them in the Death Sagas with lead, steel, blood, and death! And if you all feel as I do, you will pay the same. But, make no mistake, this is not just an unreasonable disagreement between the Republic and us. This is a fight between good and evil, and the good only wins when we put evil to death!"

The crowd exploded in uncontrollable cheer, collectively chanting, "Baron Black! Baron Black! Baron Black!"

Baron Black brought the crowd under control, then directed his attention to Alexander Wolfgang.

"Alexander Wolfgang," started Baron Black.

The crowd now shifted their attention to Mr. Wolfgang, and the mogul of Apex Diamonds flushed not in the slightest. He was a man of grit.

"Mr. Wolfgang, by now, you already know that Marshall Stryfe has long been plotting a way to strip Noble Haven of its sovereignty and assimilate your land and finances into Republic holdings. And he cares not for the slight this presents to those across the water. He intends the same for the lands of all these people you see here. And I have come to learn even your daughter has been marked for death…labeled as an outlaw to be shot down on sight. So, tell me, Wolfgang, will you and the people of Noble Haven stand idly by as your aristocratic way of life is stripped from you and your children are murdered?" asked Baron Black so acidly, knowing this would enrage Alexander Wolfgang.

Across the room, Bianca Wolfgang's face contorted in shock at hearing her father's name, knowing it was solely his love for her that brought him here. She tried to catch a glimpse of her father but failed with the throngs of people and soldiers blocking her view. Yet, she continued to feel waves of emotion wash over her.

Wolfgang looked back at Baron Black, digesting all he had just been told, relieved and angered by the revelation—relieved to know his daughter was still alive and angered at the brashness that inevitably led to her status as an outlaw. The anger quickly waned as he rejoiced in the fact that she was alive.

Wolfgang continued to study Baron Black as he internally decided how to respond. Finally, he picked up a shot glass, downed it in one gulp, stood up, looked around the hall, and then back to Baron Black.

"Baron Black, a great man once said, 'Money is an interesting luxury, nothing more.' And at my age, I've known the pleasures of nearly every luxury there is. But the best of them, such as a daughter's kiss or a man's freedom of choice, are luxuries I would kill and die for. And I will keep fighting to keep that luxury. And the luxury of choice and one's freedom are luxuries all should know."

Feeling sentimental, Wolfgang momentarily paused, thinking of Bianca before adding, "So, before death takes me, I would like to know again the tenderness of my daughter's kiss upon my cheek a final time, just as I would know the thrill of killing those who now seek to kill her. So, count me among you. Count me among everyone here!" Wolfgang waved his hand out to the people around him as they all began to clap and cheer.

Bianca sat at her table, still unable to see her father, but her eyes began to water after hearing his words.

Noticing her getting emotional, NoLove said two words: "Mob up."

She looked at NoLove, solemnly nodded, and immediately stiffened up.

The crowd continued to cheer as Baron Black looked at Alexander Wolfgang with noticeable respect—respect for an aristocrat that was now a rebel.

"Many of you here I know," Baron Black started. "And many of you I've come to know over the years. Thus, I know where you stand, and that is we stand together against Republic oppression! But there are some among you here who stand against the Republic but apart from *us*."

At this, people in the crowd immediately began looking around with scrutiny, wondering who were the people Baron Black was speaking of. They didn't have to wonder for long.

"I'm speaking of this new group of upstarts," began Baron Black as he walked back across the stage.

Fat Pockets bristled in his seat, trying to see who these upstarts were. His instincts told him that these were the bandits who brought murder and mayhem to Keystone.

When Baron Black reached the other end of the stage, he looked directly at NoLove and his band. NoLove returned the stare from his table as Baron Black held out his hand—palm up—and aimed directly at him.

"Ladies and gentlemen, let me introduce you to the Mob."

NoLove and his men now had the full attention of everyone in the hall. NoLove stood up and tipped his hat to all those present. He then returned his attention to Baron Black and spoke for all to hear.

"It is an honor to be here among you all, such solid men and women. My name is NoLove, and as you have been made aware by our gracious host, I represent the Mob, and I now speak to you on behalf of the Mob, who, like all of you here, have *no love* for the Republic."

Several pockets of the crowd laughed at his pun.

At hearing the name NoLove, Alkada sought a clear line of sight to him, and sure enough, it was the man he knew from The Fort. However, the circumstances differed—the person he once considered a respected soldier was now an enemy.

Silence began to settle in for a moment before Baron Black broke it.

"So, NoLove, you are an outlaw? We are *all* outlaws here. You say you are free? We are all free here. But the most important question now is: Are you a revolutionary like all of us here? Or are you and this Mob merely a flash in the pan, barely worth our notice?" asked Baron Black, well aware of the salts between the Mob and the Shynes. He needed to unify the Mob into the movement and vilify the Shynes into a ceasefire for now.

"Baron Black and all the other distinguished guests here," started NoLove, now addressing the whole hall, "I realize our introduction may have been a bit heinous…like the murders in Keystone, the massacre in Reach Providence, or the killings in Shameless. Yes, we claim all that, and I do not now stand before you in regret, nor offer apologies for those acts. We are the Mob, and like you all here, we also have an agenda that we will see to its fruition. However, I see now that our agenda, to a certain degree, is aligned with yours, which is first and foremost to be free. This, in my eyes, makes us friends, and the struggles of my friends are struggles of mine. So, to answer your question, yes, we are outlaws. We do not recognize Republic law, and yes, we are revolutionaries alongside you all. Death is all I offer the oppressor, for we stand with the oppressed. And the Mob is no mere flash in the pan, by the way. I assure you all, the Mob is here to stay."

While Baron Black nodded his acceptance at NoLove's statement, the crowd immediately cheered.

As NoLove sat back down, TwoFace took a swig of wine and passed the bottle to NoLove, patting him on the shoulder as he whispered, "Mob shit."

"Then, you are now counted among us," said Baron Black. "But know this, NoLove. The Mob is now with us, or you will fall before us. For we are for the whole of the people and not the selfish needs of the few."

Having made his point, Baron Black now needed to amplify his influence on their next course of action. "Friends and comrades, I want you to know it is not my intention to lead you. I intend to make you all aware of the approaching encroachment of a despotic regime seeking to cast its shadow on our way of life. And by giving you this awareness, I now ask you what we intend to do. I say we band together and bring war to the Republic that rivals the days of the Death Sagas, and if not, you can succumb to the push of the Republic and become slaves. But in this slavery, I will not join you. However, in freedom, I ask that you all join *me*!"

The crowd broke loose. "Freedom or Death" and "Death to Stryfe" was shouted out in unison. The shouts trampled throughout the hall like a living thing before Baron Black called for silence and began to speak again.

"This brings me to my final guest of the evening. An honored man whose father fought at my side in the Death Sagas and died for the very liberties the Republic is trying again to take away. Ladies and gentlemen, allow me to introduce to you Alkada of Shynetown."

Instantly electrified, the crowd gasped and whispered, and there were looks of shock on people's faces. Murmurs could be heard everywhere.

"Don't they mark their faces with their kills?"

"They're savages."

"They cut people's heads off."

A surge of excitement took control of the whole hall as people stood to their feet and looked about to catch a glimpse of the legendary Shynes seated at the back of the hall.

Alkada gave a quick sign for StreetLife and the scraps to remain seated while he and HardBody stood up and approached the stage, walking down the middle aisle for all to see. The silence now was like no other time during the night. They looked like the coming of death and madness, the scarred faces of Alkada and HardBody instantly bringing to life the truth of rumors swirling around the plains about the Shynes.

NoLove looked around to see the man he had come to know in The Fort and knew it wasn't by chance that he was here.

Elvira looked through the crowd to see Alkada, her heart now heavy with feelings of love and hate for him, harboring a secret between them that he knew nothing about. Diablo saw the distress on his daughter's face and smiled.

Alkada and HardBody now stood only about twenty feet from the stage when Baron Black asked the question on every person's mind in the hall.

"So, Alkada, where do you and the people of Red Rock stand

on this?"

Alkada and HardBody both beamed directly at Baron Black, the two of them the center of everyone's attention. Although the Shynes were widely known, they were rarely seen due to a "kill on sight" decree issued by the Republic for atrocities they suffered at the hands of the Shynes during the Death Sagas. Thus, whenever a Shyne was spotted outside of Red Rock, it was mostly to deliver death to whoever was foolish enough to cross them.

Alkada looked around the hall, taking in all the looks of wonder, respect, and fear. He then responded to Baron Black and all others in the hall.

"Baron Black, just so we are crystal-like, I'm sure you know, as I've told your captain, it is a personal matter that has brought me to your lands. And it is a matter I reckons you know I will deal with regardless of who or what."

Alkada paused, looking directly at NoLove, only to find him looking directly at him.

"Now, in regards to the Republic," Alkada continued, "I speak for all Shynes when I say we will stand with you just as my father did before me. And to all of you here that would form under the banner of Baron Black, my decree to you is the Shynes will never betray you, snitch on you, or abandon you under penalty of death, for these are crimes no man or woman can come back from or be forgiven of once committed. And for anyone who dares commit such a crime on a Shyne, trust that their head will come to rest on a pike in Shynetown," Alkada said, again letting his eyes come to rest on NoLove.

"Ah, Alkada, you are just like your father. Thus, I know your given word is as stone. But what of the Rollacks and Billies of Red Rock? Will they, too, raise guns up against the Republic?"

Alkada looked back to StreetLife, as did the rest of the crowd as StreetLife stood up to answer.

"In honor and respect to the memory of Pistol Pete and on Pete, you can count on the Rollacks," StreetLife announced.

Baron Black nodded, then looked back to Alkada. "And the Billies?"

"Trust that after what the Republic did to S.I., I'm sure the Billies will stand strong the trey way."

"Then the people of Red Rock now stand counted among us," announced Baron Black.

Alkada nodded and then looked up at Baron Black, giving him the loyalty salute of war taught to him by his father—a clenched left fist brought across the right of his chest, the right clenched fist brought over the left arm, a bowing of the head, then dropping the arms down in an X and unclenching the fists with palms up in offering. This gesture symbolized: *As long as we wage war, you have my loyalty and trust unto death.*

"Raaahhhh."

Just then, Skully ripped through the silence of the hall, causing many in the crowd to shudder and jump, looking overhead as the massive black eagle with red plumage came to land on Alkada's shoulder. It flapped its enormous regal wings, giving Alkada the appearance of an angel of death as if he and Skully were one complete entity. The spectacle enthralled the crowd.

Baron Black was utterly shocked by the ancient gesture that he had not seen displayed in ages, more precisely, since the days of the Death Sagas. He felt an immediate kinship and admiration for Alkada and saluted him back in kind, followed by his son and a few older soldiers on the stage who knew what the gesture meant.

Although unaware of what the gesture meant, the crowd knew they had all just witnessed some mystic and obscure piece of rustic history reenacted before their very eyes.

The crowd exploded in chaos with cheers of camaraderie. "Freedom," "Baron Black," and even "Alkada" could be heard shouted as numerous people roared on, trying to imitate the salute they had just seen, thirsting to be a part of the legacy that Baron Black and Alkada had awoken.

It took a moment for Baron Black to regain control over the hall, and that control came only with several blasts of shotguns in the air. When everyone quieted down, Baron Black again began his delivery. It was obvious Alkada had just unified the movement with his oath to all, but Baron Black still had to gain control of its direction.

"Ladies and gentlemen, or comrades as we now are, let this gathering be our declaration of war against the Republic. However, we mustn't get ahead of ourselves, for those who fail to plan, plan to fail. So, plan we shall. We will reconvene here in three days to decide our methods of attack. Until then, enjoy my lands, accept my hospitality, and take and learn what you will from my technological advancements. As well, I advise you to mix and mingle; get to know the men and women you are about to kill and die for during battle. My special and honored guest, you will no longer be sequestered in your chambers."

Baron Black paused, looking directly to Alkada and then NoLove before continuing.

"As I am aware, there may be personal vendettas among some of you. But, keep in mind, I take no sides of one comrade over the other. So, understand there will be a cessation of hostilities while in the sanctuary of the Freedom Compound, and this law is enforced by penalty of death for any who seek to disregard it. Therefore, respect my home as you would have it respect you," concluded Baron Black, leaving the stage.

He signaled the start of a massive celebration as shouts of "Freedom or Death" could be heard throughout the hall.

Chapter Twenty-Four

The meeting hall was instantly turned into a lavish event. In true gala-like fashion, a band took to the stage, playing music and setting a mood of merriment.

Baron Black made his way through the crowd with his son as his only escort, embracing old friends and comrades he knew and shaking hands with the people he didn't. Wine of the finest kind flowed freely, accompanied by the best delicacies. They were carried on platters by beautiful servants, and the scent of the highest quality of Kush wafted through the air—surely compliments of El Chablo.

Now that they had formally introduced themselves to the playing field and were accepted as players, NoLove and his band made their way through the crowd in true Mob swagger. They headed to one of many bars spread throughout the hall. Along the way, they were stopped, admired, and greeted for their allegiance to the cause. As they approached the bar, the Diamond Princess held fast to NoLove's arm, tightening her grip as a voice called

Avery Brown

out to her.

"Bianca."

Upon hearing her name, the Diamond Princess already knew the owner of that voice, and in it, she heard the feelings and emotion, the love and relief in knowing she was still alive.

"Bianca," the voice called again, this time sterner, more forceful, and at closer proximity.

Unable to ignore it any longer, she finally turned around to confront her father.

NoLove, TwoFace, and Goon all turned in unison with Bianca, now standing face-to-face with Alexander Wolfgang. He stepped forward as if to pull his daughter away from the company of men, reaching out like a father aimed at protecting his child. He wanted to hold her, to console her. But he was stopped mid-stride as Bianca stepped forward to meet him, pressing her hand to his chest to keep them apart while still holding on to NoLove's arm with her other hand. Before he could speak, she did.

"Father, I love you, and I love Mother. I always will. Be sure to tell her. But the life I live now is the life I choose to live. I will always hold you dear to my heart, and you will always be my father, but NoLove is my daddy now."

She stepped closer to her father's chest, releasing NoLove's arm as she did. He held her for a moment as he always did, remembering his beautiful daughter as a child, not wanting to let go of her or the memory. She then kissed his cheek and turned away, no longer the daughter he knew, and took NoLove's arm as they proceeded to walk away.

Wolfgang stared daggers at NoLove, rage burning up inside of him. Then, just at that moment, NoLove turned back, looked Alexander Wolfgang dead in the eyes, and winked at him.

306

Consumed with hate, Alexander started toward NoLove but was stopped as a hand clamped down on his shoulder from behind. Alexander furiously turned around to be greeted by the smiling face of Diablo Vasa, who had witnessed the whole affair.

Diablo faced Alexander Wolfgang, father to father, and said, "Wolfgang, do not let your emotions supersede your intelligence. What you have just experienced is what *all* fathers of daughters experience. And that is when a father is told he is no longer his daughter's one and only love because another man has become her first love. The father's pain is in letting go, yet there is joy in still holding on. Come, let us share a drink. I am Diablo Vasa, father of Elvira Vasa, and trust me when I say I know exactly how you feel right now."

Wolfgang looked at the man and knew he spoke the truth. His anger started to wane when he realized this man had obviously experienced what he felt.

"Elvira... Isn't she also the infamous Evila?" asked Wolfgang with a grin, recalling what he heard of this father and daughter team.

"Yes, she is," responded Diablo, "but she is still my daughter," he added as the two men began to laugh, becoming fast friends.

***

Alkada, StreetLife, and HardBody held council at a bar off to the side, away from the main crowd, as A1 and London looked on.

Alkada grinned at the wide berth given them by those who passed them. He could see in the guests' faces that they were amazed and fascinated yet still fearful of being in such close

307

proximity with Shynes. Everyone knew the Shynes were notorious for killing and taking the heads of their enemies—an age-old barbaric practice passed down through the generations in their native homeland somewhere across the water. This was coupled with the knowledge that the scar tattoos on their faces confirmed how many heads a Shyne had taken.

Alkada had two long scars on the right side of his face, although his legend spoke of many more killings. HardBody, on the other hand, sported well over twenty scars, and his reputation for taking lives was well known. He was often called *The Death Penalty of Shyne*. They both displayed their scars proudly like medals earned on the battlefield. The aura that surrounded them radiated loyalty to one another.

Skully was perched on Alkada's shoulder, giving an evil eye or snapping its beak at anyone who lingered or stared for too long, urging them to keep it moving by spreading his wings menacingly.

"Dig, bros," Streetlife said. "I'm 'bout to pull up on El Chablo and see what we can get on the table for some work. I know you Shynes don't allow the nose candy. Still, the Kush is all good, as well we 'bout to go to war together. So, we need to secure some diplomacy between our lands for travel purposes."

"That sounds about right," agreed Alkada. "If we shop together, we should get a nice ticket on what we coppin'. Wars cost money, and judgin' by the size of this crowd, we're going to need plenty of it. Just don't lose focus on why we're here. Leave the scraps with me."

Alkada paused, looking through the crowd. After finding who he was looking for, he directed all their attention that way with a nod.

"That's NoLove in all black with the dame on his arm. I'm assuming one of the other two is TwoFace?" he asked HardBody.

"Yeah, TwoFace is the taller one," HardBody confirmed. "It's been a while since I saw him last, but you never forget a man who reflects the same glint of death in his eyes as you. We both play for keeps, and second place in our race only wins you a coffin," HardBody added.

"Well, I reckons you go take a look at the competition—" started Alkada, cut short by Elvira, who stepped right in the middle of their huddle.

"Is this a private party, or just no girls allowed?" asked Elvira, placing her hands on the chest of both HardBody and StreetLife, pushing them away until she was standing face to face with Alkada.

Her olive skin, long black tresses, brown eyes, and stallion body immediately raised an ambivalent sensation in Alkada that he quickly suppressed.

"What's up, Elvira? You ready to let HardBody get some of that pussy now? I know it's fire from the way Alkada used to chase it," laughed HardBody as he removed her hand from his chest and pushed it down toward his dick.

Just as fast as a snake's movement, Elvira snatched her hand away and seductively responded, "How bad do you want it?"

"Bad enough to kill for it," HardBody answered, now fully engaged in the flirtation. "Just pick 'em, and I'll sick 'em."

Elvira swiftly raised a sly eye and pointed a finger directly at Alkada's chest. "As soon as you kill Alkada, you can have every hole on my body."

At this statement, Skully snapped his sharp beak at Elvira, but she didn't flinch in the least.

"Be nice," she simply commanded, pointing her finger at the bird.

Skully again snapped at her fingers but missed.

Alkada sent a mental note to Skully, and with much fanfare, Skully leaped into the air.

"Come on, Elvira. Kill Alkada for you? Never that. You know it's bros before hoes!" HardBody said with acid in his voice as her comment had raised his ire.

"Well, HardBody, I suggest you find a hoe to fuck…as I'm sure with a face like yours, hoes are all you fuck. So, I guess Alkada will remain the only Shyne that knows the feel of this pussy," sassed Elvira, waving hands dismissively at HardBody and StreetLife.

Alkada broke in, dispelling the tension between them,

"What's up, Elvira? Ain't nobody beating that pussy, right? I guess you miss me."

"*Hahaha!* Alkada, ain't nobody beat this pussy like you since you. So, now, I let bitches lick me down until you're ready to start dicking me back down proper."

StreetLife shook his head and walked away, followed by HardBody. A1 and London were caught up in the sexual banter between Alkada and Elvira, the lust apparent on their faces as they stared at Elvira's body.

"So, how have you been, Alkada? And what has brought you so far out of your little cubby hole in Shynetown? Surely more than this meeting of minds assembled by Baron Black. And judging by your flashy words, I figure you're headhunting," said Elvira, pressing her body up against his.

Alkada rubbed at the shadow of a beard growing between his scars, wondering how much he should tell her. It had been years since he last saw her, yet seeing her briefly—even after all these years—ignited all the old passion between them, which Alkada forced back down. But feeling her body against his, he admitted to himself had it not been Yemi, it surely would've been her he now called wife.

Since there was still a degree of trust between them, he answered calmly, "A matter of loyalty."

"Psst, you and your loyalty, Alkada. Are you not tired of running about the land, putting heads on sticks? Or does the wolf inside of you still control the man without?" she asked, cutting to the center of Alkada.

Alkada grinned. *She always knew how to rile me up,* he thought.

"Elvira, you know more than anyone that a wolf does what a wolf does. And I reckons when I stop being a wolf, I stop being alive, and I'm not ready to be dead, regardless of how many people may want that."

Elvira looked at Alkada, a man who still had her heart even now after all the years that had passed. She reached out and touched his face, running her fingertips over his scars. She knew she would still kill for this man and die for him if need be, and in that instant of emotional revelation, she made her decision. She would tell him. He deserved to know. She owed him that much.

"Whatever, Alkada, I guess it isn't enough to kill yourself, so you've turned to now making kids killers," she said, pointing her chin toward A1 and London.

"Perhaps it's the kids that I'm killing for. But look, Evie, you already know the script. You kill a Shyne, and you will know the touch of Shyne vengeance, period! It's not magic; it's not madness. It's mandatory."

"Please, you tell that to yourself to make it make sense in your mind, but you and I know you are still unable to control the urge to take a life," she said, trying to block out memories of a time when they were the deepest lovers—memories he triggered by calling her Evie, a name he created for her when he was deep inside of her.

"Surely, you will shed no tears over lives lost. Not you, the Dragon Lady, daughter of Diablo Vasa," said Alkada with a grin, knowing she was no daisy to death.

Elvira simply waved her hand to the comment.

"Anyway, listen to me, Alkada. I need you to come to my chamber tonight. There is an urgent matter I need to make you aware of."

Alkada could tell by her tone that it was serious and nodded his adherence that he would come.

Elvira nodded in return. She then grabbed his shirt and brought her lips to his, kissing him deeply and passionately.

After, she leaned into his ear and whispered, "I know whoever she is, she has your heart. But know that even in that, you will always have mine."

Elvira turned and walked away, her eyes as wet as her pussy.

Alkada watched her go, feeling prodded by a mixture of emotions, but he pushed them all away. Yemi was the only flame that burned within him now. She was his wife and life, now and forevermore. Elvira was a fire from his past, and he would not rekindle those flames.

At that moment, Alkada spotted NoLove just as NoLove spotted him. NoLove whispered something to Bianca and Goon. They instantly became alert, looking in Alkada's direction as they proceeded towards him.

A1 and London also beamed at NoLove and stiffened up, standing at either side of Alkada, but he swiftly said something to them, and they stepped aside. NoLove also indicated for Goon and Bianca to hold up while he went to Alkada for a one-on-one.

NoLove weaved through the crowd, finally reaching Alkada at the bar.

"What's up, Alkada? It's been a while. How long you been home?" NoLove asked, referring to their time in The Fort.

"What's up, NoLove? I'm good. Been out for a while now. Just takin' it light," Alkada answered.

"Yeah, I just got out myself," NoLove said.

"So I've heard. I also hear you all are makin' a name for yourselves all over the place. I'm guessin' the aim is to make the Mob a household name, kinda like the Shynes," Alkada said with a grin.

"Perhaps. Who knows. We may be bigger than the Shynes after it's all said and done," NoLove responded.

"Is that right? Well, one thing is for certain, you won't be alive to see it. I reckons you know you killed a Shyne back in Keystone. And in knowin' that, you know I gotta have your head for it," Alkada expressed, calm but confident.

NoLove simply nodded.

"Alkada, what's understood don't need to be explained. But just so you know, soldier to soldier, it was nothin' personal with your people—nothin' beyond him being in the wrong place at the wrong time and havin' what I came for. Now, seeing how I respect you, I'm not 'bout to make excuses for it. That would be a bitch move, and you and I ain't the bitch type. Shynes gonna do what Shynes do, and the Mob gonna do what we do. And no matter how you look at it, as of right now, I'm one up on you 'cause ain't nothin' you Shynes can do to bring a dead man back," said NoLove, grinning at Alkada with a perceived edge in their verbal exchange.

"You're right about that, NoLove. Unfortunately, I can't bring Leggs back. But I figure when I send you to him and cut your fuckin' head off, I'll feel a lot better about the matter."

"Well, Alkada, you're welcome to try, and you're sure to die. Maybe then you can be reunited with Leggs. And the both of you can wait in the afterlife for me to get there!"

"Is that right?" Alkada asked rhetorically.

"Exactly right," NoLove answered.

"That's mighty kind of you because I tend to be missin' Leggs already. And you see the kid?" asked Alkada, pointing to A1 staring daggers at NoLove. "That's Leggs' son, and I reckons he really misses his pa."

NoLove looked over at A1, tipped his hat, and winked. He then raised his trigger finger and pressed his thumb down, taking an imaginary shot at A1, then returned his attention to Alkada.

"Bruh, anyone who comes for me gets the gun from me, whether short, tall, big, small, young, or old. I kill 'em all. Dig? Now, I'm 'bout to mosey on and enjoy the night, but I'm sure we'll be settlin' up real soon. And as I said...it's one zip, my way."

Alkada only smiled, looked at A1, and called him over with a tilting of his head.

"Say, A1," started Alkada as A1 joined them. "This here is NoLove, a soldier I met durin' my time at The Fort. He's also one of the men involved in killin' your daddy, and he says he reckons to reunite us with him. Imagine that. Well, what do you say, A1? I say why don't we reunite him with one of his brothers," Alkada said as he reached for the sack on A1's hip.

Alkada opened the sack and pushed it toward NoLove, who peered inside to see Swindle's severed head looking up at him with cold, dead eyes that screamed: *You left me.*

NoLove stared with widened eyes at the head, both shocked and disgusted—his earlier air of arrogance and edge replaced by anger and hate.

Seeing that the head had its desired effect, Alkada continued on with a play of words.

"I believe you called him Swindle. Well, I guess you can say we swindled him out of his head."

A1 chuckled at the pun, feeling a sense of victory.

"You care to say anything to him? Hi, bye, or see you soon?" joked Alkada.

NoLove was still at a loss for words. Consumed with rage, he stared with hatred at Alkada.

"I got a question for you, NoLove. When we were in The Fort, you went hard on prisoners, pigs, or whoever. Truth be told, the Mob was one of the few that put the Shynes to the test, mostly because ya stuck together and didn't come apart when the pressure was on. But here it is, out in the free world, you left a man behind, and we were able to come along, break him out, and take his fucking head off. And if we did it, that means you should've done it. Then maybe Swindle wouldn't be dead yet. But if it makes you feel any better, we killed the law dawgs that had him, too, and left their dead bodies in the bush to feed the buzzards. So, this makes us even at one to one, or by my count, one down and three to go," Alkada said, retying the sack and handing it back to A1.

NoLove looked at Alkada, fury rising inside of him—not only because his brother's head was in the hands of an enemy but also because Alkada was right about what he said. He had left a brother behind, and because of that, Swindle was dead. He glanced at A1, wanting to kill them both right where they stood.

A1 winked as he shot him a bird, twirling his middle finger, flashing the diamond ring he had also taken from Swindle.

"Shyne shit," he boasted as he clipped the sack containing Swindle's head back to his waist.

"Ya gonna answer for that," said NoLove, his voice all acid.

"You gonna answer for Leggs," Alkada shot back.

"I'm lookin' forward to the moment," NoLove responded.

"And I reckons to deliver it," countered Alkada.

"Bartender!" NoLove barked. "Give me two shots of MDK."

The bartender looked at NoLove and then Alkada, baffled by the demand for such a ritualistic drink since all those in the hall were now on the same side. Nonetheless, the bartender did as he was told and prepared the dark libation, knowing that when two men ordered this drink, they were entering into a pact that the salts between them could only be melted by the murder, death, or killing of the other.

"Make it quick!" added Alkada.

The bartender hurried to gather all the necessary ingredients for the hellish drink, which is said to contain black whiskey, scorpion venom, the blood, sweat, and tears of a man tortured to death, and the final scream of the dying. All this the bartender put into a bottle like he was performing a magic show as Alkada and NoLove looked on, devoid of emotion.

To those on the outside looking in, the engagement between Alkada and NoLove appeared to be nothing more than a reunion of old pals. But for those who knew better, this was a meeting of murderers discussing the death dealing of each other.

When the bartender finished making the drink, he set two shot glasses down on the bar, one before each man. He then poured the vile nectar into both of their glasses before finally placing a dagger on the bar. His order now complete, he stepped back and watched in fascination as the dramatic ceremony between them played out.

NoLove initiated the first act without hesitation— grabbing the dagger, pricking his finger, and allowing several drops of blood to drip into the glass. He then tapped the side of the glass in offering. NoLove then placed the dagger on the bar and slid it to Alkada. Alkada repeated the ritual and tapped the side of his glass two times, indicating acceptance.

The dripping of the blood was said to enhance the hatred and malevolent intent in the hearts of the two men who drank it for each other, assuring things would never settle between them until one lay dead.

NoLove passed his drink to Alkada, who accepted. Alkada then passed his drink to NoLove, who also accepted. They tapped glasses as NoLove started the toast, looking Alkada dead in the eyes as he spoke.

"Until I kill you or you kill me."

"Peace between us there will never be," Alkada ended.

They then gulped down the demonic drink laced with each other's blood, sealing the pact between them, both men now knowing the hate they felt for one another as their enemy's blood coursed through their bodies.

NoLove then walked back to Goon and Bianca, knowing they had watched the entire exchange. He spoke a couple of words to them, and they both immediately locked in on A1, looking directly at the sack on his hip.

Goon's face contorted with uncontrolled anger as he started to walk toward Alkada, snatching his arm away from NoLove's grip. But just then, two Brigade soldiers who were also watching stepped in front of Goon, fingers on the triggers of two double-barrel shotguns. They shook their heads at Goon, letting him know there would be no altercations in the hall.

Goon continued to stare daggers at Alkada and A1. Alkada stared back and raised his fist to his neck, lifting his chin as he stuck out his thumb and slowly pulled it across his neck while smiling at Goon. Next, Alkada pointed at Goon's head and then at the sack on A1's hip containing Swindle's head.

"Alkada, how are you?" asked a familiar voice as Alkada turned around to see Elvira's father, a man who at times was also like a father to him.

"Diablo, I'm well," responded Alkada excitedly, only taking a second to look back at Goon and wink before turning his back to him as he and Diablo embraced.

"Good, good. Alkada, let me introduce you to Alexander Wolfgang," said Diablo as Wolfgang stepped forward from behind to shake hands with Alkada.

"Alkada, a lot is going on in the Plains, a lot that needs to be discussed. So, come. Let us talk on it. It's been quite some time since you and I convened. I miss you as a father misses his favorite son," said Diablo, taking Alkada under his wing as they laughed at the comment while walking off into the crowd in search of a table, followed by A1 and London.

***

El Chablo was holding the crowd in his section of the hall now turned into a shindig. Two scantily dressed women were seated on his lap, and two more women sat on either side of him in a VIP lounge area of the hall. One of the women on his lap put a blunt filled with the most upscale Kush around to his lips as another woman poured him some wine.

People sat and stood all around him, caught up in the lore that was El Chablo as he told stories of how he managed to escape from the Fort not once but twice, all the while maintaining his role as the biggest drug lord around, bar none.

Marshall Stryfe, so outraged by his escapes and continuation of his drug empire, changed the bounty on him from "wanted dead or alive" to "wanted dead only," vowing he would not suffer the humiliation of another escape. But little did Stryfe know that his escapes would not have been possible without the help of one of his own, and this was a secret El Chablo would take to his grave, for El Chablo was not one to reveal secrets. However, he was plenty flashy about the benefits of having them.

Nonetheless, El Chablo was a man of vast resources and deadly as a rattler when challenged or crossed, a fact many Republic soldiers and enemies found out too late.

Music continued to play throughout the hall, keeping everyone's mood upbeat. StreetLife made his way through the masses of people until he was less than ten feet from El Chablo, at which time he was halted from getting any closer.

El Chablo's lieutenant only relented when El Chablo urged him to step aside and allow StreetLife through.

"StreetLife!" El Chablo shouted, taking StreetLife's outstretched hand into both of his and shaking it vigorously. "Sit, sit," he insisted while waving aside the women to his right to make room for StreetLife.

StreetLife was a bit surprised El Chablo knew him by name.

"So, StreetLife, I finally get to meet you!"

The onlookers and groupies were equally impressed that El Chablo showed this gunslinger who spoke with the Shynes so much respect.

"You are with Alkada, but where he is Shyne, you are Rollack. Same tree, just different branches. Am I right?" asked El Chablo.

"Yeah, that's one way of putting it."

"Those Shynes are some crazy muthafuckas. They cut off heads and cut their faces. Those people are the devil's children, and since you are of the same tree, I'm sure some of this craziness is in you, too," said El Chablo, leaning in to grin at StreetLife before continuing. "But this is good, not at all a bad thing. From what I've heard and seen, any tree with Shyne blood is strong, loyal, and fearless. All good attributes are needed and necessary to make it in this world. StreetLife, I already know who you are, your reputation for doing good business, and how you don't fold when caught. Not to mention, the infamous company you keep speaks volumes for the man you must be. For surely in the life we live, a bullet would've been found its way into our brains if we were some bullshit."

El Chablo flagged a waitress who was all too eager to serve him.

"Bring me bottles. I want everyone around me to have a bottle in their hand," said El Chablo, smacking the waitress on her ass as she fluttered off.

Meanwhile, the woman sitting on his lap put the "el" joint to his lips, and El Chablo inhaled deeply. Finally, he blew the smoke back in her face, which she anxiously inhaled through her nose. El Chablo then returned his attention to StreetLife.

"Streets, if I may call you that?"

StreetLife nodded yes.

"You wish to talk business. I can see the ambition in your eyes. You have a hustler's spirit, but now is not the time for that. We have three days to do that. Besides, I only do business with my comrades and friends. Our position in this impending war makes us comrades, but our time tonight and over the few days will make us friends," expressed El Chablo as he passed StreetLife the Fronto leaf-rolled "el" packed with Kush.

StreetLife took the "el", pulled deeply, and immediately started coughing from the impact of the Kush hitting his lungs like a shotgun blast.

El Chablo burst out in laughter.

"Ahh, my friend, I thought you would have an iron lung."

El Chablo continued to laugh as he patted StreetLife on the back.

At the same time, StreetLife beat himself on the chest, laughing in between coughs. And just like that, StreetLife met the legend that was El Chablo, totally unaware that in this meeting, his legend would begin.

***

Fat Pockets sat at his table with a buffet of food displayed before him. There was everything from lobster tails, steaks, barbecue lamb, fried chicken, sides of skins, peppers, dips, and desserts of all sorts. Several people from the plains were seated at his table, listening as he prattled on about how he ran Keystone, a place well known for its decadence and debauchery. He was indeed in his element, flexing with an audience as Nancy sat quietly beside him.

"Now, listen here, and understand me clear. My name ain't Dead Dockets or Red Rockets. They call me Fat Pockets for a reason. I'm the big beast from back East, and I get to the bread like the Shynes get at a head, and when this shit goes ka-boom with the Republic, a lot of jokers gonna get dead. And Fat Pockets ain't gone be one of 'em. I move with the beat, laughing at suckers being made to bite the street. Ain't nothing sweet 'bout me. Pockets ain't a bitch to be dipped. And any Tamer or Republic bitch come 'round me, his ass gettin' flipped!" Fat Pockets stated boldly as the men at his table nodded emphatically to what he said.

A server brought him a fresh bowl of crawfish and set it down before him. As the server walked off, Fat Pockets looked over at Nancy and shifted his eyes to the bowl. Before she could even react to the suggestive lead, she knew Fat Pockets was about to shine for the crowd. And shine, he did.

"Bitch, what the fuck you lookin' at me for?!" he barked at Nancy, arresting the attention of everyone at the table. "Bitch, you starin' at me like the food gonna jump in my mouth on its own. You best come to life before I put a hand to you. You know a boss doesn't eat; a boss gets fed. Now, get right, right now!"

Nancy immediately began to serve Fat Pockets, plucking a crawfish from the bowl and feeding it to him, then wiping his chin as juice from the morsel squirted out of his mouth. Fat Pockets smiled like a king being fed grapes while looking around at the faces at the table to be sure they saw the whole scene that had just played out. Still holding the floor, he went on. He couldn't resist.

"See, fellas, ain't nothin' change 'cause I ain't home on the range and out on these plains. Because when Fat Pockets gets a bitch, bet you a bitch be got. And if she tries to leave, she'll be slapped, stabbed, or shot," said Fat Pockets, now receiving a few nods of praise as he broke down the science of pimping.

"That's this hoe problem," said Fat Pockets, holding a hand to Nancy. "I done took her ass from there to here. A couple of suckas done tried to get in her ear. Now she swears maybe she ain't a hoe no mo', and maybe she could be a real bitch. Bitch, please! That's like a wooden doll thinking he could one day be a real boy!" finished Fat Pockets.

The men at his table began to laugh in fellowship as he snapped his fingers, and Nancy fed him another delicacy from the table. She then looked up as Black Baron and his son reached their table.

When Baron Black waved his hand, everyone respectfully rose from the table and melted into the numerous crowds around them, except for Fat Pockets and Nancy, whose eyes were glued to the captain.

"Mayor Fat Pockets, I'm glad to see the food is to your liking. May I join you?" asked Baron Black.

"Shit, it's your world. I'm just a squirrel!" Fat Pockets responded.

"Or a fox," countered Baron Black as he sat down. "In any event, Fat Pockets, let's talk…you and me, man to man. You may excuse your assistant," Baron Black stated, leaving no room for refusal.

Fat Pockets was not stupid, peeping game instantly and knowing that daddy was throwing a diversion to give his son an opportunity to shark pimp on Nancy. Ever the chess player, Fat Pockets played on with no pressure, stepping into the moment and laying down boss swag. He turned to Nancy and spat the player pimp lingo he was known for.

"Say, Nancy, while Baron Black and I talk about things to come and what's to be done, why don't you take five and show his son why they call you magic mouth back in Keystone. But don't get too full because I'm gonna have a mouthful for you later on tonight."

Fat Pockets looked directly at Captain BB and winked as he ushered Nancy up. Nancy flushed with embarrassment and reached out to take the captain's outstretched arm.

When the pair walked off into the crowds, Baron Black turned to Fat Pockets and asked, "So, Fat Pockets, are you ready for war?"

***

The hall was now in full swing. The wine flowed, Kush burned, and cheer was heard and felt. The women moved in swarms, and a world of hedonism and debauchery was unleashed at all levels.

HardBody paid no attention to it all as he walked through the crowd. He was on a whole different mission, and its outcome meant life or death. So, he had no time to stutter-step. Finally spotting TwoFace, it was time to get to it. He cleared his mind and embraced his gift of mental focus.

TwoFace had his back to the crowd, talking to two females at the bar. HardBody would be approaching on TwoFace's nine.

Good enough, thought HardBody.

He pulled up at the opposite side of the bar, blocking out all the gasps and stares his scarred face collected, even from the bartender who seemed afraid to take his order.

"Two shots—whiskey and rum," HardBody said.

The bartender, visibly shaken, placed two shot glasses in front of HardBody and poured the requested drinks steadily, then backed off immediately without even collecting his coins.

"Time to see what you're made of, kid," uttered HardBody as he fished out a bone cracker bullet he had hidden away for such an occasion.

HardBody was good with any bullet; he mostly handed out headshots. Still, bone crackers pretty much always insured death, even if only hitting the center mass. But that was not the issue now. What HardBody needed was inside the bullet—the high-grade gunpowder used to propel it and the minced crystal shards it contained that detonated into splinter explosions inside the body after the initial penetration. Coated with acid, these same shards caused the organs to rupture. But even all this was irrelevant at the moment, for he was using it differently.

HardBody bit the tip of the bullet off and poured the contents of the shell into the shot of whiskey. For some reason, the contents made an excellent incendiary when he combined them. He watched as the liquor instantly started to fizz up. When it stopped, he poured in the rum, which acted as a primer. He topped the concoction with the empty shot glass, pushing it down until it became wedged in place. While shaking it up, he felt the glass tighten with pressure—a makeshift flash bang that would sound just like a gunshot.

HardBody took another look at TwoFace, careful not to stare. A gunslinger could always feel when he was being watched. It was a survival instinct.

TwoFace was still distracted, jaw jacking with the broads.

HardBody approached first from behind and then, turning at the bar's edge, went up to TwoFace from the side. When he was about ten feet away, he shook the glass a final time, tossed it up in the air to land midway between them, and then watched for the reaction. The next nanosecond, millisecond, and everything in between would be locked in his memory.

Blam!

The glasses hit the ground and went off like a gunshot, causing several people to jump, startled as if shooting had commenced. But the only person HardBody saw was TwoFace, who moved almost too fast for the naked eye to detect. His whole body worked in concert, moving in one fluid motion. Ducking and spinning toward the sound of the shot, he moved instinctively, reaching his right hand over his left on his cross clutch for guns that weren't there.

You're fast, kid, thought HardBody as he watched the drama he orchestrated play out.

Brigade soldiers were there in seconds, their guns drawn. They were ready to kill whoever dared to fire a weapon, especially since everyone had to relinquish all arms upon entering Freedom Compound.

HardBody stuck his hands in the air, pointing a finger at the shattered gasses on the ground.

"My bad, fellas. The firewater got me kinda saucy," he said.

The soldiers continued to keep their guns aimed at his head while patting him and TwoFace down roughly and thoroughly but found nothing and understood even less of what really happened. They remained wary, only reholstering when the lead soldier did and circulated back into the crowd, leaving HardBody and TwoFace to their reunion.

"TwoFace!" shouted HardBody, now facing him. "I see you're still fast as a snake sprung from the coil."

They both sat down at the bar, the two women forgotten.

"HardBody, what's up, bro? You ain't dead yet?"

"Nah, bro, I can't find anybody up to the task," said HardBody, wondering if TwoFace knew he had just been sized up.

"Well, Hards, you found me. So, your search is over. I know you and Alkada are here for what we did to your people in Keystone."

"You already know. I got a spot for you right here," said HardBody, pointing to one of the few unscarred places on his face.

"Nah, bro, TwoFace ain't 'bout to be a scar on your face, but I tell you what. When you try to make it happen, I promise you will die a believer."

"Is that how you feel, TwoFace?"

"Ain't no other way to feel about it. You and I know death-dealing more than most. We live by the gun, whether it's you tatting your face up or me notching my gun handles. You know the saying: *If you kill one man, kill one hundred. It's all the same.*"

"*Besides, they can only hang you once,*" finished HardBody.

"That's right. A bullet in the head will kill 'em dead. It's never personal, only..."

"Heavy metal," they said in unison.

"Well, I'm glad you feel that way, TwoFace, especially since we made your bro Swindle a believer."

TwoFace immediately became alert, knowing Swindle was already dead and gone. Emotions began to swell up in him for the death of his cousin. Still, he fought them back and looked HardBody in the eyes. HardBody returned the stare with a smile, uttering two words.

"Heavy metal," HardBody said.

TwoFace nodded his head in agreement. "He was my cousin."

"Leggs was my Shyne," stated HardBody.

"How did he go out?"

"Like a soldier," answered HardBody. "What about Leggs?"

"The same."

"So, I guess we can do no less than play this script out," said HardBody.

"Oh, bro, that's on the Mob. We mos' def' gon' rock the bells about this. You got away in the Barren Straights," said TwoFace, thinking about the last time they met.

HardBody laughed. "Nah, son, you just got lucky. Tamers hit the town before we could get to it," he retorted. "I guess that's what happens when you got a face too easy to trace, and the mouths of men constantly leak."

"Yeah, I heard about you in the Flatlands. They say you put one right through Skinner's eye, and that was a fast son of a bitch!"

"Not fast enough," said HardBody, pointing to a scar that ran down the left side of his face from temple to cheek. "But, shit, you talk about Skinner and me… as I've been hearing, you've been giving 'em to the dirt yourself. Say you gave it to the James brothers up in Cedar Creek, two against one. Now, how'd you pull that off?"

"Oh, you'll find out soon enough."

"Heavy fuckin' metal. Tell you what, kid. I can't wait to blow your brains out," said HardBody with a half-laugh and a sinister smile.

TwoFace laughed. "I know that's right. But I bet you I'm up to the challenge, and I reckons my face will be the last one you see before I deliver you to whomever it is you Shynes pray to!"

At that moment, someone tapped HardBody on the shoulder

from behind, and he turned around to find a beautiful woman looking at him. He was amazed by her beauty. She was brown-skinned with the ass of a horse, cherry in the face, pretty brown eyes, and two ponytails braided down her back. She had an aura that spoke of all manner of carnal desires. She looked seductively at HardBody, admiring his scars with her pretty brown eyes.

"Are you the Shyne they call HardBody?" she asked timidly yet sensually.

HardBody grinned before answering, "Yes, love. I'm HardBody, the fastest gun alive."

"For now," TwoFace added over his shoulder before he spun around to face the young lady, who looked confused by the statement.

"Don't mind my friend here, love. The kid thinks he's got what it takes to kill me, but that's what all these people thought, too," said HardBody, pointing at the scars on his face.

He winked, and his swagger again enamored the woman as a sinister twinkle danced in her eyes.

"Well, fellas," she said as she twirled the end of one of her braids between her fingers, still a bit hesitant.

"Come on, sweetheart, what's on your mind?" TwoFace pressed.

"I'm looking for a gunslinger, but I'm not looking for his gun to bust too fast. You feel me? I've heard a lot about you, HardBody, and I want to know if you live up to the hype of your name."

"Well, if he doesn't live up to the hype of his, you come right back and let me show you that I live up to mine," TwoFace insisted.

"Who are you?" she asked, now looking at TwoFace.

"My name is TwoFace, the Fool, and I roll with the Mob."

He noticed a glimmer of recognition in her eyes when he said his name. Still, the interest wasn't as vivid as the interest she showed in HardBody.

"Oh, I've heard of you. They say you're fast, but most say HardBody is faster," she responded, a naughty thought forming in her mind. "Fellas, it's not the guns on your waist that I'm interested in, but the one between your legs I'm tryna set off."

HardBody shrugged and responded, "Blacksnake is in the building."

"Rifle in the air," TwoFace said, meeting her gaze.

HardBody and TwoFace then looked at each other and said in unison, "Soldier to soldier."

The girl then smiled and grabbed both HardBody and TwoFace by the wrist, pulling them off in search of a more private place.

Chapter Twenty-Five

Alkada left the hall after seeing StreetLife was good in the presence of El Chablo. He told A1 and London to post up with him. They were young, but they needed to start being exposed to life outside of Shynetown. Knowing how to and how not to move could mean life or death on the Plains. Besides that, he figured they would all link in the morning and go from there. It was still early, at least as far as parties go. The hall was one big soirée, and it was barely past twelve. He thought of finding HardBody, but he knew he could handle it himself.

As he walked the immaculate grounds of Freedom Compound, Alkada had a lot to ponder. He had just pledged his loyalty as well as that of Shynetown to Baron Black in waging war against the Republic without even so much as a word to the Shyne Council. No matter what, he would honor his word. Diablo Vasa and Alexander Wolfgang were already approaching him sideways regarding his daughter being with NoLove. But Alkada was not one for engaging in sordid affairs or the twisted agendas that drove them. Yet, he could already tell this war would have many battles fought in places that eyes couldn't see. Nonetheless, it was blatantly clear that the Shynes, in fact, the whole Red Rock—had become a major piece on the chessboard.

He reached out to Skully, seeing through his eyes and feeling the euphoria of the night sky in his mind as Skully circled above Freedom Compound. All was well.

The connection was broken when a servant tugged at Alkada's arm. Opening his eyes, he focused on the servant woman, one of the many fluttering to and fro while tending to those they served diligently.

"Alkada," said the servant, "the mistress, Elvira, begs an audience with you."

She held out her hand in the direction of Elvira's chambers, indicating for Alkada to follow her as she began to walk.

Despite the enormity of the compound, they reached Elvira's chambers in moments. At that time, the servant opened the doors inward and held out her hand for Alkada to enter. Once he did, she pulled the doors closed behind him.

The room was dimly lit yet immaculate, befitting Elvira's sophistication and taste for fashion—her flair for the finest of everything. It was a circular room with a small fireplace in which a crackling fire danced. Fortunately, the wind that blew through the open windows offset the heat. Alkada's cursory scan of the room stopped at Elvira, who was standing on a bearskin rug and looking out the window.

She was wearing a red, see-through nightgown, a necklace, and nothing else. She turned around to face Alkada, her nipples hardened by the breeze. They pointed at Alkada like two black fingertips protruding from her pert, olive-toned breasts. Her shaved pussy offered a warmth that Alkada's heart remembered but his mind was fighting to forget. Their past love was an obvious elephant in the room that grew bigger as Alkada took in Elvira's amazing body. Her black hair, brown eyes, full lips, and hips were as perfect as he remembered.

Elvira was also rambling through the romantic remnants of their past in her mind as she left the window to approach Alkada. The breeze blew her veil attire to the side, revealing even more of her body. She stopped at the side of the massive sleigh bed, grabbing a bottle of wine perched in a bucket of ice at the bedside. She looked at Alkada and broke the silence as she reached for two glasses.

"I guess you finally got tired of the festivities, Kada."

"As I already told you, Evie, it's a matter of loyalty that has brought me here, not festivity," he answered, realizing she already had him slipping by again calling her Evie.

He knew this was her intent as he noticed the slightest hint of a grin on her face.

She poured two glasses of wine, set the bottle back into the bucket, and grabbed a piece of ice. Opening her sheer negligee, she seductively ran the ice cube from her neck down to the top of her navel, then placed what was left in her mouth.

"Have you seen this, Kada? Ice without snow or freezing weather. Baron Black is resourceful if nothing else."

"Yes, he is. He's managed to get all of us here at one time. That speaks volumes of both his cunning and vision. But what do you want to tell me, Ev—?" Alkada paused, catching himself and stiffening up. "Elvira, what's on your mind? Surely you didn't call me here to discuss Baron Black's ice-makin' abilities," said Alkada, watching her as if she were an approaching snake.

"Damn, Kada, I didn't know I needed a reason to share a simple drink with a man I can't stop loving."

Now standing before him, she handed him a glass of wine.

Alkada took the glass with a sly eye, bringing it to his nose and sniffing it for poison.

"Alkada, you insult me with your suspicions," she hissed.

"No, Elvira, I know you, and I know you sent many men to their maker this way. The sweet death you called it, remember?"

Elvira smiled in her evil way, reflecting on the times when she and Alkada had not only been lovers but co-killers, as well. She reached for Alkada's glass and brought it to her lips, sipping indulgently on the wine.

Alkada now did the same as Elvira laid her head on his broad chest.

"Your heart still beats so strong, Kada," she said as she reached up and caressed his neck.

Alkada could feel his desire stir, but he pushed the feeling back down. *I have a wife and a family,* he reminded himself. *I will not give in to the carnal urge.*

"What do you want, Elvira?" he pressed, setting his now empty glass down before grabbing her by the shoulders and easing her back off his body.

He still felt a rise of passionate emotion within despite his best efforts to resist it.

"What's wrong, Kada? Have you become so monastic that you can't even share a moment of warmth and comfort with a woman you once loved?" Elvira snapped.

"That was in the past, and I'm not the same man I was back then."

"That's right. Back then, you were the mighty killer Alkada, manslayer, measured by the number of heads taken. Lost in loyalty and ritualism until I came along and changed you. I took you from a love of killing and vengeance over losses you couldn't let go of and taught you how to love me."

"I love my wife now, Elvira."

"Fuck your wife!" she hissed as she threw the glass of wine at him, which missed his head and shattered on the door behind him.

"Your wife?! Your wife?! Where was she when you were a mad dog spilling blood across the Plains like a river runs with water? She may well be your wife now, but that's only due to the spoils of my labor. Before me, you only knew the love of a gun. I taught you about the love between a man and a woman. I am the woman you first told 'I love you'. I trained you, Alkada. I loved you."

"And you left me," Alkada shot back.

Elvira went silent, stuck in the moment.

"Well, I guess that's when your wife came along and found you!" barked Elvira, now enraged.

"She is also the mother of my daughter," Alkada added.

"Well, I am the mother of your son!" Elvira snapped.

The information hit Alkada like a gunshot. He struggled to maintain his composure as he processed what she had just said, instantly remembering the deal he had made with Mugasa's spirit and the mischievous laughter after striking the deal.

I was played for a fool, and my son's soul will pay the price for my foolishness, he thought, suddenly overtaken with rage.

Quick as lightning, Alkada reached out and grabbed Elvira's neck with both hands in an iron grip, squeezing mercilessly. Elvira tried to pry his hands loose but failed. She struck out like a cat in a frenzy, raking her clawed hand across his face, drawing blood in four distinct lines.

Alkada barely noticed as he lifted her off her feet by her throat, choking the life out of her. She kicked her feet wildly, fighting the blackness beginning to overtake her vision.

Then a voice of a spirit exploded in his mind: *Stop!*

He wasn't sure if it was Dempaku or Mugasa, but the command broke him out of his blind fury, and he threw her against a wall. She landed in a heap, steadying herself with one hand on the floor while holding her neck with the other and gasping for air.

"Yes, my beloved Kada, your daughter has a brother," Elvira creaked, getting back to her feet.

"Why didn't you tell me about him?" he pressed, advancing upon her, tasting his blood as it ran down his face.

Elvira regained some of her confidence and spoke as much with her response.

Laughing, she asked, "Why should I have? So that you could've taken him away and raised him to praise those Dempaku witches as you do? Fuck those black bitches!" she blurted and spat on the ground in marked defiance.

Alkada shot out his hand, back smacking her against the wall, causing the back of her head to smash into a mirror behind her. Another open hand slap sent her back to the ground. Alkada looked into the shattered mirror to see his scratched face covered in blood looking back at him.

A knock came to the door, and a second later, the servant pushed her way into the room.

"Is everything okay?"

"Leave us or be a part of this," Alkada warned over his shoulder without turning around.

The servant caught a glimpse of Elvira on the floor and started for her, but Elvira halted her with her palm and shooed her away. The servant looked from Elvira back to Alkada, then quietly closed the doors and left.

Alkada went and stood over her, squatting down to look her in the face as she bled from her mouth and the back of her head. She was leery but not frightened.

"Would you kill me, Kada? The mother of your son?"

"Killin' you is not killin' him," he answered and punched her in the face, rattling her jaw.

She was beautiful and built for battle. She shook off the blows and spoke steadily.

"Kada, can't you see? I just wanted a better life for him than the lives we got to live," she pleaded, holding her arms up in front of her face to deflect further blows.

"Bitch! He's my son. I have a right! Where is he, and what's his name?" pressed Alkada as he recalled Mugasa's laughter again.

When Elvira hesitated to answer, he slapped her once more. Then, he pieced her with two quick jabs, left and right.

"Answer me, bitch, or as sure as you stop me from meeting him, you will never see him again!"

Then he shot a hand around her neck with snake quickness, pinning her to the wall and banging her head repeatedly.

"Answer me, bitch!"

She began to cry.

"Save your tears for your father," said Alkada as he tightened his grip, bringing his face within an inch of hers, his tone filled with rage. "See, Elvira, just as you know the evil in me, I, too, know the evil in you. And I know beneath all that beauty that you truly are the Dragon Lady with the blackest heart. Now, answer me."

"His name is Caserian," she gasped.

Alkada loosened his grip.

"He's being schooled in Noble Haven," she admitted.

"You fucking viper! You have taken my son from me!"

At that moment, Alkada noticed the locket around her neck. He released her throat and snatched the locket, opening it as blood dripped down into it from his raked face. He studied the faces within it—a picture of Elvira's mother and a picture of a young boy. Alkada knew this was his son, yet he still wanted to hear it from her.

"Is this him?"

Elvira nodded yes, and Alkada shoved the locket into his pocket. He then looked back at Elvira and back-smacked her. She rose on an elbow as Alkada stood up, looking down at her. He then spit in her face and headed to the door.

Elvira knew she deserved it, but she was a proud woman, and having the man she still loved spit his hatred in her face was too much for her to bear. Her rage grew as the spit ran down her face.

"I am Elvira Vasa," she shrieked, rising to her feet. "I am the daughter of Diablo Vasa. You will not turn your back on me!"

Alkada turned around to see a deranged woman charging at him, hands raised like claws, eyes of pure insanity. She was no longer Elvira—this was Evila. When she got within arms' reach, he slapped her. Yet, she came on. The scene was reminiscent of a mountain lion attacking a grizzly bear.

She swiped at his face, just grazing his eyes. Again, he slapped her, this time to the bed. She snatched at his shirt as she fell back, pulling him with her. She hit the bed with Alkada falling

338

on top of her. She swiped at his face again, adding more scratches. Alkada grimaced at the electric pain he felt and began smacking her back and forth, but still, she raged on, oblivious to the pain.

"I hate you, Alkada! I fucking hate you!" she yelled.

Again, he smacked her, yet this only empowered her further, filling her with a poignant rage. When she rolled over, she was now on top of Alkada, fighting to get her fingernails into his eyes. But Alkada held both of her wrists as she looked down at his face, at which point she cracked. Her hate, anger, and fury were gone, and she gave in to her want, need, and love for him.

"Alkada, why do you hate me when I love you so?" she pleaded.

In the heat of the moment, Alkada, too, broke. He finally succumbed to the feelings he had been fighting since he first saw her shortly after arriving at the compound. And for a moment, the world melted away, and she was Evie—a woman he once loved…and, as it turned out, the mother of his son. Alkada wavered, and Elvira pounced.

"I love you, Alkada," she said, bringing her lips down to his as she began to kiss him deeply, passionately, the taste of blood and salty tears mingling on their tongues.

Her passion ignited his, and he didn't fight the kiss. It felt too right, too familiar. Elvira pushed on, ripping away his shirt and undressing him, careful not to take her mouth from his in fear that she wouldn't be able to reconnect. She could feel his manhood rising, and she welcomed what would follow.

But Alkada's hatred suddenly resurfaced for what she had done. Alkada knew he could not make love to her, but he would violate her. He sat up, pushing Elvira's body back off the bed as he stood with her.

"Get on your knees," he demanded.

Elvira immediately did as she was ordered.

He then grabbed a handful of her hair and snatched her head back. She stiffened to the sudden jolt of pain in her neck, but she didn't resist. Instead, she looked up into his face, and her eyes met his. She saw now he was the mad dog she had domesticated long ago. She remembered his feel, smell, and magnetic aura.

"You betrayed me, Elvira, and there is a price for your betrayal. This is only the beginning of it," he gritted.

Elvira heard the words and knew he meant what he said, but payment be damned. She reached into Alkada's pants, releasing his manhood. Greedily, she took it into her mouth and began sucking him down, feeling him grow in her mouth. She brought her hands up to stroke and hold him steady, but Alkada swatted her hands away. This would not be tender; this would not be loving. No, this would be raw and defiling to her very core.

"Suck it deep, bitch!" Alkada barked as he shoved her full lips down to the base of him, forcing the head of his cock down her throat.

She choked and gagged on his dick, but she didn't attempt to stop. He held the back of her head and fucked her face, unrelenting as her eyes watered and she gasped for breath. But she didn't care about the indignity or wretchedness with which he handled her nor the discomfort. Her only care was that she had him, or at least a measure of him.

His manhood began to pulse in her mouth as he continued forcing her head to bob up and down. Finally, knowing he was about to release, she placed her hands on his knees to brace for it as she continued to suck.

Alkada released into her mouth, pushing himself, once again, deep into her throat. While holding her head steady, he released semen into her mouth that she felt pool at the back of her throat. Elvira looked up into his eyes as if awaiting instructions.

"Swallow it!" he barked, and she obeyed, feeling the hot cum cascade down her throat.

She was voracious in trying to get it all down. So wolfish and insatiable was her want for this man. When Alkada finally pulled himself from her throat, some of his seed fell to the floor.

Again, Elvira looked up at him.

"Eat it!" he roared, still holding her by the hair at the back of her head.

He forced her face to the floor, and she licked up his spilled semen. She couldn't care less about the humiliation and degradation; she was only thankful for the euphoria of the moment.

Alkada released her head. "Get up," he snapped.

Elvira rose from her knees, standing before him as Alkada stepped to her side. She prayed he wasn't done with her, and her prayers were answered when Alkada ripped the see-through material off her body and tossed it on the bed before her.

"Bend over," he said, grabbing her by the back of her neck and shoving her onto the bed.

She fell to her hands and knees. Then Alkada, still stiff from her oral, grabbed her at the hips, parted her ass cheeks, and pushed deep into her waiting pussy.

The heat and tightness of her interior brought back a flood of love and emotion they once shared. It had been years since a man last entered her, and even in that instance, it was nothing like this. Elvira knew now, beyond all doubt, that she loved this man unconditionally.

Alkada grabbed a fist full of her hair and proceeded to dick her down. Elvira was lost in the throes of passion and elation. She started to orgasm immediately, throwing her ass back to meet Alkada's forward thrust.

"Alkada… Alkada, I love you," she moaned.

Alkada pulled her head further back as if to snap her neck, and as he made her ass clap, he barked, "Shut up, bitch! Take it!"

Alkada thought of his wife again. Rage and guilt overwhelmed him at the betrayal he was now committing. He pulled himself out of her hungry pussy and pushed her down on her stomach.

"Nooo, Kada, give it back to me!" Elvira begged as she lay flat on her stomach, her body convulsing, still in the clutches of climax.

Alkada ignored her. Falling onto her back, he began to sodomize her, plunging into her anally. She hollered out in initial pain during the first few strokes and then started to moan with oncoming pleasurable pain. But there would be no more pleasure as Alkada plunged deeper into her ass.

He reached for her discarded negligee, tied it around her neck, and began choking her from behind while continuously forcing himself in and out of her.

She gasped as Alkada hissed in her ear, "You deceitful bitch. I should murder you!"

Again, Elvira started to gasp, reaching for her neck as the unrelenting sodomy continued, only relenting enough to catch her breath before choking her again.

"Know this, Elvira!" Alkada once more whispered in her ear. "This is not love, you evil bitch! This is violation. I am the violator, and you are the violated! Shyne shit, bitch!"

Alkada felt himself about to cum again and pushed deeper still. He smashed her head repeatedly up and down on the bed as he released inside of her from the raw sexual aggression. Finally, they came together—Elvira nearly passing out from being choked.

Alkada finished cumming in her and then pulled out, shoving her aside as if she were a rag doll. He stood up and started to get dressed while Elvira remained half-conscious on the bed, ravaged and trying to get her body back under her own control.

When Alkada was dressed and made his way to the door, he stopped short and asked, "Tell me, Elvira, what have you told my son of his father?"

"That you were killed out in the Plains."

Again, rage flared up in Alkada, but he checked it and continued for the door.

"Kada," she called out to him in a way that forced him to turn and face her. "What of my locket?" she asked, holding up a shaking hand.

Alkada dug into his pocket and produced the locket he had yapped from her. He opened it and snapped the locket in half, throwing the picture of her mother and the necklace back at her, keeping the other half with the photo of his son.

As she began to weep, Alkada turned back toward the door and stepped out into the cool night air, leaving the door wide open to her chambers as he walked away.

A daughter of Dempaku, and now, a son of Mugasa, he thought, totally oblivious of the servant who fluttered past him into the room and gasped at the sight of Elvira's face.

Chapter Twenty-Six

As roosters started to crow all over Freedom Compound, announcing the start of the new day, Alkada laid in the bed of the villa given to him and his comrades for the duration of their time in Freedom Compound. It was a spacious, clean, and immaculate five-bedroom villa with various amenities, like hot and cold running water and an apparatus that allowed you to stand under it while pressured water rained down on you. The agriculture and technological advancements of Freedom Compound were impressive, to say the least.

Aside from the snores of his men that could be heard humming throughout the villa, it was a quiet morning. The scraps were left with StreetLife for the night. Surely, they had their first real taste of drink, smoke, and women. So, they would be out for a while, and he'd let them sleep. They had earned it.

Rising from the bed, Alkada walked into the basin to clean himself. Looking in the mirror, he saw crusted and dried blood in the scratches across both sides of his face, further proof that last night was real if he even thought to question it as a dream.

Clean, relieved, and refreshed, Alkada walked out into the lounge area to find HardBody studying a map. HardBody looked up at him from the table, instantly noticing the scratches that were now bright red.

"What's up, bro? You and Evie back on ya rough sex shit? What the fuck happened to your face?"

Alkada dug into his pocket and answered Hardbody by tossing him half of the locket he had.

"Who's the kid?" asked HardBody. "He looks familiar for some reason."

"He should. He's my son," Alkada answered solemnly.

The look of perplexity on HardBody's face was apparent. Being Alkada was the closest thing he had to a brother, it's no way he'd had a son without him knowing. Then just as quickly, his wonderment was replaced with understanding, made obvious by his following comment.

"See, bruh, that's why I just dick 'em and slip 'em!" HardBody stated as he took another look at the face in the locket before tossing it back to Alkada. "How old is he?"

"By my best guess, I'd say anywhere from ten to fifteen at the most," answered Alkada as he took a seat at the table, placing the locket down between them.

HardBody started to speak, but Alkada held up his hand for silence as he closed his eyes and reached out to Skully, making the connection to look down on Freedom Compound through Skully's eyes.

Finally, he sent the command: *Come.*

He broke the connection and returned his attention to HardBody.

"So, what did you learn last night?" HardBody asked.

"Other than the fact that I have a son, I engaged NoLove and pushed down on him 'bout killing Leggs in Keystone. He admitted it was his doin', said it wasn't personal. Just wrong place, wrong time. Didn't much matter either way. I told him I needed his head for it, and then we showed him Swindle's head to let him know ain't no surrender. So, we shared a drink of MDK to make it official," reported Alkada.

HardBody nodded his understanding that the script was now set in stone, and the show would go on.

"Aside from that," Alkada continued, "I was introduced to Alexander Wolfgang by Diablo Vasa, at which point Wolfgang said he'd be willing to pay pretty and proper like for the return of his daughter and the demise of the men who have her. What about you? Did you get up on TwoFace, and, more importantly, can you take him?"

HardBody shrugged. "The kid's fast for sure, but ain't no prizes for second place in this race." *Right over left*, he thought, recollecting the kid's draw.

"I was just studying the map, and I'm figuring the Roughs, which is 'bout a day's ride northeast of here, would be a proper place to handle things with the Mob. It's an old mining town on the fringes of being a ghost town. It was filled with drifters the last time I went through there. Not much will be said 'bout any killings goin' on, that's for sure."

"Okay, you're the point man, so it is what it is," Alkada responded.

"So, bro, I guess aside from dealing with the Mob, we are also about to go to war with the Republic?" asked HardBody in a way that a little brother would ask his big brother a question.

"That's about the size of it, bro. It's only a matter of time before the tyranny of the Republic will find its way to Shynetown or the whole Red Rock, for that matter. And you know those Republic cocksuckers stay gunning for Shynes. So, I figure it'll be better if we stand in solidarity and fight with the many rather than wait to be conquered standing with the few."

"Dig, big bro. You know I'm wit'chu, right or wrong. You're the boss; I'm just part of the force. But real spit, bro, this war is gonna get real dirty. Not to mention you gon' catch hell gettin' Shyne council to lock in on this."

"Maybe, but I know Elias will always be with us. He came up with pops, so he'll vote our way on principle. Old man Stan's bitch-ass is gonna be a problem, though."

"Anyway, fuck all that. You know I got'cha back, bro. I don't have the sight and awareness that you do, at least not as strong, but I can feel certain things."

"Bro, we've been doing this together since we were scraps. What's on your mind, HardBody? Split the middle," Alkada said impatiently.

"Bro, that's just it. It's nothin' I can say with any certainty. It's more a feeling than a knowing, but I will say this: The events going on aren't just ego-driven or a mere force of wills between men. This war has been brewin' a long time. There will be blood, Alkada. The skies will rain red with it before this is all over with, and even that red rain will be black by the time it stops."

Alkada looked at HardBody, his mild consternation now gone and replaced with slight surprise that HardBody was picking up on the same vibe as him. Yet, even though HardBody couldn't pinpoint or accurately articulate what he felt, Alkada could— although not with exact precision since it was difficult to describe something that superseded the physical realm. Nonetheless, he knew that the true hand of something black and evil was building around this impending war.

"Raaaaaah," Skully shrieked, landing on the window ledge and flapping his enormous wings, commanding attention as he always did upon his arrival.

Alkada held out his arm, and Skully came, snapping his neck back as the tail of a plump field mouse disappeared down his gullet. He set Skully down on the table, reached for the quill HardBody was using, and began writing down the two messages Skully would deliver. Afterwards, Alkada lodged them into two small capsules he carried for just such occasions. He then looked back at Skully, re-establishing the link between them. Their bond was solidified by years of training, nurturing, dedication, and loyalty to one another, as well as ancient mystic practices passed down through the generations of Shyne bloodlines in the training of familiars. So cemented was the synchronicity between their spirits and the synergy between their minds that Alkada was able to give him orders by simply pushing words and commands from his mind directly into Skully's.

Seek. Deliver. Return.

Skully received the words with full comprehension.

Be swift. Go unseen.

"Raaaaah," Skully shrieked at the last two commands to tell Alkada they were unnecessary.

There was a special relationship between these two apex predators. So attuned was Skully to Alkada that he could locate anyone with Alkada's blood in their veins and any other Shyne bonded by the pact to Dempaku. If Alkada did have a son, surely this would be the test to prove it.

As always, HardBody watched the ritual play out between the two with admiration and envy. Alkada whispered a final word to Skully as he hopped back to the window ledge, and again, with a flap of his enormous wings and a parting screech, he took flight, leaping into the dawn sky.

"Bro, that's my word; I gotta get a fuckin' bird," HardBody boasted.

Alkada laughed, knowing that HardBody's lust for death-dealing had taken him so far from his innate connection to Dempaku needed to hone a familiar that it would never happen. To develop the kind of connection he had with Skully, one needed to garner a sturdy spiritual relationship with nature, animals, and elements. Alkada often wondered how HardBody had not yet fallen victim to the maddening for all the lives he'd taken.

"Bro, just stick to what you do best—gunslingin' and head huntin'."

A moment later, two scantily clad women emerged from the backroom, passing Alkada and HardBody as they headed for the door.

After they left, StreetLife, smoking a cigar, came out of the backroom where the two females had just emerged. He walked over and joined Alkada and HardBody at the table.

"I saw you choppin' it up with El Chablo last night! What's his position?" asked Alkada.

StreetLife started shaking his head back and forth while rubbing his eyes with the palms of his hands in an attempt to loosen up the haze that still lingered from last night.

"He's a wild and crazy guy, but all in all, bullshit aside, I believe we have a friend and ally in him, as well as a new plug," StreetLife answered as he sucked on his cigar, blowing out the smoke and grinning with a hustler's ambition.

"A new plug, huh? I know that's right," said Alkada.

"Yeah, bro, you keep your eye on the dollar," added HardBody.

"Sex, money, and murder. That's the Rollack lifestyle, bay-bro," StreetLife responded.

***

At that exact moment, a very dissimilar meeting was taking place among the Mob. Converged at the breakfast table in their villa that the servants had set before leaving, they were about to eat—all except Goon, who was pacing the room and rattling on about his feelings over what had taken place last night.

"Bro, they had his fuckin' head in a sack! A fuckin' sack!" Goon shouted. "What type of caveman shit is that?!"

"That's what the Shynes do," responded NoLove.

"What the fuck you mean, 'that's what the Shynes do'? I don't give a fuck what the Shynes do. We can feed 'em pie in the sky when they die. That was Swindle, bruh—one of our fuckin' brothers! And now we just gonna let them gallivant around this bitch with Swindle's head in a sack, talkin' 'bout we next like we ain't talkin' 'bout shit?! TwoFace, that was your fuckin' cousin, and here you are, eatin' pancakes like you don't want no type of straightening 'bout this shit! I don't know what the fuck ya want, but I want some smoke," blurted Goon as he continued pacing back and forth.

Bianca and TwoFace remained quiet as Goon vented, but NoLove had listened to enough of the song and dance and stood up to address it.

"Shut the fuck up!" NoLove barked, stopping Goon in his tracks as the two men stared at each other. "The Shynes kill; the Mob kills. Who cares where a bullet goes once your casket closes? Now, you know the Shynes are playin' for keeps. Ain't no rules to this shit. We ain't give a fuck 'bout killing a Shyne and don't give a fuck 'bout killin' any more of 'em. So why do you think they should give a fuck about killin' us? Now, I reckons we'll get a chance to settle up over Swindle soon enough, and when that chance comes, there will only be two sides to that meeting—the quick and the dead. So, quit your bellyaching and decide what part of the story you gonna be on. Because when the time comes, I don't know 'bout you, but I intend to deliver the moment the Mob way," finished NoLove as he sat back down.

"Mob shit," said TwoFace.

"Mob shit," seconded Bianca.

"Mob shit," grumbled Goon as he came to the table and sat down with the others.

"And just so you know, if they get your heads, the sack is only the beginning. The end is your head on a pike in somebody's yard in Shynetown," added TwoFace.

"Fuckin' savages!" Goon spat.

"Savages, sadists, or soldiers, it's guns up, bruh. And if you fail to fire, you will be given to the dirt," said NoLove.

"Okay, we all get the message. As I see it, we got 'bout two more days out here. So what's on our agenda?" asked TwoFace, returning the floor to NoLove.

"Well, Baron Black says we are to meet one final time, which will probably be a meeting of committance," NoLove responded.

"So are we gonna commit to this war?" Goon asked.

"I don't see how we can't, bro. We're not strong enough to take on the Republic on our own, and we would be surrounded by people who are. We'd be overrun as a matter of principle. Basically, it's plain to see our situation and the position of it. It's either get down or lay down, and after seeing the respect that Baron Black gets around here, not siding with him would leave us in somewhat of an imbroglio," answered NoLove.

"True that," TwoFace agreed.

"True that?! Stop flexin'! Two, you don't even know what an imbroglio means," sneered Goon, still a bit miffed about Swindle's head.

"Well, Goon, what NoLove means is we would be in a complicated situation, a conundrum, a jam were we not to take Baron Black's side in this. And the word is imbroglio, pronounced imbrol-yo," said Bianca in all her sophistication, not bothering to look up from her plate.

"Oh, so you're an educated bitch," snapped Goon before going on. "So how'd it feel to see your daddy last night?" he added with a sly grin at NoLove.

NoLove said nothing, allowing Bianca to handle the moment on her own.

Bianca put her fork down and finally looked up to face Goon.

"No, Goon, I'm an educated woman and a Mob bitch, and my daddy is sitting at this table with my Mob brothers," responded Bianca with an edge in her voice, shutting Goon down from any further retort.

NoLove smiled at the exchange and then said, "Dig as long as we are here, let's be sure to bump shoulders with the neighbors. So, as soon as the final meeting is over, we'll skin-out and make our way to the Bluff, then link up with Foot. The Mob is here, and we are here to stay."

***

Captain BB awoke with Nancy in his arms, just as he was in hers. They lay in the bed of his private quarters. The sun had risen and was shooting beams of light throughout the bedroom.

His mind was spinning. He couldn't explain it, but already he knew he loved this woman. *I'm not letting her go no matter what,* he compassionately thought while holding her.

The things she'd done to him, said to him, and promised him, there was no way he would relinquish her back to Fat Pockets. At that moment, Captain BB knew he needed to talk to his father, but not just yet.

As Nancy began to stir, he knew he wanted more of her. He needed to get back inside of her—to feel her warmth, her tongue, her love. When their eyes met, Nancy spoke as she started to rise from the bed only to be gripped by Captain BB's arms.

"I must leave. Fat Pockets will have the skin off my back," she said to Captain BB, intentionally letting her eyes start to water, then watched as the anger rose in him, just as she intended.

"Fat Pockets be damned! You belong to me now!" he said, his desperation apparent. "I can keep you safe. I *will* keep you safe. Just tell me this is what you want, and it will be done."

Nancy looked at Captain BB as a crocodile tear rolled down her cheek, and she nodded yes.

Captain BB was overwhelmed with emotion, so much so that he looked at Nancy, feeling every bit of the man he was, and without a second's hesitation, he said, "I love you, Nancy."

Nancy put a finger to his lips and responded, "Show me."

She thought to herself, *Gotcha, as* she took Captain BB into her mouth and began to rock his world.

***

Fat Pockets had called out Nancy's name as he washed his face. Stepping out of the bathroom into the dining area, he found a mouthwatering brunch already set for him. Like the night before, there was an assortment of dishes: chicken, duck, lamb, and seasonings he had never tasted. He called Nancy's name again, knowing she would not answer. She had not come back last night.

Fat Pockets laughed to himself as he sat down. Captain BB was a sucker for love, and Nancy loved to suck.

Two suckers, Fat Pockets thought to himself as he chuckled at the humor of it.

Fat Pockets wiped his nose with hoes, so he never fretted when a chick re-chose, as the saying goes. His next one was always his best one. And he'd catch again; he always did. He'd bring the hoe out a bitch no matter how deep it hid, but Fat Pockets would make Captain BB pay one way or another. No way would he let a tender dick, hoe-lover get the best of him.

There was a knock on his door.

"Enter!" Fat Pockets called out.

In walked a female Sanchie woman. She was a beautiful woman—a little thick but curvy with it, barely a touch taller than Fat Pockets. She wore her hair in one long braid down to her ass, which was the style of the Plains. Fat Pocket had to admit to himself that she was most definitely a looker, and she looked to be about twenty-five or thereabouts. She stepped into his quarters with a smile that lit up the room.

"Greetings, Fat Pockets. Are all of our accommodations to your liking?"

"Oh, yes, indeed so," started Fat Pockets slyly. "You cooks here in Freedom Compound are the best."

The woman smiled and responded, "Oh, no, I'm not a cook. I'm more of the proprietor around here to make sure all our special guests' needs are met."

"Ah, so you're a proprietress," Fat Pockets corrected himself.

The woman smiled and nodded. "I'll be sure to make Baron Black aware that you're pleased with your stay thus far."

"Yes, of course. Please forgive me for assuming you were a cook. But, yes, everything is splendid. I dare say outstanding. Baron Black has spared no expense, and I greatly appreciate that."

"Yes, my uncle doesn't," she said, stepping back toward the door. "But please, do not hesitate to ask for whatever you may need," she offered.

The woman had spoken of that Fat Pockets was sure. However, he had heard nothing beyond, "my uncle..." Upon hearing that, Fat Pockets' mind was like a flower in bloom. He connected the dots, realizing if the Black Baron were her uncle, then Captain BB was her cousin. Thus, he found the crux of his revenge.

Fat Pockets strikes back, bitch, he immediately thought.

Fat Pockets hit the limp, about to spit his mackidocious shit; he lit a blunt clip and pushed like a pimp.

"Whoa, love," he started, touching his fingertips to the open air between them to pause her step. "Well, there is something I need," said Fat Pockets as he took a long toke of the Kush and then stubbed it out, exhaling the smoke in her direction.

"Yes, and what is that?" asked the woman, eager to please as she slightly inhaled the secondhand smoke.

"Well, it appears my traveling companion, for lack of a better word, has wandered off, and I'd so hate to eat breakfast alone. Yet, here it is, I have been blessed with waking up to a lovely breakfast and an even lovelier woman standing before me. My dear, you have brought more brightness into this room than the very sun shining outside of it. I can only hope you won't mind sitting for a moment and partaking in this beautiful morning with me, with your beautiful self. Perhaps you'll tell me about the many delicacies I'm about to eat."

Fat Pockets pulled out a chair with one hand while holding out his other for the woman to sit down. In his mind, Fat Pockets was thinking, *Bite the apple, Eve.*

The charms of this devoir, charismatic, and robust man instantly took in the woman as she stepped toward the table.

"Well, I guess I can have a bite or two with you," she said, smiling while placing her hand in his.

After she was seated, Fat Pockets pushed her chair under the table, then took a seat across from her.

"And what is your name, love?" Fat Pockets asked.

"Maritzah," she answered sweetly.

"Ahh, Lady Maritzah," he said, kissing the back of her hand, then patting it gently with his as he got comfortable.

Fat Pockets was in his element as he spoke words as smooth as the Kush now stimulating his mind and tickling hers.

"It is an honor to meet you, Maritzah. Hopefully, my company will be as pleasurable as the food before us, or as you are before me," he said, following up with a wink.

Maritzah blushed under such flirtations, already feeling at ease with the man.

"Fat Pockets, I'm sure a man of your status is used to good food and many women," said Maritzah, slightly grinning with a raised brow to Fat Pockets.

So shorty wanna push game? thought Fat Pockets.

"Yes, love, you're right about that, and you already be knowing I'm the beast from back East, understand me? However, there's a big difference between good, great, and the best. As you can see," said Fat Pockets, pausing to rub his stomach's wide girth, "I eat good food and have had great food, but the food out here is the best. And as for the latter part of your statement, I'm Fat Pockets, love, and I cherry-pick every chick I get. But there's a big difference between women and a woman. Play your cards right, and I might show you what I treat a woman like."

Fat Pockets reached across the table and caressed Maritzah's cheek with his fingertips.

Maritzah giggled, liking the feel of his touch on her as she turned bright red. Seeing the effect he was having on her, Fat Pockets pimped on.

"So, tell me, Maritzah, how can I make a woman like you a part of my world?"

Again, Maritzah blushed, answering shyly, "Are you for real, Fat Pockets?"

Fat Pockets smiled like a crocodile looking at a bunny that had stumbled into his pond while thinking, *My next one is always my best one.*

Chapter Twenty-Seven

Captain Hammer was tired of waiting as he sat in his tent, the heat bearing down on them like an oppressive force. It had been two days since Drake had left, venturing out to Freedom Compound, even though his true intent remained a mystery.

Drake is truly a sinister sort, thought Hammer.

He wreaked betrayal and cross as if he had been splashed with piss and sour milk. But he was also backed by Marshall Stryfe, so he couldn't be touched—at least not by him and not yet anyway.

Yet, Captain Hammer knew Marshall Stryfe well. He wouldn't suffer failure, and should the dandy Drake fail, his ass was grass.

Dandy Drake. Hammer liked the sound of that.

As Captain Hammer sat in his smoldering tent, his thoughts drifted to Alkada. He felt a tingle in the socket where his eye had once been but was now gone—taken like the eye of Odin. And the man who was responsible for its taking was out and about somewhere on the Plains.

The captain began to seethe at his desk, revenge at the forefront of his mind. He looked down at the map before him, already deciding on the action he was about to pursue.

"Private!" he called out.

Immediately, a soldier pulled back the tarp and entered the tent.

"Captain, sir," said the soldier, saluting and standing at attention, awaiting his orders.

"Soldier, tell Lieutenant LaDue to ready the men for marching. As soon as the sun sets, we are to leave," commanded Hammer.

"And our direction, sir?" asked the soldier.

"We are heading into the Roughs. I refuse to sit here stationed and skulking among the rocks like some prairie rodent when there's killing to be done."

"Yes, sir," said the private, his eyes raised in shock at knowing they were going deeper into the Baron Plains.

It was bad enough that they were already on Baron Black's land, and now, they would push further.

This isn't good, thought the soldier.

Captain Hammer read the soldier's mind by the apprehension on his face and the wavering in his voice. Captain Hammer stood up, unholstered his sidearm, and raised it to aim right at the soldier. He cocked back the hammer, now holding his gun less than three feet away from the soldier's face.

"Private, do you have a problem with the orders I've just given you? Because if you do, I can relieve you of duty right now and pay you your severance fee," said Captain Hammer.

"No, sir, I have no problems, sir," answered the soldier, desperately trying to control his bladder.

"Are you sure?" asked Captain Hammer as he stepped around the desk to the soldier, pushing the barrel of his gun into the soldier's temple.

"Absolutely, Captain," answered the private as coolly as he could.

Captain Hammer studied the soldier for a few seconds, his gun still firmly pressed to the man's skull, ready to blow his brains out. Then, rubbing his beard as if finally satisfied, he uncocked his gun, pulled it away from the man's face, and re-holstered it.

"Good answer, soldier. For a second there, I thought I was about to kill a coward and deserter. Now, carry on. You have your orders," finished the captain, nodding toward the tent's entrance.

The private gave a final salute and turned to exit the tent, supremely shaken at how close he had come to dying.

***

Marshall Stryfe sat at the window of his office, looking down at the streets of Independence, admiring the civility that he saw before him. He watched as the people—or rather the sheeple, as he called them—went to and fro, living their best lives. This very existence of calm and social solace was due to his engineering, drive, determination, and refusal to relent to the vision passed down to him.

By embracing that vision and pushing it, he now ruled the Republic. But this was only the beginning. It was now time to take over the plains, succeeding where his predecessors had failed—at any and all costs, foregoing the misgivings of his general and captain. There would be no more negotiations and no compromising. There would only be submission. The Plains people would obey or perish for their defiance, and Baron Black would hang like a flag, blowing in the wind over Town Square for all to see the fate that awaited anybody who opposed Republic law.

Yes, the time was at hand. He was the man. This was his moment, and the Republic was the machine that would deliver it, making all kneel before him.

Today, he ruled the Civilized Republic, tomorrow, the Plains, and, ultimately, the world.

"Mr. Happy," he shouted toward the door of his office.

Mr. Happy appeared a moment later, all too eager to do the bidding of Marshall Stryfe. He walked in to find the maniacal Marshall sitting in his chair, looking out the window.

"Yes, Marshall Stryfe," announced Mr. Happy.

Marshall Stryfe continued to gaze out of the window, not even giving Mr. Happy the respect of facing him. Then, talking over his shoulder, he said, "Mr. Happy, report to General Lynch and tell him to ready the army and prepare for war. It is time to take the plains."

"Yes, sir," responded Mr. Happy.

"And another thing, Mr. Happy," started Stryfe.

"Yes, sir?"

"From this point on, you will refer to me as Master Stryfe," he stated matter-of-factly.

"Yes, sir, Marsha—I mean, Master Stryfe," said Mr. Happy, quickly making the adjustment.

Marshall Stryfe then dismissed him with a flicker of his hand, still engrossed in the view from his office window as he thought to himself, *Yes, Master Stryfe. I like the way that sounds. Master Stryfe and all the world his minions.*

***

Baron Black was in his study, contemplating the recent events taking place in his lands and those that were sure to come. A knock at his door brought his racing thoughts to a halt.

"Enter!" shouted Baron Black as he leaned back in his chair, waiting to see who was calling upon him.

A moment later, his captain walked in, and one glance at his son's face told Baron Black they needed to talk. With the war in the offing, he could not afford to have his most trusted man preoccupied with emotional holds. He would deal with all issues of distraction now.

"Ah, my captain. Before we begin to speak, as I look upon your face, I can see it is much that distresses you. So, tell me, do you now stand before me as my son or my captain? And keep in mind that you have been and continue to be a blessing to me in both aspects."

Captain BB raised his head with a nod, always appreciative of his father's praise.

"Both," he answered.

Baron Black also nodded and pointed to the seat on the other side of his desk, indicating for his son and captain to sit.

"Okay, being you come before me as both captain and son, let me first address my captain, as the time of war is fast approaching. Then I will deal with my son," said Baron Black.

Captain BB nodded in agreement.

"Good. Now report, Captain," Baron Black ordered.

"Yes, sir. I have just been made aware that a small battalion of Republic soldiers has been sighted moving out of the Barren

Canyons into the Barren Hills. It is also said Captain Hammer himself is leading the battalion. I've prepared the brigade, and we'll take them as soon as you give the word. There are no more than fifty men in their troop. They will easily be overtaken!"

"No," stated Baron Black. "I know this Captain Hammer. He is a brave man and far from a fool, but nonetheless, it is his lust for revenge that now motivates him. I figure he knows Alkada is about, and the chance to get him back for what was done to him is proving too much for Captain Hammer to resist. There is a lot of bad blood between them, but Captain Hammer's hubris in marching so deep into our lands will prove to be his undoing in the future. Leave them be. They will go no further than the Roughs with so little a force. And think, my captain…if Captain Hammer, now so consumed with revenge, would encroach this close with so little and not be challenged, just imagine how deep he will come with many thinking us to be sweet. He is now building a flaw that we will fully exploit later when it is time to crush them once and for all."

Baron Black paused to ensure his captain fully understood what he stated but also wanted to illuminate a flaw in his perception.

"Captain, at the beginning of your report, I noticed that you said Captain Hammer has only fifty men, implying his force was little more than a few crumbs to be swept from the table. But if you look deeper, you will see that Captain Hammer now hunts one of the deadliest men alive in one of the most hostile lands for him to be in. Again, that is his flaw but also an indication that he is fearless and cunning. More importantly, let's say each of his men is equal to ten of yours. Well, now, my captain, his now seemingly paltry force of fifty men will become five hundred in confrontation. Remember, Captain, it is the quality of your men that matters most on the battlefield. The quantity only looks good from a distance. Remember that. There is no room for arrogance when you are responsible for deciding who lives and who dies," instructed Baron Black.

Captain BB nodded, understanding the duality in his father's logic: Give them a small step now so they'll step into a big trap later, and be sure you can handle whatever falls into your trap.

Leader and captain exchanged appraising looks. Now done with that particular issue, they were ready to address the next.

As Captain BB thought it through, Baron Black asked, "What's next?"

"We have an arrival of another guest by the name of Francis Drake, who has requested an audience with you. He says he knows information that could be of the utmost importance to you, and he will only share it face to face."

"Do you believe him, Captain?" cut in Baron Black, looking intently at his son for the answer.

"To his credit, he was the one who made me aware that Captain Hammer was leading that troop of soldiers I just mentioned, which turned out to be accurate," answered Captain BB.

"So he is a spy?"

"More than likely," answered Captain BB.

Baron Black shook his head in forbiddance before elaborating.

"I hate spies. Their whole existence is based on a willingness to betray with disloyalty those to who they pledge their loyalty. Where is he now?"

"He's being held in private quarters as a guest for the

moment."

"Well, keep it that way for now. But do not allow him to walk about freely, and be sure he knows he is intentionally being treated in this fashion. We'll let him fester in the thoughts of his treachery. He will provide some amusing entertainment at the parting banquet." Baron Black smiled, his devious mind already spinning as he looked at his son. "Is there anything else, Captain?"

"No, not anything regarding me being your captain. However, I need your advice as my father," Captain BB answered.

Baron Black leaned back in his chair and steepled his fingers as he looked at his son knowingly.

"Who is she, my son?"

"The woman that accompanies Fat Pockets," he responded promptly.

Baron Black raised an eyebrow in surprise, again shaking his head as he let out a sigh of agitation.

"Son, there comes many loves in life, and ultimately, you must choose the one of all time. Since your mother's death, my only love has been for my people and the lands they walk on, making them one and the same in my eyes and heart. So, trust me, my son, I know what love is and what love is not. If you truly love this woman, then claim her. If you only lust her, then fuck her and send her on. But always remember this simple, simple truth I now tell you: a whore is a whore, nothing less, and can be made into nothing more," said Baron Black, reflecting on how Fat Pockets treated the woman. "So, my son, be careful what you ask for because you never know what you may have to give up for it. Either way, I will have no harm brought to Fat Pockets. He is too essential a piece to our cause. I will not put your desire for an unquenchable whore before that of our people. Nonetheless, my son, if this is a bitch you can't resist, you will go to Fat Pockets and give him the respect of offering him the opportunity to engage you in the 'affair of honor.' He will undoubtedly decline, and you will have this woman. Lastly, know that fruit hanging from a tree often looks sweet to eat. Still, the sourness can never be known until you bite into it."

"Yes, Father," said Captain BB, barely able to contain himself, totally disregarding the jewel of his father's words.

"Also, send notice to our elite guests that we are to meet in private later for a formal convocation of sorts."

"Yes, Father, and the reason for the meeting?" asked Captain BB.

"I'm seeking to get a solidified commitment to our cause," answered Baron Black.

"Yes, sir. I'll have Maritzah tend to this Francis Drake. And I'm sure Maritzah will see that they will all be ready when you send for them."

Captain BB rose from his seat, saluted his leader, and left the study to anticipate his meeting with Fat Pockets. He was ready to make his declaration.

Chapter Twenty-Eight

It was mid-day, and Alkada and A1 were walking about Freedom Compound when an angered voice called out to him. It was a father's anger, enraged over a slight done to his daughter.

"Alkada! Alkada!" the voice barked as it got closer.

Finally, Alkada turned around to be confronted by Diablo Vasa, who was charging at Alkada in fury as if to strike him.

A1 stepped forward, but he was held back by the blocking arm of Alkada.

"Alkada, how dare you put your hands on my daughter?!" barked Diablo Vasa, now standing less than two feet away from him.

Alkada blankly looked at Diablo while turning both sides of his face so he could see the scars Elvira inflicted on him.

"Diablo, your daughter has put her hands on me—"

"Doesn't matter!" Diablo raged, blinded by his love for his daughter. "Alkada, should you ever put your hands on my daughter again, it will be the end of you!"

Diablo Vasa clenched and unclenched his hands into fists.

"Diablo, you have been like a father to me at a time when I had no father…and it is because Elvira is your daughter that she is even still alive to enrage you rather than dead to grieve you," responded Alkada solemnly.

The two men stood like granite statues, looking at each other, eye to eye. The threats were sent and received both ways and meant.

Alkada went on to break the violently charged silence between them.

"Diablo, you know me, and you know I respect you just as my father did. And believe me, I understand your rage and hatred for me now as the father of the daughter I violated. But, tell me, Diablo, is your rage and hatred equal to mine at the discovery that I was denied the knowledge of my own son's existence? Even you know this is a violation punishable by death. Yet, your daughter still draws breath."

Diablo took a step back, cocking his head to the side in disbelief as his eyes widened in astonishment—understanding and clarity gripping him. They were momentarily frozen in time like two lions that now knew there was a lion cub between them created from both their blood.

Diablo stood erect. He stared into Alkada's eyes, nodded, then abruptly turned on his heel and walked away.

Alkada watched as he walked off, then uttered to A1, "Well, that went a lot easier than I expected."

"How you figure?" asked A1, looking up at Alkada for an answer.

"Because, scrap, if you ever put your hands on Nefertiti the way I put my hands on Elvira, I'll put you in the ground," answered Alkada, still looking after Diablo.

He then looked down at A1, placing a hand on his shoulder, and gave him some "applesauce."

"Look here, A1, I can teach you the gun, and I can teach you Dempaku. But the learnin' of a woman is a lesson you must learn on your own because no one will be there with you when you got your dick inside of her, feel me?"

A1 nodded.

"Understand this, A1…you are the future of Shyne life. You, my daughter, Ammo, Savage, Mandu, Gunna, Shotta, MadMax, Rum, Platinum, Dread, Bandanna, and Drummer-Boi are the next generation of Shyne culture, and that's gotta be preserved and maintained at all cost and by all means necessary. Shyne love, loyalty, honor, and respect. Make sure you mean it when you say it, and make sure it's respected when it's heard. We move in Shyne silence, and when opposed, you push Shyne violence. Above all else, you never let a Shyne murder go unanswered. My father and yours gave me the game and the hood, and my loyalty to them is why I now stand here beside you. You got that?"

A1 nodded more enthusiastically this time.

"For most, Shyne killing is what we do. Living the life of a gunslinger but killing for your fellow Shyne is what we live for once you proclaim yourself to be a Shyne. So, for every head you collect, you put it in the front yard or give it to the family of the Shyne for who you took it. Now, if you take it for yourself like the one you already got, you place it in your front yard in front of the headstone of the fallen. So every day you wake up to it, you know to yourself before anybody else that you're Shyne tight and real right. And anyone who passes your house will know the same. But you're not a Shyne until you take a life for a Shyne.

Blood on your knife, head on a pike. If it's real, then it's right. And when death comes for you, you embrace it like a Shyne soldier. No fear because you know your death will be avenged if it was taken unrighteously. You gettin' all this, scrap? This is major applesauce you're bein' served," said Alkada.

"Yeah, I'm gettin' it all," A1 answered, eager to hear more. "What about the oath? My mom says Leggs put you to the oath. What did she mean by that? And why did my father choose you?"

A1 instantly perceived the mixed emotions stirring up in Alkada but was unable to discern them.

"Yes, your father did choose me, didn't he? Well, scrap, in the event where a Shyne is killed or murdered in any way that we don't respect—like being shot in the back, killed while unarmed, or killed by the law, we gotta have blood back for that. And if you're put to the oath, you must take the head of the person who did it and place it in front of the grave of the fallen Shyne or give it to his family to do so."

"What about if you're dead before you can put someone to the oath, or what if you're killed trying to fulfill the oath?" asked A1.

Alkada looked down at A1, seeing himself in the scrap. He remembered when he asked his father these very same questions when he was coming up. At that moment, he knew A1 would carry on tradition.

"That's a good question. Well, when two Shynes meet and form a bond, it is usually already written between them that the oath is the pact bonding them."

"Like you and HardBody?" A1 cut in.

"Sorta. But the bond between HardBody and me is deeper than most. The same blood flows in our veins, and I'm sure that when I die, HardBody or Ammo will take heads about it. And if they're not alive, then I now put you to the oath. Do you accept?"

"Why wouldn't I?" responded A1, feeling proud he was even considered.

Again, Alkada looked at A1, and again, he was caught up in the déjà vu of the moment when his father had put him to the oath, and he accepted it instantly—just like A1 did.

"Okay, you are now put to the oath by me once you are officially a Shyne. Another part of the oath is if a Shyne dies and has put no man to the oath before his death, then the oath is by law to be upheld by the firstborn child. The oath applies to women just as it applies to men," instructed Alkada.

A1 nodded, reflecting on the scars that marked so many women's faces in Shynetown—Alkada's wife being one of the most prominent.

"Okay, so I got a head. Now when do I get my scar?"

"Dig, scrap. A scar can only be given to you by Petra, the Queen Sista," Alkada answered.

"Why is that?" A1 wanted to know.

"'The 'why' is a little more applesauce than you're ready for right now. But I will tell you this much: you will earn your scar only if Dempaku wants you scarred, and if you get scarred, it is a decision you have to make on your own. You will also have to determine the course of your spiritual journey as much as your physical one."

Alkada's train of thought momentarily trailed off as he reminisced on when he received his first scar and how he had gotten to that point.

When he snapped out of his reverie, he said to A1, "But know this, when the time comes for you to choose, keep in mind that some sacrifices require more than blood can pay for. And you'll do well to remember this: your life here on earth is deep. Nonetheless, we all die, but if you die doing a deed for a great cause, your memory will live on forever. So, in short—no guts, no glory, scrap!" Alkada stressed to A1.

The two men turned around at that moment to the sound of a horse galloping up behind them.

HardBody was riding a black mustang, charging right at them. He pulled hard on the reins when he got about twenty feet away from them, causing the mustang to stand up on his hind legs and mewl loudly as it came to a stop. HardBody then pushed it forward to walk in step with A1 and Alkada.

"Bro, these mustangs are fast as fuck!" said HardBody, looking down at his comrades as they walked forward.

"Maybe we should steal some," said Alkada, looking up at HardBody and grinning as he thought back to when they would take horses for fun as kids. A glance at HardBody told him he, too, remembered those times.

"Say, bro, Baron Black says he needs to speak with you this afternoon. Something 'bout getting everybody on one solid accord."

Alkada nodded.

HardBody then spoke to A1. "Aye, scrap, looks like Alkada is givin' you some applesauce."

A1 nodded.

"Yeah, he gave me some a long time ago, and look at me now. I done ran out of face space and still got a long way to go. Anyway, I'll let you two finish your walkabout. Shyne love," HardBody shouted as he pulled the reins of the mustang and raced off.

"Shyne love," they both responded.

A1 immediately picked up on his conversation with Alkada, thirsty to learn all he could.

"Why is it you only have two scars on your face but four heads in your yard?"

"I only have two scars because the first two mattered the most, and the rest I've taken simply mattered—whether taken for families or comrades. However, what my scars mean for me has nothing to do with what your scars will mean for you. Dig, scrap. Time is, time was, and time will always be. You know what I mean, scrap?"

A1 shook his head that he didn't.

"Good, but when you do, be sure you explain to the Shyne that comes behind you."

A1 nodded.

"Now, this first scar was for my father, who fought alongside your father in the Death Sagas and was killed at the hands of the Republic," explained Alkada, pointing to the long scar on the right side of his face. "It's because of this scar there will never be peace between the Republic and me, or any law dawgs, for that matter. And this scar," Alkada said, pointing to the scar right beneath the first one. "I got this one for killing the man who killed my brother, S.I., leader of the Billies."

"S.I. Yeah, I heard a lot about him. He died holdin' court in the streets rather than be sent back to The Fort. But why would you get a scar for him? He wasn't even Shyne. He was Nine Trey."

Faster than striking lightning, Alkada snatched A1 by the scruff of his shirt and brought him within an inch of his face.

"Listen, scrap, before all these lines were drawn and fools started being all stain crazy, we were all one—one solid movement that was one for all and all for one. Shynes, Billies,

Blazers, Villains, Eight-Treys, Black Lions, Brims, Amenta, we were all one! Although we were different branches with different agendas, we were all part of the same tree," barked Alkada before shoving A1 back. "Maybe we'll get back to that united greatness of a nation one day."

A1's stark silence told Alkada he'd gotten his point across. Now he'd teach him the power of unity.

"Scrap, you define Shyne. Shyne doesn't define you. S.I. was as much a part of me as I am of him, and as long as I'm alive, he will never die. I walked with him, ate food with him, and spilled blood for him. So, when we said Shyne to Nine, we solidified the bond between Shynes and Billies. You got me, scrap?"

"I got you, big bro," A1 responded.

"Good. Now, there is one more thing I want you to know. In this war that is sure to start, I can already tell there will be many battles fought where eyes can't see and ears can't hear. So, you be sure to remember that if ever I'm not around and things don't play out according to plan, always stick to the Shyne code of conduct."

"You mean politics?"

"Exactly that. Now, dig, that's enough applesauce for today. I reckons we get back and see what's on Baron Black's mind," finished Alkada as they headed back toward the compound.

***

So caught up in spinning his web around Maritzah, Fat Pockets had all but forgotten about Nancy. Maritzah had left after they shared brunch but immediately returned after handling her duties around the compound. Chief among those duties was making the upper echelon visitors aware of the private audience they were to have with Baron Black that afternoon.

And Fat Pockets could tell she was all too eager to be back in his presence, just as he was eager to have her there. Truth be told, she was helpless against the parlance of Fat Pocket's pimpish vernacular and bold swagger. He was a man unlike any she had ever encountered.

They spoke on many different topics, from food to economics, even discussing how Fat Pockets could maximize his profits by buying homegrown and shipping out instead of losing by shopping abroad. Yes, Fat Pockets immediately saw the potential in this woman. She needed to be sitting in his corner office instead of selling ass on his corners. Although she could surely pull a dollar either way, the former was more befitting a woman of her caliber. Besides, he was smart enough to know Baron Black wouldn't allow for the latter. It was time to dangle the carrot and reel her into the stable.

"Maritzah, I could really use a woman like you to help me manage my day-to-day operations," suggested Fat Pockets. "Tell me, love, would you be interested in coming back to Keystone with me?"

The bait is cast, he thought, seeing the sparkle of interest in her eyes.

"I would love to visit Keystone with you, but with so much going on here, and war on the horizon, I don't think my uncle would allow me to go," she answered sadly.

Time for firm finesse, Fat Pockets thought to himself.

If he was to have this woman, he needed to start programming her. He stood up and looked down at her as she looked up at him with admiration.

"Maritzah, I hear what you're saying, but I didn't hear you answer my question."

"Well, yes, I would come with you if there was a way," she answered.

"There's always a way," Fat Pockets said, then walked into the washroom to prepare for his meeting with Baron Black.

Maritzah rose from the table to follow him—just as Fat Pockets had anticipated.

"What do you mean?" she asked, eager and excited, following Fat Pockets like a puppy.

"What I mean is..." He turned around to take one of her hands into both of his. "...if you want to go, I'll make it happen."

He brought her hand to his lips and kissed it. Again, she blushed at the words and flirtatious attention from Fat Pockets.

"Yes, of course," she answered, overwhelmed by the possibility.

"Say no more," Fat Pockets answered with a wink.

Just then, somebody knocked on the door to his quarters, causing both to look back at the door. The interruption angered Fat Pockets because he was about to press the moment.

"Hey, love, why don't you go ahead and get my water ready while I see who it is."

Maritzah nodded, stepping into the washroom. Her enthusiasm to do so was quite apparent. Fat Pockets smiled, knowing he would soon have this woman eating out of his hand.

As he reached the door and opened it, he was only slightly surprised to find Captain BB standing there with a velvet box tucked under his arm and a stony look of grimness on his face. Unshaken by the display, Fat Pockets greeted the man with a courteous smile, knowing he was about to shine.

"Captain BB, to what do I owe the pleasure of your visit?" Fat Pockets asked, stepping back from the door to allow Captain BB to step in.

Captain BB nodded at the acknowledgment yet was resolute in his purpose as he entered the room and faced Fat Pockets.

"Fat Pockets, with all due respect, I am here to profess my love and claim to Nancy. However, should you seek to take issue, I offer you the 'Affair of Honor.'"

Captain BB removed the velvet box from under his arm and held it up between them. He then pulled the lid back to reveal two pistols inside.

Fat Pockets took one look into the box and burst into uncontrollable laughter so hearty that he had to hold on to a nearby table and steady himself until the hysterics subsided. He laughed so hysterically that his eyes were watering, and his sides were aching. Once Fat Pockets settled his laughter, he looked at the captain and his opened box, noticing Captain BB's marked irritation at his response.

"Do you then decline the 'Affair of Honor'?" persisted the captain while looking at Fat Pockets, who was holding his hurting sides as if this matter of love were all a joke.

Again, Fat Pockets erupted into another bout of laughter as he closed the top of the box with the tip of his finger.

"Captain BB, not only do I decline, but I've done put Nancy out of my mind. So, if she's now your problem, that means she's no longer mine. Only a fool would duel over something so used," stated Fat Pockets ever so callously.

Amused by the emotions playing across the captain's face, Fat Pockets decided to press on and check the young, tender dick captain.

"Listen here, loverboy, I'm the big beast from back East, and I don't love these hoes. They come and go like the wind blows.

Some play, some stay, some run away. But ain't no hoe can say she runs my day, dig. Nancy was a weed to me, but you made her a rose. Just like some hoes choose, and others get chose. I respect the game and laugh at lames. When I talk to the clouds, they give me rain. You understand me, loverboy? My pimpin' is official. I fuck for free, while Lucys you pay to see. I'm not meeting you. You're meeting me."

Captain BB started to interject to the tongue-lashing he was receiving, but Fat Pockets shot up his finger for silence, stopping the captain's tongue as he went on.

"Listen up, loverboy, the two most important days of your life are the day you are born and the day you find out why. After that, life is ten percent what happens to you and ninety percent of how you react to it. Now, that jewel was for free, and this jewel is from me. You either pimp hard or get scarred."

At that moment, Maritzah emerged from the washroom, announcing, "Fat Pockets, your water is ready."

It was a voice all too familiar to Captain BB. When he saw his cousin emerge from the washroom, he immediately looked at Fat Pockets, flushed with anger.

Fat Pockets looked at him and winked.

When Maritzah saw the captain, she instantly became excited, stepping past Fat Pockets and running to give her cousin a hug.

"Lil BB!" she sang, immediately establishing the emotional bond between them as she lovely addressed him with a name only meant for him.

"I've made all the guests aware of the meeting as you have instructed," she voiced, now noticing the slight tension in the air between her cousin and Fat Pockets. "Oh, I guess you two have business to discuss," she said, turning to Fat Pockets. "Should you need me, just send for me. Also, I have a special surprise for you tonight. It's being prepared as we speak. A family lamb recipe," she said, smiling as she leaned over and kissed Fat Pockets on the cheek. She then looked to her cousin, and while wagging an authoritative finger, she spat, "Play nice!"

When she exited the room, Captain BB looked at Fat Pockets and said, "Fat Pockets, be warned. Maritzah is my favorite cousin, but we were raised as brother and sister. So, be sure you keep this in mind when dealing with her."

Not to be outdone in a duel of words, Fat Pockets countered by grabbing Captain BB by the arm and aiming him toward the door Maritzah just walked through.

"Well, loverboy, Nancy was my favorite hoe, and where I come from, an even swap ain't no swindle. Now, you be sure to keep that in mind the next time you think about mine, and if that don't set you proper, remember the jewel I just gave you."

Fat Pockets paused as they reached the door, and Captain BB stepped out.

Even though he ended up claiming Nancy, he couldn't help but feel that Fat Pockets won this minor battle of egos. It was validated when Fat Pockets glared at him, smiled, and uttered a final jewel:

"Remember the next time you try to step on a pimp that this time, you stepped in shit," he said before slamming the door in his face, not giving Captain BB a chance to respond.

Captain BB turned to walk away, only stopping for a moment when he heard clear as day on the other side of the door, the mayor of Keystone roar, "Fat Pockets, bitch!"

Chapter Twenty-Nine

Baron Black and his captain awaited the arrival of their guests in the conference room. This was a meeting to solidify the course of the coming war and the parts that all would play. All the lands within the Barren Plains were already aligned with Baron Black's cause and call to war.

This was now a call to the independent lands around the Barren Plains and the people who ruled them. These were the minds behind the power.

Like most of Baron Black's fortress, the meeting room was elegant. It was located in a tower within the compound. The room had two large windows that provided an east and west view of Freedom Compound and a massive round table in the center made of fine mahogany, encircled by seven identical chairs. The chairs were for the heads of each of the claimed lands. Their accompanying seconds would be allowed to stand behind them. The guests were all given the guidelines by messengers that they were only to be accompanied by one other.

All the guests arrived within moments of each other due to the servants who were dispatched to escort the called upon guests to the meeting. This meant no one would have to wait for the arrival of anyone else.

These were very powerful people, all known to be ardently violent in defense of their land, people, and way of life. This meeting would reveal a lot about all parties involved.

Alexander Wolfgang was first to arrive. Being he had no second, he came alone, followed by Diablo Vasa and his daughter, who appeared slightly distraught and detached. The bruises on her face spoke volumes of the whispers floating around the compound regarding Elvira and Alkada engaging in more than a lover's quarrel last night. Yet, that was of no concern here.

Nonetheless, Captain BB made eye contact with Elvira, his look indicating he had heard what happened. Elvira rolled her eyes in irritation at the captain, then looked away as they both stood as seconds to their fathers.

NoLove and TwoFace stepped into the room next, instantly assessing how they were situated. NoLove sat down as TwoFace remained standing to his right.

Then came Alkada and HardBody, with Alkada sitting down and HardBody standing to his side. The tension between Alkada and Elvira was evident as the scratches across Alkada's face went unattended, bearing truth to the gossip. They stared daggers at each other from across the table as TwoFace and HardBody nodded to acknowledge each other.

Fat Pockets blustered in next, and to everybody's surprise, he had Maritzah in tow. Baron Black spoke tenderly at his niece from his chair, like a father to his daughter.

"Ah, Maritzah, this meeting is not for you, my dear. Still, I truly appreciate you seeing to the attendance of those I requested," he said, waving his hand to usher her to the door.

Maritzah looked at her uncle and then to Fat Pockets before giving a curtsey and starting. But Fat Pockets grabbed her hand, holding her in place.

"Baron Black, with all due respect, I brought Maritzah here as my second. Unfortunately, my original ho—I mean, second has fallen under the sway of your captain."

Fat Pockets paused and held his free hand out to Captain BB while everybody around the table tuned into the drama unfolding. Fat Pockets saw that he had created a moment, so he owned it. As he addressed Baron Black, his focus remained on Captain BB.

"Now, distraught as I was, dear Baron Black, I am not one to stand in the way of true love, and if Nancy has now chosen the solace and security of Captain BB, I must respect her decision. A decision, mind you, I was forced to make only earlier today when your captain came to my quarters and made me an offer in contest to his claim for Nancy's hand. As I'm sure you can imagine, this left me in quite a conundrum. However, God has sought to bless me with meeting your lovely niece, Maritzah." Fat Pockets again stopped so everyone could admire Maritzah as he pulled her forward to stand next to him, then continued.

"And a blessing she is truly proving to be in my time of need. So much so that I may have also been struck by the same arrow that has pierced Captain BB's heart, for I, too, feel the teasing of love every time I look at Maritzah. I dare say it was love at first sight."

Fat Pockets had set the scene and knew it was time for the coup de grace.

"Baron Black, again with all due respect, Maritzah has

agreed—with your permission, of course—to accompany me back to Keystone to aid and improve upon the position Nancy has now left vacant to my great loss and regret," Fat Pockets said, turning away from Captain BB to look at Baron Black. "Surely, Baron Black, you will see fair to extend me the same respect in obtaining Maritzah that I've extended you in releasing Nancy, for as the saying goes: Fair exchange is no robbery," ended Fat Pockets with a winning grin.

The room suddenly went quiet as everybody awaited Baron Black's decision, knowing it would speak highly of his fairness now and in matters to come. However, it was equally apparent to all that Captain BB was out of his league going against Fat Pockets when it came to women. The look of his embarrassment could not be missed. He'd fallen for a whore, and Fat Pockets now made him pay for it in spades. And the irony of the matter was just as blatant. Fat Pockets had lost a rock but found a diamond, and he just boxed out all possibility of being unable to keep it, lest Baron Black would be made to look emotionally weak.

Baron Black had already reasoned that his son had been played, and nothing could be done about that now. His foot was already in the shit, and Baron Black was building a nation. So, personal feelings had no place in the matter. Baron Black knew he had to be impartial and show that he wouldn't make decisions based on favoritism, either for his son or his captain. His son needed to learn a lesson, and Fat Pockets needed to be warned.

"Of course, Fat Pockets, the respect you have given shall be reciprocated. So, as you ask, you shall receive. Nancy will be very well taken care of and respected with no harm whatsoever to come to her under the penalty of death. Thus, I expect no less of you with my niece in Keystone, for surely you would give your life before you let any harm befall her. Are we agreed on this?" asked Baron Black with a wolf's grin.

"But of course," responded Fat Pockets with a fox's smile.

It was a smile he now shared as he looked first to Maritzah and then to Captain BB, seeing that they were both red in the face but for two altogether different reasons—Captain BB's out of anger and embarrassment and Maritzah's out of excitement and anticipation.

The matter was settled just as El Chablo and his lieutenant entered the room, the last guests to arrive. El Chablo carried with him the same air of power as Baron Black.

Now that all were present, the doors to the conference room were closed, and all leaders were seated except El Chablo. Noticing this, Baron Black addressed the matter.

"El Chablo, will you not join us and be seated?" asked Baron Black, holding his upturned hand out toward the empty seat.

After clasping his hands behind his back and looking down at the empty seat like he was gathering his thoughts, El Chablo looked again to Baron Black and said, "As I look around this room, I see men and women of the highest caliber. But as I look at individuals seated at this round table, I see many things."

He began to walk around the table, giving an assessment of each person he stopped next to, starting with Alkada.

"Alkada, in you, I see loyalty, pride, and strength. You step in the same manner your father did. In you, Wolfgang, I see a man in his final years but ready to fight—driven by love, a father's love for a daughter who has gone astray. In you, Fat Pockets, I see the ambition of men, an ambition to live life according to his own whims."

El Chablo then walked over to Diablo Vasa, placing a hand

on his shoulder.

"In you, my old friend, I see power. And in you, NoLove, I see all of us in the room twenty, and in some cases, thirty years ago with fire and desire in our eyes and the tenacity to follow our minds and hearts and become… And in you, Baron Black, I see the visionary that brings us all together, and in that *us*, I see revolution," stated El Chablo, concluding the full circle around the table.

"Ah, El Chablo, I never knew you to be such a diviner," interjected Baron Black. "Then again, one doesn't become one of the Republic's most wanted without some touch of clairvoyance on how to stay that way. First, however, tell me, El Chablo, what is it you see when you stand before the mirror?" asked Baron Black, knowing all present wanted to know the answer to this question.

El Chablo looked Baron Black dead in the eyes, and at that moment, they knew they were both giants among men.

"Again, as I look at all of you here, a single word comes to my mind, and that word is hope," El Chablo responded. "A hope that all of us here will get along and look at each other as equals. You all know the nature of my business, and I make no apologies about it. But to answer your question more directly, when I look in the mirror, I see an opportunist always. However, should we all come together to do this thing, do not think that after we have achieved our goal and brought the Republic to its knees, it will then be El Chablo's turn. I am an outlaw now and forever," El Chablo declared, making eye contact with all six men seated at the table before proceeding. "So, what I need to know before I sit down, Baron Black, is in your vision for new world order. Where does an outlaw stand?"

The question was paramount, and it hung above them in the air like an anvil waiting to be dropped. Everybody was now looking at Baron Black, awaiting an answer. They knew that the wrong answer could be the deal-breaker for several parties, if not all parties, gathered. As the moment lingered on, NoLove now stood up, as did Diablo, the gesture making their position blatantly obvious—not that they were against Baron Black, but that they, too, were outlaws.

Baron Black locked eyes with El Chablo from across the table as the unseen yet felt pendulum began to swing between them. This was a question they all wanted to ask, and El Chablo had asked it.

Baron Black sat back in his chair, his eyes cutting to NoLove, then to Diablo, who was also looking at him. Finally, Baron Black nodded to himself. He had to make this work.

"El Chablo, you have put a question to me that you should've put to *us*," answered Baron Black as he waved out his hand to everybody at the table. "Because that is a question I alone cannot answer. The table you see before you is round, so any question put to it will go around it till everybody has their say. Then, and only then, will we collectively decide on whatever the matter is at hand. But I now say to all of you here that I am an outlaw, and as such, I respect the outlaw code. However, we can't just be a nation of outlaws, with our only way of life being banditry. Nonetheless, whatever a man does in his own lands is his business," finished Baron Black, and at this, both NoLove and Diablo sat down.

The unseen pendulum stopped, and everybody now looked at El Chablo, gauging to see if this was the right answer.

El Chablo looked down at the empty seat, then looked at all those gathered around the table, nodding his head from shoulder to shoulder, deciding. He took a final look around the room and then sat down.

And just like that, the alliance was formed.

***

Baron Black began the meeting with firm clarity.

"Comrades, as I have just made clear, every person sitting at this table is equal to the person beside them," Baron Black stated sternly, officially opening the meeting. "And if any of you are captured, killed, or just dies as life dictates that we all must, then know your recognized second will take your place and your seat at the table. In the event there is no second, those of us remaining will submit the name of a person capable of taking the vacant spot that all must agree upon by way of a majority vote. Are we all in agreement on this?"

Everyone at the table nodded.

"Good. Then cast votes will be signaled by a yay or a nay. Although we all have designated seconds at our sides, only the person seated will be heard at this table. Yay or nay?"

Several yays rounded the table. However, the faces of several standing seconds spoke a silent distaste for this rule, especially that of Elvira, as she hissed and rolled her eyes.

"One final thing I feel I must address to you all," said Baron Black as he stood to his feet, looking at all seated before continuing. "I am aware of the bad blood and hostilities that loom between some of you at this table, but know that I take no sides. I respect the outlaw code and the rules of loyalty and revenge that govern that code. But when at this table, I respect us above all else. Because it is *us* that must prevail, thus *us* is my only concern, as should be yours—for as you all know, the Republic to divide *us* is the only way to defeat *us*."

Baron Black sat back down after seeing they were willing to comply with his words. He also noticed a look between Alkada and NoLove that spoke otherwise.

Baron Black placed the flats of his hands on the mahogany table and officially opened the meeting.

"Comrades, let us begin this call to war. From all my reports and gathered information, it is my understanding that Marshall Stryfe's forces boast over one hundred and fifty thousand to approximately two hundred thousand soldiers. Now, this number, although great, means nothing unless we were engaging them out in open flatlands. Still, when we introduce them to our brand of warfare in the mountains, woodlands, swamplands, and deserts, we will drastically cut the Republic's army in half, not to mention we have the advantage of attacking on lands that we know, survive, thrive, and live off. This very advantage helped us beat them back in the Death Sagas, yet I know this time we will need more than knowing how the wind will blow or the river will flow to be victorious. Therefore, I will put forth several thousand of my finest soldiers to the very front lines of our campaign," said Baron Black, pausing to let it sink into all at the table the power under his control. "I realize all of you may be unable to make such a contribution of men. Still, everyone here has something they can bring to the table. I put forth this much to show I am committed to our cause beyond words. Now, what do each of you bring to the table?" asked Baron Black, turning first to Alexander Wolfgang, an indication for him to now speak.

Wolfgang acknowledged having the floor and stood up to address all those present.

"I came here, as you all surely know by now, in search of my daughter," said Wolfgang, cutting his eyes at NoLove before going on. "I hoped to bring her home, back to Noble Haven, but instead, I have come to find my daughter is too far gone to be saved."

Baron Black started to interject, but Wolfgang held him back with a halting gesture of his hands as he continued.

"Now, I see in seeking my daughter, I have been given a chance to be a part of a revolution fighting against the very Republic that now hunts my daughter. So, if I am soon to die, then I can think of no greater cause to die for than to kill those who would see me and my lineage dead. I have no soldiers to offer. As you know, Noble Haven flies under a flag of sovereignty, which the Republic has long sought to put an end to, pausing only for fear of those I answer to. But I, myself, have my vast resources and other powerful friends who will not mind contributing to the war chest nor paying for whatever you need, and at that, the very best that can be bought. Not to mention, I offer all of Noble Haven as a base of operations for when the time comes to inevitably invade Republic City, which we will need to do," said Wolfgang, already knowing The Imperium would not like the idea of this alliance.

"Yes, Republic City must be taken," said Diablo Vasa. "This will give us sway over the entire east coast from Noble Haven to Shynetown."

This statement invited a wave of nods from everyone, especially from Diablo and Elvira. They had already pondered the taking of Republic City to stop the expansion of Republic control and expand their own.

"I also have several sources that can be cultivated for information behind our now enemy lines," offered Wolfgang.

"No!" barked Baron Black to the startlement of all those present, forcing him to explain his reasoning behind his outburst. "No spies. We will use no spies. They can never totally be trusted. The whole nature of their existence is based on lies and betrayal. This war will not be fought from the shadows. Whoever is with us will stand and be recognized with us. Please forgive me for interrupting you, Wolfgang. I just hate spies in earnest. One might even say it was the whispering of a spy that brought about the Death Sagas. Anyway, your power and financial contributions will be greatly appreciated."

As Wolfgang sat down, Diablo Vasa stood up next to speak, his daughter to his right, still looking death at Alkada.

"Gentlemen, it appears we are about to make history, but mind you all, this will be a bloody affair to rival even that of the Death Sagas, which I also partook in. But this time, we must be absolute in our pushback against the Republic because their push will, without a doubt, be absolute on us. Baron Black, as you know, my lands are to your rear. So, know that I have your back. As well, I will issue forth several thousand soldiers. Of that, half will be Sanchie riders, the finest in horseback infantry. And know that all of you seated here are now welcome in my lands."

El Chablo paid close attention to all that was being said. Aside from him, Red Rock was the only other surmountable force in the room to rival Baron Black or Diablo Vasa. And he noticed that both Diablo and Baron Black did not reveal the actual number of soldiers under their control. El Chablo decided he would play his hand just as close to the chest as they did when the time came.

NoLove was next to stand up, removing his hat as he nodded to all present, temporarily stopping at Alkada and instantly feeling the hate born between them.

"As you are all aware, I represent the Mob, and real talk, we don't yet have the numbers or resources to make much difference on the battlefield. But we will contribute to the war efforts in other ways just as effectively."

"Such as?" asked Baron Black, looking at NoLove, who was standing directly across the table from him.

NoLove knew he had to bolster up his story. These were all-powerful men, so he wanted to measure up as close as possible.

"Well, for starters, we already have people planted all across the border in Republic territory who are ready to move when given the word. In this, we will introduce and deliver a method of warfare based on terror and acts of attrition that will show no mercy. The Mob will unleash a horror that knows no bounds behind the lines of the Republic, either by the massacres of their innocents, burning down their towns, robbing their banks, or killing their leaders. We will bring the Republic to its knees with anarchy and chaos. We will make them come to fear the terrorist among them that is us."

"This is good, NoLove. The Republic needs to know the feeling of the pain it forces others to endure," said Baron Black, enthused.

Everyone else nodded in agreement to the use of such maliciousness and subterfuge.

As NoLove sat back down, Fat Pockets was next to stand. He was used to addressing crowds and talking to underlings and minions, but now he was here in a room talking to men who were larger than life—men who openly challenged a man Fat Pockets feared. And these men now all looked at Fat Pockets the same way—a look that told him: *You don't deserve to be at this table, but what are you willing to do to stay?*

"Okay," started Fat Pockets.

He glanced at Maritzah to find her gaze already locked on him. That loving glance was all he needed to muster the courage to be who he needed to be.

"Ain't no secret Marshall Stryfe got his foot on my neck, and I don't like it, but I ain't got no army of killers holdin' my lands down like everybody else here. And by the sound of it, shit is 'bout to go ka-boom for real. I'm talkin' gunplay on Sunday, so the fuck shit is unavoidable. If I don't throw in with ya, I'm sure I won't make it back to Keystone alive!"

"Plans known are plans that can be defeated, Fat Pockets," said Baron Black, smiling like a cat that had trapped a mouse.

Fat Pockets knew in an instant he was trading the devil he knew for the devil he didn't, but it was too late to back out.

I might as well push it to the limit, thought Fat Pockets.

"Well, I take it if I'm not part of the plan, I'm a dead man?" said Fat Pockets.

"Pretty much," said Diablo Vasa, who also knew the importance of locking down Keystone.

"Your commitment?" pressed Baron Black to Fat Pockets.

"Okay, so it's 'get down or lay down.' I peep the play, I recog—"

"Your commitment, Fat Pockets!" barked Baron Black, having no more patience for his stalling.

"Okay, okay, here goes. I will lay an injunction down in Keystone on any and all Republic goods."

"That is a good start, Fat Pockets, but only a start. This matter will require more than an embargo."

Fat Pockets nodded his understanding; he would not be able to half-step.

"As well, anything coming into my docks headed for the Republic is gettin' took and brought to the table."

"What else?" pressed Baron Black, prompting everyone seated at the table to now beam in on Fat Pockets.

"What more would you have?" countered Fat Pockets, already knowing what Baron Black was after.

"What about all the Republic monies and other holdings now sitting in Keystone banks?"

Fuck, thought Fat Pockets, as several brows raised at Baron Black's question. He was quick to answer but felt no pressure. Yes, he was in a den of lions, yet he knew he was the sheep they couldn't afford to eat, although he could end up dead if he denied them being fed.

"Shit, I'm gonna bring it to the table and break bread with all of ya," said Fat Pockets.

This brought several nods of appeasement from those seated at the table. Fat Pockets knew his worth, but he had to be sure they knew that he knew and would act accordingly.

"Now, understand me, I don't mind passin' the bag around as long as ya hold me down. I ain't no gunslinger or killa, but I will point the finger and get shit started. Now, you all be knowin' Keystone is a money town, and bills gotta be paid."

"Yes, of course. And I'm sure you'll find my niece very helpful in the accounting and financial dealings you may have to contend with," Baron Black added.

Again, Fat Pockets, never one to be outdone with words and his mind constantly spinning in money matters, sought to put things in their proper perspective. Yes, Maritza was Baron Black's niece, but Fat Pockets was a pimp, and he was about to pimp hard.

"Oh, no doubt. Now you see why I need her at my side. With all due respect, Baron Black, Maritzah may be your niece, but by the next time you see her, she may be my wife," Fat Pockets said, grinning at Baron Black.

An awkward moment of silence was interrupted by a gasp from Maritzah, who was inwardly shocked yet outwardly trying hard to hold her composure.

"Now, I may have some Republic soldiers still lingering around in Keystone in light of the performance of murder that just took place courtesy of the Mob," said Fat Pockets, again looking towards NoLove and TwoFace, who only snickered. "Anyway, I'm sure I'll have that to deal with when I slide back East, and I'm talkin' the lead way. On another note, we're gonna have to hold that northern border against Republic invasion because they may try to flood in from Republic City. Fact being, we both border the mountains, and there are often supply ships on my docks bound for Republic City at any given time. But, as I said, I will be pushing down on all of that," ended Fat Pockets as he sat back down.

Alkada stood up next, claiming the floor. A large man, two long scars laced his face while well over twenty crisscrossed HardBody's. Their scars were a testament, tribute, and symbol to who they were, what they were about, and what they were capable of.

"I'm sure all of you here know me or know of me. I am Shyne, and the hate I hold for the Republic is held by all of mine who claim Shyne. I've lost many comrades to the Republic in the Death Sagas. Most notably, my father, Elijah, who fell during the Death Sagas, and my pal, S.I., leader of the Billies, who was murdered by a Republic regime born from the Death Sagas."

Alkada paused as a wave of emotion washed over him at the memory of S.I.

"I got blood back for him, just as I did for my father, but this blood came at a high price. Fact being, because of things I've done, every Shyne man, woman, and child is marked for death by the Republic. Were Marshall Stryfe given his way, he and Hammer would see every Shyne extinguished from existence, and I can't give them that. I've taken many Republic heads, and if this war to come is any indication, I will take many more. Some of you here knew and fought alongside my father, as I will now fight alongside you. I don't have legions of soldiers to offer, but I do have the Platinum Army of Shyne. Each soldier is a general's rank with extensive and explicit experience in warfare and killing. They lead from the front and are disciplined in the art of malicious murder, sniping, ambushing, tracking, and scouting. And as you all know, our specialty is taking heads," said Alkada, then locked eyes with NoLove for a fraction of a second before continuing. "My men are adaptable to any landscape, any warlike settings, and will move and remain militant under the hardest conditions. Trust that no man can lead the line like a Shyne. Even if I'm killed, my men will remain loyal to you until victory or death."

"What about the rest of Red Rock? Will they also stand with our cause as you do?" asked Baron Black.

"Yes, do you speak for the Billies and Rollacks, as well?" added Diablo Vasa.

"I speak to you now the same as I did last night. All of Red Rock will contribute to what is being discussed. The Billies and Rollacks will also stand and be counted among us, just as my comrade StreetLife told you he would. But I can't give you an exact count of how many until I return to Red Rock."

"Alkada, I hope you are right because if we are to be successful, we will need everyone in Red Rock to muster up the courage. I stress this only because I've heard there may be tensions in Red Rock," Baron Black stated.

Alkada knew Baron Black was referring to the fray between the Shynes and the Billies. It was slight, but nonetheless, blood had been spilled. Had it not been for the intervention by S.I. to establish the truce between Alkada and one of his own, things would've been a lot messier. But that was Red Rock's business and not the people's concern who now sat around him.

"Baron Black, the people of Red Rock are all brothers and sisters, and sometimes siblings have differences that must be settled. Fashion Red Rock as a tree, a mighty redwood, the Shynes, Billies, Rollacks, and many others as branches. To bring harm to any one of these branches would inevitably harm the tree. And should the tree fall, then we all fall. Thus, I say to you all, whatever you may hear of Red Rock, we are always all together as we are always a tree," concluded Alkada as he sat down to a round of nods.

Alkada was a man of sterner stuff—a man to be believed, a man to be followed, a man not to be questioned. *You have grown well, Alkada,* thought Baron Black as he nodded and studied him.

Finally, El Chablo stood up to address the room.

"I see everyone here has truly committed to the cause. So, I can do no less. I will put forth a full army of infantry and an army of riders, all numbering in the thousands," said El Chablo, raising one eye to Baron Black before going on. "I will also put forth my naval fleet for attack by sea."

Several brows raised at this revelation, totally unaware of El Chablo's naval fleet.

El Chablo picked up on the surprise and continued in true hustler swag that represented all he stood for. "Comrades, you all look surprised, but surely you had to suspect that had we not assembled here today, I was already planning for war against the Republic. I was going at Marshall Stryfe straight up. I'm eating good in the streets, and ain't nobody tellin' me and mine how to trap a dime. The world just ain't big enough for the both of us. And the bread I'm gettin' ain't gonna stop till my casket drops. Yet, I'm glad to know others feel as I do about the capitalist pigs of the Republic. The Death Sagas was a lesson to us all on how far the Republic will go and how merciless they can be. It is now time to show them that a blade cuts two ways," said El Chablo as he sat down.

"Agreed," said Baron Black. "Is three months enough time for you all to prepare?"

"Yay," they uttered in unison.

"Good. Then, ladies and gentlemen, our meeting has come to an end. Tomorrow, there will be a parting feast and a special event in the banquet hall. I look forward to seeing you all then," said Baron Black, rising to his feet along with everyone else.

"Halt," barked Diablo Vasa, arresting everyone's attention. "I have a final question. What is to be our name, our banner that identifies us to the Republic?"

Looks went around the table as the brainstorming for a name began. Then, finally, Alexander Wolfgang stood up to put forth the moniker that would come to signify them.

"May I suggest 'The Democracy of the Plains Alliance,' or the DPA, if you will."

All nodded in concurrence as the call rounded the table in a vote, and thus, the DPA had been formed.

Everyone now rose, their respected seconds at their sides, and began to leave the conference room.

"Alkada," called Baron Black, stopping him as he and HardBody headed for the door.

Alkada stopped and turned to Baron Black.

"Can you stay for a moment? I'd like to have a word with you."

Alkada nodded as Diablo Vasa nodded to him in passing, followed by Elvira, who deliberately bumped Alkada as she passed him while on the heels of her father.

Alkada nodded to HardBody that he was good, and HardBody left the room, followed by Captain BB. When everyone was gone, the doors were closed, and Alkada and Baron Black were left alone.

"Alkada, I know and understand that you have been put to the oath regarding the salts between you and the Mob. Once, a long time ago, your father explained this oath to me and the specifics involved. So, I would not disrespect you or his memory by trying to persuade you from it. I already know your loyalty to it. Looking at you now, I am reminded of your father. You have that same grit and stubbornness—defiance and willingness to kill and die for your beliefs when blood is the only payment. I get that. Although I take no sides in settling the matter between you and the Mob, I am hoping you will be victorious in that when this war starts, you are at my side. I say this out of respect for you and the memory of your father, who died fighting at my side. Thus, I am obligated to tell you, as I know both you and the Mob are headed to the Roughs to handle what must be done. Know that Captain Hammer is also about, headed toward the Roughs, as well. So, you are warned. Now, you spoke of how the people of Red Rock, although they may be of different branches, are all of the same tree. Trust that your analogy was not wasted on me, for we both know the significance of what you said. I am now asking you to be a branch on my tree—the tree we have planted today upon this very table," said Baron Black as he laid his palm down on the round table, awaiting Alkada's response.

"Baron Black, know that I respect you just like my father did, and you have my loyalty until death. But I am bonded by my oath, just as my scars are bonded to my face. This salt between the Mob and me can only end with blood, the same way it started. Thank you for telling me about Captain Hammer. Perhaps Dempaku will bless me with his death, as well. And however things go, I've given you my word that whether I live or die, a Shyne will be at your side when you sound the call to war."

Baron Black nodded, then, stepping in closer, he placed his hand on Alkada's shoulder.

"As your father used to say, there is nothing like being on the front line with a Shyne. But, unfortunately, Alkada, I know your father is no longer among us. I hope you can respect this coming from me, but were Elijah still here today, I am sure he would be proud of the man you have become."

Alkada already had the utmost respect for Baron Black, but that respect was now amplified. Baron Black, a man his father held dear, spoke to him as his own father once did, bringing on memories too numerous to count: the passing of his first gun, the first head he severed, his first scar. Alkada nodded his head, shaking the pain of his dead father away. He then placed his hand on Baron Black's shoulder the same way Baron had grabbed his.

"Baron Black, your words are respected beyond any response I could articulate, but know that I now look at you the same way

I looked upon my father. And *after* I deal with my oath, I will follow you just the same."

Baron Black nodded and saluted. He pushed as far as he could. He patted Alkada's back as they left the room together.

Chapter Thirty

Judge Grimlock sat in his chamber, brooding over the turn of events while sipping brandy and watching through his window as the sun began to set over Independence. He found out about Marshall Stryfe's impending call for war on the Barren Plains—a region where the first war was so monstrous that it would forever be marked as the Death Sagas.

The Barren Plains is a mass of land that can't be tamed or controlled. At least not with aggression. The Death Sagas proved that. But here is this fool about to repeat history, thought Grimlock, embittered by Marshall Stryfe's thirst for absolute rule.

Stryfe was blind to the fact that the people he was trying to rule over would rather die than surrender.

Salt was all the Republic knew to use, whereas Grimlock knew honey was what was needed. Men like El Chablo, Baron Black, Diablo Vasa, and the notorious Shynes could not be subdued or conquered by force. They were to either be killed or left alone.

The strength of these men was rooted in their faith and beliefs. Their beliefs were in their blood, and their blood gave spirit to all that they stood for. These were true men of charisma born to lead, so even in killing them, you would only be killing a man and making him a martyr—a legend never to be forgotten, and his ideas made all the stronger to the people who followed them.

If this man is left to his own devices, he will be the ruin of the Republic! What conqueror doesn't at least attempt to understand the very people he seeks to subjugate? Divide and conquer! It's a simple formula that has worked time and time again. Shit, it's how the Civilized Republic was born and formed! And now this backward thinker is straying from tradition, only to get the reverse effect with his antics! Instead of driving the Plains people apart with pressure, he's galvanizing them!

Grimlock grew more infuriated with each passing thought.

If the rumors Grimlock heard about a great meeting at Freedom Compound were true, then the Plains people must have cast aside their differences, and they now knew that collectively they could withstand the might of the Republic. It was only a matter of time before withstanding turned to challenge, and this had to be avoided at all costs. However, all wasn't lost, at least not for Grimlock. Indeed, he had a powerful friend down bottom who owed him a favor—who owed him his life actually, since no one escaped from The Fort without Grimlock's approval. Yet, this man had done it twice, or rather Grimlock allowed it to happen twice, much to the embarrassment of Marshall Stryfe. Grimlock was pleased with himself about that.

For all Grimlock knew, he'd never figure an alliance between Baron Black and El Chablo possible. One man was an idealist and the other an opportunist, and both were extremes in their spectrums. But surely, different sides of the same coin they were. Nonetheless, Grimlock knew something had to be done about them, or Marshall Stryfe, or all of them, for that matter.

Grimlock knew that the first law of nature was self-preservation. He didn't become the high judge of the Civilized Republic being idle or slack. In his years of judging the courts, he created his own power, cultivated resources, and entrenched himself in the very fabric of the Republic. He kept many secrets, which brought and maintained his status in the upper echelons of Republic society, a status that left him revered and feared, with a lot of favors owed to him. Now it was time to call in a few of those favors.

There was a knock on the door of his office.

"Enter," announced Judge Grimlock, spinning around in his chair, looking away from his view to observe his secretary stepping into his chambers.

"Grim, I was about to leave. Do you need anything done before I go?" she asked.

"Ah, my beautiful Hilda," said Grimlock, leaning back in his chair and admiring the woman before him.

She was a lovely woman of mixed descent with a Noble Haven upbringing. A very shapely woman with raven black hair and oily black eyes shaped like almonds, hinting at her far eastern ethnicity. She was no more than twenty-five and every bit as exotic and neurotic as she looked, bringing the judge to an aroused state every time he laid eyes on her.

"Hilda, it appears this brandy has given me quite a swelling in my nethers. Please, come be a good pet and suck on it until the swelling goes down," said Grimlock with a wink of his eye.

Hilda immediately closed the door to the judge's chambers,

and smiling, she closed the distance between them. Walking around his desk, she grabbed the glass of brandy from his hand, took a sip, handed it back to him, and pushed his legs apart with her thigh. She then got down on her knees and took the judge in her mouth, giving him oral ecstasy for the next fifteen minutes.

Feeling himself about to erupt, he placed his hand gently on the top of her head as he released in her mouth, patting her on the head as he finished.

Life is good, but Marshall Stryfe's death will make it grand! he thought as he took another swig of his brandy and passed it to Hilda.

"Anything else, Grim?" asked Hilda as she downed the rest of the brandy.

"No, love, you've done me good already. Just be sure to send that telegraph off I gave you earlier in the day and clear my schedule for tomorrow and the following days. I have a few favors I need to call in."

"Okay, Grim. Is it anything I can help you with?" Hilda purred, now standing behind Grimlock and massaging his temples.

"*Ha-ha*, you just did, my dear, Hilda, although the next time we tangle, I'd much rather you sit on me than spit on me."

"Sure, Grim," she replied as she kissed his cheek and fluttered out of the office, leaving Grimlock to his solitude and thoughts.

If El Chablo is unable to meet my needs down bottom, perhaps there's another that can, he thought slyly.

***

Simon Thorn, or the Weasel as he was more commonly

known, had been in Republic City for a few days now, awaiting confirmation and details on his undertakings in Independence. He was ecstatic when it finally came. Now he could get back to his wife and daughters and enjoy some of the money he just made. God knew he could afford it.

They don't call me the Weasel for nothing, he thought as he looked at the message he had received from the desk clerk.

WHAT YOU ASKED HAS BEEN ARRANGED. TWO WEEKS FROM TODAY, ON FRIDAY, BE AT ARMGALE TRAIN STATION IN REACH PROVIDENCE—THE 3:10 OUT OF INDEPENDENCE. YOUR PACKAGE WILL BE DELIVERED. KEEP IN MIND, YOUR SILENCE GOES HAND-IN-HAND WITH YOUR HAPPINESS AS WELL AS THAT OF YOUR FAMILY. MY BEST TO YOUR WIFE & DAUGHTERS.

— GRIM

The desk clerk watched as the Weasel read the message that had arrived for him by telegraph. He, too, had read it just as the Weasel was now reading it. Yet, he was puzzled by the Weasel's reaction because he knew to some degree, the message harbored a threat to his family.

The threat was real, but so was the money. Simon Thorn was no fool, though. His deal with Judge Grimlock was a secret he would take to the grave—one of many.

Secrets were such powerful things, and often enough, people were willing to pay for the secrets of others. Perhaps one day, he would be able to send Judge Grimlock such a message as the one he had received today, but it wouldn't be any time soon.

One step at a time…and I will make Grimlock rue the day, the Weasel thought to himself cunningly.

Simon stepped out of the hotel lobby into the fresh air of the day, greeted by clear skies and cool breezes that announced the coming of fall. He noticed that Republic City was alive with activity: wagons going to and fro, groups of soldiers on the march, saloons and storefronts bustling and packed with patrons. The gossip and chatter were charged with electricity. Something was amiss.

The Weasel spotted a paperboy on the corner and flagged him down.

"Hey, kid, pass me a paper," he said, flinging the kid a coin three times the paper's worth.

"Thanks, mister!" the kid cheered, happy for such a tip.

"Beat it, kid," responded the Weasel as he unfolded the paper to the front page of *Republic Speaks*.

MARSHALL STRYFE DECLARES WAR ON THE BARREN PLAINS!!!

The Weasel didn't need to read the paper to know what was coming, tossing it to the street as he made his way to the telegraph station. *Shit!* Grimlock had told him in so many words. The Weasel needed to get to his family in Noble Haven and decide which side of the war he would be on. The sooner he sent Foot a message, the sooner he'd be headed home.

***

SECOND FRIDAY FROM NOW, BE AT ARMGALE STATION IN REACH PROVIDENCE—THE 3:10. YOUR PACKAGE WILL BE THERE.

— THE WEASEL

Foot read the message several times until he had memorized it. He had just gotten to the Bluff and situated himself in the Rose Hotel. There was still no word from NoLove, but Foot was confident he could handle it himself. Plus, he couldn't imagine NoLove or TwoFace being killed and the news of their deaths not spreading like wildfire. He was certain he would hear something soon, and sure enough, news of the war was circulating fast and changing the feel of the streets. The air had a certain tenseness that had not been there before.

Foot turned to the desk clerk on duty, asking, "Is this the only message for me?"

"That's the only one I gave you, isn't it?" snorted the desk clerk in response as he went back to sorting the other messages, giving Foot his back.

Foot looked at the desk clerk, perplexed at how he had been so chumped off as other patrons began to snicker at him.

"What the fuck?" Foot muttered under his breath.

Reaching over the counter, Foot grabbed the clerk by the scruff of his neck and spun him around. With the desk clerk now facing him, Foot swung his arm wide and open-handedly slapped the shit out of him, sending him a step back into the message rack behind him. Numerous messages fell out of their slots and onto the ground. Foot again grabbed the clerk and pulled him forward as he let loose another slap. Next, he reached for his gun, cocked back the hammer, and stuck it in the clerk's mouth, totally oblivious to the patrons gathering to watch the drama play out.

"Now, listen up, you fucking guppy. My name is Foot, and I don't take no sass from no fuck-boy desk clerk. You understand me?!"

The desk clerk, unable to talk with the barrel of Foot's gun jammed in his mouth, vigorously nodded his head up and down and managed an, "Uhm-hmm."

"Good," Foot said as he uncocked his gun and removed it from the clerk's mouth, shoving him back before turning to the crowd.

"Listen up!" Foot shouted, addressing everyone in the hotel lobby. "The Bluff is now under Mob control and protection. Y'all got that? We run the Bluff!" Foot then looked back at the desk clerk. "You understand me, guppy?"

Again, the desk clerk emphatically agreed while nodding his head.

"Bitch, answer me. I don't speak in nods."

"Yes, sir, I understand!"

"Good. Now, I reckons you pass that along to everybody you encounter today. That goes for all of you, as well," Foot ordered, pointing at the crowd.

"So, let's try this again so I can be sure you and I are crystal," said Foot to the desk clerk. "Is this the only message you got for me?" he asked again, holding up the telegraph, his other hand gripping his gun handle.

"Yes, sir, Mr. Foot, sir. I'll be sure to notify you the instant a new one arrives, sir," answered the desk clerk in his most servile voice.

"Well, much obliged. I'd really appreciate that, and ain't no need of you calling me sir and mister. I'm an outlaw, for God's sake, and we just established you's a bitch when I put my gun in your mouth. But so long as you're a bitch with respect, you'll stay alive. Now, if and when anybody comes this way claiming to be my brother or the Mob, you be sure to show them the same respect. Savvy?"

"Yes, sir—I mean, understood, Foot," the clerk responded cautiously.

Pleased with his performance and the clerk's responses, Foot flipped him a coin as he started to walk off, then stopped mid-stride.

"I'll be in my room 112. Send me a menu, a paper, and while you're at it, find me a Lucy with big tits."

He tossed the desk clerk another coin and continued to walk off. Several of the patrons immediately sidestepped Foot to get out of his way as he walked by.

The Bluff is only the beginning, thought Foot, ignoring the onlookers who gawked at him.

*****

Caserian was barely awake. Buried deep under the blankets that covered his bed to stay warm from the chill that waited outside his window, he tried hard to go back to sleep, but the incessant tapping on his window made it impossible for him to drift off.

The sun wasn't up yet. It was Saturday, and he had no lessons. Caserian wanted to do nothing more than sleep, but the tapping became too much to be ignored. In that realization, Caserian asked himself why he was hearing tapping anyway. Then, removing the blanket from his head, Caserian opened his eyes to see a massive black eagle streaked with snatches of red plumage perched on his window ledge, staring directly at him like it was judging him—looking at him as much as looking through him.

Now sitting up in bed, Caserian was momentarily frozen with fear and alive with wonder. Yet, at the same time, he felt an instant connection with this enormous predatorial bird. He broke the fear that gripped him and walked toward the window as if hypnotized. He undid the latch to open the window and immediately stepped back as Skully entered the room, bringing with him a thrust of cool morning air. Again, their eyes met and locked, and a connection was established between them. It was surreal and completely metaphysical.

Finally finding his voice, Caserian spoke to the bird.

"What are you doing here?" he asked, stepping away from the bird.

Skully shrieked loudly, causing Caserian to cover his ears and back away, bumping into the dresser behind him as Skully spread his massive wings, filling the small room with his entirety. He hopped forward, then lifted his taloned foot, indicating for Caserian to grab the capsule attached to his leg.

Caserian felt courage and curiosity rise up within him as he gingerly reached for the capsule, unfastening its latch.

"Rahhhhh," Skully shrieked, re-paralyzing Caserian for a moment.

After ruffling his wings, Skully reached forward and placed one of his massive wings on Caserian's face, and in an instant, a jolt shot through Cesarian's body. At the same time, a jolt shot through two other people—all three miles apart, yet for a moment, all connected.

A father whispered, "Son," a sister uttered, "My brother," and

Caserian spoke as the reverberation of the shock dissipated.

"Father? Sister?"

Skully then hopped back to the window ledge and looked Caserian in the eye, both knowing this would not be the last time they saw each other.

"Rahhhhhhh," Skully shrieked a final time before leaping back into the dark morning sky with a massive flap of his wings, the force toppling several items on Caserian's dresser.

Caserian bolted to the window in awe, watching the bird soar away until he was little more than a dot in the distant sky. Once Caserian could no longer see him, he turned his attention back to the capsule in his hand. He pulled it apart to read the message inside.

KNOW THE TRUTH OF WHO YOU TRULY ARE, YOUR FAMILY, YOUR BLOODLINE. I KNOW YOU HAVE QUESTIONS. COME TO SHYNETOWN AND KNOW THE ANSWERS IN TRUTH INSTEAD OF THE LIES YOU'VE BEEN TOLD.

— YOUR FATHER, ALKADA

Caserian couldn't believe what he had just read, but believe it, he did. He always knew deep down inside there was more to him, more to his life than what he'd been told—or rather not told—by his mother. Even here in Noble Haven, with kids from everywhere, he always felt like an outsider. It was nothing they pressed upon him, as much as he felt like an outcast. He thought differently, and now it all made sense. For as long as he could remember, he knew something was being hidden from him, and now he had evidence to support his suspicion.

He heard about the Shynes before; all the world had, so he thought. He could still remember being told as a child: Be good, or the Shynes will get you. It would scare him into being good or going to sleep or whatever his mother wanted him to do. And to now discover he was of the stock that he had always been told were a savage lot of bloodthirsty killers who cut off people's heads and drank their blood, it boggled him. There were no Shyne children in Noble Haven, so there was no one to help gain the guarantees on fact or fiction.

Caserian just knew the Shynes were always described as dark and feral—loners lost to a ritualistic way of life. A life of guns, knives, and bullets. Yet, in receiving this message—from a giant bird, no less—he instantly felt a kinship to these people. He felt a calling deep within him to be counted among them, and instantly, the feeling consumed and overwhelmed him. So much so that he was willing to go to Shynetown to have his questions answered. He would know this Alkada who claimed now to be his father after all these years of being told his father had been killed in some type of skirmish with Republic soldiers.

Caserian was alive with excitement and anticipation. He immediately began to scramble around the room, collecting and gathering up his possessions for a trip he already knew would be one way. He was finally about to know the answers to so many questions. Who was this Alkada—a name that already felt paramount to him? And a sister?

All of this was revealed when the bird touched him, and even more, another name that of late had begun to press down on him like a force. The force whispered to his soul and, at times, even whispered to him deep in his dreams promises of sweet indulgences if Caserian embraced the dark touch. Always the sibilant voice expressed a desire for him when he slept, and always with a name. And that name was Mugasa. Yes, Caserian would have answers. The answers his mother couldn't or wouldn't give him.

***

Francis Drake sat in his room in a state of frustration. It had been nearly two days since he arrived in Freedom Compound, and even though his every need was seen to, he wasn't allowed to leave the room. And for all the talk of him being a guest, he felt like little more than a pampered prisoner.

When he entered the compound, he found it lit with activity, a clear indication that something was amiss. He knew trying to assassinate Baron Black would be next to impossible. It would be nothing short of a suicide mission, which was not in Drake's planning. But he figured he would at least be able to talk to him. Things were heating up, and Drake needed to know how to play and whom to play out. Just then, his door opened.

"Hello," said the attendant as she stepped inside his room.

"Hello," he responded to the woman who had introduced herself as Maritzah days prior.

"I hope all has been to your liking. I'm here to let you know that you are now permitted to leave your room. You have also been invited to join Baron Black at tonight's dinner, which starts in about one hour, at which time you will have the audience with Baron Black that you seek. A servant will be set outside your door to escort you to the banquet hall when you are ready," said Maritzah.

"Well, thank you very much. It's truly nice to be appreciated.

So, as soon as I bathe and get myself together, I will be headed your way," Francis responded, only slightly letting his irritation show at his treatment thus far.

Maritzah curtly nodded, smiled, and left.

Francis merely nodded. It was about time they started showing him some respect. He had waited two days, so they could now wait for him.

Chapter Thirty-One

The banquet hall filled quickly, just as it had three days earlier. The only difference now was that there was no feeling of tension or apprehension in the air—no looks of disdain or contempt for each other. The three days of congregating had given everybody a chance to get to know each other. Thus, everybody in the hall now embraced one another as comrades on the crest of waging war together.

Trivial hostilities were forgotten for the most part. However, the pressure between the Shynes and the Mob was apparent to those who knew the particulars between them. Still, true civility was respected and maintained by all.

Like before, as the premier guests arrived, they were seated up front, right before the stage. Servants fluttered about through the crowd, seeing to the needs of over five hundred people in the hall. The mood was jovial in earnest, a stark contrast to what was to come.

As usual, Wolfgang arrived first, promptness no doubt born

from decades of business dealings. Diablo Vasa and his daughter were next to arrive. They joined Wolfgang at his table, shaking hands and smiling among the throngs of people before sitting down.

Elvira maintained a composure of controlled rage, knowing servants had spread the word of her violation and ass-kicking at the hands of Alkada. Captain BB looking at her with a knowing grin only infuriated her more. She decided that no matter what, she would kill Alkada, even if she had to die doing it.

NoLove was next to arrive with the Mob in tow. He nodded to the many people he had become acquainted with over the past few days. They were seated a few tables over from Bianca's father and the Vasas. As they passed them, Bianca reached down, hugged her father, and told him that she loved him. Wolfgang embraced his daughter and said the same. NoLove paused in his step, allowing them to pass a few words between them and nodding his respect to Diablo Vasa as he waited. Bianca was back on his arm a few moments later, and they were seated.

El Chablo was next to arrive, dressed in full military garb and flanked by his lieutenant, announcing to all that he was ready for war. Several throngs of people began to clap at his arrival, to which El Chablo threw up his hands in acceptance of the praise before he sat down.

Fat Pockets strolled into the hall next, dressed to impress with Maritzah draped on his arm. She was wearing an elegant red gown that stuck to her body, and her hair was out, causing black tresses to fall down her shoulders and back. A beautiful diamond necklace adorned her neck, obviously a gift from Fat Pockets that sent a clear message to all that she, like the necklace, belonged to him.

Yet, to his credit, when Fat Pockets was shown to his table between Diablo Vasa and NoLove, he pulled out the chair for Maritzah to sit. He then proceeded to pour her a glass of wine. Fat Pockets was careful to show her the utmost respect and attentiveness, which many noticed.

Nancy, seated at Captain BB's table, was engulfed with envy to see this man whom she had been a slave to treat this woman with such high regard. In contrast, Fat Pockets had always handled her with nothing but disregard and disdain. The display truly caused Nancy's ire to flare. As if she had spoken her thoughts aloud, Fat Pockets turned to catch Nancy staring at him with daggers in her eyes.

Ever the player, Fat Pockets smiled and winked at Nancy as he sat down and kissed Maritzah on the cheek, making her blush devil red as she waved and smiled to the many servants she had bossed over throughout her many years as head hostess.

Alkada was the next and final arrival, flanked by StreetLife and HardBody to his right, London and A1 coming up the rear. Like always, they could hear the gasps, feel the stares, and note the whispers as dozens of eyes fell upon the scars on the faces of Alkada and HardBody. Many people not only stood but also saluted in the ancient way they had witnessed by Alkada, signifying their allegiance and loyalty in the upcoming war.

Alkada nodded his acknowledgment to all who he passed while being shown to his table. As he approached Diablo's table, he also stood, placed his hands on Alkada's shoulders, pulled him close, kissed him on his neck, and spoke directly into his ear.

"You are my son as your son is my grandson," said Diablo.

And just like that, the salt was melted between them.

However, that was hardly the case with Elvira. When she

locked eyes with Alkada, she gave him a hateful gaze, refusing to stand and greet him.

HardBody, falling in step behind Alkada, paused at the table, kicking the top of Elvira's foot, breaking the death trance between her and Alkada as he spoke to her. "What's up, Evie?"

Elvira shifted her death gaze to him.

"So what's up? Are you ready to have my baby now?" he asked, grinning.

StreetLife heard the comment and began shaking his head while pulling HardBody away.

Fat Pockets stood up as the Shynes passed his table and offered a bottle of wine, which HardBody snatched as they continued to mosey by without stopping. Finally, Alkada reached NoLove's table, and NoLove, along with his brothers, stood up as Alkada and his men approached.

The rumored salts between the Shynes and the Mob were now common knowledge to all at Freedom Compound. However, everyone knew that nobody would violate the peace pact that Baron Black had in place.

Alkada and NoLove were face to face. TwoFace and HardBody gave acknowledging nods as StreetLife and Goon sized each other up.

"What's up, NoLove? There's a place called the Roughs not too far from here," started Alkada.

"I know the place," NoLove answered pompously, feeling his hatred rise.

"Good. So, let's say we meet there so I can settle up on the heads you owe me?"

"That sounds alright to me, bruh, 'cept you won't be gettin' no more heads. But I intend on pullin' some blood up out'cha, and I reckons Leggs is getting lonely waitin' on ya to join him. Ain't that right, kid?" said NoLove to A1, reaching out to pat A1 on the head. "I'm sure you miss your pa, don't cha?" NoLove chuckled.

A1 smacked his hand away. Immediately, security swooped down, and Alkada and his men pushed on as the Mob sat down.

Now passing El Chablo's table, he stood up to greet them.

"Ah, Alkada and StreetLife, I see suns to guns truly does exist between you two!" He patted both on their shoulders. "StreetLife, join me at my table. There are a few things we need to discuss before our departure tomorrow. Surely Alkada won't mind," El Chablo added.

"Go ahead, bro. I'm gonna polly with El Chablo here," StreetLife said, turning to Alkada, then reached his hand out to receive the weed El Chablo was already passing him.

Alkada nodded in agreeance and pushed on to their table. Once they were seated, Baron Black entered the banquet hall, and it erupted in cheer.

Shouts of "Baron Black!" and "We are with you!" could be heard throughout the hall, followed by a crescendo of "Fuck the Republic!" and "We will rise up!" All this praise and belief was heaped on Baron Black as he approached the stage. Baron Black waved and shook hands with all he passed along the way. Stopping at each table of his honored guests, he embraced and saluted them before stepping onto the stage flanked by his captain. Like El Chablo, Baron Black was dressed in full military regalia, clearly projecting his state of mind.

Francis Drake watched it all from his table, very much impressed by what he saw. Everybody who was anybody was in this hall and standing together as one.

Marshall Stryfe needs to know this immediately, he thought.

Baron Black, ever the showman, stepped to the podium, raising his hands for silence over the pandemonium raging in the hall. When the crowd finally went silent and settled down, he began his spiel.

"Friends, family, and countrymen alike," started Baron Black in his baritone voice, his words reaching the ears of every person in the hall. "And even more importantly, now comrades, know that I do not stand here before you as an opportunist or an optimist. No, I stand before you as a realist. I stand before you as a revolutionary. I stand before you as a freedom fighter who would fight and kill the fascist pigs of the Republic that now seek to dictate how we are to live. I stand before you not as a leader, but I will lead the charge for what we all believe is our right—and that is to live, die, and do as we please. By the Republic, I have been labeled an 'outlaw' because I have chosen to live outside the oppressive law of the Republic, and if the same can be said of all of you before me, then I guess we are a nation of pariahs. But I ask you, is it not better to be a pariah rather than a Republic slave? Are you with me?" roared Baron Black.

"We are with you!" the crowd shouted.

"Good, because I am with you," responded Baron Black.

El Chablo leaned over to StreetLife and whispered, "He is one hell of a speaker."

"Yes, he mos' def' can control the crowd," StreetLife responded as Baron Black continued.

"Ladies and gentlemen, I have another honored guest I would like to present to you tonight," said Baron Black as he stepped back from the podium. "Comrades, let me introduce you to Francis Drake of the Republic!"

There were no cheers. The hall went deadly quiet as eyes

sought the man Baron Black referred to.

Drake was awestruck at hearing his name announced from the stage. He was caught further off guard as several security guards surrounded him at the table to escort him to the stage. Feeling backed into a corner, he rose from his seat and reluctantly followed the guards.

As Drake topped the final steps of the stage, Baron Black held out his hand to him, indicating for Francis Drake to take the podium. Drake was dumbfounded as he took ginger steps toward the stand. When he reached it, Baron Black spoke to him.

"Sir Francis Drake, I believe you came here to speak with me about some information, as you told my captain," said Baron Black, pointing his finger toward Drake for him to address the crowd, then sat down next to his captain.

Drake stuttered momentarily, knowing the hundreds of eyes now beaming on him already hated him. He turned around to face Baron Black.

"Eh, yeh, yes, but I th—thought I would be given a private audience with you."

Baron Black erupted in laughter from his seat.

"A private audience, you say. Tell me, Drake, why would you need that? Did you not just witness that we are all comrades here? There are no secrets among comrades. Therefore, there is nothing you can tell me that cannot be said here for all my comrades to hear. The only reason I can see you wanting a private audience is because you are either a spy or an assassin. So, tell me, Drake, which one are you? And be forewarned, in Freedom Compound, spy or assassin are both titles that can have you put to death."

The banquet hall was already silent, but now there was a certain menace in the air.

"So, which are you, Francis Drake? Or do you prefer 'The Drake' as you are more commonly known? I know exactly who you are," grinned Baron Black, rising from his seat and approaching Francis Drake.

Drake looked out at the crowd and then back to Baron Black while backing away from the podium.

"You are a snake, Drake," hissed Baron Black as he drew near, nodding to the two soldiers who had crept up behind Drake and grabbed him by the arms.

Drake began to wiggle and jerk, fighting to free his arms from the soldiers' grip.

Baron sent a signal to his captain, and Captain BB stood up, grabbed the chair he was using, and brought it to his father at the front of the stage.

"Be seated," ordered Baron Black, and Drake was thrust into the chair behind him.

"Tie him up, hands behind his back," ordered Baron Black as he looked out into the crowd to see all eyes on him, everybody enthralled in what was playing out before them.

"Baron Black, please," started Drake before being slapped silent by Captain BB.

Baron Black nodded as he turned to face the crowd.

"Comrades," he started, "this man is a spy and assassin for the Republic, and we have no need for either here— for the whole nature of their existence is based on betrayal." Baron Black placed his hand on Drake's shoulder and patted it. "So, Drake, it is obvious you are either here to betray your Republic or learn what you can and betray us to your Republic," said Baron Black as he waved his hand out toward the crowd, indicating the "us" he was referring to.

"Either way, Drake, you cannot be trusted. But alas, perhaps I am being too hasty in my bias. So, let me ask my comrades. Comrades, can this man be trusted?" Baron asked the crowd.

"Death! Death!" was all that returned to Baron Black.

"Ahh, you see, Drake, the crowd has spoken," said Baron Black, just as he had hoped.

"No, no, you got it all wrong. I've come to offer you my services," yelled Drake, now starting to panic.

He tried to rise out of the chair but was pulled back down forcibly by the guards.

"Please, Baron Black, I swear I'd never betray you. I'm here to help you. I can tell Marshall Stryfe whatever you want me to, and he would believe me. Please, let me work for you!"

Shwapp!

Baron Black back smacked Drake, and again, the crowd started to chant threats of death toward Drake.

"Silence, betrayer! You are a Republic whore, and we cannot use you. But in my mercy not to put you to death as you hear my comrades calling for, I will give you a message to take back to Marshall Stryfe from all of us who you see here before you. And that message is that we, the people of the Democracy Plains Alliance, will not be enslaved by the tyranny you represent."

It was the first time the crowd had heard the movement's name. Yet, all embraced it as shouts of "Democracy" instantly began to reverberate throughout the hall.

Baron Black held out his hand, and his captain passed him a large buck knife. Again, the banquet hall fell silent, and the crowd sat transfixed with anticipation of what was to come as Baron Black began tending to his gruesome work. Ripping off Drake's shirt, Baron Black stood before the seated man and got to it.

"So, spy, you want something to report? Well, report this," he said and nodded to his captain.

Captain BB grabbed a handful of Drake's hair and pulled his head back from behind.

"Arrggh, stop! Please! Arrgghh, stop!" hollered Drake as his mutilation began. "Stop this, please! You can't do this! You can't... Grahhh!"

Drake raged and jerked in his chair, now unable to yell as Baron Black applied pressure to his neck using his forearm, which forced Drake to open his mouth. Baron Black then dug his knife into Drake's mouth and began cutting his tongue out. Pain shot through Drake's body as the knife's serrated edge tore through his gums and teeth, severing the nerves and roots that held them in place.

Once Baron Black was done, he grabbed the tongue, snatching it from the little piece of skin that held it, and threw it on the stage floor.

Baron Black could hear the gasps behind him from the crowd witnessing the macabre horror show playing out before them. Again, Baron Black tended to his grisly work, carving out a final message for the Republic in a single word. Now done with his butchery, Baron Black addressed the crowd while blood dripped from his hands.

"Now, betrayer, go back to your Republic. Tell them that we, the Democracy of the Plains Alliance, have one word for them and one word only," said Baron Black.

He then ordered the soldiers to stand Drake up so all could see the single word he carved in Drake's chest—a word that would speak volumes of what was to come:

Upon seeing this, the crowd lost all control as the shouts started instantly.

"War!"

"War!"

"DPA!"

"Baron Black!"

"Freedom!"

Everyone cheered while looking up at a disfigured and mutilated Drake.

Having proven his point, Baron Black nodded, and Drake was immediately carried away.

Fat Pocket sat with his mouth open, thinking, *Shit just went ka-boom!*

HardBody smiled, thinking to himself, *Shyne shit!* Then he raised a bottle of wine in salute, took a long swig, and passed it to

Alkada, who did the same.

The Mob looked to Baron Black, and all stood and saluted him.

El Chablo nodded emphatically in respect and salutes as he passed the Kush to StreetLife after taking a long inhale.

"You can't come back from that," he said.

"No the fuck you can't," StreetLife responded.

Diablo Vasa and his daughter raised their glasses in a toast as Wolfgang stood up and clapped along with the crowd, amazed by it all.

"Jolly good show! Jolly good show, indeed!" Wolfgang shouted.

Baron Black looked out among the masses, embracing their cheer, harnessing the energy, feeling the roar, and living in the moment of it. These were his comrades, and together they had drawn first blood.

***

The rest of the night played out much the same way it did when they met in the banquet hall upon arrival. Music, wine, Kush, good food, women, true camaraderie, and people mixing and mingling. Baron Black circulated the crowd, receiving much backslapping and praise for his show of bravado earlier in the evening. He wished everyone a safe departure on the morrow and looked forward to the campaign of war they were about to wage. He also spoke with the honored guests, finalizing their plans and exchanging input and suggestions with a tentative agreement to reconvene in three months.

Chapter Thirty-Two

The day of departures from Freedom Compound was just as busy as the arrivals. Wagons being loaded lined the streets. Horses were being saddled, and arrangements were being made. Soldiers were a heavy presence, walking all about as guests were issued back their weapons upon leaving.

Baron Black demanded that there be at least a four-hour delay on the departures of the Shynes and the Mob, with soldiers posted along the route between Freedom Compound to the Roughs to ensure there would be no ambush by either side. Yet, this proved unnecessary since the Mob rode out at sunrise, and it was now midday. The rest of his honored guests were just awakening after a long night of varied indulgences.

El Chablo briefly spoke with Baron Black before he and his troops headed back southeast to the Benta Territories. The weather was mild and bright, making for easy riding no matter the direction.

Baron Black issued a small contingent of soldiers to escort

Alexander Wolfgang back to Noble Haven despite his insistence that he didn't need them. Although a proud man, Wolfgang was a man relieved and broken. He was relieved to know his daughter was still alive but broken that she was no longer the daughter he remembered, now an outlaw wanted by the Republic. She would be a soldier in the war to come. Nonetheless, she was his daughter, and because of her, he would be a part of the war that loomed in the near future.

Fat Pockets barked orders to his handlers as they loaded his stagecoach for the trip back to Keystone, all the while doting over Maritzah, who was always at his side. They had been inseparable ever since the meeting where he claimed her, his massive diamond necklace ever-present around her neck, a symbol of his commitment to her.

They were approached by Baron Black, Captain BB, and Nancy as Baron Black felt the need to make Fat Pockets fully aware of his love for Maritzah and the importance of her well-being.

"Fat Pockets," Baron Black called out, Captain BB and Nancy flanking him.

Fat Pockets turned around to find the trio standing before him. Baron Black extended his hand to shake Fat Pockets' as Fat Pockets simultaneously reached out for his.

"Fat Pockets, as you depart from my lands, please know that you take with you my niece and my blessings. I hope you respect and understand the significance of both," Baron Black said grimly while firmly squeezing Fat Pockets' hand before letting go.

Fat Pockets smiled, first looking Baron Black in the eyes and then directing his gaze to Captain BB and Nancy as he thought to himself, *My turn.*

"Baron Black, with all due respect, please know and believe that Maritzah will be in good hands that Nancy never was," Fat Pockets responded with a grin.

Captain BB took a step forward but was halted by a hand gesture from Baron Black as Fat Pockets went on.

"See, Baron Black, when you know better, you do better. And as you no doubt know, in choosing Maritzah, I have done great. I am thankful that you have given me your blessing in taking your niece. And to that, I would add that I leave as your comrade and hope to return as your family. Isn't that right, love?" asked Fat Pockets to Maritzah, who was holding his arm.

"Yes, Papi," said Maritzah, excitedly kissing him on the cheek.

Fat Pockets looked at Captain BB and Nancy, checking to see if his words were as cutting as he meant them to be. And sure enough, both their faces were as red as a bleeding heart.

Baron Black said nothing, knowing his son needed to be taught a lesson for his selfishness in falling in love with another man's whore.

Maritzah then stepped forward, looking at the men who were biologically her uncle and cousin but emotionally like a father and brother to her. Both of her parents and her siblings were killed in the Death Sagas. So, Baron Black and Captain BB were her only living blood family. Tears welled up in her eyes as the reality hit her that she would be leaving them. She started speaking to them as Fat Pockets turned back to the wagon.

"Uncpa, thank you for letting me go. I love you so much," Maritzah said as she wrapped her arms around his neck in a warm, tender embrace.

Baron Black hugged her back, hating he had to let this girl he raised as his daughter go with this "thing" called Fat Pockets.

Maritzah then turned to Captain BB. "I will miss you so much, Lil BB," she said, pinching his cheeks and crying as she hugged him.

"I will miss you, too, cousin," responded Captain BB as he held back tears while memories of them climbing trees and learning to ride horses during their childhood flashed through his mind.

"Maritzah," called Fat Pockets, holding out his hand as he opened the door to the stagecoach.

Maritzah turned to Fat Pockets and nodded. She then turned back to her uncle and cousin, kissing both on the cheek. She beamed a winning smile at Nancy while flashing the diamond necklace around her neck—an accessory Nancy had never even been allowed to touch. Then she approached Fat Pockets, who helped her onto her seat like a gentleman.

Once he made sure she was secure, Fat Pockets stepped back to Baron Black and Captain BB to shake their hands, shaking first the hand of Baron Black but with far less fervor than the first time.

As he shook Captain BB's hand, he brought him closer and whispered in his ear, "My lane's wide; lames stand aside. The game is chess, so don't bring checkers to my board no mo'. Now you take care to remember that, loverboy."

Fat Pockets gritted as he released Captain BB's hand. Finally, he turned to Nancy and addressed her.

"Well, Nancy, this is where you and I part ways and say goodbye to the good ol' days. Of course, Keystone won't be the same without you, but at least now you're 'round people who don't know about you," he said with a wink and chuckle.

Nancy flushed red with anger at his words and what they

implied, then scampered off.

"Fat Pockets," interjected Baron Black, ending any further drama, "I'm sending a contingent of soldiers with you back to Keystone to, as you say, 'hold you down' and flush out any Republic soldiers that may still be in Keystone upon your return. As well as to ascertain how many soldiers will be needed to patrol and hold your northern borders between Republic City and Keystone. Lieutenant Piya here…" said Baron Black of a short, stocky man standing at his side with one shotgun strapped to his back and twin six-shooters on his hips, "…will be at your command and in command of the troop. I trust you will find him to be adequate in situations that require violence. He will help you get things in order," finished Baron Black.

"Very much obliged. As I said, I just need all the muscle for the tussle, and trust, I'll do my part," responded Fat Pockets.

"Fat Pockets," called Maritzah from the open door of the coach, now eager to leave.

Fat Pockets nodded to her, then gave a final nod to Baron Black and stepped toward the waiting coach, followed by Lieutenant Piya, whose troops were already saddled up and ready to ride.

As the convoy began to move, Fat Pockets swung back the curtain of the coach, his eyes locking directly on Captain BB's. Fat Pockets grinned as he cracked the window to the coach and hurled out a shout into the air that burned Captain BB to his core, a final stab as he left Freedom Compound to all who heard.

"Fat Pockets, bitch!"

Obnoxious laughter followed the taunt that, to Captain BB's ears, seemed to last for as long as the coach could be seen.

Next, Diablo Vasa and Elvira pulled up to Baron Black and

Captain BB on the two massive stallions they had arrived on, ready to depart back to their mountain fortress.

"Baron Black, Captain BB, I salute you," started Diablo, looking down at the father and son. "And know that your back will be covered as long as Diablo Vasa is alive," he said.

That may not be for much longer, thought Elvira, who refused to speak.

Her hatred now smoldered for her father, as well, knowing that not only had he forgiven Alkada for what he did to her, but he also accepted him as his own son.

"I look forward to our alliance," Diablo added as Elvira remained aloof to the whole exchange.

"Diablo, you have long been a friend from a distance, but now we are brothers in arms," offered Baron Black as the two men clasped each other's forearms, solidifying their allegiance.

Alkada walked up, followed by A1 and London.

"Comrades," he announced to the group.

As he and Elvira made eye contact, Elvira rolled her eyes and sucked her teeth at his presence. She immediately snatched the reins of her horse, striking leather to its behind.

"Yah-yah!" she shouted and galloped off.

Diablo and Alkada knew the meaning of her abrupt departure, as did everyone else, but nobody spoke on it. Instead, Alkada and Diablo clasped arms in salute, and Diablo took off behind his daughter.

Baron Black now looked at Alkada to again attempt to persuade him from his course.

"Alas, Alkada, I know you have affairs to tend to with the Mob, and I respect that, but as I have already expressed to you, I hope you are at my side when the war comes."

"As do I," Alkada responded.

Baron Black stepped before Alkada face to face and placed his hands on his shoulders. "Alkada, you are a man truly after your own father's heart, but may I remind you, as I'm sure you remember, your father died fighting for a cause he believed in, which was higher than himself, and that fight was against oppression and tyranny. This is a good cause to die for, Alkada, not vendettas."

Alkada nodded his head in respect. "My father taught me first and foremost to always be loyal to my beliefs and my given word—whether in matters of oppression, tyranny, or vendettas. If I am loyal to my beliefs, is that not worth dying for? And would you, Baron Black, respect me as you do my father's memory were I disloyal to my given word?"

"Alkada, you put forth a logic for which I cannot argue. I am sure your father would be proud of the man you've become. So, aim true, my young son, and be safe."

Alkada nodded and embraced Baron Black and Captain BB, as did A1 and London, and they parted ways.

Baron Black thought as they walked away, then turned to his captain and said, "Were you not my son, a man could ask for no greater a son than Alkada. May he be to you as his father was to me," said Baron Black as he clapped his son on the back. "Come, my captain, let us prepare for war."

***

Captain Hammer arrived in the Roughs under the cover of night. The Roughs was a small mining town, long forgotten and left desolate once all its gold had been dug out. Now, it was only a shallow shell of the town it once was. It had only one major road that led in and out of it. The remnants of people still there were those too poor to go anywhere else and made a living off the handouts and travelers that often came through their town just looking for a place to rest up and feed and water their horses.

As Captain Hammer entered the town, he realized a massive labyrinth of little streets encircled themselves, a sort of mazed city. Hammer also noticed several stagecoaches making their way from Freedom Compound earlier in the day.

They headed northeast and east with at least two military escorts. He had already lost too many soldiers with the fiasco in Shameless to try again at open combat, especially behind enemy lines as they were. Yet, he made markings of their heading, which, as he surmised, were to either Noble Haven, Keystone, or both.

Whatever took place at Freedom Compound was big and had brought in people from all over. It must've been serious, and Captain Hammer wanted to know why. All he needed to capture was one person who had attended the meeting, and he would torture them until they told all they knew. And this little shantytown was the perfect place to post up, as it was a central passageway for people of the plains. All Hammer had to do was wait, and sooner or later, a fly of the right size would land in his web. As he rubbed the eye patch over his missing eye, he hoped and prayed that the fly's name was Alkada.

***

The moon was full and bright in the sky, with far too many stars to count illuminating the night—perfect for what Nefertiti was going to attempt. Since she first learned of Dempaku as a child, she had always felt a connection, heightened empowerment,

438

and awareness of the energy of Dempaku felt but unseen. Her spiritual sensory was way beyond most, if not all, of her Dempaku sisters, except for her Queen Sista, Petra. Nefertiti's knowledge and inclination for ritualism came naturally. However, she had learned to frequently fake naivety so as not to hurt the feelings of her elders when they taught her things she knew instinctively. Her ability to perceive, understand and touch the supernatural power of Dempaku was at times astonishing to others. But, in her mind, it was simple navigation of elements, energy, science, and faith. Yet, she would really put herself to the test in what she was about to attempt.

Come what may, Nefertiti was going to speak with Dempaku—a feat said to only have been performed by the most accomplished and proficient Dempaku practitioners. There have been many calamities for many poor souls who had attempted this very act— from strokes to comas, and on several occasions, even death, for it was said nobody speaks to Dempaku unless Dempaku wishes an audience with you. Nefertiti didn't care, though. She would know. Always her curiosity pushed her to take risks, and tonight would be her riskiest.

Nefertiti cracked the door to her room, and pushing her senses forward, she felt for her mother. She could feel her sleeping, holding the feeling to be sure. She then closed and locked her door and opened the two windows in her room, feeling the night's cool air blow in. Next, she poured a circle of revelation on the floor before her bed, using the powder from the bones of ancestors she had grounded herself. She then lit a candle and held it out before her, seeing which way the wind would blow into her room, determining which direction Dempaku might come from so Nefertiti would be sure to face the deity upon arrival. Giving your back to Dempaku's coming could cost you your life.

Nefertiti then set the candle down before the circle and stepped inside it. She sat cross-legged, facing the window that the flame flickered in front of, then reached for her bowl that contained some rocks, dirt, grass, and leaves from her front yard. Next, she added water from a nearby stream. Pausing again, she studied the flame, which continued to blow strong toward her from the window she faced.

Good sign, she thought.

Pulling a needle from her pocket, she pricked her finger and let a few drops of blood fall into the bowl. She stirred the mixture until the water took on a murky hue. She then picked up the bowl, brought it before her lips, and spoke a few simple words.

"For Dempaku, I bow," she said, then sipped from the bowl and spit the liquid at the candle's flame. This would push her scent to Dempaku's realm.

Instantly, the atmosphere in the room changed. Not cold, not hot, just heavier. She could feel it moving against her skin. Nefertiti smiled inwardly. She was right in knowing when all the elements of the earth were combined, a doorway to the Never could be opened. She was being guided strictly by instinct now. She was not nervous, just focused.

She stilled herself, concentrating on the burning flame till her eyes closed and her mind cleared. She put forth the prayer of Dempaku, and at that moment, she was transcended into the vastness of her mind. Nefertiti had entered into the Never, the realm of Dempaku.

As far as Nefertiti knew, this was a connection not even her mother could make at this age or even now. A connection that not even the Queen Sista Petra knew Nefertiti could make, for if she had, she would've prohibited her from doing such a thing unguided.

Nefertiti reached deeper into the Never, opening her soul to the touch of Dempaku.

Opening her mind from deep, deep within her anima, she called out, "Dempaku."

In an instant, the wind began to blow through her window into her face, thickening the already intensified air. A force completely physically engulfed Nefertiti. She could feel energy literally vibrate through every inch of her flesh. Again, she knew not to press, but her will to know pushed her, and again, she called out.

"Dempaku."

This time, she was answered.

"Ah, the Child Queen," said a sensuous voice in Nefertiti's mind.

Nefertiti was only briefly astonished before her body was again seized in paralysis by the overwhelming power of Dempaku. She felt elevated.

"Such power dwells within you, my child... A power that allows me to speak right into your mind and soul as I have done with none before you," whispered Dempaku in a voice heard and felt.

Nefertiti surrendered all her will to her goddess, giving into the euphoria. Still, even in the clutches of such elation, Nefertiti remembered her reason for calling upon Dempaku—the flash in her mind that had shown her a face with the whisper of a brother. Nefertiti needed to know. She knew her heart, mind, and soul were laid bare like glass before Dempaku; no thought unseen or secret unknown. Unable to contain her eagerness any longer,

Nefertiti pressed forward.

"Dempaku... The face I saw, who is he to me? Do I have a brother? I ask of you the proof of truth."

Only a moment lingered before she heard a response to her inquiry.

"Silence, little one. So bold and brazen, you are just like your father... Just like your bloodline. I chose well with you, but do not think yourself so precious that I won't take your life from you in this very instant and bring you to do now for me what is prophesied of your future?"

Nefertiti felt a relocking of her body, but gone now was the euphoria, replaced now with searing pain, the likes of which Nefertiti had never felt. Every hair on her body felt like a dagger slowly sinking into her skin. Her mind and soul began to burn as if hot embers of coal and smoke filled her lungs, choking off her breath. Nefertiti was dying. Although she had never experienced death before, she knew this was it. She fought back the panic, pushed away from the fear, and went deeper into herself. Holding fast to her faith, the words just came to her.

"Dempaku, I am bowed."

Immediately, the pain started to dissipate, and words began to flow into Nefertiti's mind as if Dempaku had whispered them in her ear.

"Yes, Child Queen, you are bowed. Bowed before all to whom you believe, and you will ask of me nothing and be told by me all you are to do."

Nefertiti could feel the euphoria returning, yet the pain remained bonded to her memory. Even the feeling of her beating heart returned that she hadn't noticed stopped.

"Know this, child; you are the daughter of Alkada. True just as the face you saw is the son of Alkada, and it is a twin flame that burns between you. Yet, as your soul is claimed by me, the soul of the face you saw belongs to another. Ask your father if you would seek to know the truth of it all, Child Queen. For he is the one who allowed himself to fall to the trickery of the other. Be warned, Child Queen. Do not let this trickery befall you, lest you be brought to me before need be. There is a spark of a cat's curiosity in you, a passion for knowing what must first be understood. No matter the power within you, respect always your Queen Sista and never call upon me again before your scratching, lest you come again to the Never, never to leave again, my child. Your proof in truth comes on the wings of a feather, as your guardian will come by the spirit of a Sista. Safu, young daughter."

In that instant, Dempaku was gone, and Nefertiti felt as if she were slammed back into her body. All her senses were back. She was drenched in sweat and gasping for air, now released from whatever supernatural force held her. Her candle had burned down into a puddle of wax, yet her time in the Never only lasted a few brief moments. It was said that time in the Never flowed differently from that of the earthly plane. But yet and still, not only had she gone to the Never and back, she had communed with Dempaku, a feat some died when they tried. Nefertiti smiled at her success, and instantly the memory of her pain flashed through her.

"Dempaku, I'm bowed," she uttered quickly, knowing her moment of hubris caused the pain.

The rustling of feathers turned her attention to the window, only to be greeted by Skully's massive frame as if he had materialized out of the night sky. Nefertiti attempted to get up, only to fall back down, dizzy from her ordeal in the Never.

Skully flapped his wings and came to Nefertiti's aid, allowing her to steady herself as she wrapped her arms around his neck and hugged him.

"Raahhh," Skully shrieked mildly so as not to upset the child and then began hopping around, eager to deliver his message and get back to Alkada as he raised his taloned foot.

Nefertiti snatched the capsule from his raised leg as she had so many times before, eager to know the message Skully was to leave. Once she got it, Skully jumped back to the window ledge and, with another leap, became part of the night without so much as a look back.

Nefertiti sat on her bed and opened the capsule to reveal a note and locket snapped in half with the picture of a young boy's face. Nefertiti was transfixed as she stared at the picture, knowing this was her brother—the face in the flash. She stared intensely at the locket, seeing her father in him. Everything about him spoke of Alkada. In this young boy's face was a life connected to her father, connected to her. Gripping the locket tightly, she read the note.

DEAREST NEFERTITI,

KNOW THAT I LOVE YOU AND YOUR MOTHER DEARLY. BUT SHYNE IS THE LIFE I LIVE, AS DOES YOUR MOTHER AND AS WILL YOU. IF I DON'T RETURN, KNOW THAT YOU HAVE A BROTHER. AND JUST AS YOU HOLD THE LOCKET I HAVE SENT YOU. I TRUST YOU WILL ONE DAY MEET HIM. LET HIM KNOW I DIDN'T KNOW HE EXISTED, AND I'M SORRY FOR WHAT I'VE DONE TO HIS SOUL. SHOULD I DIE, IT IS WRITTEN HARDBODY, AMMO, AND A1 ARE PUT TO THE OATH. LOVE, YOUR FATHER.

—ALKADA

Nefertiti now had the proof in truth, just like she asked, and it was brought to her on the wings of the feather as Dempaku predicted. Nefertiti read the note over and over again, trying to understand and wanting to know more.

Still feeling drained from her step into the Never, she laid down on her bed, feeling and welcoming the cooling breeze of the night that blew through her windows. Finally, she drifted off to sleep with the locket held tight in her hand. Her final thoughts before sleep took her were, *I have a brother... I have a brother.*

***

Petra awoke from her sleep with a simple knowing of events. Nefertiti, the Child Queen of prophecy, was now announced, recognized, and brought to the fact by Dempaku in the Never. Such a fire-hearted child Nefertiti was. Then there was Alkada, the father of Dempaku's chosen child and father to Mugasa's morning star, and with a child on the way to be claimed by both.

"My, my, Alkada, you truly are a man of a great legacy," Petra whispered, getting up from her bed and walking to the open window.

She stuck her hand out into the air, feeling that war was coming and blood would flow. After pulling her hand back inside, Petra spoke Dempaku's prayer, thinking to herself, *Come what may, the Shynes will be ready.*

To Be Continued…